To my husband & sons,
You guys are the jelly to my doughnut.

A DIARY OF A DEITY NOVEL

THE RISING

LORYN MOORE

TABLE OF CONTENTS

Mackayla 1

Singed 5

Disturbance 18

Clandestine 39

Impossible 64

Subterfuge 73

Sacrifices 98

Shadows 109

Inauguration Night 136

Vacant 163

Fallout 181

Tormented 197

The Rising 222

Fatigue 245

Blindsided.. 262

Alachary... 283

Revelation.. 300

Elucidation.. 320

Solace.. 330

Explosive... 341

Liberation.. 351

Combat... 358

Reunion... 368

Bound... 380

ACKNOWLEDGEMENTS.. 390

ABOUT THE AUTHOR... 391

OTHER BOOKS BY LORYN MOORE 393

PROLOGUE

Mackayla

A cold ripple wove through the air as Mack's heels clicked on the white marble floors of the Valerian palace. This wasn't the typical breeze of a cool spring day in Valeria. Instead, it moved through the white-washed halls like a specter, shifting her gauzy, blue dress and sending a chill down her spine. She spun around, her breath catching as the muscles of her throat constricted. Her whole body tensed as realization clicked into place. This was something much more sinister.

She turned back around and began to run, the slender muscles of her thighs coiling and releasing. The tall columns that lined the external border of the throne room, open to the fresh air, blurred with the speed of her movement. She dug into the pocket of her loose-fitted dress, and her fingers wrapped around the small, spherical device she sought.

She grasped it and powered it up with a mere whisper of her time magic. Then, without another thought, she hurled it a few yards in front of her. It hit the floor with a metallic clang and bounced across the tiles. Instantly, a silvery sheen erupted from its near-invisible eye—a portal materialized before her. She ran full speed straight for it, taking a final giant leap into the silvery, mercurial surface. A split second later, she skidded to a halt inside a different kind of place, chest heaving. One moment, birds chirped, and a warm breeze rustled from the open air of the throne room, and the next, the drone of busy voices filled her ears.

Voices that abruptly stopped.

All the eyes in the room, filled with dozens of deities, fixed on her. She had appeared in the middle of the central headquarters of the Prophecy Aversion Branch of their godly government, commonly known as the PAB, the open portal humming behind her. Golden strings of prophecies glistened overhead, floating like ribbons caught in a breeze. The large, holographic simulators they used to predict all possible prophetic outcomes whirred.

Grief swelled inside her as every single deity in the room stared at her, the weight of their expectations heavy in the air. Her father, their king, and Peacekeeper of the Twelve Realms was dead. She'd felt his departure the instant it had happened just moments before. And there she was, fighting for composure. She must look like a wraith, some terrifying omen, she thought. An assessment that wasn't far off from the truth.

A few faces began to shift from confusion to panic, but only the select few lucky enough to count themselves as upper-caste deities. They were the gods with the most substantial power among their ranks. The rest still hadn't caught on, hadn't realized just how bad things had gotten.

The prophecy—the one Mack and her husband, along with Gabryel, had fought to keep secret for so many years— had all come crumbling down around them. Only a handful of their most trusted allies in the PAB even knew of its existence, and they'd been working around the clock since Bekka's disappearance to keep this very outcome from happening.

Maybe they'd played it all wrong, she thought, as her mind raced to make sense of it all. But they'd done all the mitigation measures by the book. They'd worked tirelessly to ensure the security of their borders and Bekka's ignorance of it. The prophecy should have been dead in the water. It should have been impossible.

And yet, here they were.

Gabryel was dead, and her daughter, a novice creator with no experience in war or anything even remotely resembling it, was the only option to claim the Peacekeeper's mantle. And, Ascended have mercy on them all, she was woefully unprepared to take on that role.

Mack could hear her father's voice echo in her mind, *"Destiny will find its way through any crack you allow to exist. Some things are inevitable unless sacrifices are made. It's for the greater good, Mackayla."*

Her stomach churned as she ran through the lines of the prophecy in her mind. She'd memorized them decades ago, when the seer had first spoken them, first recorded them in their archives. A hot poker of pain seared her belly as she remembered everything they'd done to keep it quiet. It hadn't been a matter of choice, she reminded herself. It had been the only way to keep Bekka safe.

Mack opened her mouth to speak but shut it again, feeling like she'd lost her voice. A first for her, to be sure, and she shook her head, at a loss. Eyes began to flick around the room, everyone seeking an explanation, but Mack couldn't seem to find the words amid her grief and fear.

Finally, after what felt like an eternity of stunned silence, her husband's voice boomed through the crowd. Killian's tall, lean frame appeared from behind the cluster of seers and time deities. His shoes clicked on the silvery glass floor as he moved towards her.

"It's as we feared, isn't it, Mack? Gabryel's gone?"

She felt the threat of tears spring into the backs of her eyes but forced them away. When she nodded her confirmation, the room erupted in chaos. She let the mayhem crash around her. Did nothing to stop it.

After all, it wouldn't be long before the rest of the Twelve Realms followed.

CHAPTER 1

REMI

Singed

Remi's hands trembled as her finger hovered over her portable comm device, a message from her parents blinking an alert on its transparent, glass screen. She could feel the slim bead of the microphone pressed onto her temple, hyper-aware of its presence.

Press the damned button, you coward, she thought, chewing on her cheek. Unfortunately, her finger refused to move. She had the sickening feeling that she wouldn't like what they had to say.

It had been just over two weeks since her wedding, a knot of grief swelling at the memory of everything that had happened that day. Her sister, kidnapped and vanished without a trace.

After they'd picked through the decimated remnants of the ceremony and realized that Bekka was gone, her family's eerie calm had infuriated her beyond reason. She'd demanded that she be allowed to assist in the effort to locate her twin, her best friend, the one person she loved most in this world. She'd begged and pleaded, but they'd refused.

"Gabryel will find her," they'd said. *"You have other responsibilities,"* they'd insisted. Then, they'd pushed her out of Valeria and forced her to go to Bicaidia with her new husband, where she would assume her new role as princess-in-waiting.

Why?

Because of duty, honor, and to maintain the stability of the Twelve Realms. In other words, to keep up the appearance that they had it all under control.

And just how well had that turned out? She mused, bitterness leaching into every pore of her body.

Her beloved grandfather had died, ascended to the next phase of his life far too young. And what of her sister? Gone to who knew where. She shook her head, anger and a sticky kind of grief beginning to mingle with the bitterness now.

She wasn't some naive child. She knew her parents had to have *some idea* where her sister was. They just weren't sharing it with her.

She chucked her comm device onto her modest, but comfortable bed. Striding over to the massive floor-to-ceiling window that overlooked the high-desert outside, she surveyed one of the best views the Bicaidian palace had to offer. The red dirt seemed to pick up the pinks and oranges of the sunset, the dots of green trees cutting into the otherwise monotonous tones. The rocky mountains that surrounded her new home were beautiful and rugged, but it offered no respite from her grief and worry.

She sighed, keeping her back to her comm device just a bit longer. Because she knew, deep down, what the message from her parents would contain. Her request to return home to Valeria and assist in finding her sister would be denied. There was almost no point in listening to it.

But she knew herself better than that. So, unable to resist her curiosity, she turned and looked at the comm device discarded in the center of her bed. She couldn't help but hold onto a tiny sliver of hope that maybe, just maybe, they would surprise her.

It was that kernel of hope that had her stiffening her spine. Had her striding to the bed. Had her retrieving the device.

Sucking in a deep breath, she started the message. A holo beam appeared from the screen, projecting her father's face into the empty space above her comforter. Despite her anger with him, a pang of familiar comfort centered in her belly. But when his words filled her mind, all that warmth and all longing to see him disappeared as quickly as it had come.

"Remi," her father said through the bead on her temple, "I know you mean well and wish to help your sister, but we have things under control here. We need you in Bicaidia. With your grandfather gone, we can't afford to withdraw any of our assets in leadership roles abroad. So you will stay there and do your duty. You know your role; you know your responsibilities. *See to them*, and we'll keep you abreast of any developments regarding your sister."

The message blinked off, and Remi felt her jaw clench in reaction to her father's words. Hot, furious rage seared through her as the holo dissipated and the message ended. They were unbelievable! Cold, callous, and utterly uninterested in anything but their precious power. She growled, the sound low in her throat. She could feel her skin beginning to heat, the fire that burned eternal inside her bucking against her constant restraint.

She seethed. Why wouldn't they at least let her help? Bekka meant more to Remi than any damned duty that she might have. Her responsibility was to her family first. Only once Bekka was safe could she even begin to focus on anything related to Bicaidia. She couldn't see why they didn't understand that.

Heat crawled beneath the surface of her skin as she railed against them in her mind. Her chest heaved. She needed something to hit, someone she could blame for everything that had happened since her cursed wedding.

Her mind flashed back to her last memory of her sister. Sweat dripping down Bekka's face, small cuts lining it as she cried helpless tears of terror, her body bare and exposed. Then the blast and the blackness that had followed. Remi hadn't realized what was happening. She'd thought maybe someone was protecting them all from Bekka's newfound power. But then, her sister had disappeared, evaporated into thin air.

Had Remi known what would happen, she would have fought through the agony of her damaged leg and run to her sister's rescue. She would have done anything, even unleash her own gift in a crowded room of unconscious deities, just to keep Bekka safe. But she'd been too slow. Too dim-witted and confused to do anything to stop it.

Now? Now, she just had to sit here and twiddle her thumbs while everyone but her took care of it. Her breath came in ragged pants as she paced, her internal fire burning hotter with each passing second. She could feel herself losing control, the anger taking over bit-by-bit, but she couldn't bring herself to care.

She felt the fury coil tight in her chest, just before a slice of grief speared through her. She sunk to her knees, tears springing to her eyes as she let out a desperate scream of pain.

Then, at last, fire exploded from her body in a blast of flames, instantly engulfing her brand-new room and all of her belongings. Her sheer, mint-colored curtains erupted, burning to cinders in seconds. The soft, peach bed cover with its green vines snaking along its surface was ablaze before she could even register the change.

She'd lost control, she knew, as her magic took over and unleashed its special brand of devastation.

The door to her chambers blasted straight off the hinges and into the hallway as she cried, sobs racking her body. All of the pain, grief, and anger coalesced into a single moment of agony that she couldn't escape. It was all that existed. Nothing else mattered. Not control, not the voice inside that told her that she had to stop... nothing.

The heat emanating from her body melted the walls, the glass of the windows, and the adobe stone floors. The flames tore out from her chambers and into the rooms surrounding hers. Her cries turned into keening as she wrestled with the knowledge that she would never see her grandfather again. She might never see her sister again either. As she wailed, she heard shouts coming from the hall, her mind barely registering them.

Then, she heard a voice pierce through the drone of her pain. "Remi!" it shouted, and a pang of familiarity shot through her. She forced her hands from her face and dragged her gaze toward the source of that voice. Tears and massive flames blurred her vision, and she blinked, squinting as a silhouette of a tall, broad shouldered god came into focus.

It was Thayne. Her husband.

His dark, intense eyes locked onto hers, and that connection tethered her back to reality. She shook her head, coming back to herself and recognizing the full extent of the damage for the first time. Her mind reeled as she realized that she wasn't stopping. Fire still pulsed from within her, spreading through the room and the nearby sections of the palace with abandon. Horror flashed in her mind as she realized what she was doing. She'd let the pain take over. She'd given up control, something she'd vowed would never happen.

Now, desperate to stop herself, she fought to contain it. But that tenuous control that she had always managed to maintain felt slippery and insubstantial. As she tried and failed to get ahold of herself, to grab the rope of magic that coiled inside her and yank it taught, panic took hold. She didn't know how to fix this; she couldn't seem to stop.

Her eyes met his, the harrowing depths of his dark irises seeming to comprehend what had gone wrong without her even having to say. He stood in the doorway; his hands extended as dark, billowing clouds flowed from them. They swirled up, licking across the ceiling, sizzling on contact with the fire as they began to dump rain inside her room.

The droplets evaporated at first, unable to make it past the inferno of her blaze, but he kept pressing, matching his magic to hers. It took precious minutes for his power to gain ground, but it did. He was cooling the flames and extinguishing them one small modicum at a time.

With every precious inch his storm gained, he advanced closer to her. "Keep going, Thayne! Don't stop!" she begged, her body still engulfed in flames. She needed his storm to put out her blaze, to combat her magic and help her regain her control.

He did as she asked, and his large frame filled her vision as he approached. At first the rain sizzled and turned to steam when it touched her skin, but he clenched his fist and the clouds inside the incinerated room darkened. A downpour unlike anything she'd ever seen before cascaded from above them and little by little, her fire weakened. Then, she felt it, cool water soaking her skin in seconds.

Her shoulders sagged in relief as water pooled around her. She slicked her sopping hair back with two hands and sucked in ragged breaths as the rain ceased. A few seconds later, Thayne dropped to his knees beside her. He smelled like petrichor and fresh rain, his long, dark brown hair dry despite the deluge.

She looked up into his face, her eyes still stinging and raw from the tears. He reached out a tentative hand, placed it on her cheek, hissing in pain as he did. Her skin still held the fiery heat of her power beneath its surface. "Remi, you can stop now. It's OK. You're not alone. You don't have to be alone."

His words rattled against her ears, her mind latching onto them as she took in the charred blackness of her chambers. Guilt wrapped around her like a shroud, and as it did, she found that rope, gripped it, and yanked it taut. Then, the last vestiges of her fire cooled under her skin, and she let out an exhausted groan.

"I'm sorry...Thank you," she whispered. He'd come to her rescue, or her doom, depending on who else had come with him. After all, in their laws, a dangerous, uncontrollable deity should be shackled with a governor chip, regardless of their royal or Nefaric status.

"I have you," he replied with a soothing voice. Seeming to guess the direction of her thoughts, he added, "Don't' worry. It's just me."

With that, she fell forward. Thayne wrapped his arms around her, and she thanked the Ascended that her powers didn't burn anything that came into direct contact with her skin, like her clothes. Her limbs felt doughy and loose as he helped her to her feet, water soaking the floor. Smoke and steam still sizzled around them, and blackened char swallowed the rooms at least two deep on either side of hers. The floor felt unstable beneath her feet as Thayne led her out of her ruined room and into the destroyed hall.

Suddenly, a voice broke through the thrumming in her ears. "No, no, no! This can't be happening. You've got to be kidding me!"

Remi shifted her focus and found the source of the voice. It was a tall goddess, all lean limbs and golden-bronze skin. She glowed with the usual ethereal shine of a goddess, but she seemed brighter somehow, more vivid as she stared in disbelief at the ruined room two doors down from Remi's. A god wearing a perfectly tailored black suit stood beside her, his dark hair smoothed back from his face. He slid his arm around her shoulder, tucking her close to his side.

Thayne maneuvered Remi toward the pair of deities, staring into the goddess's ruined room. Then, shifting to support Remi's weight with one arm, he placed his hand on the god's shoulder, pulling the pair's attention to him. "We'll sort this out later. This whole wing needs to be evacuated. The structure isn't stable."

"Of course," the god answered before he turned his focus on the goddess. "Come, Ellarah. Let's go." With one mournful look back at her room, she allowed herself to be led away from it.

Certain she couldn't feel any more guilty if she tried, Remi rested her weight on Thayne's shoulder and vowed to make it up to the goddess later.

The floor seemed to sway as Thayne led them down the hall, turned two corners, and guided them onto stable ground once more. Once away from the charred damage she'd caused, Remi began to feel some of her strength flow back into her legs. She pressed a hand to Thayne's shoulder, indicating that she could handle this on her own, her momentary lapse in control behind her.

He let go of her as a rush of deities surrounded them. They hurtled questions. What had happened? Had there been an attack? How bad was the damage? Who did they need to smite? She was pretty certain that the last one was a joke, but then one could never be too sure.

She felt each question as though it were an accusation and tried to stand tall and not wince. It wasn't altogether uncommon that a high-powered deity lost control and caused some kind of a disaster. Though, it typically happened at the inception of their powers and rarely to a member of the royal family.

The royal-caste was held to a different standard, after all. They were expected to be level-headed and keep their cool even under the direst circumstances. Great, she thought, eyes straight forward, daring anyone to meet her stare. But instead of throwing her to the wolves, Thayne gestured to the gathering crowd and directed them down the hallway, away from Remi.

Once they were out of earshot, he leaned closer to her and said, "I should take care of this now before it gets out of hand."

She could hear the hum of all those curious voices and feel their eyes on her. "I understand."

"You know, I'll be here if you need anything." He waited, his intense eyes boring into her as though searching for evidence that she wouldn't combust again.

She nodded in response. "Thank you. Go do what you need to do. I'll be fine." He paused a beat, examining her before he decided that she meant what she said. Then he turned and started down the hall.

As he left, she could hear his voice boom out over the hum of his frenzied subjects. "We can discuss what happened at length later, but no one is under attack. Right now, we just need to get repairs started." He turned the corner, giving her one last concerned look before he disappeared.

Alone in the corridor now, Remi let out a long breath and pressed her back onto the cool stone wall. A combination of relief, shame, and guilt pooled in her belly, overtaking the anger. For now, at least.

"What in the Twelve Hells am I doing?" she groaned, letting her head fall into her hands as her soaked clothes dripped on the floor.

A voice drew her out of her shame-spiral. "So, uh, that was your handiwork, I take it?"

Her head shot up, stunned as she faced the leggy, golden goddess and the slick, dark-haired god from a moment ago. Crossing her arms over her chest and resting her head against the wall, Remi let out a long sigh. Unsure what else to say, she went with, "You got me. Guilty as charged."

They watched her with blatant curiosity before they moved closer. "You pack quite a punch," the god observed, seeming more impressed than upset.

"Comes with the territory," Remi muttered, still not sure where this was going or why these two had stuck around when the rest of them had followed their prince to do his bidding. "So, why are you two still here? Shouldn't you be with Thayne, sorting this whole mess out too?" Though deep down, Remi knew she owed them more than her prickly side, like, say, an apology, she couldn't seem to bring herself to do it. She still felt raw, and she wasn't ready to deal with anyone else's emotions right now. Not before she worked out her own enough to keep herself calm.

"Thayne asked us to stick around and keep an eye on you," the goddess said.

Remi's eyes narrowed in confusion. That was funny because she'd been standing right there the whole time, and she hadn't heard him say anything to that effect. So, she tilted her head asking the unspoken question, "When did he say that?"

"Well, it was more a look than actual words," the goddess said. "But I'm a pro at reading them. Thayne's looks, I mean. It's just something that happens when you've known someone since infancy, you know?" When Remi didn't respond within one millisecond, the goddess continued, "So, want to talk about what happened back there?" She hitched a finger over her shoulder.

"Not really," Remi replied, wishing to all the gods that these two would just leave her alone until she felt capable of dealing with people again. Alas, it was not meant to be.

"Okay, if you don't want to talk about it, how about I guess?" the goddess asked. Before Remi could bite her head off and send her scurrying away like a frightened rabbit, she continued, "So, here it is. Someone called you a meany face, and you don't take kindly to insults of such a serious nature.

So…," she mouthed *boom* and mimed an explosion with her hands.

The god led out a low chuckle, his adoring gaze fixed on the beautiful goddess. Remi stared at the goddess with a confused expression for a stunned moment before a bark of laughter escaped her lips. "Wow, you're such a good guesser," Remi said, her response dripping with sarcasm.

Rolling her eyes in mock acceptance of the compliment, the goddess pressed a hand to her chest. "I know. I have a gift."

Unable to help it, Remi's face split into a smile as she shook her head. On impulse, she leaned forward and extended a hand in greeting. "I'm Remi."

A stunning, white smile spread across the goddess's face. "I was at your wedding, though we didn't get a chance to meet. I'm Ellarah." They shook, Ellarah inclining her head in deference to Remi's title as they did.

She looked over to the god, who seemed like the silent broody type, and held out a hand. She couldn't help but notice that he was the polar opposite of the girl with him. Pale and dark-haired, sharp featured with vivid eyes. "I'm Riven," he said, taking her hand, also inclining his head in respect. "Thayne, Ellarah, and I have been friends since before any of us can remember."

Remi knitted her brows together and pointed between the two. "You're not together?"

Ellarah's stunning face split into another smile. "Oh, no, we are *definitely* together." They looked at each other, the combination of affection and reverence unmistakable.

Feeling the tension in her shoulders relax with the ease of the conversation, Remi let out a sigh. "I'm sorry about your room. I promise I'll replace everything."

Ellarah waved it off, though she gnawed on her bottom lip in concern. "It was just clothes and electronics. It's a good thing there are so many empty rooms in that wing, or else this whole situation could have been a lot worse. As it is, you just messed up a few empty guest rooms, along with mine, of course."

Remi's spine straightened in horror. She hadn't even thought of that until just this moment. Ascended, what if there had been other deities in there? Lower-caste or servant-caste gods and goddesses who couldn't have withstood her magic? She let out an involuntary shudder, grateful that she hadn't gone full nuclear and that Thayne had gotten there in time to help her out of it.

"You're right; it could have been a lot worse," Remi allowed, raking a hand over her face in a combination of relief and horror.

"Hey, look," Ellarah said, her voice dropping into a more comforting tone. "There's a lot going on right now, especially for you."

Remi looked back at her, arching a brow, daring her to elaborate. To her utter astonishment, Ellarah did. "I mean, after everything that happened with Gabryel and your sister, who could blame you?"

It would appear that this goddess had no fear of royalty and also very little concern for stepping on anyone's toes. It was actually somewhat refreshing. Letting her guard down just a little, Remi inclined her head in agreement looking between her new companions. "It's just…we still don't know where Bekka is." She gnawed her lip as fear and worry crept their way back into the forefront of her mind. "And I feel helpless. No one will let me do anything about it. Instead, I'm stuck here with no idea what's happening."

Ellarah shot Riven a quick but meaningful look as though she were asking his opinion on something. She raised her brows in question while he gave his head a quick shake. She narrowed her eyes in apparent disagreement, and then he caved, nodding in acquiescence.

The whole exchange took maybe a few seconds, and then Ellarah turned back to her. "You mean, you haven't heard the rumors? Like nothing about your sister's whereabouts, at all?"

Her words seemed to echo through Remi's mind. Her pulse raced. "What rumors? What are you talking about? Do you know something?"

Ellarah held up a manicured finger. "I don't really *know* anything per se—" Remi opened her mouth to argue, but Ellarah beat her to it "—but I might know a way we can find out. We have certain…connections." Ellarah peered down the hall either way as though checking for eavesdroppers. When she saw nothing, she stepped closer, and dropping her voice to a whisper, said, "Not of the official sort. Off the record and not of the savory variety either, if you catch my meaning."

Foreign spies or criminals, Remi thought, her mind whirring as she took in everything that they implied. This could be her chance to help her sister, but was she willing to get wrapped up in something unsavory to do it?

Who was she kidding? There was no line that she wouldn't cross to find her sister, no matter how distasteful. Besides, this would mean that she wouldn't require permission from her family to do it. Maybe, she could find Bekka and bring her back herself.

She leaned closer and whispered, "Tell me."

CHAPTER 2

BEKKA

Disturbance

"A re you sure about this?" I asked, squinting down at the portable comm device and holo that Damion had commandeered for this mission—it was a sphere, no larger than 2 inches in circumference. Projected from a small eye was a life-sized image of a large, four-legged creature, unlike anything I had ever seen. It looked like a horse; only it was zigged-zagged with contrasting black and white stripes running the length of its body.

"I'm sure," Damion, the Moldizean god of the hunt and the resident expert on all land-bound creatures in Moldize, confirmed.

I frowned at the image. "But its ass looks like a hypnotic spiral."

Damion let out a begrudging laugh. "OK, I'll give you that. But that serves a purpose."

"What possible purpose does *that* serve?" I pointed at the aforementioned ass for emphasis. Damion chewed on his cheek, amused as I continued, "It seems like we're serving them to the lions and hyenas on a silver platter. So, I guess if that's their purpose, then well played, Mr. God of the Hunt. Well played."

He chuckled and shook his head at me. "It confuses the biting flies that carry disease, which Sybil will create later today."

"Ew," I said, scrunching up my nose. "Remind me again, why in Twelve Hells do we need biting flies?"

"The same reason why the god of pestilence will re-create the fungus needed for mold to form. In all things, there is a balance." When I only gaped at him in disgust, he said, "Just be happy you don't have to create them."

I paused for a few beats, just for maximum effect, before I replied with a dry, "I say again. Ew."

Damion looked down his long, straight nose at me. His curly blond hair was half-pulled up in a ponytail, while the rest hung loose around his shoulders. He rubbed a hand over his scrubby beard as he prepared to lecture me. Again. "All of these creatures exist in many of the other realms, zebras included. As I said, all creatures have their place—"

"I know, I know," I interrupted, waving a hand. "But baiting you never gets old." I tossed a wicked grin in his direction. "You should stop making it so easy."

He opened his mouth to reply but then shut it and shook his head. "Your professionalism leaves something to be desired." I wondered if he regretted asking for my help with repopulating the animals on the planet. But then his lips twitched into a begrudging smile, and I knew he wasn't angry.

I pursed my own as though thoughtful and nodded. "It does. It really does." Before he could chastise me further, I called my power forward and pushed it outwards. My body glowed blue, and my skin hummed, my core heating into a toasty warmth as it vibrated with magic. The ease with which I could handle my creation gift comforted me. I held up my hand and let it loose, the magic dancing along the riverbank.

Damion did the same, his coppery magic dancing next to my own and beginning to take form. His gift as a god of the hunt allowed him to create any non-sentient animals he desired. He'd asked for my help because he was the only hunter left in Moldize, and repopulating an entire planet proved to be a tall order, even for a god as powerful as him.

Rather than gawk at him all day, I decided to focus on my own magic. Ignoring him for the moment, I looked down at the picture and then forced my power to comply with that image. The stream of my magic twisted upwards into translucent, blue, horse-shaped creatures. Then, the blue silhouettes solidified as zebras, their yips echoing off the hills around me. Damion and I continued, magic flowing freely as more and more zebras appeared, galloping along the shoreline. I had counted three hundred by the time he held up his hand for us to stop.

I obeyed, turning to Damion to ask, "What's next?" We started down the list. First, him, projecting a 3D life-sized image with statistics and rationed quantities, and then both of us, creating it. We worked quickly, enjoying the peacefulness of the savannah, free of any distractions.

It had been an entire month since we'd saved Moldize and its home planet of Myzhrele from certain destruction via the explosion of their sun. But it would be a while yet before the surviving humans and animals migrated this far north. I glanced up at the glowing orb in the sky and basked in the comfortable warmth of the day. I liked to imagine that people everywhere on this planet did the same, relieved to be given a second chance at life.

Damion showed me another image, this time of a massive cat. It had a bobbed tail, deep orange fur, and long, protruding teeth from its upper jaw. This wasn't a creature we had in

Valeria either, and I squinted, memorizing the lines of the creature's body. "What's this one called?"

"It's a saber-toothed tiger, native to this part of Moldize. It dwells mostly in the hills surrounding the Savannah and will come down here for water or prey if needed," Damion explained.

I nodded, understanding *tiger* well enough. We did have those in Valeria after all. "How many?" I asked, noting that no count accompanied this photograph.

"For now, let's go with a hundred," he answered, his tone decisive. "That should be enough for today. We can revisit them later." Damion had ensured that the initial quantities were low for both of our benefits; after all, creating thousands of living creatures with instincts and minds of their own drained one's power reserve to damn near empty. For now, we would just let nature take its course and revisit the populations in a few mortal years.

"You got it," I answered. I shook out my hands and exhaled, releasing my power once more. It flowed as did his. No Moldizean wards blocked us despite our presence in the mortal realm. That was one of the first changes I made after we'd rebuilt the sun. All deities could access their powers in this place without the threat of repercussion. We were just expected to use discretion, which was how it worked in all the other civilized realms.

A few moments later and the tigers were complete. They looked stunned, crouched low, surprised to be alive. Then something clicked. They roared, hissed at each other, and fled off in opposite directions. It made sense since most cats had a tendency to be solitary creatures.

Spent, I sat down in the tall grass and watched, enjoying the sight of my surroundings. "It really is beautiful here," I said, wiping a thin sheen of sweat off my brow. We were perched on a hill overlooking the valley below. A steady, flowing river cut straight through the middle of it, and soft green and tan grass waved in the gentle breeze. Hills and rocky outcroppings surrounded us, and I sighed at the restfulness of it all.

"We couldn't have done it without you," Damion said, sitting down next to me.

"Nah, it was a team effort," I said, wiping the sweat from my brow with the back of my hand. It was the truth too. As a creation deity, I alone could create new planets, solar systems, galaxies, and even universes. I was also the only living being who could create sentient life, with a soul, like humans. Similar to a hunter, I could also create living creatures, even those without souls. But other stuff—like water, vegetation, healthy soil, a breathable atmosphere, fire & micro-organisms—was not my realm of responsibility. And all of those things were critical when it came to sustaining life.

That's where the hunt, agriculture and botany, water, air, land, and many other deities came into play. They rid the planet of radiation, conjured the plants and the waters, and balanced the animal life to ensure that the natural world operated smoothly. As Damion had said, there was a balance in all things, even in the roles of the gods.

Creating life was not easy at all. Actually, creating anything was difficult, and it always took a lot of energy to accomplish. The more complex the creation was, the harder it was to create. That's why, at the moment, I felt like I'd transversed the entire planet on foot.

But all the exhaustion and effort was worth it. Once we finished with this Savannah, we would have restored the planet's surface to about 90% of its former glory. We planned to be done with the last 10% by the end of the week. Then it would be up to the seasonal and weather deities, along with many others, to maintain the surface conditions. And my job would be done.

We finished our break and spent another hour working until, at last, Damion had no more pictures for me. I shielded my eyes from the sun that hung low in the sky. "That's it for today?" I asked.

"For now," Damion replied. "Why don't you make us a portal back to Castle Molo?" Creators were one of a handful of deities powerful enough to create portals between the mortal and immortal dimensions.

"You got it, boss," I teased. Obeying his request, I made awkward squiggly motions with my hands. Damion rolled his eyes because I could have just pointed, and the result would have been the same. But where was the fun in that?

I grinned at him and unleashed my magic amid my ridiculous hand gestures. Blue power swirled in front of us, crackled like lightning, and then settled into a circular doorway. On one side was the mortal realm where we stood now, and on the other, I could see the grand hall of Castle Molo.

Damion stepped through, and I started to follow him but stopped short when a flash of movement caught my eye.

My breath stalled in my throat as Arrick came into view on the other side of the portal. My power crackled between us, but I could still see him clearly. He stood with his hands slipped into his pockets, and his green eyes stared at me with an intensity that made my stomach roil. He wore his shaggy dark hair brushed back and sported a fitted t-shirt with snug jeans. He looked incredible. I mentally slapped myself at the thought, my lady parts betraying the better sense my brain had to offer. But, I had to remember, we weren't on speaking terms at the moment.

Our eyes locked for a split-second, and electricity skittered down my spine. Pointedly, I looked away and stepped through the portal and into his home. I dissolved the doorway behind me with a thought, the heat of Arrick's gaze on me unmistakable.

I swallowed hard, my throat bobbing, and observed haughtily. "You're back."

"I am," he answered, his voice as warm and velvety as hot chocolate.

Refusing to behave like a coward, I forced myself to look at him once more. The minute our eyes locked, I regretted it. Even now, even after the massive blowout of a fight we'd had, I still felt it—that tug. Like he was the sun, and I was a helpless planet caught in his magnetic pull. But I had no intention of letting him see that. So instead, I held his gaze with as much defiance as I could muster and asked, "You plan to stick around this time?"

He nodded slowly. "The underworld is settled now, so I'll be here for the foreseeable future." Two weeks ago, Arrick had left under the guise of necessity. Something about heaven and hell and his responsibilities as a death deity. But I had my suspicions that the real reason was to avoid me. "Are you disappointed by that?" he asked, searching my face.

My spine stiffened. "It's your home," I replied, deflecting the issue. "I can hardly keep you from it."

I registered hurt in his expression before he composed it. "Look, Bekka, when you're ready to talk about this," he gestured to each of us before he finished with, "you know where to find me." His fists clenched as a black mist swirled, forming a portal of his own. Then, with one smoldering glare at me, he walked through it, disappearing just as quickly as he'd come.

I let out a long-suffering sigh and nearly jumped out of my skin when Damion asked, "When are you going to cut him some slack?"

I snapped. "No offense, but I don't see how that's any of your business."

Damion held up his hands in surrender. "You're right; it's not. But he's not the only one you're hurting. You know that, right?"

I sighed. "Yeah, I know. I'm sorry if our disagreement is making things uncomfortable for everyone." Disagreement was the understatement of the millennia for what had happened between us, I thought, my mood grim.

Damion rubbed the back of his neck. "It's not just that. Though I'll admit, we all breathed a sigh of relief when he went to the underworld."

My brows pinched together. "Then what do you mean?"

"This disagreement is hurting you too. We can all see it." Damion stared straight ahead as we began to walk towards the dining hall. I marveled at how close I had become with both him and Erykha, the Moldizean science goddess and Damion's sort-of wife, after only a few short weeks. I considered both her and Damion to be friends and confidantes. But there were limitations to what I was willing to discuss with them. One of those limitations was Arrick, because he was their son, which made anything I might have to say awkward as hell.

I sighed. "Is it OK if we not talk about this right now? It's a little more complicated than me cutting Arrick some slack; I promise you that." The truth was that Arrick and I were at an impasse. Things had blown up between us, and I wasn't sure how we were going to fix it. My belly knotted as I remembered the awful words that I had hurled at him in anger.

He had taken the abuse, his eyes like green fire before he had blown up at me in turn, losing his patience with me and his temper along with it. The reality was that we had a long way to go before things were resolved between us. There were too many hurt feelings and too much injured pride to simply apologize and move forward.

Damion gave a solemn nod. "You're right. I didn't mean to overstep. It's just that I hate seeing you both this miserable. We all do."

"Noted," I answered with a quick nod before I expertly changed the subject. "Now, let's talk about food. What do you think Nanthia made us tonight? I'm crossing my fingers for lobster." We turned the corner and walked down a hallway filled with doors.

Damion pursed his lips as we reached the end of the hall. "I don't think you're going to like what's on the menu tonight." He reached out, ready to grasp the doorknob that led into the dining hall, but his hand hesitated. He cut his eyes to me. "You have to promise me that you'll forgive me for this." Without further delay and before I had the chance to question what he meant by that, he turned the knob and pushed the door open.

Inside the room and seated at the large dining room table were Deklan, Caden, Erykha, Lilja, and Arrick. My mind screamed *"ambush,"* and panic rushed through me. I gave Damion a betrayed look, mouth agape and eyes wide with horror. If this was what I thought it was, then Damion would be second on my shit list, right below Arrick.

Erykha sat closest to where I stood and pulled out a chair, beckoning for me to sit. I held my ground. "What's going on here?" I asked, clenching my fists at my side.

Damion rested his hand on my shoulder. "Please, Bekka, have a seat. We need to talk." His voice was low and soothing.

Dread crawled up my spine as I shook my head and pressed my lips together. As I took in the kind sympathy on each of their faces, realization hit me—I knew what this was about, and I wanted no part of it. "No. I don't want to talk about this."

Concern flashed over Erykha and Lilja's expressions, and they each cast nervous glances at Arrick. Caden and Deklan looked stone-faced, as though they didn't want to be here any more than I did. At least someone was on my side, I thought bitterly.

When Erykha spoke, her voice was a gentle caress over my ragged nerves, "Bekka, we've given you as much time as we can, but—"

"But what?" I snapped. "We aren't even done fixing Moldize yet! Can't you at least give me that before we do this?" I waved my hand at them and scowled at their concerned expressions.

Damion shook his head beside me. "I'm sorry, Bekka, but Erykha's right. We're out of time."

I bristled. "What is that supposed to mean?"

Arrick leaned back in his seat, one ankle resting on the opposite knee, hands clasped in his lap. He looked relaxed and authoritative when he answered, "It means that Gabryel is gone, and we need to talk about what comes next. If we don't do it now, then we might not get another chance."

Grief swelled inside my chest faster than I could process it. It choked me as I tried to breathe through my body's visceral reaction to this callous reminder of my grandpa's death. I shook my head. "Please, I'm not ready. I need more time."

Tears formed at the corner of my eyes and I swiped at them angrily. That was the reason why I didn't want to talk about it. My emotions still ran too high. Every time I even tried to broach the subject of my loss, I turned into a hysterical, blubbering idiot.

Recognizing my distress, Lilja, Arrick's little sister, rose from her seat and came to stand in front of me. She didn't speak, only wrapped her thin, lanky, pre-teen arms around my waist and squeezed. Her empathy cracked something inside of me, and the dam broke. Tears slipped unbidden down my cheeks as I sniffed and hiccuped, trying to rein myself in again.

When my shoulders stopped shaking, and I no longer shuddered like a lost puppy, she whispered, "I know it isn't fair, and I know you're sad. But things are happening, and we're worried. Please, sit down and talk to us."

Lilja was young, right on the cusp of puberty, but she was a perceptive kid. There was something about the soft understanding written in her young, sweet eyes that chiseled away at my armor. I found myself nodding before I realized that I had agreed to anything.

She twined her slender, delicate fingers into mine and pulled me to the table. I took the seat next to Erykha, the one she had originally offered. I tried to ignore the fact that Arrick sat next to me as Lilja took the chair on the other side of her mother. I fixed my swollen eyes on Erykha. "What does she mean? What's happening?"

Erykha pressed her palms to the table and grimaced almost imperceptibly, but I still caught it. I could tell from her hesitation that she didn't want to upset me, but it was clear that whatever news she had was bound to do just that.

Arrick spoke from the seat next to me, having no such qualms, "There's unrest. Everyone in the Twelve Realms has learned of Gabryel's ascension, and there have been rumblings."

I knew the gods would figure out that their Peacekeeper was gone soon enough, but I had hoped that the upper-caste and royal gods would keep it secret. And that maybe their inclination towards secrecy would buy me some time to grieve and prepare. But if Moldize had already heard rumblings, then it was safe to say that the cat was out of the bag. I ran a nervous hand down my braid. "What kind of rumblings?"

"Gabryel had a lot of enemies. Many of whom resented the Peacekeeper's council and its laws. They see his absence and his apparent lack of a willing heir as an opportunity."

My whole body tensed at his words, knowing what was next. I was my grandpa's heir. The last creation deity left in the multiverse and the only being powerful enough to step into his place and keep order in the Twelve Realms. The only one powerful enough to become their Peacekeeper.

Damion leaned forward, voice soft as he said, "It's time for you to come out of your self-imposed exile. You need to go home to Valeria and take your rightful place as his heir."

I resisted the urge to lean over and hurl all over the black marble floor. Instead, I settled for shaking my head in denial. "I can't," I whispered, shame threatening to swallow me whole.

Deklan spoke up then, "What do you mean you can't?" His words were curt with no trace of soft emotion, only cold logic. It seemed I'd misread his discomfort earlier, and he wasn't as much on my side as annoyed by this entire exercise.

My head snapped up, and I glared at him. "You wouldn't understand."

"You don't have a choice anymore," he said. "Shit is happening, and you can't bury your head in the sand and pretend like it isn't."

Anger pulsed through me, and I shot out of my chair, sending it screeching backward as blue power swelled around me. It filled the room with static electricity, and I knew I should get it leashed, get it under control. But at the moment, I just didn't care. I sniped back at him. "What would you know about it? You've lived in the immortal realm all of what? One second? And now you're an expert?"

Deklan and Caden were long-lost relatives of the original creator of this realm, Afriel. They'd just recently learned of their heritage, and after they traveled here with Arrick and me on our mission to fix the sun, they had decided to stay with what remained of their family.

Deklan rose to his feet, accepting my challenge head-on. "You're his only heir. So, I guess my question is, what don't you understand about that?"

I bared my teeth at him. Clearly, the demigod had a death wish. It took every ounce of self-control I had to stop myself from leaping across the table and throttling him. Instead, I opened my mouth to give him a verbal lashing to end all lashings, but Erykha beat me to it. "Time out!" She slapped a hand onto the table in command. "Let's not fight amongst ourselves. We're all on the same side here."

"She's right." Caden rose to clap a hand on his brother's shoulder. He pulled him back into his seat, and Deklan clenched his jaw, his frustration with me clear. Finally, Caden spoke again, "Bekka, you say we don't understand. But what is it that we don't understand? What are we missing?"

I closed my hands into fists, and my power evaporated. I felt drained now, the fight in me dissipating as quickly as my magic. The truth was, the anger felt good. Better than the pain that assaulted every fiber of my being. Wearily, I slumped back into my chair, and as I did, Arrick shoved it forward and saved me from falling on my ass. I chose not to acknowledge the gesture.

Instead, I contemplated Caden's question and came to one conclusion. There was too much to explain. Everything had gone so wrong on that fateful day when I was supposed to save the Moldizean's mortal planet from extinction. Instead, my power had guttered, flying away like a bird released from its life-long cage. Drained and on the brink of death, my grandpa had gifted his power to me and sacrificed his own life to save mine. I had begged him to stop and then pleaded with Arrick to make him stop. But neither of the hard-headed bastards had listened to me.

As I sat in silence, still debating my answer, I glanced at Arrick through my lashes. This last part was what our fight had been about. I'd blamed him for everything that had gone wrong that day; screamed that he should have let me die and saved my grandpa instead. Told him that I would never forgive him.

The very next morning, I awoke to find a note slipped under the door.

Sorry for leaving, but I need to do my duties as the Moldizean God of Death. Will see you later.

A.

We hadn't spoken since. At least, not until today.

After a long pause, I gave them the answer that had plagued me for so long. "Because what happened to my grandpa is my fault."

Everyone around the table froze. Every face wore a mask of complete shock. Clearly, this was not what they had expected me to say.

Hell, it was not what I'd expected to say.

I looked down at my hands and then at Arrick. His stare was intense, boring into me, and I could guess what he was thinking at that moment. That fight. That awful fight. I winced at the memory.

Damion was the first to speak. "Bekka, that wasn't your fault. There must have been some piece to the prophecy that we didn't know about. Something we didn't understand or didn't realize."

I shook my head, adamant that it had been my responsibility. "But it is my fault, don't you see? I chose to stay here. I chose to live out the prophecy and face it on my own, and now he's dead because of it!" Tears swelled in my eyes again. I swiped them away, frustrated by my inability to keep my emotions under control.

Caden shook his head, his white-blond hair rustling in its long ponytail as he moved. "But if you hadn't, then everyone in Itoriah would be dead. What would have happened to Niko and Kaleb if you hadn't stayed? Not to mention the millions of other people that we don't even know about. Do you really think you should have walked away? Do you regret helping us that much?"

My heart squeezed, and I rushed to explain the thoughts that had warred in my mind since that night. "No, of course not. Of course, I don't regret helping you. It's just...I just—" I struggled with the words that would make them understand, that would make them comprehend the guilt that plagued me. The feeling of complete and utter failure that enveloped me like a shroud. The shame that dogged me every time I even thought about returning home. But the words weren't there. The last thing I wanted was pity, and if I told them any of that, that was precisely what I would get.

The smooth tenor of Arrick's voice broke through the dull roar of my thoughts. "What Gabryel did that day, it was his choice. He chose you over himself."

"Don't you think I know that?" I yelled, unable to control the rush of emotion any longer. "But think about how my family will see this. Hell, think about how all of Valeria will see this. It doesn't matter that I know we did the right thing here. All they'll know is that I chose to help the one universe they loathe over keeping my own people safe. My actions robbed them of their ruler and the multiverse's Peacekeeper! Now they're stuck with me." I broke off, shaking my head again. I was a piss-poor substitute for my grandpa, and everyone with half a brain in their skull knew it. When I continued, my voice was under control. "With everything that's happened, how can I ever face them?"

Erykha laid her hand over mine, the knuckles of my clenched fist white against the dark wood of the table. Then, cutting to the meat of the issue, she asked, "You don't think Gabryel made the right choice, do you?"

"No, I don't," I said. "He should have let me go. If he had, then everyone else would be safe right now, and we wouldn't be in this insane mess." And I wouldn't be the ridiculously under-qualified heir to his throne, I thought as I looked down and let out a long sigh. Because that was the other problem—I was nowhere near ready to take on the task of policing the Twelve Realms. We needed someone who knew what they were doing. Not some twenty-something goddess with powers barely over a month old who didn't know the first thing about maintaining the integrity of a vast kingdom. The task was way out of my league, and I damn well knew it.

Arrick shook his head. "You're wrong. Gabryel was not the type of god who made mistakes or took decisions lightly. If he gifted you his power, he did it because he knew you could handle it."

"He's right, Bekka. Gabryel never did anything without thinking through all possible outcomes," Damion agreed.

I pulled my hands from Erykha's and rested my elbows on the table, dropping my head and rubbing my temples. "That may be true, but it doesn't change the fact that I doubt I'll be welcomed back to Valeria with open arms. And even if I wanted to go, how would we get there? We're completely cut off from them."

Before my grandpa left our world, he had doubled down on the security wards surrounding Valeria. We'd checked right after I'd rebuilt the sun. It was an absolute fortress for any realm that didn't have an open portal already in place, which Moldize did not.

Arrick shifted in his chair. "We've been working on a plan for that since Gabryel ascended. We almost have the details hammered out. We were going to wait to tell you until you had a chance to grieve a little longer, but the situation has changed. Things are getting bad out there, Bekka."

I locked eyes with him. "What is it you're dancing around? What's the problem? Just tell me because it seems like you're talking about more than just rumblings."

Arrick's gaze flicked to his parents before it settled back on me. "It's the Nefarals. We've heard talk of insurrection from at least six of the Twelve Realms."

I swallowed hard, my throat pulsing. A prickle of fear raced down my spine. My grandfather had conquered them over 900 years before in the War of the Nefarals. Then, he and his allies, tired of watching the Nefaric powers infect and destroy realm-after-realm, had declared war on them. The fight had been long and bloody, but Gabryel had come out on top. Since then, the Nefaric deities, once the most powerful across the Twelve Realms, had been under intense scrutiny and regulation.

He leashed their gifts, suppressing them and no longer allowing them to run free. Since then, all of the realms had prospered without the threat of destruction. But now, Gabryel, the driving force that kept everyone in check, was gone. And no one liked to live in a cage. Now that that cage had been knocked ajar, I hated to imagine how they planned to escape and what revenge they'd take.

"But there's something else—" Arrick broke off, clearing his throat and looking out the window opposite our side of the table.

Something about his tone made me look up, nerves pricking at the back of my neck. "What? What else?"

Arrick swallowed and locked his eyes on mine. "The worst of it is in Bicaidia. There are more Nefarals there than in any other realm. It could get ugly if we don't act right now."

Arrick's aforementioned *something else* hit me like a... "Remi," I whispered, eyes wide. My twin sister lived in Bicaidia. She had married the prince of the kingdom, Thayne, just as my powers came to be, and this disaster happened with my grandfather.

My heart raced—this wasn't just some vague threat or mysterious whispering. They forced me to talk about this because my sister was at risk, and the danger was real. Maybe even imminent.

Could I risk letting Bicaidia get overthrown by the Nefaric Pillar of Power? All because I was too damned scared to claim my seat as my grandpa's heir? I shuddered to think about it.

Arrick nodded gravely. Leaning closer to me as though to impress the importance of his next point, he said, "Remi would be at the center of it. There's no way that an insurrection led by the Bicaidian Nefarals would allow the royal family get away unscathed. At minimum, they'd imprison her and use her against your family."

I stared at him, letting his warning sink in. The truth was that Arrick was as much a Nefaral as anyone and was the leader of the Nefaric Pillar here in Moldize. His powerful death deity magic cemented that status. I wondered if he had any empathy for this budding insurrection. If he did, I couldn't read it in his dire expression.

Blood roared in my ears, and a ballad of curses played on repeat in my mind as blind panic set in. They were right; I couldn't stay here and screw around anymore. We had to get back to Valeria. We had to keep the Nefarals in check. I could only hope that my presence—my power—was enough to deter them from their current course of action. If it wasn't, then I didn't know what I or what any of us would do. But my best guess was that it would drag us into a war like we hadn't seen in nearly a millennium.

I sucked in a breath and calmed my racing heart. Blue power licked up my arms as anger pulsed through me. No one was going to touch a hair on my sister's gorgeous head. "Tell me," I demanded, at last able to think clearly past the panic. "You said you had a plan, so, what's our way into Valeria?"

"We aren't going to Valeria," Arrick corrected, a slow grin spreading across his face.

I scrunched up my nose in confusion. "Wait, what?" I asked, drawing a total blank.

Erykha answered, "Like you said, we're completely cut off from them. Plus, we've lost all contact with any spies we had there. So, there's no way in."

I grew more irritated by the second. "Then what the hell are we going to do?"

Damion smiled at me now, the look eerily similar to his son's. His voice was filled with confidence when he said, "We have limited but effective communication access to the other realms, and we have allies positioned in many of them too. We plan to send word to Bicaidia and then travel through that universe to get back into Valeria."

I considered, weighing the pros and cons of such a plan, and after a while, I decided that it was a solid idea. "One question," I interrupted, holding up a single digit. "How do we plan to get to Bicaidia? Communications access is not the same as a portal for travel, and there's no open portal between Moldize and any of the other Twelve Realms."

Arrick shrugged a broad shoulder. "We have a few options."

"Which are?" I asked, raising my brows.

"You can contact your sister," Erykha rushed to explain, the words eddying out of her quicker than seemed natural. I eyed her in confusion. But, she continued, unfazed by my bafflement. "That would be the best and the easiest way. Do you think she would agree to help you? Maybe she could convince the royals to open a portal with us if we explained the situation."

I squared my shoulders with confidence. "She'll help." Despite everything that had happened, I knew my twin would never leave me hanging when I needed her. But then a thought hit me, and I hedged. "But she's barely lived there for a month. So she may not have the influence she would need to convince the pillar leaders or the royals there to side with us. And I can't speak to what Thayne would do, should she need his help. We barely know him."

Pillar was shorthand for Pillars of Power. There were six, and they spanned across all of the Twelve Realms, each pillar containing many sects within them. The most powerful deity in each pillar, elected by the sects they oversaw, ruled their home realm in conjunction with the royal family. Any creation of a new portal to another realm would require their approval, along with a royal decree.

I chewed on my nail, doubt creeping into my previously certain demeanor. Remi would try, of course, but could she convince them to make it happen?

"What's the other option?" I asked. All the Moldizean deities at the table grimaced, and I knew it wasn't going to be good.

"Let's try this one first," Erykha suggested soberly,

Oh boy, this does not bode well, I thought. "Oh no," I wagged my finger. "You need to tell me the other plan right now. I want to know what I'm getting into, should the first option fail."

Arrick rubbed a hand over the back of his neck. "We can use the path I usually do when I navigate through the realms. It's how I got you out of Valeria the last time."

I scratched my head as I tried to remember. Unfortunately, everything from the moment I came into my powers at my sister's wedding until I awoke here was a complete blank. I had nothing. "I have no idea how you managed that. I was unconscious," I pointed out.

"We took a detour," Arrick answered vaguely. I waited for him to elaborate, but he said no more. I surveyed each of the faces around me. Lilja was carefully looking at a spot on the ceiling. Not helpful. Erykha was looking out the window, avoiding my gaze, and Damion was staring at the ground. Not helpful either. Caden and Deklan looked just as confused and annoyed as I felt. Apparently, no one had filled them in on the backup plan either.

Deklan leaned forward. "Would you stop being cute and just tell us what the damn detour entails, Arrick?"

"Yes." I pointed to Deklan. "What he said."

Arrick's lips twitched in amusement. "Cute?" He murmured, "That's a first." He shook his head as though to clear it. "Fine, but for the record, it's not my first choice."

"Just spit it out!" Caden exclaimed, raising his voice well beyond its usual, measured tenor. For a split second, I could have sworn the soft sheen of light that surrounded him pulsed brighter. But I blinked, and the effect was gone.

Arrick did as he requested. "We can go through the underworld." We all froze as his words hit home. Something told me we wouldn't be so lucky as to get to go through heaven. Then, after a brief pause, he clarified, "Specifically, hell."

Called it, I thought, finding pleasure in my rightness despite the horror that this plan elicited.

Arrick continued his explanation, "The wards will be too strong to create a portal into Bicaidia directly for any of us. Bicaidian heaven is also too heavily guarded. But, on the other hand, hell is where my powers are strongest, and it's also the least warded entry point. So I should be able to make a portal into the underworld, then we can find our way to a portal to the immortal realm from there. No one ever uses the portals into or out of hell from the immortal realms, so we should be able to go through one unnoticed."

He had a point. We had the same kind of portals scattered throughout all of the habitable planets in Valeria, yet we never used them. There was no reason to, since we didn't have a death god there.

Deklan looked to the sky as though speaking to the great beyond, and asked, "Why can't it ever be simple?"

The demigod had a damned good point.

CHAPTER 3

REMI

Clandestine

A knock on Remi's door had her leaping up from her new, not burnt to a crisp bed and running to the threshold. She yanked the handle and pulled it open to reveal Ellarah.

Remi felt breathless with hopeful anticipation at the sight of her newfound ally. Stepping aside, she gestured for her to come inside. Ellarah obliged, her long legs eating up the floorspace with her cavalier stride. Before Remi could even open her mouth to ask what she'd learned, Ellarah started talking, "Just as promised, I did a little digging." She stopped in front of the large picture window and crossed her arms, back facing Remi. "Everyone's acting real cagey about it, though. I had to get a little creative before I found someone willing to talk."

Remi felt her pulse in her ears but didn't let her anxiety show. "What did you find out?"

Ellarah's shoulders rose and then fell, an audible sigh releasing in time with the physical gesture. "Nothing, well, not yet at least." She turned from the window and faced Remi, who stood straight and still, her body having condensed into the consistency of stone, bracing for the disappointment she sensed coming.

Ellarah's eyes seemed to travel the length of Remi as though assessing her suitability. For what, Remi couldn't even begin to guess, nor did she care at the moment. Her deflating hope felt like a living, breathing entity, swallowing her insides into a vacuum of despair.

But before Remi could spiral further, Ellarah's face split into an exquisite grin, her eyes alight with intrigue. "But, you should know something soon enough. I got you a meeting of the clandestine variety. It starts in about, oh…Ummm…" she peeked outside at the moon to gauge the time and then turned back. "A few minutes, give or take. So, we need to be quick about this. No time for idle chit-chat."

With that, Ellarah pulled a smooth, round orb from the pocket of her loose-fitted black silk trousers and tossed it from hand to hand. "The coordinates are already punched in, and it's ready to go. You just need to power it up."

She tossed it across the room, and Remi caught it with ease. "Who—what?" She cleared her throat and shook her head, trying to get her thoughts in order. "Who am I meeting? What should I expect?"

Ellarah stepped closer; her footfalls softened by the thick-spun rug beneath them. "They didn't give me a name. All I know is that if you want this meeting to happen, there are rules. No names, no caste or pillar positions, no comm device, and you have to leave the instaportal here. You will be 100% alone. The payout, though…" She sucked air through her teeth. "My source claims to know where Bekka is and says he is in communication with her."

Remi's whole body ignited, figuratively, of course, at the prospect of learning the truth behind her sister's disappearance and at the fact that Ellarah's source believed her to be alive.

She looked longingly at the metallic device in her hand as she took in the full ramifications of everything else Ellarah had said. Alone, no comm device, no names, no means for a quick escape.

Suspicion crept into her mind then. Could she be walking into some kind of a trap? Someone had kidnaped her sister, and Remi was just going to waltz into an unknown location to meet with someone who wouldn't even give her their name? She thought about telling Thayne but then dismissed that idea out of hand. They might be married, but their relationship was little more than a cordial friendship at this point, regardless of how he'd come to her rescue just days earlier.

Still, this had all the makings of a terrible idea at best or an ambush at worst, and yet…it was the only shot she had to learn what had happened to her sister. If what this person promised was true, then she might even be able to talk to her. Maybe bring her home. Was there even a choice? She thought, knowing the answer deep down.

With that question answered in her mind, Remi sent a spark of magic into the metallic orb and rolled it across the floor. Within seconds, a portal flashed to life before her. She blinked as the fire that the orb had absorbed from her receded, leaving nothing but a buzzing, circular blackness in its wake.

Judging by the void in front of them, Ellarah had cloaked their location from the portal, which would give them privacy until she stepped through it. She turned back to her companion, her partner in crime. Remi's skin felt clammy, and her breaths were shallow with nerves. "If I'm not back in an hour—"

Ellarah's eyes darted to the portal and then back to Remi. "Don't worry," she said, her voice soft and reassuring. "Thayne and I will come looking for you. But presuming that things do go smoothly, I'll send a domicile to the closest intrastate breezeway. Come find me the second you're back, okay?"

For the first time, Remi spotted concern in her new friend's expression. It had her doubting the wisdom of this once more. But then the image of her sister flashed in her mind, her face pale and sweat-soaked with exhaustion. Just as it had been the last moment she'd seen her, and her resolve stiffened.

She was a powerful fire goddess, capable of taking care of herself and anyone who dared to cross her. Moreover, she was a high-ranking member of the Bicaidian and Valerian royal-castes, with connections that defied anyone to harm her. You'd have to have a serious death wish to do anything of the sort.

With one last determined nod at Ellarah, Remi pulled the comm device from the pocket of her snug, forest-green trousers. She tossed it onto her four-postered bed before she spun on her heel and stepped through the blackness. As she did, a cool steam enveloped her limbs, rippling the fabric of her loose silk tank top before she passed through and into the meeting location.

Sound exploded around her, and the heat of many bodies crammed close together warmed her skin. Dim lights and interspersed flashes of brightness whirled through the lower-caste nightclub. Music thrummed while deities danced around her, their ethereal light glowing brighter as many of them released fragments of their magic into the atmosphere.

Party doses of power glowed overhead. She could see dancing wolves made of flame from a fire deity, water dolphins leaping through the air from a water god, and raw energy swirling, flashing bright sparks of colorful magic above.

Taking a moment to orient herself, she blinked. Not the clandestine meeting space she'd imagined, though she did feel comforted by the public nature of it. Then, mind fixed on her goal, she pushed through the crowd.

She could see a metal stairway at the edge of the dance floor that led to a loft-style balcony. Gods and goddesses alike leaned over the rail, dancing in time with the beat of the music. But when she reached the top of the stairs, she spotted rich, velvety cushioned couches surrounding thick, wooden tables. As she drew closer, she saw what topped them. Drinks made with the most potent Bicaidian liquor, powders, and crystals that she knew contained illegal substances. Cross-magicking, as it was known.

Energy gods' magic was pure, untamed power that could be melded into a plethora of uses. But for the most part, they supplied the raw energy needed to fuel technology in both the mortal and immortal realms. Cross-magicking, though, was one of their magic's less savory uses.

To accomplish it, they harnessed that raw power into crystals and powders that, when ingested, boosted any god's natural magic. From what she'd been told, the resulting rush of energy and power produced a high unlike any other. Addicting and dangerous, depending on who took the stuff. Her grandpa had banned the substance hundreds of years ago, but it was hard to enforce when underground clubs like this one popped up all over the Twelve Realms and then disappeared the next day.

Finding a bare place on the railing, she squeezed between pulsating bodies and peered into the crowd below. Her eyes scanned the party with intensity, trying to find the deity who'd summoned her here. But she could see no one who didn't seem to be partaking in the revelry below. She let out an irritated sigh, the music turning grating on her ears now.

That was when a low, deep voice seemed to crawl inside her. "Princess. You came."

It wasn't next to her or behind her but inside her mind. She tried not to let this unsettle her, but she knew what she was dealing with now—a consciousness deity, a Nefaral, and no average example of one either. He had to carry a high-power level to break through her well-formed mental barriers.

Since he was already inside her head, she answered him mind-to-mind. "I see you like to make an entrance."

A low laugh sounded, and the music seemed to quiet, the party fading as his voice grew in her mind. "You're right; I do."

"Where are you?" Remi silently asked, dispensing with the pithy back-and-forth. She didn't have time for that. She only cared what he had to say about her sister, dammit.

"Did you come alone? No comm devices, no portals? Don't bother lying. I've got my claws in you, so I'll know if you do."

Remi sucked in a surprised breath of pain when he raked those not so metaphorical claws across her brain. Straightening her spine, she answered with a simple, "Yes."

"Very good," he replied, "She follows instructions." Before she could snarl at him, he said, "Follow the balcony to the edge of the building. You'll see a door. Open it." She hesitated. Who knew where that door would lead? Would it take her from the relative safety of the public club? Would it put her in danger? Then his voice rang out once more. "It's the only way you'll learn anything about your sister."

He was right. He *was* in her head, and he knew just what to say to make her obey.

She swallowed her reservations. Glancing along either side of the balcony, she spotted a door through the haze of intoxicated deities. She moved to it quickly, pushing past a few gods and goddesses caught in the throes of passion, mouths locked and hands roaming over each other's bodies. Averting her eyes, she fixed her gaze on the door, and when she approached it, she pushed it open.

Cool night air whipped her hair around her and she recognized the river rushing below. The glowing water lapped beneath her, a stream of colorful, cleansing bacteria dancing in its depths despite the darkness of the night.

Then the voice sounded once more, only this time, it was from right next to her. "There you are."

She spun, heart in her throat, and saw a god standing there. His hands were planted on the railing that enclosed the balcony to the building behind them. Her pulse slowed as he remained still, making no move toward her.

"My apologies for the mind games, Princess. But I had to make sure you held up your end of the bargain. Royals can't be trusted on their word alone." He turned to her then, his hazel eyes bright. He seemed to enjoy the intrigue of their interlude.

Ignoring his insult to her character, Remi began to rebuild the walls in her psyche. He'd penetrated them once, but after he'd departed, she had no intention of letting him in again. She lifted her chin and asked, "You say you have word of my sister?"

A long pause passed as his gaze raked over her body, and a feral grin spread across his mouth. A chill ran up her back, her neck prickling with gooseflesh, but she didn't dare react. She didn't like the way he appraised her, but before her misgivings could grow into full-blown panic, his eyes fixed back to hers and his face split into a charming grin. "I do."

He held up his hand as magic began swirling around his fingertips, as though he were pulling something forth from her subconscious, something she couldn't see before. After a few seconds, it solidified into a small, white square. Paper, Remi realized. A letter.

Unusual in an era where all communication was digital, but it was by far the most secure way to communicate. Paper meant that even the most advanced hackers couldn't get ahold of it. So, whoever had sent this communique wanted its contents kept secret. Remi's eyes locked onto it like it was made of pure magnetism. "Who are you? And where did you get that?"

A low laugh rumbled through his throat, echoing off the walls. He wagged an arrogant finger at her. "No, no, Princess. No questions. This," he held the letter up for clarification, "could land me in a cell in the Peacekeeper's prison for the rest of my life. So, I think I'll hang on to my name and those of my contacts if it's all the same to you."

Remi lowered her voice. "What do you mean? Why would a letter land you in prison?"

"It's not so much the letter as where it's from and who gave it to me." She stared at him, deciding to use silence as her strategy once more. Finally, after a brief hesitation, he spoke, seeming to savor the illegality, "It's from Moldize. Sent directly from the royal family themselves."

This time, Remi didn't bother to temper her astonishment. Instead, her eyes widened, and she stopped breathing for a few seconds. Her brain rebelled at this revelation. Moldize? This meeting was supposed to be about Bekka; what did Moldize have to do with anything? Unless…

"Who wrote the letter? The Moldizean royals?" Remi asked, thinking that she already knew the answer. The reason why her parents had been so cagey about her helping them with their search for Bekka was starting to make sense. This even shed some light on what might have happened to her grandpa. Was this some kind of a ransom note? She wondered, fear alighting in her mind as she tried not to panic.

He shook his head, his dark, wavy hair shifting in the breeze. "No, not the royals." She could tell his pause was for dramatic effect. She resisted the urge to pummel the answer out of him. Finally, after an excruciatingly long second, he said, "It's from your sister."

Without hesitation, she held out her hand. "Give it to me. Right now."

A low chuckle rumbled again as he reached out his hand and, to her immense surprise, did as she requested. "Pleasure doing business with you, princess. You'll be in touch soon, I'm sure."

As soon as the note passed into her possession, his material body began to dissolve. Consciousness deities couldn't translocate, but they could cloak themselves and move outside the visual abilities of the other gods.

When he disappeared entirely, her mind whirred as she tried to piece together what this could all mean, what it would mean for her, if the Moldizeans had indeed taken her sister.

As she fingered the cool paper of the letter, she fought her need to open it right then and there. She had no idea if that slippery snake of a consciousness deity was still lurking nearby. She didn't want to read anything this explosive in front of any witnesses. There could be spies anywhere.

So, she slipped the note into her pocket and hurried back through the illicit nightclub. She moved fast, pushing through the throngs of inebriated gods and goddesses. She took two steps at a time down the stairs and hurried to the door that served as an entrance, checking over her shoulder as she went.

When she burst into the cool night air, she spun a quick circle to get her bearings. They were on the far edge of the capital city of Helverta. A long way from the castle, near a collection of abandoned buildings once used for technology production that had become outdated. Most of these buildings had yet to be repurposed because the royals had allocated their resources to more critical matters.

She turned to the north, towards the rocky mountain range, their tips just visible in the distance above the city skyscape surrounding her, and began walking.

She made it about a dozen blocks before she started to see signs of habitation and links to the intrastate breezeway. She passed a few energy stations, a shop that boasted an update to the latest trans-dimensional portal technology, and finally, the official embassy for the Nefaric Pillar of Power. She shivered as she strode past the tall, stone building. It seemed out of place to her, with its extravagant columns, dragon statues, and spiky metal gate that surrounded the compound.

But the real problem wasn't the building, she thought; it's the Nefarals themselves. They enjoyed far too much power here for her taste if tonight were any indication. Her grandfather would never have allowed them to have that much power in her home realm of Valeria, considering what they'd done with it centuries ago. But, of course, they'd run unchecked back then. That wasn't the case now, thanks to the Peacekeeper's laws. But despite the governor chips embedded in their necks, she still didn't trust them.

She let out a sigh of gratitude to Ellarah when she finally found the breezeway entrance and saw her domicile floating about fifty feet above her head. She closed her eyes and sent out a small pulse of heat, a magical signature that her domicile would pick up on. And it did, the sleek vehicle descending to rest in front of her a few seconds later. Pressing her thumb against the reader and sending another tiny spark prompted the door to open. She slid into the luxurious interior and entered the coordinates for the palace into the holo control panel.

Following her instructions, the domicile merged into the non-existent traffic in the sky. Its engine latched onto the magnetic ley-lines that served as the godly superhighway throughout all the immortal realms.

While magic had always been tantamount to the gods' way of life, technology had helped fill the gaps between the lower and upper-caste deities. Domiciles were a perfect example of advancement from the Science & Technology Pillar of Power. They allowed gods without translocation-friendly gifts, such as fire deities, to get around with ease in their realms.

As they flew over the buildings of Helverta, quiet, peaceful music swirled around her, and the lights of the city blurred. She could feel the letter burning a hole in her pocket. She wanted to rip it out and read it right then, but she knew she needed to wait until she was in the privacy of her bed-chamber. After all, there were security camera feeds all over this city, and she couldn't risk any of them catching a glimpse of that letter. At least, not before she knew what it said and had a plan on how to deal with it.

Two minutes later and a smooth, robotic voice flowed out of the speakers. "You have reached your destination." The domicile settled onto the ground, the entrance of the stunning adobe-style palace not ten feet away from her. It glowed with power, the energy force field that cloaked it providing both protection and a beacon of strength to their people.

Remi all but fell out the door of her domicile in her rush to get inside. When she reached tall, wooden doors, she pressed a shaky hand to the imprint reader and lined her face up to the scanner. She sent a pulse of magic and waited until the security system cleared her for entry before she burst inside. Shutting the door behind her, she ran down the empty halls, trying her best to keep her footfalls silent.

When she, at last, reached her bed-chamber, the security lock executed another painfully slow facial and power scan before the door sprung open. She pulled the letter from inside her pocket as she spun into the threshold and closed the door behind her.

A sound in the dark made her freeze in her tracks. Her heart leapt into her throat as a smooth, deep voice rumbled, "At the risk of sounding like an overbearing, alpha-male douchebag, can I ask where you've been?"

It was Thayne.

Her mouth went dry as she took in his large, well-muscled frame. He wore black fitted pants paired with a charcoal undershirt, and his hair was loose around his shoulders. His well-muscled arms were crossed over his chest, and his dark, slanted eyes were trained on her.

Her pulse skittered in surprise at his presence as she debated the wisdom of confirming that he *was* an overbearing alpha male. He had entered her private room without her permission, after all. Though douchebag seemed a bit harsh, considering what he'd done for her just days before during her incineration incident.

Before she could say anything, Thayne pushed off the wall and prowled closer to her. His thick, hair was as smooth as silk and was so dark that it seemed to absorb even the brightest light. "Remi, where were you? You left without telling anyone." He paused, waiting for a reply. Instinct and common sense told her that he wouldn't like the answer, if she gave him an honest one. So, she said nothing. Instead, she watched him carefully, sensing suspicion rolling off of him in waves and found herself resenting his inquisition.

Eyes trained onto his, she held his stare, not backing down an inch as he stepped right into her space bubble. She didn't owe him an explanation. He wasn't her keeper or her master, and he had no right to treat her like some disobedient child. Deciding that she valued her privacy, she lied. "I was restless, so I went out to get some air. I took a stroll along the riverwalk."

Thayne uncrossed his arms and ran a thumb over his eyebrow. His expression held a combination of amusement and annoyance. "You're a terrible liar. You know that, right?"

She glared at his cocky smile and opened her mouth to argue, but he laid a fingertip on her lips to stop her.

"How about instead of feeding me another line of bullshit, you tell me what this is?" He removed his hand from her lips and grasped her wrist, tugging her hand up to indicate the letter she'd crumpled in her fist the moment she'd seen him in her room. She cursed inwardly. She should have slipped it back into her pocket. But she hadn't wanted to draw unintended attention to it.

Frustrated with herself, she knew that he wouldn't be letting this go anytime soon. A paper missive was unusual enough that he wouldn't just forget it. She opened her mouth, intending to lie once more. But Thayne gave a firm shake of his head. "Don't," he growled.

She pressed her lips together, annoyed at having been given an order—a feeling she'd grown all too familiar with in her recent experiences. One she'd come to hate more than just about anything. His fingers were still locked around her wrist, and she could feel the weight of his stare.

He tightened his grip. "I know you don't think so, but you can trust me."

She stepped closer, a challenge in her expression. The move brought their bodies mere inches apart, and she looked at him from beneath her lashes. He might be an alpha, but he wasn't the only one. She injected as much sickly sweetness as she could into her words. "How do I know I won't live to regret it if I do decide to trust you?"

She watched with satisfaction as his eyes darkened at the closeness of their bodies and the suggestiveness of her eyes. The truth was, she had no intention of letting him in on her secret without some assurances. He was the high prince of Bicaidia, and he'd sworn to uphold the laws of his realm. How could she be sure that he would bend them for her sake?

She kept her face sober as she inhaled the scent of his body, tangy electricity, and petrichor. Then, with their eyes locked in what felt like an eternal power of wills, she tried to gauge what he would do next. As she did, she found that he was more of an enigma than she'd expected. She could see pride, mixing with anger and also, no small amount of curiosity in those depthless eyes.

Then, without warning, static electricity filled the room, and she saw lightning dance down his arms before alighting his fingertips still wrapped around her wrist. She hissed in shock when the electrical current hit her skin. After a brief hesitation, he dropped it and grasped her other hand, the one without the letter. Again, his lightning stung, but she'd braced herself this time, realizing what he planned to do just before he spoke, "Is it a binding you want? If so, then it's yours."

Still tingling from current rushing through her limbs and the gesture itself, she hesitated. Accepting a binding would give her the protection she needed, but binding him to this big of a secret made her feel uneasy. She paused, not alighting her internal flame but thinking over her next move instead. Having his help with whatever came next would prove useful, considering his prominent position in this realm. She may be their princess, but that wasn't official yet, and he far outranked her in the respect he commanded here.

Then there was the issue of her sister. She could be trapped in Moldize, far away from anyone who loved and cared for her. In constant danger or fear for her life. And if this were a ransom note, as she suspected, then she'd need his help bringing it to the pillars and his parents. They'd be far more likely to listen to him than anything she had to say.

Her mind worked quickly as she tried to weigh the pros against the cons of taking him up on his offer. Breaking a binding carried a steep penalty, one paid in flesh and pain. She knew that he wouldn't do this if she told him that the letter came from Moldize. Which was precisely what she should do, she thought. Yet, she held her tongue.

Before she could change her mind, she called her magic to her. Flames ignited her arm and the palm of the hand he held. She felt a slight pang of satisfaction when he hissed in his breath at the sting of her magic. "A binding it is," she agreed.

The magic swirled up each of their forearms and held them together for a moment, awaiting further instructions. She then spoke the words that would tether his fate to hers, at least when it came to this matter, "Whatever is in this letter, we will handle it together. No action will be taken nor will its contents or origin be spoken of to anyone unless we both agree to it first." When he nodded his agreement to her bond, the magic absorbed into their skin. A faint shade of lightning swirled up her arm while one of fire crept up his. It would be invisible to anyone but them.

Now that she had a binding with him, unbreakable by either of them lest they wish to be subjected to extreme torment, she felt assured that he would be on her side. She could only hope that he wouldn't blow a gasket with fury once he realized what she'd bound him to.

Releasing his hand, Remi brushed past him and moved to the table that doubled as her desk on the far end of her room, near the picture window. She tossed over her shoulder, "I'm not sure what this will say, but it's a letter from my sister."

She could feel his looming presence beside her as she unfolded the paper and smoothed it out.

His voice was low as he asked, "Where did you get this? No one's heard from Bekka since the wedding."

She tapped the letter with a burgundy painted nail. "This is where I went tonight. To get my hands on this."

Thayne's dark eyes narrowed. He gestured to her discarded comm device, still laying on her bed. "In the middle of the night, without your comm device, and without telling anyone?"

Remi flushed with irritation, and she worked hard to control the fire that swelled within her. "Like you said, this was the first inkling we've gotten that my sister might be alive. So as far as I'm concerned, it was worth taking a risk to get it."

He didn't reply. Instead, he gaped at her. The look suggested that she was either stupid or insane. Or maybe both. Before she could give him the verbal lashing she desired, a pounding on her door had her head whipping in its direction.

It lasted mere seconds before the precipice swung open, and Ellarah burst inside. Her wide eyes fixed on Remi and she let out a sigh of relief. "Oh, thank the Ascended! You found the domicile. You were supposed to come to get me the second you got back. What gives?" Then her eyes traveled to the god standing on the other side of Remi, and she snapped her mouth shut. "Shit," she muttered, looking guilty now. "Any chance you can pretend you didn't hear any of that?" She asked Thayne, who glared at his friend from over Remi's shoulder.

"Not likely," he replied. "And for Ascended sake, Ellarah, I wanted you to look out for her, not let her go into dangerous situations without backup and without telling *me!*"

Remi growled. At this rate, she'd never read her sister's letter. "She didn't let me do anything, Thayne. I make my own decisions. I'm a big girl, and every morning I put on my big girl pants and decide how I want to live my life. I did it for many years before we ever got married. Now, will you two stop bickering so we can read this letter?"

Thayne's jaw flexed with irritation. "Fine," he bit out. "But we'll discuss this in more detail later." His eyes fixed on Ellarah, letting her know that he didn't plan to drop this anytime soon.

Resisting the urge to roll her eyes, Remi turned back to her desk and smoothed the paper once again. When her gaze focused on the writing, her heart leapt with instant hope. It was Bekka's handwriting. The Nefaral hadn't been lying.

Anchoring her palms on the desk and bending her head, Remi began to read. Both Thayne and Ellarah peered over her shoulder and did the same. She couldn't say why she hadn't asked Ellarah for the same binding Thayne had given her, probably because Ellarah was just as deep into this as she was. She had been the one to arrange the meeting, after all. Add to that the fact that she didn't have the same obligation to Bicaidian law that Thayne did as a high prince. So it made it easier to trust her.

Dear Remi,

I have so much to tell you. I hope that we'll have time soon to talk about everything that's happened since your wedding. But for now, I must keep this short and stick to the pertinent details.

I assume you've heard that our grandpa is gone. He ascended a few weeks ago. I'm guessing you don't know all the details surrounding the circumstances, but I can say that he gave up his life to save me. He gifted me his power, entrusting me to use it well. That's the reason I'm writing to you now. I'm currently safe and protected in Moldize but without a way to return home to Valeria. As you know, Moldize's banishment has cut them off from all potential allies that could help me get back home, which is what I must do, and quickly.

There has been talk of a Nefaral uprising. Our intelligence tells us that the epicenter of this rebellion is in Bicaidia. I'm afraid of what will happen next if I do not get back home soon. As I'm sure you've realized by now, I am our grandpa's heir and the only creation deity left in the multiverse. And I'm the only one who has a chance to stop what comes next before it starts.

So, I need to ask for your help, with full knowledge of the challenges that surround this request. And for that, I am sorry. But Valeria is locked down. There is no quick way in for us from here. So, we must travel to another realm and use their portal to get home instead. You're the only one I can trust with this task.

I need you to use your new position in Bicaidia to convince the royals and the pillar leadership to open a portal with the Moldizean deities. I swear on all that we both love and cherish that they aren't what we thought they were. They have no intention of harming any Bicaidians. We merely wish to pass through so that I can go home and save us all from an inevitable catastrophe.

I feel compelled to tell you that this is in Bicaidia's best interest as well. Without my intervention, war seems inevitable. But maybe, with your help, we can stop it in its tracks.

Respond with your answer as quickly as you can. Leave it behind the faceplate of the facial scanner outside your bedroom. We will see to the rest.

With all my love and well-wishes,
Rebekkah
PS – You're the toughest bitch I know. So, trust me when I say, you've got this.

Remi had stopped breathing. The surge of emotions coursing through her left her in a state of semi-paralysis. She didn't realize she needed air until her chest began to burn and black spots danced in front of her eyes. She gulped in one greedy breath after another as a tangle of incomprehensible thoughts tumbled through her brain. She'd thought her grandfather had been murdered and Bekka kidnapped, so she'd expected a ransom letter written in her sister's hand… but that wasn't what she'd gotten at all.

Instead, she'd just learned that her grandpa had gifted Bekka his power and sacrificed himself to save her. But why would he do that? She wondered, her mind grasping at plausible explanations. What in the Twelve Hells had happened, that would have forced him to do something like that? Her mind reeled, and she pinched the bridge of her nose as she fought to calm her racing thoughts.

Thayne's hand on her shoulder caused her to jump. She swallowed, her mouth dry and looked up into her husband's deep, brown eyes and asked, "What is she talking about? A Nefaral uprising? Here in Bicaidia? Have you heard anything about that?"

Thayne's jaw flexed, his eyes flicking towards her window before he nodded. "Yes, there have been rumors of unrest in the Nefaric pillar." Brushing that aside with the swipe of his hand, he continued, "But that's not the most concerning part of this letter. This came from Moldize. How did you get it? And who gave it to you?" She could see his mood darkening, a combination of anger and betrayal flashing in his eyes. Yep, he was definitely mad about the binding, she thought, refusing to let herself feel guilty.

In answer to his question, Remi flicked her eyes to Ellarah before she could stop herself. The returning glare that Ellarah shot her could have scalded the depths of Valerian hell. Thayne turned his ire on Ellarah then, and Remi could see that he was gearing up for a fight. So, she stepped between them and held up a hand, pressing it onto the firm muscles of his chest to still him. "I didn't get this from Ellarah. She just helped me find someone who knew something about my sister. There was no way she could've known that this came from Moldize until now."

He seemed to vibrate with anger, but to his credit, he held it in check. "Fine, but that still doesn't answer my other question. Who gave this to you?"

Remi pressed her lips together, growing annoyed. She didn't want to waste time on pointless questions that she had no meaningful answers to right now. Instead, she wanted to figure out how they would help her sister; she wanted to come up with a plan. But she knew that avoiding his question would only delay her desire, so she answered with the truth. "I don't know. A consciousness deity, male. Tall, dark hair, hazel eyes, powerful. He didn't tell me his name."

Thayne dragged a hand over his face and turned to look out the window into the blackness outside. "That describes about a two dozen gods I can think of off the top of my head, and even more I can't think of."

Trying to steer the conversation back to her priorities, Remi picked up the letter. "Who he was doesn't matter right now. This is what matters. What Bekka said about the Nefarals, the uprising, and needing our help. We need to do something. We have to help her prevent a war from happening."

Thayne turned back to her, appealing to both Remi and Ellarah now. "Look, there's nothing to worry about with the Nefarals. We have everything well under control."

Remi's eyes fixed back on the letter as a sick feeling pooled in her belly. Call it intuition, but the urgency in Bekka's words would indicate that the Bicaidian royals and pillars had nothing under control. "Are you sure about that?"

"I have every confidence in the leadershi—" Thayne began, but Ellarah cleared her throat, interrupting the high prince of Bicaidia—a move that took serious guts from someone in Ellarah's position, which made Remi like her even more.

"Are you sure about that, Thayne?" she whispered, her voice breathy with nerves. "There's been talk throughout the

Realm since Gabryel's death. It seems to be getting more organized and gaining steam, not losing it."

Thayne stared at her, apparently unsure how to respond to being both interrupted and contradicted. He usually seemed so damned confident and self-assured. If Remi weren't so concerned with helping her sister, she might have enjoyed seeing him caught off-guard for a change.

He clenched his fists. "Why haven't you brought these concerns to my parents, or the pillar leadership, or Twelve Hells, Ellarah, to me?"

Ellarah blanched under his scrutiny, but she didn't back down. "I thought you knew. I was under the impression that you were still taking action against it. I didn't realize that you thought you'd already quashed it, because you definitely haven't."

Remi spoke up before Thayne could reply, "So, that means Bekka's right, and Bicaidia could be in danger, doesn't it?"

Thayne shook his head, adamant in his position. "Our best intelligence tells us that it's a few disgruntled, lower-caste Nefs causing trouble. The leader of the Nefaric pillar and all of the sect leaders have assured us that they have it under control. We plan to use your inauguration ceremony as a chance to show that we are all unified under the same banner. Everyone from all of the pillars and each of the sect leaders will be in attendance."

Remi and Ellarah both stared at him, dumbfounded. All of the most powerful and influential people in Bicaida together in one place? In the middle of a potential uprising? Granted, she would remain the princess-in-waiting until her inauguration made it official. But that was all just ceremonial. An unnecessary and antiquated tradition that seemed like a massive risk, given the new information in Bekka's letter.

Her clothing became suffocating as she realized that she would be front and center during the event. Had they even planned to warn her of the potential danger before they paraded her around the party like a tarted-up trophy? She wondered, grinding her teeth.

Ellarah shook her head. "This is insane! I'm telling you that your intelligence is wrong, and you can see the same in Bekka's letter. We can't afford to endanger ourselves just to play politics!"

Remi couldn't help but agree. It seemed unwise to ignore the Nefaric gods and the threat they posed. After all, they had once ruled and terrorized the multiverse, subjecting deities like all three of them, along with all mortal beings, to their sick whims.

He shook his head and looked back at the letter. "You don't understand. The intelligence is solid, verified. They aren't going to agree with Bekka's overwrought warnings. They're going to continue as planned with the inauguration and use it as their show of unity with both Valeria and the Peacekeeper's law."

Remi shook her head, exasperated at the insanity of everything he was saying. "Maybe you're wrong. We have to at least show them Bekka's letter. Maybe they'll change their mind and cancel the inauguration. I mean, maybe they'll even grant my sister's request."

Thayne groaned, paused for a moment, and squinted at the paper on the desk. "I know you want to help your sister, Remi. But there is one thing that we haven't considered yet. How can we be sure that this note comes from her at all? This could be some Moldizean trick, and no one is going to trust anything that comes from Moldize. Period. You both know that as well as I do."

Remi frowned and looked down at the letter, considering. Her mind went through the options and, though she hated to admit it, Thayne had a point. She felt a sickening sense of defeat wash over her. "Then what the hell are we supposed to do? This comes from Bekka; I just know it. She's asking me for help, and I can't let her down, not when so much is at stake."

Thayne continued, "It's possible that this is Moldize's way of breaking their exile now that Gabryel is dead. That realm is filled with uncontrolled Nefarals; we all know that. If we create a portal and let them loose—" He looked at her, his eyes pleading with her to consider this possibility. "There's no telling what terrible things they might do."

Remi thought through what he proposed, but something didn't make sense. She looked down at the paper once more and scanned through the letter until she found what she was looking for. She pointed to the postscript at the bottom of the page. "No, this is definitely from Bekka. This line here. It's something we used to say to each other when we were teenagers. A sisterly code of sorts. No one else would know to say it but her."

"You're willing to bet the stability of our realm on *that*?" Thayne questioned, staring at the words she'd indicated skeptically.

"I am," she said, her tone brooking no argument. Then she continued, brushing her fingers over his for emphasis. "Please, Thayne, I know they think they have the Nefarals under control, but we should still bring this to the pillar leaders and your parents right away. They need to hear what Bekka has to say, and Ellarah can corroborate it. You know the only shot we have to open a portal is with their approval. There's no other way."

Once everyone knew of Bekka's warning and her willingness to claim her seat as Gabryel's heir, maybe it would give them what they needed to sell Bekka's plan. Her sister, the only creator left in the multiverse, back in the seat of power would only strengthen the Bicaidians' position both politically and against the Nefarals.

Ellarah cleared her throat, drawing their attention to her. When Remi's eyes locked onto her new friend, her expression was filled with sympathy. "I agree that we need to tell them about the seriousness of the Nefaric threat. But as for showing them the letter and telling them about the portal?" She shook her head. "We can't do that. They'll never agree to it. They're too afraid of the Moldizean gods to open any kind of a portal between our realms. If we tell them about it now, all we'd be doing is tipping them off that Moldize is looking to get access to Bicaidia, and by default, Valeria. So they'd redouble security and do anything they could to stop it. Then we'd never be able to help your sister."

Remi slammed her fist onto the desk in frustration. She could feel the heat building inside her, that familiar tug of her magic fighting to be off its constant leash. She took a breath to calm the feeling of helplessness that washed over her. Then she leveled an accusing glare on her partners in crime. "We have to do something! We can't just let my sister stay in exile while the rogue Nefarals grow bolder here. And without a Peacekeeper in the seat of power, they will."

She glared from Ellarah to Thayne and back, a little surprised when they shared a look with each other. She hadn't known them long enough to master their method of non-verbal communication. But she learned from her previous experience that they knew each other well enough for that. So, when they each focused back on her, their expressions filled with subterfuge, she crossed her arms over her chest and narrowed her eyes. "What is it?"

Thayne spoke first, his voice low with secrecy, "There are other ways to get things done, outside of the pillar leaders or the Royals, you know? And it will have the benefit of being faster and a hell of a lot more private."

Remi tried to hide the shock that rocketed through her at this suggestion. Was he seriously suggesting that they go around the Bicaidian leadership and open an unsanctioned portal from Moldize into Bicaidia? She stared at him in disbelief. If they were caught, such action carried a steep price, even for a royal prince. Death, via the surface of the sun.

Trying to make sure she hadn't just lost her grip on reality, she looked at Ellarah for confirmation. When Ellarah nodded in agreement with him, she was confident she'd gone mad. This was the last thing she would have expected either of them to suggest. Shaking her head to clear it, Remi asked, "But wouldn't that be breaking Peacekeeper law?"

A grin as wicked as sin spread across Thayne's lips, but it was Ellarah who spoke next, "That's only if we get caught, and we have no intention of letting that happen."

Remi's mind reeled, still too astonished to comprehend what she was hearing. "You can't be serious," she whispered, afraid to speak too loud, lest they be overheard.

Ellarah turned to Thayne, pretending as though Remi hadn't just spoken. "You know we can't do this alone. We'll need help."

Thayne nodded, fingers brushing over his full lips in thought. "Who did you have in mind?"

"Riven," she replied, as she paced toward Remi's bed and then back to the desk, in full scheming mode. "I know he's a Nef, but we can trust him. He's the one who helped me get this letter in the first place. Besides, he's the only person we can count on for discretion with the power we need to make this happen."

Thayne crossed an arm over his chest and eyed her. "I should've known he'd be involved with this." Waving that aside, he nodded his head. "You know I'd trust Riven with my life. But for Remi's sake, we ask whoever helps us for a binding. We have to make sure this stays quiet."

Ellarah nodded in agreement conspiratorially. Then, after a full minute of stunned silence, Remi came out of her stupor and hissed, "You two can't be serious! This could get us all killed!"

They both turned their attention to Remi then, Thayne stepping closer to brush a reassuring hand down her bare arm. Gooseflesh rippled on her skin in response as he said, "Look, I'll talk to my parents and the pillars about the Nefarals. I can at least convince them to double up on security at the inauguration. That should take care of the internal threat without increasing our transuniversal travel security. That way, Ellarah and I can work around it…with a little help that is. And then, once we pull this off, which we will, you'll have your sister back."

Her mouth opened and then closed like a fish sucking air as she tried to think of something to say. But she couldn't seem to bring herself to argue against it, no matter how stupidly dangerous this idea was. If it worked, and they seemed confident it would, then her sister would be home, the Twelve Realms safe, and the Nefarals stopped in their tracks.

Damn, she thought, how could I say no to that?

CHAPTER 4

BEKKA

Impossible

I strode down the indistinguishable Moldizean halls, feeling as I always did—like they were a maze created to screw with anyone who dared to traverse them. I scrunched up my nose as I reached an intersection with yet another identical row of doors down it. I sighed, following the instructions that Lilja had given me. "Keep right," I muttered to myself. "All rights, no lefts. Just follow the directions, Bekka." I turned right and continued at a steady pace, my footfalls quiet on the marble floor.

It had been a full day since the intervention staged by my Moldizean friends, and I was a jumble of nerves. Shortly after that meeting of the minds, I had drafted a letter and sent it to Remi, asking for her help. I was assured that it would find her by Erykha, Damion, and Arrick, but my patience was already waning.

I didn't like how much I worried over what her response would be, hoping that it was in our favor. Praying to the

Ascended that she would heed my warning and let us help her. I also prayed that helping us would not cause her any harm. Moldize was banished for a reason, and I knew that better than anyone.

But while I waited for word from her, I decided that it was time for me to confront a devil of a different sort. I stopped at a door that was different from the rest, though equally unfamiliar. I'd never been to this particular room before, and now that I was here, my nerves were getting the better of me.

I could feel my heart in my ears as I squared my shoulders and knocked on Arrick's door. I sucked in a breath and waited, listening for any sounds of movement beyond the threshold. A short moment later and I heard feet shuffling towards the precipice. I held my breath as the door swung open.

He stood before me in all his glory, shirtless. I groaned inwardly and tried not to gawk...or drool. His abs, shoulders, and pecks must have been sculpted without considering the poor goddesses who'd be driven wild by their sheer perfection. His golden tanned skin gleamed in the light of the hall and I resisted the urge to step forward and wrap his hard body into my arms and press my lips to his.

"Hey," I said instead, a little dumbstruck as all thoughts evaporated from my mind like water from the desert. I would not be able to concentrate on my reason for coming here if Arrick remained half-naked.

His hair was tousled and adorably messy, as though he'd just woken up. He ran a hand through it. "Hey back," he replied. No smile, eyes simmering pools of velvety green.

The silence lingered for a moment, and I licked my lips to wet them. "Can we talk?"

He dipped his head in acknowledgment and opened the door further for me to enter while turning and walking into the shadows of the room beyond. As he did, he commanded the lights on and what I saw amazed me. This wasn't just a bedroom. This was a loft, as stylish and luxurious as any in Valeria. A sectional couch was positioned in the far corner, while an open, eat-in kitchen was situated on the opposite wall. Windows that overlooked the village below the castle lined the entire back wall. I could see a large spiral staircase in the far back corner, leading to an open bedroom.

I followed him to the plush leather sectional as he sat down in the corner seat. I didn't miss that it was as far away from me as he could manage. Rather than address that elephant in the room, I blurted, "Can you please put a shirt on?" I waved a hand to encompass his naked upper body. "This is a little distracting."

The corner of his mouth twitched upward as a single brow arched. "Distracting?"

I held up a finger in warning. "Yes. But try not to be too smug about it."

He shook his head, the ghost of a smile still playing about his lips as he rose from the couch. His eyes locked onto mine as he chuckled. "I'll do my best. Make yourself at home. There's coffee in the kitchen and fruit in the fridge." My mouth watered as he made his way up the stairway and to his bedroom. However, I couldn't tell if it was from his proposition of coffee or the shapely curve of his ass under his sleek pajama bottoms.

Deciding that it was just the coffee, *yeah, right*, I meandered over to his kitchen and set a pot to brew. The machine had just started to sputter when he re-emerged in jeans and a fitted t-shirt. I sighed in relief and leaned on the counter, waiting for the coffeemaker to feed my addiction.

He pulled up a stool and sat down, eyeing me as though he didn't trust my intentions. If I had to pick a word to describe his demeanor, I'd say suspicious. "What are you doing here, Bekka?"

A little shot of regret pulsed through me, but I ignored it, and with a disapproving scowl on my face, I said, "That's not a very polite way to greet a guest. You should try to be more welcoming. It's the courteous thing to do, you know."

"I'll make a note of that," Arrick mused. "But it doesn't answer my question."

The coffeemaker finished its cycle, and I grabbed a cup from the metal tree on the counter and poured. I turned to Arrick and offered him the cup. I saw it as a peace offering, small as it might be.

He nodded, and I handed the mug to him. When he clasped his hand around it, our fingers brushed, and I felt that pull once more. The undeniable thrill that pulsed through me whenever I was near him. I batted it down and poured myself another mug.

I turned to face him again, and he raised his brows expectantly. "So, are you going to answer, or are you just planning to give me the silent treatment up close and personal now?"

My lips twitched in spite of myself. He was a witty bastard; I'd give him that. "I'm getting to it."

"Which one?" He asked, sipping the dark liquid, eyes on me. I watched as his lips touched the rim, envious of their contact with the inanimate object. I had such conflicting emotions about this guy.

"The first one," I confirmed.

"I'm glad to hear it. So…?"

"I want to talk about…what happened," I explained, the words stilted in my discomfort. The sad and sorry truth of it was that I had missed him. Despite my seething anger towards him at the time, I had missed the closeness we shared, our conversations, the intimacy I felt with him that had nothing to do with the mind-blowing sex. Though admittedly, I had missed that too.

But there was a part of me that was still angry with him and still unable to forget the day my grandpa died and everything that had happened. I just couldn't pinpoint why.

Why couldn't I just let him off the hook? Of course, logically, I knew that my grandpa's death hadn't been his fault. But still.

He frowned, and his eyes flashed. "You mean the fight where you told me that I killed your grandfather? And where you blamed me for not listening to you and berated me for not letting you die?"

I blanched as he recounted the words that I had launched at him like a blast of magic. Each landing harder than the last. I swallowed my sip of coffee and winced, both from his words and the heat. I cleared my throat. "Yeah, that."

"I'm all ears," he replied, resting his forearms on the counter.

"I've had some time to think," I started, wrapping my hands around the mug to absorb the warmth I felt there. "And I just wanted to say that I'm sorry for what I said and for how I treated you. I shouldn't have blamed you for what happened. I'm just so damn…I don't know, angry? I feel like a failure and an imposter all rolled into one. And when I'm not angry and feeling inadequate, I'm overwhelmed with guilt and shame. It's like a constant assault. It never lets up." I paused for a moment, breathing hard as I felt my eyes sting. I blinked, and the sensation abated, thank the Ascended. The last thing I wanted to do was shed what he might interpret as manipulative tears. I swallowed and finished saying, "You were just there when it all happened, and that made you a convenient target."

He paused as he absorbed all that I had revealed and pressed his lips together. He remained silent for a while, and I could see him struggle as he let my words sink in. "Do you still think I betrayed you?"

I shrugged helplessly. "I don't know what I think anymore." I chewed on my lip and tapped my mug as I thought through what I wanted to say next. "Sometimes, I wonder what would have happened if my grandpa had never shown up. Would my power have failed me at all? Or was it because he showed up that I almost died? Sometimes, I'm so sure that I could have finished that sun if I hadn't created that shield to protect you from him...if he hadn't just acted instead of listening to us first. And other times, I want to rage against the full might of the Ascended for not sending our seers a better vision. Then there's the part that bothers me the most. I am angry with my grandfather. Like if he were here, I think I would hammer his chest with my fists and scream at him for getting involved, for trying to stop me."

I used a spoon to swirl the liquid in my cup as a distraction, unwilling to look Arrick in the eyes just yet. I still felt raw, vulnerable, and exposed. I'd just aired all of my dirty laundry, and now he had the chance to rifle through it. I didn't know how he would react.

Without warning, he reached across the counter and rested his fingers on my wrist. I paused my fidgeting and looked up into those depthless, green eyes. His voice was sad when he said, "That's a lot of anger to hold onto."

I let out a long, shuddering breath, relieved not to see judgment in those eyes, but understanding. "I know it."

"Anything I can do to help?" Arrick asked, and the simple gesture of kindness threatened to break me. I didn't deserve it after what I had accused him of.

I shook my head. "All I wanted you to know is that I was wrong to blame you. I used you as my personal punching bag, even though it's not really you that I'm angry with. It's everything and everyone, whether they deserve it or not. I shouldn't have taken it out on you."

He nodded and released my wrist as his hand settled back on his mug. "For what it's worth, you weren't wrong with what you said to me before." He looked up at the ceiling and shook his head. "I'm probably an idiot for saying this since it will make you angry with me all over again. But the truth is that I'm not sure I could have stopped what he set in motion when he gifted you his power. All I know for sure is that I didn't want to try. I chose you, Bekka, just like he did." His eyes were greener than I'd ever seen them as he refocused his gaze on mine. My heart constricted as he said, "I'll always choose you."

I let out a shuddering breath and looked away. "I know," I breathed, unable to stop the heavy pounding of my heart. This was the other reason why I had come here today. To talk about us. The relationship that had grown between us despite my best efforts to deny it.

I braced myself for what I had to say, knowing he wouldn't like it, and gestured from me to him. "But we jumped into this, you and me I mean, under all the pressure that surrounded the prophecy and the idea that we might never see each other again. I just need some time and space to think, to make sure that this is the right decision for me. That I'm not just clinging to you because you're all I have left, and I want the comfort you give me. I want to be sure that this is real and that I'm choosing you because it's what I want. Not what I think I need. Does that make any sense at all?" I asked, desperate for him to understand me.

Rather than speak, Arrick stood and walked around the counter. He stepped right into my space bubble and brushed his fingers up my arms, sending tiny shivers of pleasure down my spine.

I tilted my head back and looked up at him as he whispered, "I know what I want, and that won't change." His eyes bore into mine and I felt as though I could fall into them, lose myself forever in their depths. He leaned closer, breath brushing over my ear and every muscle in my body seized with anticipation. Then, his deep voice reverberated through me as he spoke, "But if time is what you need, then I'll make sure you have it. Time is what I've been giving you, Bekka. That's why I didn't confront you before this conversation, even if I wanted to pin you down to make you listen to me." His mouth parted in a sexy smirk, and I felt my legs turn to jelly. "I understand that Gabryel was important to you, and I can imagine how overwhelmed you were with everything that happened in such a short time. Especially since you never knew about the prophecy. But, just know that I won't make it easy for you to say no to me."

My words were breathy as I asked, "So, does that mean you're ok with it? With me wanting to take a step back?" I waited for his response, my shoulders tense with uncertainty. I knew he had feelings for me, he'd told me as much before, and I'd just asked him for what amounted to a break.

His gaze hovered at my lips and then tracked back up to my eyes. He dropped his forehead to press against mine and groaned with frustration, the sound softer than I would have expected, considering what I was asking of him. "I understand. Just don't take too long, Bekka, I'm not a patient god." With that, he released my arms and stepped back, leaving me cold and shakey in his wake.

I sighed, wanting to wrap my hands around his neck and pull his mouth down to mine. I wanted to taste him, to feel his body on me, but I knew it wasn't a good idea. Because this request wasn't just about sorting out my feelings, it was also about what happened next. If or when I made it back to Valeria, our relationship was doomed. I was going to be Peacekeeper of the Twelve Realms, and Arrick was a Moldizean Nefaral. Our love, if that's what this was, would be impossible. He was someone that my family and my people would never accept.

Despite that, there was a tiny spark of hope that clawed inside my stomach. An undeniable attraction that kept me holding onto to him, no matter how many times I thought about breaking it off for good. Maybe I was just being stubborn, but something kept bringing me back to him, like a cross-magicking addict aching for her next fix.

I paused for a beat, my heart squeezing as I struggled to regain my composure. "I should go," I whispered, running a hand down my braid to calm myself. Preferably before I broke down and wound up in his bed.

"I'll show you out." He moved toward the door. He opened it for me, and I brushed past him and into the hallway.

"One question," I said, turning back to face him. "Will you still come with me? To Bicaidia, I mean?"

He stared at me. "You really have to ask me that?

I shrugged my brows in response.

"Of course. You couldn't keep me from your side, even if you tried."

I smiled in spite of myself. "Just checking." Then I turned on my heel and strode down the hall. I heard the soft click of his door behind me and wondered if I had just made a monumental mistake pushing him away like that. In the turmoil of emotions pulsing through me, it was hard to tell.

CHAPTER 5

REMI

Subterfuge

Remi sat on the windowsill at the far edge of her room, looking over a vast canyon filled with shrubby green trees and red-tinted rocks. It was warm and dry outside, the sun hanging low in the sky, and she propped her window open to enjoy the fresh air. Thanks to her fire goddess powers, the heat never bothered her.

She could feel the buzz and hum of the magical energy that powered the immortal realms brush over her skin. The air felt charged, electrified, and the beauty around her was as vivid as the periwinkle sky.

She sat with her legs outstretched and a book settled on her lap that served as a necessary distraction while she waited to hear from Thayne or Ellarah. It was an erotica novel from the Bicaidian mortal realm that made her blush deeper with every page she turned. These people were freaky, she thought, and she couldn't stop a rush of heat from creeping up her neck. Granted, she was no virgin. It would kill her parents and shock her sister to know that, but what happened in this book? Well, that was another matter entirely.

It had been a long time since she had shared a man's bed. The last time was in the Valerian mortal realm with a human male and far away from the prying eyes of her family. She had known, even then, that one day she would be forced to marry to forge an alliance. But she refused to leave the decision of who her "first" would be to her parents and trans-universal politics. As far as she was concerned, it was none of their business anyway.

Sex was natural, and as she saw it, a necessary part of life. Unfortunately, she and her new husband had yet to take that step. That wasn't unusual in their situation, Nuptial law gave them up to one year to consummate their marriage before the contract became void. And while Thayne defined the word sexy, that didn't change the fact that they barely knew each other. Also, it didn't help that they hadn't spoken since the night she'd gotten Bekka's letter a few days earlier. She couldn't be certain, but she had the distinct impression that he'd been avoiding her. She had a feeling she might know why, but she didn't want to think about that at the moment.

A knock sounded at the door, and she swung her legs off the sill and rested her feet on the floor. "Come in," she called.

Ellarah slipped inside and shut the door behind her with a soft click. She spun on her booted heel, and her eyes fixed on the book in Remi's hand. She cocked a wicked brow. "Am I interrupting something?"

Remi looked down at the scandalous cover of the novel, and she let a lascivious grin part her lips. "Yes, definitely, but I'll allow it since we had plans anyway."

Remi rose to her feet as Ellarah got right down to business. "Okay, so Thayne has already brought the concerns about the Nefarals to the royals and the pillar leadership. He convinced them to triple security at the inauguration, so we can rest easy there. But that leaves the next part of the plan."

"Oh, you mean the difficult part?" Remi asked.

Ellarah pointed at her. "Yep, that's the one. Now hurry up and get ready. We have a meeting to get to, and I promised Thayne we wouldn't be late. You need to meet the new recruits. Well, you already know Riven, but you haven't met the other one." Ellarah scrunched her nose up on the last two words, and Remi wondered if that look of semi-distaste had been intentional or not.

As she eyed her new friend trying to decide, she noticed Ellarah's attire for the first time. She was bundled up compared to Remi's flowy trousers and tank. So Remi looked pointedly outside at the warm, sunny weather. "What gives?"

"Thayne didn't fill you in?"

"No," she said, unwanted guilt springing into her gut. If her suspicions were correct, and he had been avoiding her, then it was definitely her fault, no matter how much she hated to admit it. It was the binding. She knew it, deep down. She'd cornered him into keeping a dangerous secret and helping her, under pain of torment. Probably not the best way to earn her new husband's trust.

Unaware of Remi's internal self-flagellation, Ellarah continued talking, "We're going to the mortal realm. Less prying eyes, more privacy." She eyed Remi up and down, gesturing to her outfit. "That isn't gonna cut it. You'll need boots and a coat, at least."

Remi moved to her new armoire that had been filled with new, unsinged clothes. Thayne had sent them via a servant-caste god to replace the old ones she'd burnt to a crisp. She flung open its doors and pulled out a long charcoal coat and navy scarf, trying to tone down the brighter color of her sky-blue trousers. Next, she pulled on boots, and checking Ellarah's outfit, she grabbed a knit hat and sleek leather gloves.

Looking her over, Ellarah nodded her approval. "Good enough for me," she said, sliding the instaportal from her pocket. She pumped a small blast of her energy magic into the orb and rolled it across the floor. A flash of raw magic illuminated the room, and then the portal appeared. The pool of liquid silver shimmered in front of them. Nerves skittered down Remi's spine as she realized that this was the moment of truth. They were meeting accomplices, where they would make an actual plan to break Peacekeeper law and open a portal into Moldize.

"You ready?" Ellarah asked, looking at Remi in a way that told her she meant the question in reference to more than just walking through a portal into the Bicaidian mortal realm.

Remi wondered if she'd lost her mind, and if she was really going to go through with this insane plan. But instead of voicing any of her concerns aloud, she nodded, not letting an ounce of her misgivings show. "No turning back now."

With that as the final word, she walked straight through the portal. A bell jingled overhead as Remi's hands connected with a door. A mortal door. She pushed it open, Ellarah just behind her, and a blast of freezing wind hit her face. Snow swirled around them, blanketing the roads and sidewalks, as the wind howled, whistling between the tall, industrial buildings on either side of the pedestrian walkway.

If any human saw them, it would appear that they'd just come out of the shop behind them. A simple but effective disguise for trans-dimensional travel, she thought, groaning in discomfort at the chill that seemed to pierce through her jacket. The abrupt change in weather made her wish that she could call her magic to her, ignite her flame and warm her body, but no such luck.

Bicaidian law prohibited the frivolous use of magic in the mortal realm. The original creators had formed humanity in their own image for a variety of reasons, but the main one was so that the gods could walk amongst them unnoticed. No one wanted the kind of notoriety that would come with revealing themselves to humans, so they all used their magic only when absolutely necessary in the mortal realm.

A brief moment passed before Ellarah's voice cut through the blizzard. "This way! It's not far!"

Remi nodded, following Ellarah as they hurried down the walkway. They made it about three blocks before Ellarah turned, approaching an old-fashioned-looking brick building. She yanked the door open and gestured for Remi to enter first—a kindness Remi could have kissed her for; otherwise, she was afraid that even her fiery core would have frozen to death.

Inside was dim, illuminated by faux candle chandeliers. She looked around and noticed that the brick on the outside continued inside, and a large wooden desk dominated the front lobby. Cozy-looking, colorful couches and chairs were arranged in artful positions, with coffee tables to hold drinks or booted feet.

Ellarah walked straight up to the front desk, to the human girl positioned behind it. She wore glasses that Remi knew doubled as comm devices here in the mortal realm. She offered them a warm smile. "Welcome to Highborn Virtual Reality Cafe. May I have your reservation number?"

Ellarah propped her hip on the top of the desk and leaned on it, offering the receptionist an award-winning smile that left her blinking in amazement. Gods tended to have that effect on humans. Even without their ethereal light, they still emanated power, and some part of the human subconscious seemed to pick up on that.

Remi's lips twitched as Ellarah answered the flustered receptionist. "13847. I believe it's under Thayne if I'm not mistaken."

The woman blushed a deep pink at the mention of Remi's husband's name and cleared her throat. "Oh, right. The VIP combat room. The rest of your party arrived just a little while ago." The poor woman looked like she might keel over from either nerves or pure awe, it was hard to tell. She bent down to pick up something from beneath the desk and then dropped it.

Clearing her throat, she picked it up again and laid her haul on the tabletop—a glass strip that served as a key and two blacked-out pairs of goggles. "Your session will start in ten minutes. The room is down the hall, up the stairs, and then it's the first door on the right. Enjoy!"

Ellarah and Remi gathered the paraphernalia and followed her instructions. When they arrived at the door, Remi used the key to open it. The moment she stepped inside the room, her mouth dropped open. She'd never visited a VR café before, so she had no basis for comparison. But this place was incredible. The brick carried through to this room, too, and the ceilings were at least a hundred feet tall.

Large stone structures served as realistic-looking ruins, with halls and perches that filled the room. Carefully scattered debris ate up the remaining floor space, adding to the sense that they were, in fact, in the middle of a real combat zone. Along the left wall, Remi could see a weapons selection that would put most armies to shame. Laser and pulse guns, electroshock weapons, grenades, and protective gear. All replicas, sure, but state of the art copies nonetheless.

For a civilization that hadn't had a war in decades, they sure still liked to play at it, she thought as Thayne strode around one of the stone structures. Somehow, he looked even more handsome than usual in his wool peacoat and knit beanie, his hair falling loose beneath it and his sharp, high cheekbones making him look like some kind of tragic hero. When their eyes locked, she could have sworn she felt the temperature drop a few degrees before he fixed a smile on Ellarah. No smile for her, she noted, and tamped down the guilt that she didn't want to feel.

Riven turned the corner then and Remi fixed her attention on him, relieved for the distraction from her husband. "How long did you reserve this room for, Thayne? If you have it for the evening, then we should make use of it once we're done with whatever you have planned," Riven suggested, eyeing the weapons in interest.

Thayne smiled, shaking his head. "Let's see if you're still in the mood to screw around after you've heard everything we have to say."

"That sounds ominous," Riven answered, his slick hair gleaming in the light as his gaze landed on Ellarah. His eyes lit up at the sight of her and he strode toward them, his gait unhurried and a lazy smile on his face. "Hey, baby," he drawled to his girlfriend.

When he reached her, he slid an arm around Ellarah's waist and bent down to kiss her lips, a gentle finger tilting her chin up to meet him. Kissing completed, he smiled at Remi. "Hey Remi, good to see you again."

She offered him a warm smile, trying not to worry about Thayne's coldness towards her. He'd agreed to help her just a couple of days ago, and he hadn't seemed angry when he'd left that evening. But she had to admit that, in that moment, he seemed different, distant, and like if he had the choice, he wouldn't have anything to do with her. That damn binding, she thought, knowing for certain that she hadn't just been imagining things. He really had been avoiding her. She could tell by the way he carefully avoided meeting her eye.

Keeping her demeanor calm and collected, she turned to Ellarah and Riven. "So, where's this new recruit I've heard so little about?" She injected a little vinegar in her words, just for her husband. He might have been angry with her, but he could have at least had the decency to fill her in on who else they planned to tell her secret to.

But instead of Ellarah or Riven answering her inquiry, another voice rang out from somewhere within the ruins. "You're all such disappointments. You never even mentioned me?" Female, cultured, and well-educated. She sounded like someone who'd been born and bred within the upper-caste of godly society, which shouldn't be a surprise. Thayne was a royal. Most of the people he interacted with were either upper-caste or within the servant-caste.

When the newcomer stepped around from behind a large stone column, Remi had to focus on keeping her mouth closed. Silken blond hair fell in perfect waves to her shoulders and full red lips spread into a saccharine smile. She seemed to emanate power and authority, both of which she bore with a kind of ease and expectation. As though she'd been born to be obeyed.

The goddess walked right up to Remi and offered her slim hand, her perfect white teeth gleaming in the dimly lit room. "I'm Madwyn of house Senagal." She paused for effect, letting the name sink in.

Remi narrowed her eyes as recognition seemed to click in her mind. "Senagal?" Remi repeated, letting the word roll over her tongue. "You mean—?"

"Yes," Madwyn interrupted. "I'm a descendant of the original creation deity of Bicaidia."

Remi felt a jolt of surprise wash over her, though she kept her face composed. Riven groaned behind her. "Must you tell that to everyone we meet who isn't from Bicaidia, sister?"

Of course, they were related. Remi had instantly seen the resemblance between the two. It was in the eyes. They were the mirror of each other—ice blue and wide with thick, black lashes. Shaking her head to regain her composure, Remi looked from one to the other. Just then, a silvery-looking snake of light slithered along the ground, sliding up Riven's leg, winding its way to his neck, where it dissolved into his skin. He sucked in a strained breath in reaction.

The pieces fell together then. Ellarah and Thayne had said that Riven was a Nef, a trustworthy one, though, and no wonder. He was the descendant of Roderick from house Senagal, the original creator and ruler of Bicaidia. Roderick had ascended many centuries before Remi's birth and his family had abdicated the throne for reasons unknown. After that, the Bicaidian pillar leadership had chosen Thayne's family, House

Aphyrsh, to assume the royal responsibilities. But, House Senagal had remained allies to the Bicaidian royals and served as generals in her grandfather's army during the last great war.

Remi also remembered hearing the stories of what a scandal it had been when two Nefaral children were born into the original creator's bloodline. One a death god, a power that had its own seedy history, and a chaos deity, which had to be Madwyn.

As far as Nefarals went, if you were going to rely on any of them, best have them be from a house with a history of loyalty to her own family's house, Daevos, and a reputation to uphold, like the Senagals. Realizing then that she had yet to shake Madwyn's hand, Remi turned back, grasping her slender fingers and shaking. The goddess inclined her head in deference to Remi's title, but the gesture seemed unnatural for her. Remi imagined that the authority she wore like a cloak made it damn near impossible for her to ever seem humbled before anyone.

"It's a pleasure to meet you," Remi said, and she meant it. It wasn't every day she had the opportunity to meet someone with a family history as storied as her own.

"The pleasure is all mine," Madwyn crooned, continuing as she released Remi's hand. "You know, I was at your wedding, and I've been dying to meet you ever since. But Thayne here asked me to give you a little time. According to him, I can be a bit much." She shot him a glare that had Remi stifling a grin.

A lazy smile spread over Thayne's lips in response. "And I stand by that assessment, Madwyn." It seemed his coldness was reserved solely for Remi, and it felt like a slap in the face. Even incinerating her room and endangering castle residents hadn't elicited this kind of a reaction from him.

"We all stand by it," Riven added, arm still looped around Ellarah's waist. For the first time, Remi noticed the sullen expression on Ellarah's face. It was as if, with the arrival of Madwyn, she seemed to sink into herself.

Remi made a mental note to ask her about it later as Thayne gestured for them all to follow. "The game will start any minute, and I've located a blind spot in the security cameras where we can talk in private." He turned his back to them and began walking behind a stone archway with chunks blown out of it to lend to the air of semi-destruction.

They all fell into step behind him, and when Remi turned the corner, she saw a small clearing between three large stone archways. Five crates seemed to have been arranged in a circle, and Thayne moved towards one, leaning against it and facing the inside of the circle.

They all joined him. Remi picked the one across from him and leaned back, resting on her palms. Ellarah and Riven chose the one next to her, Ellarah hauling herself on top of it to sit while Riven leaned back between her legs to rest against the crate's sturdy surface.

Madwyn picked the one next to Thayne, leaving a space to Remi's right. The chaos goddess crossed her legs at the ankles and folded her arms across her chest, leaning back and eyeing Thayne with curiosity. "So, you got me here with promises of conspiracy and intrigue," she said, looking around at each of the gods positioned around her. "You know I'm a sucker for that, so I'd say it's time to pay up."

Thayne caught Remi's eye and raised his brows in question, stepping forward and into the center of the circle. The one thing Ellarah had told her in advance was to bring the letter to whatever they had planned for tonight, so she'd tucked it into the pocket of her loose trousers, hidden beneath the weight of her coat. She tilted her head in acknowledgment of his silent question. Yes, I have it, she thought, unfastening the oversized buttons on her jacket.

The room had grown warm despite the blizzard still raging outside, so she let the fabric of her coat fall to either side of her body and waited, eyeing both Ellarah and Thayne. So, Madwyn hadn't been given the full story, she observed, uncertain if she should be grateful or not. Secrecy had been part of the binding, as had mutual agreement on the next steps, and she hadn't agreed to telling anyone other than Riven. So, most likely, Thayne had kept the confidence out of self-preservation rather than respect for her wishes.

"Ellarah wouldn't give me any details either," Riven said. "So, now I'm wondering exactly what the three of you have gotten yourselves into." Remi raised her brows. That revelation took her by surprise. She didn't take Ellarah for much of a secret keeper, at least not from Riven. She thought maybe her new friend had given him bits and pieces, and not the whole story. But zero details?

Ellarah shifted under the combined scrutiny of both Riven, who looked back at her over his shoulder, and Remi, who stared at her in disbelief. "What?" She asked, clicking her tongue in annoyance. "Thayne asked me to wait until today, so I did. He made a compelling argument."

"What argument was that?" Riven asked, facing forward again and crossing his arms over his chest as he surveyed his high prince.

Thayne eyed Riven and then cracked a confident smile, allowing his lightning to encircle his fingers. "I convinced her that we needed both you and Madwyn to agree to a binding before we can talk. If you refuse, then we can play out our time in this ridiculous VR cafe, and go back to the godly realm without divulging anything, no harm done."

Madwyn's eyes seemed to glow with newfound excitement. "That serious, huh? Tell me..." she scanned her gaze from Ellarah to Remi and then to Thayne. "Is it illegal?" Her smile turned almost predatory with elation when all three of them remained silent.

After a few beats of quiet, Thayne replied, "Binding or no deal."

Riven had shifted his stance to face Ellarah, one hand on each of her thighs. Surely, he must know more than Madwyn or at least have an inkling of what this was all about. He had, after all, been the one to help them procure the letter in the first place. But it seemed that he had been just as in the dark as Ellarah had about its origins and Bekka's outrageous request.

Ellarah seemed to soften under his intense scrutiny, her golden eyes turning a little moony. But she held steady, shaking her head. "I told you, his argument was compelling. So, I'm with Thayne and Remi on this one. Binding first, then we can talk."

Madwyn and Riven shared a look as though debating the wisdom of agreeing to a promise before they knew what they would be getting into. Remi couldn't blame them. If she were in their shoes, she'd walk out the door and never look back. She'd learned a long time ago that curiosity didn't always pan out the way you wanted it to. Sometimes, you found out things you'd rather not have known about in the first place.

Madwyn pressed herself up from the crate and moved toward the center of the circle to join Thayne. She slipped off her leather gloves one at a time and tucked them into the pocket of her burgundy coat. "This is simply too intriguing. Now, I must know." On an exhale of breath, a small tendril of purple magic twisted around her fingertips. The smokey texture of it was laced with small slices of what looked like an electrical current.

Her magic called to her; she turned her focus on Riven. "Come on, little brother; you know you're just as curious as I am."

But, Riven hesitated, still seeking confirmation from Ellarah. "Give it to me straight, baby." He rested his hands on either side of her face, holding her gently as he looked into her eyes. "Is this something I want to know? Or should I walk away?"

Ellarah licked her full lips, and Remi tried her best not to stare as she deliberated. Knowing what kind of power Riven had, she understood why they needed him on their side. Ellarah had been right when she'd said as much that night; Remi had just been too overwhelmed to ask for more details.

The reality was that he was one of the few gods alive today who had the kind of magic to do what they needed to be done. Many deities could translocate within their own realms, but few could create trans-universal or trans-dimensional portals. Death gods, well, they could do both.

After what felt like an eternity, Ellarah said, "I can't say that you'd want to know, but what we need to do...it's important. And we need your help to do it."

He dropped his hands from her face and slid one through his slicked-back hair. "Shit," he muttered, taking a step back from her, and slipping his hands into his black, wool coat. "I don't know, Ellarah."

Thayne's voice interrupted them then as he spoke to both Riven and Madwyn, "The binding we're proposing won't require any action on either of your parts. You can hear what we have to say, then if you don't want to help, you can go on your way, and we'll figure something else out. All we're asking for is a vow of secrecy and silence."

Riven shook his head as though trying to clear it. Then, he turned to Thayne for a second before turning back to Ellarah. "It's really that important?"

They each nodded, the sober expressions on their faces letting him know just how serious they were. Finally, he let out a long sigh. "Fine, I'll agree to the binding." With his reticent response, he stepped into the circle, Ellarah on his heels.

Without hesitation, Remi pushed up from her own crate, moving to join her companions. She slid off her gloves and called her fire to her, flames licking up her forearms. Black mist coated Riven's hands, and a vibrant shock of white enclosed Ellarah's. Then Thayne spoke the words that would set the guidelines of the binding, "You will speak to no one of what you learn today. Everything we tell you must be kept in complete confidence unless we give you direction otherwise."

With the words spoken, they each stepped forward, moving their hands to the center of the circle until all their fingertips touched. Their magics stung as they wove around their wrists and fingers, marking them all with each other's unique magical brand.

With the pact set, Remi's mind relaxed, and after a nod from Thayne, she knew it was time to show them what they'd come here to see. Pulling the note from her pocket, she moved over to one of the crates. She unfolded it and spread it out, smoothing the wrinkles as she did. She gestured for them all to follow and she heard footsteps just before she felt their collective body warmth and their eyes peering over her shoulder.

She looked back at Riven this time. "You know how you and Ellarah agreed to help me find information on my sister?" He nodded at her, looking a little pale. "Well, you hit pay dirt. The meeting you guys arranged was with a consciousness deity, he wouldn't give me his name, but he did give me this letter."

Riven and Madwyn each stepped forward, Riven looking a little cautious and Madwyn looking almost excited. Say what you want about her, but she didn't seem to ruffle easily. It was a quality that Remi thought would come in handy, considering what they were going to ask them to do.

Before they could start reading, she continued, "According to this letter, my sister is trapped in Moldize. She's asked for my help. But I think it's best if you read it for yourselves. She explains everything better than I could."

Remi stepped aside. When they finished a few minutes later, they spun around. Riven gaped, but Madwyn seemed gleeful, or maybe just entertained. It was hard to tell with her.

"Ascended," Madwyn breathed. "You certainly don't disappoint. So, Rebekkah is alive, and she's in Moldize, of all the hideous places?" She gave a quick shudder of repulsion before she leaned forward, gleaming eyes locking onto Thayne. "Is this the part where you ask me to create an epic distraction at the palace while Ellarah sneaks you all into the travel and communications depot so that my brother can conjure a portal to Moldize?"

Thayne opened his mouth to reply, but Madwyn continued, seemingly lost in thought as she theorized, "Well, it would have to be during the inauguration ball, of course. That seems like the most opportune moment. Everyone in the entire palace, Twelve Hells, everyone in the entire realm will be distracted and partaking in the festivities. It will give me ample material to work with, and once Remi is sworn in, it will be easy for us to slip away unnoticed." She looked at Remi and beamed. "It's a good plan, my loves. Don't you think it's a good plan?"

Riven shook his head and pinched the bridge of his nose. "Don't you think you should let Thayne talk before you just assume that's what he wanted to say?"

Remi got the impression from the sickened look on his face that he hoped Thayne would shut Madwyn down and say something entirely different. She couldn't blame him, considering the potential repercussions.

"What?" Madwyn purred. "The ceremony is less than a week away, and if we're going to help Remi's sister, it's the ideal time to do it."

Thayne nodded in response and rubbed a thumb over his eyebrow. "Well, Madwyn, you took the words right out of my mouth."

A moment of silence fell between them as they all seemed to contemplate the gravity of what Madwyn had just suggested and Thayne's confirmation of it. There was no doubt that Remi wanted to help her sister, but Thayne hadn't filled her in on his apparent plan to use the inauguration as cover for it. Just two days ago, they'd discussed the danger just having the event could pose. Yet now that he had the security nailed down, he wanted to use it to obscure their own illegal activities?

If she thought about it, it made sense, but hearing someone say it out loud also made it more real. And a lot more anxiety-inducing.

Riven interrupted her thoughts. "You can't be serious." His cool blue eyes pierced them each, one by one as he took a step back from them. "This is insane. You're asking me to create a portal to another universe without permission from the pillar leadership or royal approval, and it's not just any universe. It's *Moldize*." He scoffed. "I mean, this could get us all killed."

The way he put it did make it sound bad, Remi thought. But Thayne and Ellarah knew this realm better than anyone. They'd made it clear that no pillar leader in their right mind would approve opening a portal to Moldize, no matter who requested it. Or why, for that matter. That left a plan like this one as their only option.

Thayne looked at his friend and moved to rest a hand on his shoulder to reassure him. "We're dead serious. The letter is real. The request is real. The urgency of this situation is real, and we need your help. All of you," he said, looking at Madwyn and Riven too.

Madwyn was composed. Almost eager. From what she'd said earlier, they'd have no trouble convincing her.

Riven, on the other hand, stared at them, his skin seeming to grow more pallid as he realized just how serious they were. "Have you all lost your minds?" When no one answered right away, he shook his head. "We could open a doorway, and anything or anyone could walk straight through it. How can we even be sure that this letter is authentic?"

He flung a hand in the direction of the aforementioned letter, and Remi straightened her shoulders. "We would never have brought this to you if we weren't sure it came from Bekka. First, it's in my sister's handwriting—"

"Simplistic," he snapped, waving a hand in dismissal. "That could be some kind of trick, or she could have been forced to write it."

Remi glared. "There's more," she bit out, her tone letting him know just how little she liked being interrupted. "There's the postscript. It's a code, something that only Bekka would know to say. She would never have included it if she'd been coerced. It's her way of authenticating the letter for me."

Thayne joined the conversation then, appealing to his friend. "Riven, come on. You know I'd go through the official channels if I could. But we all know it will never happen. Rebekkah would stay trapped there. If this is all true in her letter, then we can't risk letting that happen just because the leadership in our realm is afraid."

Riven's voice dropped a few octaves. "Did you ever think that maybe they're right to be afraid? Moldize was banished for a reason. We shouldn't forget that." Even if his words were delivered without any bitterness or anger, Remi could tell that he was trying not to snap at them.

"But Bekka is trapped there and we're her only chance at getting out," Remi said. "Riven, there's an uprising; talk of another great war. She is the last creator left in our realm. We need her."

Riven turned on his heel, pacing. "We need to back up—" He stopped and turned toward Remi. "—and really think about what we're talking about doing here."

Ellarah reached for Riven's hand, then rested a palm on his cheek. "I know what we're asking for is a lot to process, but you're the one who told me about the Nefs and the discontent. You said it's only going to get worse. What if what Rebekkah says is true? What if we need to act now?"

Everyone registered surprise at this new information, even the unflappable Madwyn. Ellarah had mentioned that she'd heard rumblings about a Nefaral movement, but Remi hadn't realized where they'd come from until now. Of course, it made sense. Riven was a Nef, probably the most powerful one left in Bicaidia. He'd be a valuable asset for any uprising worth its salt.

Uncertainty pooled in Riven's blue eyes. "If we get caught..." he trailed off, and Remi saw the real problem now—he wasn't concerned for himself, at least not entirely. Instead, he was worried about Ellarah. Remi's heart squeezed as she realized once again the depth of feeling they had for each other and how much it must be hurting Ellarah to put him in this position.

Ellarah met his gaze. "We need you if we're going to make this plan work."

He closed his mouth, his brows knitting together in thought as his jaw flexed. But before he could say anything else, Madwyn offered her two cents. "Come on, little brother, pull that giant stick out of your ass just this once."

Riven turned on his sister, his teeth almost bared in a snarl of anger. "You make it sound like I'm uptight, but this isn't a joke, Madwyn. I want a Peacekeeper back in the seat of power as much as anyone, but if we get caught, we'll all end up smoldering piles of ash on the surface of the sun."

Madwyn waved a hand in dismissal at his concern and rolled her eyes. "Oh, please. If we get caught, we'll run. If we need a quick escape, then we can always go through the portal instead of Rebekkah. Then you could close it behind us."

Remi swallowed the bile that rose in her throat at the idea of going to Moldize. Even under those circumstances, she wasn't sure she'd want to do that. Smoldering pile of ash or living in exile in Moldize for the rest of her life? Sadly, they came up on even ground in her mind.

Riven seemed to agree with her assessment because in response to his sister's suggestion, he spun away from the group at large. He took deep breaths, his shoulders rising and falling in time with them. After a long moment of silence, Thayne filled it. "Riven, we're counting on your help here.

Your power is the key to this going off without a hitch. Trans-dimensional portals created by energy gods are notoriously difficult to close, and we'd need more than Ellarah if we have any hope of just opening one. If anything goes amiss, then we wouldn't be able to—"

"Close it," Riven finished for him, turning back to look at them all. "And I'm the only one who has that capability. So, when you said I could opt out of this and you'd figure something out, you were lying?"

Thayne's face didn't show a trace of guilt when he replied, "Mostly, yes."

"Bastard," Riven grumbled, but Remi could see a crack in his resolve, which seemed to deepen as his gaze settled on Ellarah. When his face softened, Remi knew that they had him. Elation mingled with fear coalesced in her belly as he let out a long-suffering sigh. "Fine, I'll help if for no other reason than to make sure the four of you don't get yourselves killed."

Madwyn examined her nails, looking unsurprised by her brother's change of heart or, at a minimum, uninterested. From what Remi could tell, she wanted to get to the next part of this whole endeavor. The plotting and the scheming, which made sense, given her chaos deity instincts.

Thayne smiled wider than Remi had ever seen before, the expression transforming the hard lines of his face. He looped an arm around Riven's shoulder and squeezed him roughly. "Good, because if you'd said no, I would have had to call in that favor you owe me. And I really didn't want to waste that."

Riven smiled a devious grin, "Oh no, this counts as that favor, Thayne. We're even now."

Thayne chuckled. "Alright, fair enough," he said, as Riven moved back to Ellarah, smoothing his hair before he wrapped an arm around her waist.

Remi caught Thayne's eye, and she dipped her head in appreciation for everything he'd done and would do to help her and her sister. He might not be thrilled with her at the moment, but he still offered her a closed-mouthed smile in acceptance of her gratitude. It wasn't a lot, but it was something other than the cold shoulder and she chose to take it as a good sign.

As the light dimmed in the room and then began pulsing with random flashes to simulate explosions in battle, they spent the rest of the afternoon planning. They went through the details. They discussed how they'd gain access to the depot and who would be responsible for what pieces of the plan. They talked through everything, making sure no stone was left unturned and that all angles were covered.

Thayne further explained why they had to do this on inauguration night. With the extra security in place, there would be protection at the palace should anything go wrong, and something or someone got through before Riven could close the portal. Misdirection also was essential. While everyone was looking one way—at the celebration and the palace perimeter—it would leave the depot with a skeleton staff. It would provide them with the ideal opportunity to do what they needed to do with minimal intervention.

It made sense, Remi knew. But she still couldn't help but feel like it was all moving so fast. The inauguration was less than six days away, so they would have to move quickly.

When all the details were sorted out, they each left with their own assignments and an agreement to meet again in three days to finalize the timing and the plan. As they moved back toward the entrance of their combat room, Madwyn called out to her brother. "Riven, you're needed back home. Family business." She raised her brows at him, looking between him and Ellarah. Remi caught a distinct sense of disapproval coming from her but decided to keep her mouth shut. It was none of her business, and besides, maybe she was just misreading the situation.

But then she ran through the entire afternoon in her mind once more and realized that Ellarah and Madwyn hadn't spoken a word to each other. She pinched her brows together, certain that she must be mistaken. But she couldn't recall a single moment that they'd exchanged even the most basic pleasantries.

Riven raised Ellarah's hand to his lips and pressed a kiss to it. "I'll find you later."

He stepped away from her then, and with the flick of his hand, black mist oozed from it. His death magic, Remi realized, never having seen it on full dispay before. The last death deity in Valeria had died long before she was born, so she'd never witnessed the actual power up close.

Within seconds, a portal alighted in front of Riven and his sister, and Remi knew that while this wasn't technically against the law since no mortals were present, it was still sort of a gray area. But then again, who was she to judge, considering what she, Thayne and Ellarah had just asked them to do?

Choosing not to say anything, she watched as Madwyn turned back to her and smiled that same dazzling smile that had just a hint of wildness in it. "It was lovely to meet you, Remi." She leaned in, grasping her shoulders and kissing both of her cheeks. "Don't worry; we're going to get Rebekkah home."

With that, she spun on her heels back toward Riven. Thayne offered them both a nod in goodbye and a second later, they both disappeared into the mist. It evaporated behind them, and Ellarah let out a massive sigh.

Thayne looked at her from the corner of his eyes as they opened the door and strode into the hallway of the VR cafe. "Things are still tough between you two, huh?"

"You could say that." Ellarah shrugged a shoulder, and Remi could sense a genuine pain in the expression she wore even though sarcasm dripped from her tongue.

Thayne shook his head. "I'm sorry, Ellarah. I'm sure she'll come around."

Ellarah barked out a laugh that was anything but amused. "Come on, Thayne; you know Madwyn as well as I do. Once she's made up her mind about something, there's no changing it."

He pressed his lips together and nodded but remained silent. Remi felt a little like an intruder since she had no idea what they were talking about. What had Madwyn made her mind up about? And what did it have to do with her and Ellarah's chilly relationship?

At last, Thayne pulled an orb from his pocket, electricity dancing on its surface for a brief moment as he powered up the instaportal. "This issue between you two won't be a problem, right? You can get past it and work together in this?" Of course, if he'd asked Remi, this was something he should have verified before he brought Madwyn into their circle of trust. But all the same, at least he was asking it now.

Ellarah shook her head. "You know it's not a problem on my end, Thayne. I'll play my part, and Madwyn and I will stay out of each other's way."

With a nod, he dropped the orb, letting it roll a few feet ahead of them before it hit a closed door. The hallway was empty, and when the portal sparked to life, highlighting the door in magic, he turned, looking at Remi now. His dark eyes felt even more intense in the low-light, and he seemed to see her for the first time. But rather than say anything to her directly, he said, "I'll see you both soon." Then, before Remi could utter a single syllable, he was gone.

Ellarah and Remi stood alone in the hallway now, and Remi let out a long sigh. "He's mad at me, isn't he?"

Ellarah pressed her lips together and wagged a finger. "Oh no, I'm not touching that. I don't like getting in the middle of lover's quarrels."

Remi let out a disappointed sigh. "Fair enough, but are *you* ok? I'm not blind, you know, and I could see how cold Madwyn was with you too. Is there anything I can do to help?"

Ellarah grinned a little, coming out of her shell again with Madwyn gone. "Yes, I'm OK. You don't need to worry about me." She paused then, eyeing Remi from beneath her lashes. After a short silence, she seemed to cave. "Alright, I'll give you my take on Thayne. Yes, he does seem to be upset with you, and I think we both know why—" she broke off, leaned closer and whispered "—the binding. But that's all you're getting from me. The rest you'll need to sort out between the two of you."

She'd been dead on, but somehow being right didn't have the same effect on her it normally did. Then a thought occurred to her. He hadn't been blameless or perfect that night either. The reason they'd agreed to that binding in the first place was because he'd been in her room, uninvited. Talk about obtrusive. Besides, he'd been the one to ask for the binding, not her. Although sure, she'd known that allowing him to bind himself to her with a promise over something that could potentially get him killed hadn't been her finest moment. But she'd done it for her sister.

A new, righteous fire burning in her belly, she followed her friend through the hall and back to the front desk. Ellarah handed all five pairs of goggles and the key to the receptionist. Remi hadn't even seen her grab them. Exchange made, they left the jittery human behind and went back out into the freezing cold outside. The sun had set, and the snow had stopped, but the biting cold still had Remi gathering her coat close to her.

"So, I know that you said you're ok, but—" Remi paused, unsure how to broach this subject. She didn't want to pry, but at the same time she didn't want to be left in the dark either. "Can you tell me what the deal is with you and Madwyn? I want to understand the tension, since we're all in this together now."

Ellarah groaned, shaking her head. "It's sort of a long story." They turned down an abandoned alleyway, and Ellarah checked behind them to ensure no humans were around. She pulled her instaportal from her pocket and pulsed her magic through it. Rolling it on the ground, a flash of light issued, and a portal appeared, surrounding a metal door on the side of the VR cafe.

They twisted the knob and stepped through the doorway, landing right back in Remi's room. Ellarah picked up the orb and powered it down as Remi said, "Well, we've got time."

Stripping off their coats and throwing them onto the windowsill, Ellarah dropped backward onto Remi's bed. "Madwyn, Riven, Thayne, and I have been friends all of our lives. My parents immigrated to Bicaidia from Perenelle when I was three to help with the energy mines. They've lived in the palace ever since, so I grew up with all of them. We used to do everything together. Where you'd find one of us, you'd find the rest, and Riven and I have always had a…flirtation. That never used to bother Madwyn, but when we started dating a few months back. Well, let's just say that things have moved fast between us. Of course, we didn't plan it this way; it's just that nothing has ever felt this right before, you know?"

Remi shook her head. "No, I don't. I wish I did, though." She splayed her hands on her thighs, a little envious. "So, what went wrong with Madwyn?"

Ellarah let out a pained sigh and closed her eyes. "Let's just say she didn't approve. She didn't want her brother to end up with some middle-caste Perenellean deity. According to her, he can do better."

Remi winced. "Yikes. That's harsh." She didn't know what else to say, and she wished she was surprised, but she wasn't. Upper-caste gods, especially those with royal bloodlines, liked to make matches that increased their family's power and position. And Ellarah's middle-caste status put her at a serious disadvantage.

"Yep," Ellarah said, shaking her head. "It floored me, to be honest. We were so close before, and I thought she'd be happy to see both of us happy."

Remi could see pain wash over her face and leaned forward, wrapping her fingers around Ellarah's hand and squeezing. "I'm sorry, Ellarah," Remi said, at a loss for words now. Remi had always hated the prejudicial bullshit that came along with the caste system that ruled the Twelve Realms. But, that was just how things had always been. It was ingrained into the DNA of their society and she had no idea how to go about changing it.

She watched as Ellarah shrugged her shoulders helplessly. "There's nothing I can do about it. If she doesn't want to be friends with me anymore because I'm too low-caste for her brother, then that's up to her."

She was right, of course. There was nothing Ellarah could do to control or change Madwyn's reaction. She would just have to accept it and hope for the best. Remi felt a tug of gratitude for Ellarah at that moment. "Thanks," she said, which had Ellarah's brows rising. "I should've said it a lot earlier, but I want you to know that I appreciate what you're doing for me. And for my sister."

Ellarah waved it off. "If things are as dire as Rebekkah says, then we need her back here sooner rather than later, right?"

Remi nodded, hope blossoming in her chest. They were really going to do it. They were going to bring Bekka home.

CHAPTER 6

BEKKA

Sacrifices

"**D**o you ever take breaths between bites?" I asked, watching in mild disgust as Deklan shoveled food into his mouth across from me.

He paused and looked up from his feast, elbows spread protectively around his plate. Caden sat next to him, an amused grin on his face. He ate with similar vigor but with less aggression.

Deklan made a big show of slowing down, offering me his most steely glare, which considering his warrior past, was something to behold. When he finally swallowed, he took a long, audible inhale and then pursed his lips and blew it out. "Does that satisfy you?"

I nodded. The moment his lips twitched beneath his cold facade, I knew his ire was all pretense.

We sat in the grand hall, at the ridiculously large dining room table—the massive, arched ceilings were painted with unexplained events from Moldize's long, mysterious past.

Colors swirled together, the imagery a beautiful contrast with the white walls and black marble floors.

Compared to the enormity of the space, we clustered close together so that we could enjoy lunch in some semblance of companionship. It had been two full days since I'd sent my letter to Remi, and the reality of what I'd asked and what I needed to do had begun to sink in.

I fiddled with the sorbet melting in my bowl. I'd already finished the duck paired with candied sweet potatoes and wilted greens that had been today's fare. The Moldizeans may have been lacking in upper-caste deities who packed a powerful punch, but servant gods? They had those in spades.

As Deklan dug back into his food, I took a bite of the lemon-raspberry ice and pondered what I was getting myself into. I was going to be the next Peacekeeper. The one who held the Twelve Realms together through the sheer force of my iron will. I would be the new Gabryel. Yeah, right, iron will my ass, I thought, but suddenly, a pang of grief rocketed through me at the reminder that he was gone.

I sighed, wishing that he was here with me because, without a doubt, he would know exactly what to do in this situation. He'd be decisive; he'd quell any rebellion that came his way with no questions and zero doubts.

Me, on the other hand? I was a bundle of nervous energy and a veritable ocean of self-doubt. How was I going to make them respect me? Make them listen to me? I was an unknown quantity in the ranks of the royals and the pillar leadership of the Twelve Realms. Until last month, I was just the late-blooming and possibly defective granddaughter of the Peacekeeper, Gabryel.

Would anyone even listen to me? Arrick and his family believed that the mere presence of a powerful creator would be enough to deter what had begun with my grandpa's death, but I had doubts about that. Serious ones that had started to seep out of my psyche in the form of nightmares, each one growing more terrible than the next. Last night, I'd barely gotten three hours of sleep before I awoke in a drenched sweat, trembling like a lost puppy.

Without warning, the door at the far end of the great hall boomed open, and the crystal chandeliers overhead shuttered in reaction, tinkling like bells. I spun in my chair and watched as Arrick strode through, Erykha and Damion on his heels.

His eyes locked onto me, a hard determination in their depths. In his hands, he held a letter. "Remi replied. We just got word."

My heart quickened in my chest as their fast footfalls echoed across the marble floor. This was it. The moment of truth, and I wasn't sure I was prepared for it. I closed my eyes and steadied my breathing as Arrick pulled out the chair next to me.

Erykha moved to the seat across from me, and Damion grabbed the chair on the other side of me as Arrick unfolded the paper missive, smoothed it across the wooden table. Nervous energy swelled around me, which made me realize that no one else had read it yet.

We all leaned over the letter, except Deklan. He continued digging into the enormity that was his feast. I spared him a glance before I rolled my eyes at him. Unbelievable.

Refocusing back on the paper, I scanned it.

Bekka,
Words can't express how relieved I am that you're alive and safe. When news came of grandpa Gabryel and no word came of you, I must admit, I feared the worst.
But relief and joy aside...Moldize?? How in Twelve Hells did you end up there?! I imagine that's a long story that you'll fill me in on as soon as you get to Bicaidia.
Yes, you read that right. Thayne and I, and the rest of Bicaidia, are prepared to answer your call for aid. We'll open the portal to the coordinates of your choosing. Between 2100 and 2300 standard time on the eleventh of Ideslere...be ready. If any Moldizean should

come through with you, we'll take them into immediate holding for questioning. If the deity is a Nefaral, they will be subject to the laws of the Twelve Realms and will not be freed until that deity accepts a governor chip.

Please reply with the coordinates and your confirmation if these conditions are amenable to you.

With love,

Remi

P.S. When you're back, I expect a full explanation of everything that's transpired since my wedding night. Trust me, I'll hold you to it.

I could feel my eyes widen and my mouth drop open. I hadn't been sure that she would have the sway needed to help me. But she had. Thayne must have used his influence to convince his family and the pillar leadership to help us, because nothing else made sense.

I looked at Arrick. Our eyes locked as he slid the paper across the table to Erykha, Caden, and Deklan. "I can't believe it," I said, shaking my head in utter astonishment. A smile spread across my lips, and I covered my mouth as a bubble of surprised laughter escaped my lips. "She pulled it off."

Arrick's vibrant, green eyes seemed liquid with emotion as they locked onto mine. A lock of thick, dark hair fell over his forehead, and he brushed it back as his jaw clenched. Something was bothering him, and with a slap of realization, I knew what it was.

Remi's letter. The part about what would happen if a Nefaral crossed through the portal with me. The Peacekeeper law was clear when it came to Nefaric powers; a governor chip was required for them to operate within the Twelve Realms, period. So, if Arrick came with me, he would be forced to get one. The initial relief and excitement of getting Remi's response lessened, concern and worry taking up residence in its wake.

I shook my head, careful not to break eye contact. "You don't have to do this," I said. "I can go alone, and that's probably the smart thing to do." I could hear my heartbeat in my ears as I awaited his reply. I couldn't let him risk losing access to the full breadth of his power. I knew that his confidence, his prowess as a leader, and the core of who he was as a god, came from his power—both its rarity and its strength. I didn't want him risking that because governor chips were not removable. Once inside the neck of their host, they stayed there.

There were no removals allowed unless specifically approved by the royals, the pillar leadership, and the Peacekeeper. I recalled a story my parents had told me as a child, about how the Nefarals had resisted the chips at first. Then, they'd tried to cut them out. It hadn't ended well. The chips contained tamper-resistant measures that left anyone who tried to remove them through unofficial methods either severely injured or dead.

His jaw flexed, and his gaze hardened on me. "I'm not letting you go there alone." He rose to his feet, body hovering over mine as he gripped the back of his wooden chair. It groaned under the pressure, the wood splintering with spiderweb cracks before he released it.

I shook my head, rising to my feet as well, squaring off against him. "You heard what she said in the letter, Arrick. You can't come with me. It's not even an option."

I stepped closer to him, my breath heaving with frustration and the icy grip of fear. I already had enough to worry about, with the possibility of the uprising and even a war. I was willing to shoulder that responsibility, no matter how much it frightened me. But I couldn't stand the idea of the Bicaidians reducing Arrick to something less than what he was right now. I wouldn't be responsible for that just because he felt some…what? Affection for me? Loyalty to me? At the end of the day, it wasn't worth it. I shook my head at him. "You know what they'll do to you. I can't—I can't allow it."

He stepped forward and wrapped his strong fingers around my arms. My breath quickened as he stared into my eyes. "It's not your decision to make for me. I'm coming."

Erykha cleared her throat, causing my back to stiffen. Shit, I groaned inwardly, I'd forgotten that anyone else was in the room with us. It was his eyes—his damned hypnotic eyes. They made everything else seem to melt away until all that was left was him. I could feel the sizzle of electricity between us before he stepped away from me, the connection breaking.

We both turned our attention to Erykha, a flush of embarrassment burning up my neck. I spared a glance at Arrick, who seemed as collected and composed as he always did. Typical.

Erykha had risen to her feet as well, the letter dangling from her fingers. "She's right, Arrick. You can't go under these conditions."

His hands clenched into fists as he stepped forward, fury flashing in his eyes. As he rested his hands on the table, leaning over it, a black mist began to seep from his fingers. Temper always made control over our power tenuous, and I could tell he was close to combusting. "You're suggesting we send her in alone? We don't know how serious the situation will be five days from now, and I won't risk her. I can't."

I wanted him to come with me because I knew he would have my back, but I also knew that Erykha was right.

And so was I, damnit.

Out of all of us, Arrick was the one person who couldn't come with me no matter how much he insisted or how much I wanted him there. And believe me, I wanted him there more than I'd ever wanted anything in my entire existence.

Because I knew that this wouldn't be a temporary separation, the likelihood of ever seeing him again dropped to near zero once I got home. The very thought of this cracked something in my heart, but I didn't dare let it show. I had to protect him, to keep him from making the biggest mistake of his life, no matter what that meant for me.

After a long pause, Erykha shook her head at her son's refusal, and Damion rested a soothing hand on Arrick's shoulder. "Son," he said, drawing the angry death deity's attention to him. "Your mother's right. We need you here and at full power. We already have enough problems in Moldize without letting them clip your wings in the Twelve Realms for all eternity."

Anger still seemed to simmer within him, but the magic seeping from his fingers dissipated. He opened his mouth to speak, but Erykha beat him to it. "I'll go with Bekka until she is safe with her sister. You have my word, son. But you must stay behind. You know damn well why we can't risk you." Her words transformed, the tenor as cold as ice now, a meaning I couldn't quite place lingering beneath the surface. She gave him a stern, meaningful look that had Arrick releasing a long breath, the corded muscles in his arms flexing in time with his clenched fists.

"What's going on here that requires Arrick's attention, exactly?" Deklan asked.

All three of the Moldizean royals exchanged pained looks like this wasn't something they'd wanted to share with anyone. This didn't look or sound good. I braced myself for whatever they would say next.

Damion ran a hand through his long, blond hair. "We picked up a reading at our borders, a power pulse of some kind. We think someone is trying to penetrate our wards."

"You're kidding?" I asked though I couldn't say why. Judging by the seriousness of their expression, they weren't.

Erykha stalked over to the floor-to-ceiling windows that looked out onto the village surrounding the castle below. Her back facing us, she continued Damion's explanation and ignored my question, which worked for me since it was rhetorical anyway. "It happened for the first time just after Bekka recreated the sun. But we've had similar readings five times since, at different locations. It's like someone is inspecting our borders. They seem to be searching for a weakness." She turned back, her green gaze defiant as though daring anyone to question her. "Don't worry; they won't find one."

Deklan had the decency to look concerned when he asked, "Have you been able to track the perpetrator?" Caden remained silent, but his wide, blue eyes, the mirror image of his twin's, flicked from Erykha to Damion, his apprehension obvious. I was right there with him.

All three of the Moldizean leaders shook their heads in unison as though possessed by the same puppet master. I could see the nervousness on all their faces, though they tried to hide it.

"How serious is this?" Caden asked, his voice measured as usual, though his skin had gone a bit pale as he awaited an answer.

Damion's jaw flexed, and Arrick ran a hand over the back of his neck, both gestures I knew all too well, and I knew exactly what they meant—this wasn't good. Arrick confirmed my suspicions when he said, "Whatever or whoever it is, they pack a serious punch. The readings, they mirror the strength of Gabryel's when he got through our borders before."

The hairs on the back of my neck rose in response to this. No one else in the multiverse had that kind of power anymore. *Except me.*

My mind spun as I tried to think up different scenarios for how or why this could happen, and I realized there was one other possibility. This could be a concentrated effort. Many gods with the same power, fusing their magic and working in concert towards the same goal.

But, why now? And why would they come to Moldize of all places? Could this be part of the Nefaric uprising? Or something else entirely?

I shook my head in disbelief, "Why the hell didn't you tell me about this before now? And why would you suggest that I leave while this is still happening? I thought we were a team and that we were in this together. Why would you lie to me?"

Arrick moved to me, his body drawing close to mine. I could feel his warmth and the charge of his power, still rippling just beneath the surface. "We didn't lie to you," he answered, brushing his fingers over my cheek, the affectionate gesture a useless salve. I was furious with them, but I let him continue. "You've already done all you can to help us. The wards are strengthened and rebuilt, and Moldize is on its way to being whole and healthy again. Whatever is happening here, we can handle on our own, just as we have for centuries."

Despite his comforting touch, his words felt like a cold slap in the face, and I sucked in a breath in response. Hurt suffused me as I realized that they didn't think of me in the same way as I did of them. Maybe I'd been naive, but I thought I'd earned some level of respect here, that they would have asked me for my help with something this serious. Or, at minimum, they would have told me about it.

I ground my teeth in frustration, and I could feel my magic swell in response. I took a deep breath, leveling my temper and getting my power under control. Unlike Arrick's, mine didn't seep out in misty sheets. It exploded whenever I got too angry, and I'd rather not knock everyone fifty feet through the air right now. They might deserve a good verbal lashing, but they didn't deserve the wrath of my creation gift.

After two deep breaths to get myself under control, I asked, "How do you know that it's not an army of Nefarals out there, trying to breach your wards?"

"We don't think that's it. Based on their heat signatures, we think it's a small, concentrated force," Damion interrupted before I could really get going on my tirade. "But this is why we can't allow Arrick's power to be suppressed. We still don't know who this is or what they want, and if it comes to a fight, Arrick's the only one who could face them on even ground."

Deklan rose from his seat, pushing his food to the center of the table so he could plant his hands at the edge of it. "How long has it been since the last reading?"

Erykha crossed her arms over her chest, her eyes severe when she answered, "A few days."

My belly tensed into thick knots at this news. Only a few days? How could I just leave them behind, knowing that something suspicious, and possibly even dangerous, was happening along the border here? But then, how could I not go home, knowing that the Nefarals could stage their revolt at any moment? Starting in Bicaidia, where my sister would be in danger.

A headache began to bloom, starting from my neck and settling over my right eye. This couldn't be happening, I thought, my guts turning to slippery eels in seconds flat.

Sensing my internal conflict, Arrick enveloped my hand into his. He gave it a gentle squeeze, and my eyes found his once more. The electric green depths framed by those dark, sumptuous lashes made me want to fall into them forever, no matter how impossible it was between us.

But his deep voice pulled me out of inner turmoil. "You have to go home, Bekka. You can't worry about us. We're one realm, and we can handle ourselves. The Twelve Realms are your responsibility, and they'll fall apart if you don't go back. Of this, I'm certain. Here though, we don't even know that this is a threat. So, the choice is crystal clear. I don't doubt that you going is the right thing to do, and you shouldn't either."

I swallowed the bile rising in my throat. "But what if I leave and something happens to you?" I looked around the table at all of the people I'd grown to care for so much. My eyes swam with tears before I blinked them away. "I'd never forgive myself."

Erykha shook her head, her eyes hard as ice. I sensed an authority in her and an immense strength that rippled beneath the surface. I'd always known she had to be strong, given everything the Moldizeans had been through, but I'd never seen the tough side of her before. This was the ruler beneath the kind-hearted and determined goddess I'd come to know so well. "We can handle this. As long as Arrick, Damion, and I stick together, we'll be fine."

I looked around again, searching them for some semblance of doubt, but I saw none in any of their eyes. So, I let out a shaky breath. Well, if they're confident that they can handle this, then I guess I should be too, I thought. But a cold sense of dread had settled over me just the same, an icy pit forming in my stomach to accompany the headache.

"We're agreed then?' Erykha asked. "I'll go with Bekka and Arrick, and you stay here?" Then, when he only glowered, Erykha continued, "I know you don't like it, but it's the right thing to do, and you know it."

His jaw worked as he debated how to answer her. A long pause passed where I could hear my heart beating in the silence. Then he finally answered, "You're right, I *hate* it. But Remi's conditions and situation here give me little choice…so, I'll stay."

Though I knew it was irrational, sorrow crawled up from somewhere deep inside me. Even though this was what I wanted, the fact remained. In five days, I'd be gone, and Arrick would be out of my life for good. One question pulsed through my mind, though.

Was this an outcome I was willing to live with, or could I do something about it?

Deep down, I already knew the answer.

CHAPTER 7
REMI

Shadows

Remi popped a tender piece of prickly cactus fruit wrapped with cured meat into her mouth as she marveled at the crowd of inauguration attendees gathered in the central palace courtyard. "This is delicious," she said, pointing to the tray of pink fruit balanced on a waiter's hand as he bobbed through the crowd. "You should try some."

Ellarah frowned at her. "How can you possibly eat at a time like this?"

Remi shrugged her shoulders. "I eat when I'm nervous. It's my thing." And there was plenty to be nervous about, she thought, trying not to let those nerves overtake her. Ever since she'd sent that letter, packed with lies and half-truths, to her sister, a pit of dread had formed in her belly.

She'd made it seem like they were going through official channels to open the Moldizean portal because she knew how her sister would react if she suspected otherwise. Bekka would refuse to come, stubborn creature that she was, and that wasn't an acceptable outcome. At the time, Remi had decided that it would be better to ask for forgiveness rather than permission.

But the day of reckoning had arrived and she felt less sure about that decision. So to calm herself, she had scarfed down five prickly cactus wraps, six deep-fried seafood puffs, and four meat-filled tarts—all within twenty minutes.

She snagged another puff and downed that too, deciding that it would be less stressful if she turned her attention to her immediate surroundings rather than waste any more time second-guessing herself.

As she looked around, she saw deities decked out in their finest, spanning an extensive range of styles depending on their pillar. On one extreme, the elemental goddesses wore long, flowy dresses made of light-colored silk, satin, and chiffon, adorned with metal armbands, decorative circlets, and other accessories. In contrast, the Nefaric pillar goddesses wore bold, vibrant colors, often dark and dripping with large, sparkling jewels.

The gods' clothing aligned nicely with the goddesses from their pillars—tuxedos white with silvery-blue stitching, sashes of gold and silver draped over their shoulders. While the Nefaric gods wore dark suits with vibrant pops of color in their stitching or sashes. The only similarity held throughout all attendees was that they each wore sigils to mark their pillar affiliation. The golden, sparkling emblems dangled from their necks, a physical reminder of their station in the immortal realm.

Tiny cocktail tables dotted the courtyard with delicate flowers in crystal centerpieces. Drooping floral arrangements held together with sparkling energy magic floated through the open air, scenting it and adding to the ambiance. Servant deities with enviable artistic talents played the harp along with a few other string instruments.

This event qualified as ultra-posh, even from a royal standpoint—the kind that she had always dreaded growing up. Too bad that she'd been forced to attend due to her position.

After a few moments of silence, Remi saw Ellarah snag a glass of golden, frothy liquor from a passing tray in her periphery. She pressed the flute to her lips, sipping the liquid as though she hadn't a care in the world.

Remi eyed the beverage, concern pressing to the forefront of her mind. Alcohol seemed like an unwise decision, given their extracurricular plans for the evening.

Ellarah seemed to notice Remi's crossed arms and the bitchy, judgmental look on her face and rolled her eyes. "Relax, it's cider with vanilla foam. Here, try some. It's delicious." She offered the delicate crystal glass to Remi, who accepted it. She had worked up quite a thirst from all that food, she thought, taking a sip. The sweet-tart liquid slid down her throat, cold and fizzy, and she sighed with pleasure.

As Remi passed the flute back to Ellarah, she shifted closer so that she could keep what she said next between just them. Then, she looked up at her companion. "So, did you do it? Are we good?"

Ellarah leaned in, and her sleek hair slid forward to cover one side of her face as she whispered, "I did. We're all set. If we don't check in with the all-clear by 2300, then a letter will go to your sister."

Remi nodded, a slight smile on her lips. "Good." Over the last week, Remi had done a little plotting of her own. Nothing groundbreaking, just a tiny contingency plan. A *'just in case anything should happen'* plan.

She'd staked out her facial recognition plate after she'd put her response to Bekka behind it. Expecting to catch the mysterious consciousness deity in the act of retrieving it, she'd been surprised when someone else had come. The servant-caste goddess had been scared out of her wits at the appearance of the princess-in-waiting.

Remi had dragged her into her room and questioned her. From there, she'd coerced, or well, threatened her into giving up her contacts. It wasn't her finest moment, but desperate times and all. To her surprise yet again, the contacts didn't include the god Remi that had met that first night. But they did put her in touch with a middle-caste water goddess who had direct ties to the Moldizean royal family. Though blackmail sounded ugly, it was also an accurate descriptor of what Remi had done to secure a favor from this goddess.

After she had agreed to Remi's request to send a just-in-case letter, Remi had enlisted Ellarah's help in getting it to her. The way she figured it, it seemed safer to send Ellarah rather than drawing unnecessary attention to the goddess's illegal activities with frequent, unexplained, royal visits. With everything arranged now, she felt a little calmer.

Pleased with the solidity of the plan, Remi sipped her drink, a smile on her lips. As she did, she saw Thayne striding towards them. She raised her brows at Ellarah, an indication for her to stay quiet, and her friend pressed her lips together before taking another sip of her cider.

A moment later and Thayne rested his hand on Remi's lower back, a nicety she knew that he would only perform in public. "Sorry I got called away; I'll be a few more minutes. Are you good here?"

Remi nodded, a cool smile on her lips. His eyes seemed distant as he looked from her to the crowd, his chilly disposition toward her still well in place. She found that she didn't like how he seemed to look through her rather than at her. It chafed.

Despite that, she couldn't deny that he looked handsome tonight. He wore a well-tailored tuxedo in a green so deep it almost looked black, its golden stitching a subtle twinkle in the waning sunlight. His black shirt had been left open at the collar, and his long, silky hair had been brushed and tied back from his angular face, a thin crown sitting atop his head to denote his station. "All good here," she answered, doing her best to mirror his level of indifference. "We've been sampling hors d'oeuvres."

"Good," he answered, an absent smile on his face as he pressed a quick kiss to her hand before he departed. Another gesture that she knew was just for public consumption. When he'd turned his back, she sighed, watching him go. For some reason she couldn't pinpoint, the way he'd acted since she'd shown him the letter bothered her much more than she cared to admit.

Ellarah leaned closer then and whispered into her ear, "I see that look."

Remi dragged her eyes away from her husband as he disappeared into a crowd of deities and turned her attention back to Ellarah. "What look?" she asked, plucking a glass of cider off a tray as a waiter passed.

A devilish gleam shone in Ellarah's eyes when she replied, "The one that looks like you want to unwrap Thayne like a piece of candy and enjoy every inch of him."

Remi squinted one eye at her companion. "You're way off base there, my friend." When Ellarah arched a skeptical brow at her, she caved. "OK, so I'll admit that he has some decent qualities—"

"You mean like the shape of his ass in those trousers?" Ellarah interrupted.

Remi had just taken a sip of her cider and promptly spit it back into the flute, laughter bubbling out of her. "My goodness Ellarah, you have such a way with words." She rolled her eyes and then found him again. He emerged from a small group of deities, a broad grin on his face, and walked toward another.

Loathe as she was to admit it, Ellarah had a point. "It's just that we still haven't spoken since that night with the letter."

Ellarah narrowed her eyes. "You're kidding."

Remi shrugged, downing another sip of fizzy beverage. "I think we're both avoiding it. Or at least, I know I've been avoiding it." When Ellarah just surveyed her with crossed arms and a hint of judgement in her eyes, Remi mirrored her posture and hissed. "I already had enough on my plate this week. I didn't feel like adding a marital spat to it just yet, alright?"

Ellarah opened her mouth to argue but was interrupted when a smooth voice purred over Remi's left shoulder. "Hey, dollface!"

She and Remi both turned to face Madwyn as she prowled closer to them. Her generous hips swayed, her body sinful in a blood-red gown. The silken fabric clung to her like water, rippling over every curve she had to offer. She drew closer, pressing her hands onto Remi's shoulders and air-kissing both her cheeks with full, red lips.

Madwyn's mouth pursed in approval. "You look gorgeous! Fierce too."

Thinking it over, Remi decided that fierce was an apt description of her own attire. She looked like a warrior queen in her traditional green, flowing silk dress with a golden chest plate. Golden lace had been twined and braided into her otherwise loose red curls, and her golden sandals laced up to her knee beneath the gown.

Remi made a claw with her hand and uttered a dry, "Rawr."

Madwyn tipped back her head and laughed, the sound contagious enough that Remi grinned at her. Ellarah looked a little less than amused at Madwyn's intrusion and downed the last of her cider.

As though noticing Ellarah for the first time, Madwyn turned to appraise her with a semi-hostile expression followed by a smirk. Remi groaned inwardly as Ellarah seemed to shrink into herself in Madwyn's presence. She hated to see the way her friend disappeared whenever Riven's sister came around. She'd tried to picture them as friends about a million times since Ellarah had told her about their falling out, yet, she couldn't imagine it.

Remi found the whole rift frustrating. Mostly because after the initial shock of her brazen nature had worn off, Remi found that she liked Madwyn. She was intelligent, honest, and gave zero shits about what anyone thought of her—all enviable qualities in Remi's opinion.

But, she had the gnawing concern that Madwyn's disdain for Ellarah would hinder their otherwise budding friendship. She didn't like the way that upper-caste deities looked down on anyone below their station. While she knew that Madwyn was probably just being overprotective of her little brother, it still rubbed her the wrong way.

Just then, Riven slipped through the crowd and into view. She did an internal sigh of gratitude at his timing. It would save her from having to run interference between the goddesses on either side of her. He wore all black, as always, and the suit was well-tailored to his body. His hair was slicked back, and the angles of his face were cut into sharp relief from the lighting above.

The moment his eyes locked onto Ellarah, Remi noticed that everything about his sleek demeanor seemed to soften— from his stiffened posture to the cynical expression in his eyes. "Hey, beautiful," he drawled, wrapping his arms around her waist and drawing her in for a long kiss.

Remi cleared her throat, resisting the urge to roll her eyes, and they broke away. Then, turning to face Remi and Madwyn, he dipped his head in greeting. "Sister. Princess."

Since their first meeting, she'd learned that Madwyn and Riven were both contenders for the top job in Bicaidia's Nefaric Pillar of Power. The Nefaric Pillar's leader was an older deity, a goddess of pestilence, who looked like she might ascend at any moment.

For now, though, Riven ran the metaphysical sect, which meant he oversaw heaven, hell, and reincarnation, and everything that happened in those dimensions.

Madwyn ran the chaos sect of the Nefaric Pillar, and though Remi had known many chaos deities back home, there was something different about Madwyn. But then, Remi had felt that way about most Nefs since she'd arrived in Bicaidia—they all seemed to have far too much power and influence here for her taste. She had a feeling that was why Bicaidia had become the epicenter for the uprising her sister had warned them about.

Riven snagged a tumbler of water from a passing waiter. "So, did I interrupt anything important?" he asked, lips parting in a charming grin.

Ellarah and Madwyn eyed each other from beneath their lashes, each looking less than thrilled by the other's presence. Remi swallowed, damn the consequences, she thought before blurting in a teasing voice, "Actually, you saved us all from yet another chilly, hostile silence between your girlfriend and your sister, so thanks for that. It got so cold in here, it almost felt like we were in Ipupolca." Ellarah's eyes almost bugged out of her skull at Remi's words, but she ignored it. She had no patience for drama that everyone just pretended didn't exist.

She especially hated the fact that it seemed to be eating Ellarah alive. Madwyn, on the other hand, smiled her usual, cool smile. It seemed like nothing could ruffle her.

Riven frowned and looked between Ellarah and Madwyn. Then gaze hardening, he stepped away from Ellarah and wrapped his long, slender fingers around Madwyn's upper arm. "A word, sister?"

Behind Riven's back, Ellarah mouthed to Remi, *"What are you doing?"*

Remi mouthed back, *"I'm calling her out. She's acting like an elitist bitch."*

But before Riven could lead Madwyn more than a few steps away, presumably to a more private location, an unfamiliar voice interrupted their little *tête-à-tête*. "You two going somewhere?"

Turning, Remi saw the owner of the low, raspy voice striding toward them. He stopped next to Riven and clapped a hand on the death god's back. Riven looked like he'd eaten something bitter as the impact of the blow caused him to stumble forward a step.

"Pietyr!" Ellarah exclaimed, her voice filled with surprise. "We weren't sure you could make it." She stepped forward and shared a quick, friendly embrace with the stranger. As she stepped back, Remi looked at his smooth, gorgeous face, and then scanned his silvery suit complete with a matte black shirt. He had deep, bronze skin, like Ellarah's, and his silvery, gray eyes were fixed on Madwyn. Remi couldn't tell if it was interest, attraction, or something else that lingered in the depths of those hypnotic irises.

"My savior," Madwyn crooned, gathering the god into a hug of her own. "My brother was just about to give me another lecture about my attitude."

"Something tells me you weren't the one in need of saving, Madwyn. You can handle yourself," he replied, lips quirking in a seductive half-smile as his eyes traveled the length of Madwyn's body. She shrugged a lean, toned shoulder and raised her brows in a cocky gesture, suggesting that she agreed with his assessment.

After a brief moment passed, he turned his attention to Remi. "You must be the main event," he observed, crossing his arms over his chest and surveying her with irreverence. His silvery gaze locked onto hers and the appraising nature of it had Remi standing up straighter and squaring her shoulders. His neutral attire and lack of sigil pendant left her wondering about his pillar affiliation, yet he had an air of authority that was both appealing and unnerving. She couldn't help but wonder what kind of power he wielded that warranted so much swaggering confidence.

Refusing to let him see her off-balance, Remi smiled a sly grin of her own and offered him her hand. "Pietyr, was it?"

"That's right," he answered, taking her extended hand and pressing his lips to it. His eyes still lingered on hers, the intensity of his gaze almost feral. Despite that, she kept her eyes locked onto his, not backing down an inch.

Riven, the only one of their group who seemed less than thrilled to see Pietyr, interrupted their introduction. "I see you made it back safely from Sydonia." His voice remained calm, but his expression had darkened. Remi picked up on some definite animosity between the two, but she couldn't tell if it was outright loathing or just the result of standard male competition. However, what made the entire situation feel disconcerting was that Remi got the distinct impression that maybe Riven would have preferred it if Pietyr hadn't made it back from Sydonia at all.

She cast a covert glance at Madwyn to weigh her reaction to all this machismo posturing. As she studied the goddess's face through sips of cider, she noted that what she'd thought to be an attraction between the goddess and Pietyr seemed to take on a different texture. She realized then that the way they looked at each other wasn't sexual at all. Instead, it was the way one predator might watch another. And though Ellarah seemed to ignore the entire uncomfortable dynamic, Remi felt off-balance yet again.

There seemed to be so much damned context that she was missing. But then, that's what happened when you've only lived somewhere for a month; she reminded herself. She vowed that she would get to the bottom of everything soon enough.

She shifted her gaze back to Pietyr when he answered Riven's question, "I always do." The way he said it sounded like a threat. Her back muscles tightened as she struggled to read the room, to understand the history between these three. But she found that without someone outright explaining it to her, she could only guess.

Curiosity driving her, she asked, "So, how do you all know each other?"

"It's a long, boring story." Pietyr leaned into her conspiratorially. "Not a good party conversation." As she opened her mouth to insist, a beautiful goddess nearby raised her hand in a come-hither gesture. It caught Pietyr's attention, and he leveled an apologetic expression on the group. "Well, it's been fun, but duty calls." Then, as quickly as he'd breezed into their circle, he departed.

Remi was about to open her mouth to ask what in the Twelve Hells that was all about when a soft touch caressed her shoulder. Expecting Thayne, she turned her head but saw nothing. She frowned. She could have sworn she'd felt something.

Then a breath of air shuddered across her ear. Words flowed on it, and their clear tenor made the message unmistakable. The voice hissed in a near-silent whisper, *"Be careful tonight. The threat is closer than you think."* She sucked in a surprised breath, and all three of her friends looked at her. Judging by their confused expressions, they hadn't heard it. She ignored them as she scanned the room, searching for the source of that voice.

Was that a threat? Or a warning? She had no idea. She spun and rose onto her tiptoes, trying to get a better vantage. Her heart raced, and her palms grew clammy as anxiety pulsed through her. She intended to track down the sender of that message and ask what the hell they'd meant by it.

She knew for certain it hadn't been a consciousness deity. The thought hadn't permeated her mind. Rather, it had floated on the wind, or maybe a shadow. Then, a connection clicked in her mind, shadow deity, as she turned and crashed right into

Thayne's chest. Her eyes were on the edge of frantic when she looked up at him.

He gripped her arms to steady her and, for once, actually looked into her eyes. "Is everything OK?"

She didn't answer; instead, she stilled. Forcing her heart rate to settle a bit, she swallowed her anxiety. She could still feel someone watching her, though, and she didn't like it. Diverting her gaze from her husband, she scanned the room. She knew what she was looking for now, her eyes inspecting the ground for any sign of unanchored, inexplicable shadows.

At last, she saw it. A snake-like tendril of darkness slithering across the ground and inking its way from her to...it stopped. She looked up, and her eyes settled on Pietyr. He stood just on the other side of Thayne, his face visible over her husband's right shoulder. Her gaze locked onto his. The burning intensity of his eyes seemed to hold her in place.

Time froze. Her surroundings blurred. Voices muffled as words that could only belong to him seemed to float on the depthless shadows. "Be careful, princess. When you play with fire, you could get burned." He held her stare for another beat before he pressed a single finger to his lips. A warning to stay silent, and then slipped back into the crowd.

Reality snapped back into place around her as a gentle hand on her shoulder jolted her out of her stupor. Blinking her way back into the present, she saw Ellarah standing next to her husband. Steady now, Thayne released her from his grip. Looking between them both, they both appeared to be the picture of concern. Ellarah frowned. "Remi, are you okay? You look pale."

Her mind raced. She had no idea what to make of Pietyr's warning. He was a Nefaral, a shadow deity, and yet she understood intuitively that his words *had* been a warning, not a threat. He wouldn't have told her to be careful otherwise. But the whole experience had left her reeling. She had so many unanswered questions. Who or what should she be cautious of? And what the hell had he meant by that whole fire metaphor? Was it a reference to her abilities? Or did it have something to do with the rumors of the Nefaral rebellion? Or something else, something unknown to her?

She shook her head again, feeling a little dizzy, and cleared her throat. She took a step back, trying to give herself some more space before she answered, "I'm OK. Just nerves." It was a lie, of course. But what was she supposed to say? If Pietyr had wanted to warn them all, he would have, right? Instead, he had chosen to walk away and to tell only her of his concerns. But why? Her mind scrambled for a viable explanation, but she could think of nothing.

Ellarah stepped closer, and Remi caught sight of Madwyn and Riven just behind them. Ellarah whispered, "You're sure?"

Remi waved it away and forced a confident smile. "I'm fine. Like I said, it was just nerves. We have a lot to think about tonight." It was the only excuse she could come up with, and it had the benefit of being true.

She had to think about the ceremony tonight—the one that would cement her position as official Bicaidian royalty. But then she had to think about the other activity they had planned. The one that could earn them a one-way trip to the surface of the sun should anything go awry.

"If you say so," Ellarah said, but her eyebrows wrinkled in disbelief.

A shot of guilt singed Remi's belly. This was a feeling she'd grown accustomed to this past week, and she didn't like it one bit. It hit her then because, if she was honest, the real reason she'd decided to keep Pietyr's warning a secret was far more insidious.

She wanted to make damn sure she got her sister out of Moldize that night. And, if she told them what Pietyr had said, she worried that they'd decide he must have found out about their plan somehow. Then, they might decide it was too risky.

Maybe even call off the whole thing, and she couldn't afford to risk that outcome. They'd come too far already.

"I do," Remi confirmed, forcing her smile to remain in place. She looked at Madwyn and Riven now, who eyed her with narrowed eyes.

She averted her gaze from them before they could discern any uncertainty in her expression and turned her attention back to Ellarah and Thayne. Something told her that Madwyn would be relentless when it came to getting her way. If she decided that Remi was hiding something important, then she would keep digging until she got to the bottom of it.

To her relief, Thayne changed the subject before anyone could interrogate her further. "If you're sure you're okay, we're needed in the hall. The ceremony will start any minute now. Are you ready?"

What a loaded question, Remi thought, as she composed herself once more. She needed to relax and keep her mind clear. This was not time for panic or second thoughts, she told herself.

She would just do what Pietyr suggested. She would be careful and watch for any possible threats.

A few minutes later, Thayne dragged her into a room, shutting the door behind them. They'd left the stunning gardens, the courtyard, and the open-air hallways trimmed with adobe arches in favor of this—a miniscule coat closet.

Turning in a small circle, Remi stared up at him. "Why are we in a coat closet? I thought the ceremony was going to start soon."

"I lied. We still have some time to spare, and there's something I want to show you. Before everything happens tonight." He waved his hand to encompass their covert mission along with the legitimate and legal inauguration.

"Why did you want to show me a closet, exactly?" She asked, lips twitching in amusement despite the fact that she still felt a little uneasy from Pietyr's warning. After all, what could be so important about a coat closet? His eyes fixed on her, scanning her body in a way that felt anything but disinterested. Confusion and a little concern niggled at the back of her mind as she wondered what had triggered such an abrupt change in his attitude. But, she did find the change a welcome one.

Thayne grabbed her hand and tugged her to a back corner. "It's not just a closet," he explained, maneuvering around a few discarded boxes. Then, on a long hanging rod situated behind a rack of shelves, Thayne pulled on a hanger, and a secret door sprang open.

Remi let out a low whistle through her teeth.

"Impressed yet?" Thayne asked, white teeth flashing in a cocky smile.

She offered him a flirtatious grin of her own. "I'm way more impressed than I was a minute ago. But I wouldn't go all the way to fully impressed."

"Just give me a few minutes. I promise you won't be disappointed."

"You sound very sure of yourself," she observed, teasing.

"I am," he replied, that cocky half-grin still on his face. He tugged on her hand, and they kept moving. Finally, she allowed him to lead her up a long corridor of steep stairs with smooth, rock walls. The palace was a mixture of adobe clay and rough stone, built using the materials that their world provided. It was stunning and gave the impression of being carved into the cliffs and rocks that surrounded it. That hallway turned out to be no exception.

When they reached the top of the landing, Remi looked down the swirling staircase below and felt dizzy. Then Thayne reached out and grasped the knob of an over-sized, intricately carved wooden door. He pushed it open and led her outside into the golden light of near-sunset.

A breeze filled with fresh air hit her face, and she inhaled, relieved to be out of the claustrophobic stairwell. Following Thayne's lead, she stepped outside and onto a large, flat overhang. A few paces ahead the ground dropped into a steep cliff, a vast canyon beneath it, the view unobstructed and heartbreakingly gorgeous.

Red rocks stacked together and layered with limestone made up the bulk of the canyon, though she could see green trees popping up and adding their own color sporadically. At the base of the canyon, she could see the winding, shimmering river that split through all of Helverta, its surface alight with color.

Remi shaded her eyes with her hands and breathed out, "This is unbelievable."

Thayne nodded, also shading his eyes from the brightness of the waning sunlight. "I told you, you wouldn't be disappointed." He grinned at her before he turned back to survey the view. "This is my favorite place in Bicaidia. No one knows about it except the immediate royal family. It's on the backside of the palace, so it's protected by security as private royal property." He held out his hand for hers once more. "There's something else," he explained, angling his face to survey hers. "A tradition of sorts for all Bicaidian royalty pre-inauguration. Come with me."

After a brief hesitation, she twined her fingers into his. She found that she enjoyed the warmth and security they provided as they trailed along the precipice of the cliff, a massive drop below them. Not that the fall would kill her, but it would hurt. They walked a short distance, and on the other side of a large boulder, she saw it. An oversized, velvety blanket spread out with a bucket of ice, a bottle, and two glasses.

"Did you do this?" she asked. After the way they'd been avoiding each other, this was the last thing she ever would have expected.

He nodded, a grin on his lips once more.

Touched and also a little surprised by his thoughtfulness, she followed him to the blanket and what she presumed was sparkling wine. He gestured for her to sit, and she obeyed, cushioned by a small pillow that matched the blanket. She stretched her thin, long legs outward and leaned back to rest on her palms and enjoy the view while Thayne popped the cork and filled their glasses.

"I meant what I said before, about this being a tradition. My great, great grandfather started it. Anytime a deity from another realm marries into the royal family, we bring them here on their inauguration day. It's meant to let them see Bicaidia as we do. To start the seed of love and home that we, as natives, already have."

Remi accepted the crystal flute and took a sip. She arched a brow. "Cider?"

Thayne drank as he looked out over the vast beauty that surrounded them. "We can drink as much as we want of the real stuff after our mission is complete. Until then, better to keep our wits about us."

Remi moved the flute to her lips once more and enjoyed the crisp, cool liquid. "Couldn't have said it better myself."

They sat in silence for a few moments, watching the sun as it dropped lower in the sky. Birds chirped and cawed, adding to the overall aesthetic. When she finished her first glass, Thayne offered her another. She accepted, watching him intently as he poured, wondering if he felt the tension that seemed to coil in the silence between them.

All traces of playful flirtation seemed to be gone now, and she wished that they could return to that. But, instead, the silence held. Then, tearing her eyes away from the beauty of the view, she glanced at his hand from beneath her lashes and saw the faint tattoo there. Her mark, along with Madwyn's, Ellarah's, and Riven's.

"I'm sorry," she breathed, eyes wholly focused on him now. Earlier this week, she'd geared herself up for a confrontation, convinced that when they finally did talk, they'd have it out, that they would lay everything out on the table. And, of course, she hadn't wanted to be left without any ammunition when it happened. But now, in this place of restfulness, it seemed easier to admit that she'd wronged him that night with the letter. She'd locked him into a promise, knowing the danger of keeping it a secret. At a minimum, it was a breach of the tenuous trust they had only just begun to form. At most, it blew up any chance she had of him ever trusting her.

But then, she wondered, did she really deserve to be trusted by him? She chewed on her lip as the scent of scrubby pines and fruity sweetness blended into a pleasant aroma that didn't suit her current mood. Because now, in the silence, she could see in perfect color the things she liked least about herself. After all, was she not cut from the same cloth as her family, angry as she might be with them? Always scheming to make sure things turned out the way she wanted them to?

His dark eyes met hers then, and she saw something move in their depths. She thought for a moment he would force her to elaborate, so she took a deep breath, preparing for it. But then he turned back to look at the canyon. "Don't worry about it."

She raised her brows in shock. Taken off guard, her brain sputtered as she tried to fumble through what the hell he meant by that. But before she could puzzle it out, her surprise turned into annoyance. She blinked for a few moments before she said, "That's it?"

He turned back to face her and offered her his signature arrogant, lopsided grin. "Sure, why not?"

The ever-present fire began to burn in her belly again as she recognized the signs of her anger beginning to rear its ugly head. It flared faster than she could stop it. "Why not?" she asked, looking at him like he'd lost his mind. "*Why not?*" Her mouth opened and then closed a couple of times before her brain rebooted. "You give me the cold shoulder for a week, then you do a complete about-face and bring me here, and that's all you have to say? *Why not? Don't worry about it?*"

When he chuckled at her—chuckled, for Ascended sake—fire licked up her arms. Its flames singed the blanket they sat on before she controlled herself and extinguished it.

His eyes caught the dance of the flame, and he pressed his lips together, his expression sobering. "There's no need to get angry. I'm letting you off the hook."

"Alright, that's it," she said, rising to her feet and dusting off her dress. "No. You do not get to sit here and play the part of a benevolent husband. Not when you've barely spoken to me for a week and treated me like some infectious pestilence. So, thank you for the view and the cider, but I will see you inside." She offered him her most scathing glare before she turned on her heel and stormed off. Stopping a few paces away, she whirled back and leveled an accusing finger at him. "Besides, you were the one who was in my room that night, without my permission. So, don't act like you're blameless." She turned again and continued her exit as best she could over the rocky terrain.

She'd made it just a few steps before the crunch of his shoes, and his hand on her shoulder stopped her. She spun around, crossing her arms over her chest. "What?" she bit out, heat still raging inside her. Brimming with irritation, her thoughts burned through her brain. He was unbelievable. Where did he get off pretending he was perfect?

"Look, you're right. I have been angry with you, and I haven't sought you out since that night in your chamber because of it." He slid one hand into his pocket and dropped the other from her shoulder. "My intention wasn't to brush it or you off back there. I'd meant to just…let it go. You don't know me, and I don't know you, and the more I thought about that night, the more I realized that I might have done the same to you if our situation had been reversed. I know that you were just trying to protect yourself and your sister." He paused, waiting for her to give a response. At last, she inclined her head in acknowledgment, and he continued, "Now, let's go back and finish our bottle of cider. It's the only peace I'm going to have tonight." That charming grin of his returned. "The same goes for you too, and I'd like to spend it together."

She hesitated for a moment as the fire burning inside her cooled just a little. "What about you showing up in my room, uninvited and without my permission?"

He looked out over the canyon, the golden-pink light making his bronze skin glow. After a brief moment of contemplation, he fixed his attention back on her. "I'm sorry too. After everything that happened in your chamber...with your magic, I just wanted to check on you. See how you were doing. When I couldn't reach you, I worried. I only opened your chamber to make sure you were OK, that nothing else had happened." He gave her another crooked grin. "Trust me, I think I've paid enough for my intrusion."

She felt her lips quiver in response to that, tempted to smile despite her softening anger. "You did get more than you bargained for, I imagine."

He chuckled. "That's one way to put it." He brushed a hand down her bare arm and she could feel gooseflesh rise in its wake. "Now, will you come back with me? Please?"

After a brief consideration, she inclined her head in agreement and allowed herself to be led back to the spot they'd vacated. Once she'd settled herself back down and he'd poured her another glass-full of cider, she felt herself begin to relax again. She looked at him from the corner of her eye beneath her lashes. "For what it's worth, if I knew then what I do now, I wouldn't have accepted the binding. Or at the very least, I'd have told you about the letter's connection to Moldize first."

In the last week, he'd proved himself to be both a skilled leader and an intelligent strategist. Those were the qualities that she found herself admiring most about him, despite Ellarah's crude yet accurate observation about his ass. She also knew that he could keep a secret. Granted, this one had been forced on him, but she still thought he would have kept it, even if just for her sake.

He lifted a broad shoulder, shrugging it off. "I offered. I just didn't expect that letter to be quite so consequential. Although, I'll admit that a disclaimer would have been nice."

Her lips quirked upward as she scoffed at the ridiculousness of that request. "How would I have done that exactly? I couldn't have given a disclaimer without giving away the very thing I didn't want to disclaim." He chuckled then, the sound husky as the sun dropped further behind the skyline. She turned her face away from him and took another sip, "But, why did you ask for one in the first place. A binding, I mean? You didn't have to."

He stayed silent for a few moments as though weighing his response. After a long beat, he answered, "I wanted you to know that you could trust me." He opened his mouth to continue but then closed it.

"But why?" Remi asked, sensing that he was stopping himself short of saying what he really meant. She had no intention of letting him off the hook. Marriages in the royal godly world didn't typically consist of mutual trust or promises-kept. They existed on things like assured mutual destruction or necessity.

Thayne cleared his throat and drew up one leg, propping a forearm across it as he turned to face her. "Because I want more than a marriage of necessity or duty." He stopped, his hair rustling in the breeze as he peered at her. "I had to give up a lot when my family agreed to our betrothal."

Though she could see pain in his eyes, she still held his gaze. She knew that look, and she knew what it meant. A fist seemed to clench in her gut as she filled in the gaps for him. "There was someone else, wasn't there?" Of course, there was, she thought, an inexplicable, sticky dread crawling up her throat.

He swallowed, nodding. "That's part of the reason I've kept my distance this week. It's just been complicated."

She furrowed her brows, trying to infer his meaning. But again, she felt like the unwelcome interloper, oblivious to all the complicated inner workings of people's lives here. "How has it been complicated exactly? What's the difference between last week and the first three of our marriage?"

"The goddess I was with, we split because of the betrothal, and I think she expected me to handle the situation differently. So, she's been angry and letting me know it," he explained, his eyes never leaving hers. "But this isn't something I want you to worry about. It's done now, and I want to move forward."

Despite his assurance, a quick pang of unexpected, irrational jealousy speared her. She took a breath to steady herself because, of course, he was allowed to have a past, a history. After all, so did she. "So, that's why you've been giving me the cold shoulder? You didn't want to upset her?"

He pressed his lips together, but to his credit, he didn't flinch at the acid in her tone. "That's part of it, but I was also angry with you about the binding."

Remi's eyes turned to ice along with her tone. "You said you understood that and wanted to move forward."

He nodded, remaining calm despite her cold glare. "I do, on both counts. Look, I was with this other person before I ever knew that we would be together. The instant we confirmed our betrothal, I broke things off with her, for all of our sakes." That hadn't been that long ago, she realized. Just a few months. That wound must still be fresh for both of them. She also couldn't help but wonder who the other goddess was. Had she seen her before? Was she at the inauguration? Remi wondered, but then decided she'd rather not know.

What good would that do? Aside from creating a conflict between her and some unknown deity? At last, she unclenched fists she hadn't realized had been clenched. She breathed out and braced herself for his response when she asked, "Does it still hurt?"

Thayne raked a hand through his hair, his gaze settling over her shoulder and into the distance. "Sometimes—" He paused, the word weighty between them. "I won't apologize for my past because I can't change it. All I can do is tell you what I see for my future. Right now, I look at you, and I see possibilities, not just the duty-bound necessity that haunts most arranged marriages. I see the potential for more than that between you and me. And I'm a greedy god by nature, so I want more, and I want it with you." He reached out and ran his fingers over her cheek to smooth a stray lock of crimson hair aside.

She noted that it was the first time he'd shown her any affection that didn't come from a sense of duty, and her heart beat just a little faster. As his dark irises moved over hers, his voice grew husky, "When I look into your eyes, I can see it. Everything that we could be but aren't yet, but that all starts with trust and honesty."

Remi let his words settle and tried to gauge her feelings. She wished he'd been more upfront about his history. But then, she hadn't exactly been forthright with him either. And wasn't he entitled to his past? It wasn't as if he'd continued his previous romance after their marriage, which she knew he could have done without her knowledge.

Then there were his qualities to consider. The ones that she admired. The ones that made it easy to see herself wanting more from him than duty and necessity too. She could never be with someone she didn't see as her equal, and he was that at least. Maybe even more, she thought, not loving that notion. But it rang true in her mind. He had power, confidence, and experience in his role as high prince.

But, here he was asking for trust and honesty, something they'd both already breached within the first few weeks of their relationship. Could they just erase that and start over? She considered the possibility, realizing that trust was similar to a leap of faith—sometimes, you just had to try it to find out.

"Trust," she repeated, looking down at the blanket beneath them and considering. "What about secrets?" she asked, curious about his position on those. Because she might not be a lie to someone's face kind of goddess, but she liked her secrets and her lies of omission.

Could she give those up? Did she even want to? As she thought it over, she realized it might be nice to have someone to share those things with. She'd always been so alone before. She'd never even felt comfortable telling Bekka everything. Sometimes, everything had been too much for her sister to handle. But maybe, just maybe, she could tell him.

Thayne gave her a knowing smile. "As long as they don't affect what's between us, then you can keep all the secrets you like."

She sighed, looking away from him and pretending to consider his proposal. The truth was, she'd already made up her mind. She just wanted him to squirm a little. After a pause that had his eyes darkening with concern, she shifted her gaze to his and offered him a sly smile. "Okay, trust then. If that's really what you want, then I have a couple of things to tell you."

His brows raised in surprise. "Already?"

She shrugged. "What can I say? I'm a busy goddess. But, first, who's Pietyr? I know he's a shadow deity, but what's his story? Is he trustworthy?"

Thayne surveyed her as she sipped her cider, eyes narrowing as though trying to read her mind. Or maybe he was just wondering where the hell she was going with this line of questioning. But, he answered her just the same. "He's the leader of the shadow sect and our top spy. He's one of the few

Nefs who doesn't work for the Nefaric Pillar, instead he works for my father. So, yes, I'd say he's trustworthy."

She nodded, satisfied with that explanation. Shadow deities acted as the primary spies between realms. They gathered intel for leadership on illegal activities, assisted with any functioning PAB missions, and could walk through worlds and realms undetected. They almost never reported to the Nefaric Pillar because they needed intel from so many of the other branches to be effective. Add to that, few royal families trusted Nefs enough to let them run their own covert operations.

After a moment to consider, she explained what had happened at the cocktail party. "He sent me a warning earlier, one only I could hear. He said to be cautious tonight and that the threats are closer than we think. Then he said something about how playing with fire could get me burned." She tilted her head, examining him for any sign of reaction. "Any idea what he meant by that? I couldn't tell if he meant my power or the Nefarals we already know about. Or if there is something specific that I should be careful of?"

His eyes narrowed as he considered her question. "I have no idea what he means. He just returned today from his last mission. It was off-world, in Sydonia. He hasn't been debriefed since he arrived at the palace." The unspoken meaning was clear. If he'd been off-world, then how much could he possibly know about threats here?

"Do you think we should be worried? You don't think we should call off the plan, do you?" Remi asked, holding her breath as she waited for his reply. This was, after all, the reason she'd kept it a secret in the first place. She didn't want to call off the mission any more than she wanted to traipse around on the surface of a star. But, if this was what mutual trust looked like, then she would have to swallow her desires and hope he agreed with her assessment.

Thayne rubbed a thumb over his lip as he thought it through. Remi remained still as marble while she awaited his reply, hoping he'd be on her side. "No, I don't think so. If anything, his warning only increases the urgency for Rebekkah's return. Don't you think?"

Remi nodded her head in agreement, relief washing through her. "I do. I think having a Peacekeeper in the Twelve Realms is the best way to stave off any threats. No matter where they come from." Setting her glass down, she lay back on the blanket in relief and stared up. Wispy clouds and periwinkle sky spanned as far as the eye could see.

Thayne joined her, the length of his body mere inches from hers. He brushed a finger over hers, a question, and she opened to him, allowing his fingers to entwine with hers. As they lay there holding fast to each other, she filled him in on the water deity and her contingency note for Bekka. Though he didn't say much, she could tell he approved of the plan.

Then, after a brief silence, he asked, "Why did you tell me, about Pietyr's warning, I mean?"

She was sure that it was getting late and that they would need to go back soon, lest she miss the ceremony altogether. But she chewed over her words anyway. She wanted to make sure she chose them with care. At last, she decided to keep it simple. "Because I, too, am a greedy goddess." She rolled over onto her side to look at him. He followed her lead, and she memorized the lines of his face. So fierce, so handsome, and so damned confident, she thought. She had to admit that she found the combination sexy as all hell. Possibilities, he had said, and he was right. She could see them too. "And I don't like to share."

He laughed, the sound rich with amusement. Then he leaned forward and brushed a curled tendril of loose hair off her face. His eyes darkened, and she thought, for a fleeting moment, that he might kiss her. She would welcome it, she decided, holding her breath as a charge of electricity pulsed through her body. She looked down at his lips, full and tempting, as she drew her tongue across her own to wet them.

But then he withdrew his hand and rose onto his elbow. "We've lingered long enough. I'm sure my parents and the pillar leaders are looking for us. Are you ready?"

Remi spared one last, longing glance at the final vestige of sunset disappearing behind the cliff. Of course, they had to get back. They couldn't stay there forever. Life was a funny thing, she thought, following Thayne back to the doorway and back down the winding staircase to the deities below.

She was to be made a princess tonight. After which, they planned to break a dozen of the laws she would have just sworn to uphold.

CHAPTER 8

REMI

Inauguration Night

Remi listened as Kehlani, Thayne's mother and queen of the Bicaidian Universe, walked her through the steps of the ceremony for what felt like the hundredth time. To be honest, she was impressed at how many times she had practiced in the fifteen minutes since her alone time with Thayne. Kehlani was a powerful healer and leader of her sect in Perenelle before she married into the royal Bicaidian house of Aphyrsh hundreds of years before. Based on her thorough explanation of the ceremony, she remembered her own inauguration well.

"First, you will join Thayne, Rynard, and me on the stage. Next, you will kneel as we read the rights and the vows. Finally, you will say 'I swear' at all pauses. You memorized them all, right? The rights?" Kehlani stopped mid-instruction as though just realizing that this might be an issue. Her dark eyes held Remi's as she waited for a response.

"Yes, my lady," Remi replied. She had read and memorized them all before her marriage to Thayne. She wanted to understand her role here and know exactly what would be expected of her, down to the most minute detail. All of it had been predictable—upholding the laws of the Peacekeeper's council, overseeing the functions of the immortal realm and the pillar leaders, and ruling all of it with a fair hand. At least, that was the general gist of it. She'd trained for this her entire life, and she was ready for it.

"Wonderful," Kehlani answered, beaming at her. "Are you nervous?" She rested a hand on Remi's shoulder.

"Of course she's nervous, Kehlani. Look at her! She looks like she swallowed a slug," Rynard snapped, his large body hovering nearby. Rynard was king of Bicaidia and a god of the air, one of the primary elemental deities in Bicaidia.

Remi's lips twitched. She imagined that that was a decent enough description of her current state of mind. However, it had little to do with the responsibilities she was about to assume or the ceremony itself. Instead, it had more to do with the dozens of laws she planned to break right after that.

Kehlani swatted Rynard's arm. "She does not. She looks beautiful." Remi smiled at her gratefully as her in-laws began to bicker.

Thayne leaned down and whispered in her ear as his parents continued their argument, "You do, you know, look beautiful." Gooseflesh prickled up her arm as she looked into his eyes. She liked this attentive, flirtatious version of Thayne much more than the one she'd been subjected to earlier this week. Truth be told, if they'd been alone, she would've wound her fingers into his hair and dragged his mouth down to hers.

Both turned their heads in question as Rynard cleared his throat. A knowing smile played on the king's lips as he clarified his earlier statement. "I didn't mean you looked bad. You look wonderful."

Remi waved it away. "Oh, no offense taken. Though you are a strong observer of emotion. I am nervous."

Her new-ish in-laws cast sympathetic looks her way. Kehlani's soft voice filled the backstage room. "You know, we're sorry your parents couldn't make it."

"It's OK, really," Remi replied. "I understand. They have a lot on their plate right now. I wouldn't want to take them away from their responsibilities in Valeria." They had more important things to deal with than her inauguration…Like the massive power vacuum her grandfather's ascension had left behind. Or finding her sister, which she knew they'd still be working on at this point. If only they knew that Remi had already found her. She couldn't help but feel a gloating sense of accomplishment that she'd done it first and without any help from them.

Kehlani's comm device chimed then, and she looked down at the glowing glass screen. "They're ready for you."

Thayne flung a reassuring arm around her shoulders. "You're going to be great."

With that as the final word, Rynard, Kehlani and Thayne led her outside and back towards the throngs of gods and goddesses. They walked through the outdoor halls and back toward the central courtyard. Blooming cactus, succulents and green shrubby bushes planted in red-rocked gravel lined the halls. Finally, they turned a corner and saw the central courtyard, and she smiled in appreciation.

It had been transformed in the short time she'd been gone. A tasteful, stone stage stood as the focal point of the festivities. The sun had finished its journey behind the mountains and lights had begun to twinkle within the floating flower arrangements. The servants had moved all of the cocktail tables to the edge of the courtyard, under the covered hallways that lined it.

They'd replaced them with long, rectangular dinner tables draped in shimmering white and gold table cloths that seemed to pulse with a sheen of magical energy. Lush floral arrangements sprouted from the center of each table and dripped over one side, overflowing onto the floor. As the royal procession moved into view of the guests, the deities rose from their seats. All eyes fixed on them before the entire crowd bowed their heads in near-perfect unison, a show of respect.

Remi's legs remained steady as she ascended the steps, moving to the center of the stage. She knelt, the evergreen fabric of her dress draping around her while her breathing quickened. Heads lifted, and eyes locked onto them as Rynard's voice boomed out from beside her.

When he spoke the words that would seal her fate, Remi repeated them without hearing her own voice. Her heart seemed to pound in time with the breaths of the crowd. She realized then that this ceremony would seal her to them for the rest of her life. She would be theirs, and they would be hers.

The gravity of the responsibility had never fully sunk in until that moment, and she felt her eyes sting with emotion. She would be their high princess. Their leader. One of the privileged few who would protect them and care for their needs. She tried to pick faces out in the crowd. She wanted to see them as more than just Bicaidians. She wanted to look at them as individuals.

She saw Madwyn, Riven, and Ellarah all looking at her with gleaming eyes in the glistening lights. Then, before she even realized her mother and father-in-law had finished the first part of the rights, Thayne's large, powerful body stepped in front of her. He offered his hand, and she took it, rising to her feet.

Behind him, Kehlani held a pillow of deep, green velvet embossed with gold stitching, and atop it sat two beautiful and important pieces of jewelry. He turned, taking the first piece from the pillow with one hand and then holding her hand in the other.

When he spoke, his voice boomed out through the crowd, "The armlet, a symbol of servitude and loyalty to Bicaidia. Do you swear to practice both as high princess of this realm?"

Remi stared into his eyes, his fingers warm and steady on hers. She licked her lips to wet them as a peaceful silence traveled through the crowd, awaiting her answer. "I swear it."

He smiled at her, dimples she hadn't noticed before forming on either side of his mouth, and Remi found her nerves calming just a bit. Next, he turned back and grabbed the woven golden circlet with a green jewel placed right in the center. He held it at eye level, and she focused on it, its beauty even more immense that close up. She wanted to reach out and brush her fingers against the strands of twining metal but resisted the urge.

When Thayne spoke again, his voice was loud enough for all to hear, "This circlet is the symbol of the Bicaidian princess-ship. She who wears it will one day be queen. Will you accept the responsibilities that come with this post?"

Without hesitation this time, she answered, "I will." She knelt before him once more and he placed the circlet atop her head. Taking Thayne's offered hand, she stood, but this time amid raucous cheers. They turned to face the crowd, hands clasped together, as Rynard and Kehlani joined them. Kehlani grasped Remi's hand, and Rynard held his wife's; all linked together, they raised their arms to the sky. Amid the cheers, she heard whistles and some indelicate whooping. She couldn't hide her grin.

Crowd still cheering, they exited the stage as a unit; Remi had become the official high princess. Thayne led her to a table situated in front of the stage, the royal table. She sat next to Thayne for the proceeding feast, who recommended traditional Bicaidian dishes and foods he thought she'd enjoy. He even offered her tender morsels of meat and then a sliver of spiced chocolate torte from his own fork, which she indulged happily.

Conversation pulsed around her, and she felt a warm hum of acceptance as her new mother-in-law rose to a standing position and held up a glass of sparkling wine. Her voice carried above the drone of animated conversation as she called out, "To the new high princess of Bicaidia!"

A hammer of fists on the tables sounded, almost making Remi jump in surprise. Then a collective shout sounded, "May she be mighty! May she be bold!"

As she sat, grinning from ear-to-ear, Thayne leaned in and whispered, "This is where you chug the rest of that glass. According to Bicaidian tradition, consuming large quantities of alcohol is both mighty and bold."

His eyes twinkled as she shook her head, amused by that notion. For a second, she doubted him, wondering how drunken antics qualified as either mighty or bold, but then she shrugged and did as he requested. The party burst into applause, unaware that Thayne had traded the traditional sparkling wine for cider the moment she'd sat down at the table.

As the servant deities began to clear away dessert plates and cups of hot tea and coffee, her mood sobered. Pietyr's warning started to echo in her mind as she realized that the fun part of the night was about to end. Soon, it would be time for cocktails, dancing, and then espionage.

When all the plates had been removed, at last, the dinner tables disappeared and cleared, the servants made way for a live band on the stage and a dance floor in the courtyard. The open bar hummed with activity, located in the far back corner of the party. Servant gods and goddesses, those with minimal to no magical power, served the guests drinks as the upper crest of godly society delighted in its own celebration.

If she could've had it her way, all of the gods and goddesses in Bicaidia would have been here, enjoying this part just as much as the upper-caste gods. But no one had asked her opinion, and that sentiment was far from customary.

She sighed into Thayne's chest as they finished dancing to a slow, melodic song. They'd cleared the air between them at last, but she still couldn't help the small voice inside her head that had her wondering just who he'd been involved with before their marriage. She scanned the room, then decided it would be best not to dwell on the past; she just wanted to enjoy the party a little longer before they started breaking every major Peacekeeper law.

Unfortunately, time flew by. It was getting late, and they'd just hit the window of opportunity that she'd given Bekka. So, hating to do it, she rose onto her tiptoes and whispered in her husband's ear, "It's time, don't you think?"

He peered down at her, a few strands of his dark hair falling forward from its binding. "Madwyn said she would give us a signal. I haven't seen one yet."

She watched as Madwyn floated through the crowd. This was the part of the plan that Remi liked least. It was too *'go with the flow'* for her taste. Precision and planning were more her style.

But Remi tried not to be uncharitable about it. Instead, she observed the chaos deity, noting that everyone seemed to adore Madwyn, smiling and laughing as she breezed into their circles and made easy conversation. What they didn't notice, thanks to the dim lighting and their unsuspecting self-assuredness, was her purple, smoky power. It wafted around her like a perfume, permeating every nook and cranny of the party.

The air was tinged with it, and Remi resisted the urge to cover her mouth with her hands. She didn't want any of the effects that might arise from it, however innocuous they might be to her or those who knew what Madwyn was up to. The music changed tempo, faster and more upbeat now, signaling that it was time for the party to really get started.

Ellarah and Riven slid into step next to Thayne and Remi, claiming a small cocktail table along the hallway. Riven leaned forward, elbows resting on the table, and whispered, "Madwyn's working her magic." His eyes scanned the room and his lips quirked in a mischievous grin. "Just wait for it...any minute now. This should be interesting."

Ellarah arched a sculpted brow and murmured, "Oh Twelve Hells, Riven, what is she going to do?" This was the other part of the plan that had been left to Madwyn's sole discretion, which Remi also hadn't loved. When she'd brought this concern to Ellarah and Thayne after their last planning session, Thayne had insisted that Madwyn wasn't the type to take step-by-step instructions. She needed a little wiggle room in the plan, or else she'd create some when or where they didn't want it.

Remi watched as Madwyn snaked through the crowd. Knowing that she was the goddess of chaos didn't make Remi feel any better about this entire situation. On the contrary, she had this nauseating sense that whatever happened next, she wasn't going to like it.

Madwyn's grin spread wide as she twirled through the crowd. When she stopped at one older, uptight-looking god, the leader of the Elemental pillar, she tilted back her head and laughed. He smiled back at her, his opalescent, blue tuxedo with silvery stitching shimmering in the twinkling lights. She whispered something in his ear, pointing across the room. When he turned to follow her gesture, his eyes damn near popped out of his skull.

Remi looked over in the direction he stared, toward the dance floor. A goddess, at least his own age, was bent over and shaking her booty on another goddess. She whipped her hair from side to side and gyrated. Remi did a double-take and surveyed what had been a tame, classy party just moments before.

No longer.

Half the deities in attendance seemed lulled into a drunken party-fest while the other half were so damned uptight that they each looked like a twenty-foot poll was lodged right up their collective asses. The partiers drank from shimmery bottles of golden liquor and danced like their lives depended on it. The uptighters tried to pull their spouses or fellow pillar leaders that had turned into partiers out of the ensuing mayhem.

Remi assumed this was to preserve their dignity, which they were quickly losing. In spite of her original reservations, she let out a snort of laughter as a bra soared through the air and smacked the singer on stage in the side of his head. He was an uptighter, and his back went ramrod straight as he stared at the massive cups of the bra.

Remi looked up at Thayne, who shook his head, dimples pressed deep into his cheeks in amusement. "Well, it's safe to say Madwyn has given us a good window. It will take them hours to sort this mess out."

Ellarah hiccupped with laughter. "Well, now I don't want to leave. This is way too good to miss."

As though on cue, Madwyn turned to them, formed a perfect "O" with her lips, and then covered it with a prim hand. Despite her initial apprehension about this part of the plan, Remi couldn't help but be amused. She could even admit that maybe Thayne had been right to give Madwyn a little leeway. As this thought permeated her mind, Madwyn gave them all a finger wave, followed by a shoeing motion. Her signal that the distraction was complete. It was time to start their true mission tonight.

Thayne inclined his head, a barely visible nod of assent. "Come on, let's go before it wears off."

Ellarah downed her cider, and Riven pressed his hand onto the small of her back, leading her down a darkened hallway lining the edge of the courtyard. Thayne and Remi moved into step behind them, their gait casual as all four of them slipped out of the party unnoticed.

Once away from the crowd, they picked up the pace. The brisk tattoo of their footfalls beat against the stone floor as they hurried further from the courtyard and into the palace gardens. A large wooden door stood tall and ominous a few feet ahead, the entrance to the throne room.

Thayne reached the security scanner and sent a quick pulse of power, allowing them all access into the lavish room. Its walls were draped with gold and green banners, and the polished wood floors gleamed in the moonlight. Even in the dim lighting, Remi could make out the intricate, woven gold of the throne. Sparing it no more than a fleeting glance, they breezed past it.

Remi understood why all too well. They needed to hurry. It would take about ten minutes to get to the communications and travel depot, commonly known as the CTD, on foot. It was a small, detached building on the opposite side of the palace grounds. She remembered coming through there when she had first arrived in Bicaidia. At the time, it had been heavily occupied with both security and diplomats.

Though Ellarah had assured them that would not be a concern this time around, she couldn't help but wonder why not? Logically, she knew that the royal family had boosted external security. Extra guards were posted around the palace, atop the walls that protected it, and in the city of Helverta itself. But why hadn't they also considered internal or trans-universal security? It seemed crazy to her, but she couldn't complain. They needed lax internal security to pull off what came next.

As their quartet rushed through the near-empty palace and onto the sprawling grounds that led to the CTD, she decided not to worry about it. Instead, she followed Ellarah's lead as she led them in a circuitous pattern that seemed haphazard but wasn't. Ellarah had mapped out the security patrols beforehand and led them on the path they needed to take to avoid any guards that might happen by.

When an unexpected patrol stomped past them, they hid behind one of the many scrubby pines that lined the palace walls. Once clear, they continued on their mad dash to the CTD. Remi's palms had begun to sweat, and her hairline also grew damp. Her nerves had started to get the better of her, she realized, just as the crisp, white building that housed the CTD came into view.

Ellarah spared one glance around before they rushed from the greenery and out into the open field that led to the CTD. When they finally reached the depot, Remi's heart beat fast and steady in her chest. The distraction of avoiding detection and the urgency to get there had consumed her, pushing all thoughts of her end goal out of her mind. But now, she could feel a mixture of excitement and nerves pulsing through her entire body.

Once they reached the entrance, Ellarah held up her hand to stop them. The depot was closed that night and locked up tight, with no operators stationed inside. According to Ellarah, the only guards stationed in this area were on a rotating shift that took about twenty minutes to cycle through. This was all information that she had obtained under the pretense of her position. As palace liaison to the energy sect of the Science & Technology Pillar, she had free rein over every piece of critical technology in the palace. That included everything inside the CTD.

Ellarah took a quick look around, scanning for any unexpected guards before pulling out her comm device to check the time. Her eyes scanned the screen before she refocused on us. "Based on the schedule and our current time, we have fifteen minutes before someone comes to check this place out." She turned to Riven and slid her hand into his, squeezing. "Is that enough time?" Remi could see the nerves in her expression when he didn't answer right away. She continued, "If not, then I can buy you about five more minutes if we wait for them to come by and then go in after."

Riven shook his head. "No, I don't want to increase our chances of discovery if someone gets too curious on their patrol. I'll make fifteen work."

Ellarah squeezed his hand once more and nodded. "OK, we go." She moved forward, angling herself in front of the facial scanner and magic sensor.

But Thayne rested a hand on her shoulder, pulling her away before he shook his head. "Not you, Ellarah. I'll do it. If anything goes wrong, this should be on me." Remi felt herself melt just a little more at this show of selflessness. But deep down, she knew that if anyone should take the blame for this, it should be her. And she would have, but she didn't have the same clearance as they did. At least, not yet. So, her hands were tied.

Ellarah opened her mouth to protest, but he stepped into the scanner's active zone, and he sent a pulse of magic into it before anyone could say another word in protest. Ellarah turned away as the machinery whirred. All four of them seemed to hold their collective breaths as the lock clicked open and the door popped from its frame, offering them entry.

Thayne yanked it wide, and they all rushed inside, Riven closing it behind them. At that moment, Remi could feel some of those old doubts creeping back in. She'd wanted to do this the right way and go through the official channels. While she knew Ellarah and Thayne had been right and that this had been the only realistic way to see her sister again, sweat still prickled the back of her neck, and butterflies jumped in her belly.

Knowing that Thayne would be held responsible should anything go awry made her feel nauseous. Though, from her composed exterior, no one would guess the internal anxiety she felt. She just wished they could have found a way around the palace security measures. But according to Ellarah, there hadn't been one. Only authorized users got into the CTD, period.

Once they opened that portal and allowed her sister entry, then there was no way that the Bicaidian pillar leadership and royals wouldn't know what they'd done. She just had to hope that their ask for forgiveness rather than permission motto would suffice when it came down to it. And that Bekka's re-emergence into the Twelve Realms would be enough of a justification for the laws they'd broken. Besides, as the Peacekeeper's heir, Bekka would pardon them when she got there. They were doing this to help her and to stop a potential uprising, after all.

Remi let her breath out in a relieved *whoosh* as the lights flickered on in the CTD. They'd made it. The depot itself was a large, industrial room with an observation bay on the second floor and two massive rings used for trans-universal travel on the first floor, a glass partition separating the two areas. Ellarah and Thayne rushed toward the control panel situated near the back wall of the top floor and called up the travel holo.

"I'm shutting down travel to and from all other realms now," Ellarah explained, swiping away at the holo and tapping symbols on the control panel like a pro. This was another precaution they'd come up with to protect the Twelve Realms against any possible intrusion or Moldizean malfeasance. "Almost ready," Ellarah murmured. "Got it," she confirmed a few moments later as she pulled up a blank travel dossier, and Thayne took over, using his royal access to approve it. They didn't bother to assign it a proper name, only calling it 'the realm' before they saved the entry point. Ellarah looked at Riven, his attention on the process at hand, and said, "The coordinates are 18 z alpha red beta 20, 50, 10. You're on, babe." Remi had received those coordinates from Bekka after her agreement to help. She could only hope that they worked as expected.

Riven linked his fingers together and cracked his knuckles, then turned his head to pop his neck. He let out a long exhale before he stretched out his hands. Within seconds, black mist flowed from them like billowing smoke from a fire. It roared toward the archway and swirled around the thick metal rings, the only objects in all of Bicaidia that weren't warded against the creation of trans-universal portals.

Lightning crackled and snapped within the black cloud, and Remi's breath quickened. The archway began to glow a bright yellow, and she stepped closer to the observation bay, her hand pressed against the thick glass as she watched in breathless anticipation.

A sound behind them almost had her jumping out of her skin, and she whirled around to see what had caused the commotion. Sweat prickled along her hairline, and she prayed that they wouldn't be arrested as her eyes locked onto the doorway.

Her mouth dropped open in surprise as Madwyn slipped in behind them, the red of her dress glowing in the dim lighting. Ellarah and Thayne stared at her. Only Riven seemed unfazed by Madwyn's presence. Wasn't she supposed to be overseeing the distraction? Nerves crept down Remi's spine as she eyed the chaos deity. Also, hadn't they closed and locked the door behind them? Or had Riven left it open for his sister? She seethed. What a ridiculous, dangerous risk.

"Just wanted to see the show," Madwyn said, casual and calm, as though this wasn't a complete breach of the plan. She strolled over to the control panel, the picture of carefree relaxation, as she stood behind Ellarah and Thayne to watch Riven work. Remi bit back her desire to throttle Madwyn— that would have to come later.

Instead of worrying over what she couldn't change at that moment, she cut her attention back to Riven, watching as the lightning within his mist built up even more energy. The sound reverberated off the walls, and Remi hurried over to the windows facing the palace to check for any sign that the sound had drawn unwanted attention. To her relief, she saw only empty grounds around them.

She spun and quick-stepped back to the observation window as a loud boom issued from the arch of the fledgling portal. Thayne had moved from his spot at the control panel. He stood next to her now, and they watched in amazement as a fully-formed portal took shape. She looked at Riven, saw that a sheen of sweat slicked over his forehead and that his hands trembled. Even with the archway's assistance amping up his magic, he still looked like he was flagging.

A tremor of unease rippled through her at the sight. She knew he was more powerful than most of the Nefs she'd ever met, but was the chip in his neck going to be a problem? This wasn't something that any of them had ever cited as a concern. It had never crossed her mind. At least, not until now. She stared at him, assessing his strength and not liking what she saw. He needed to close the portal the instant Bekka came through. That had been the plan. It was also their best chance at convincing the Bicaidian leadership that they hadn't been entirely reckless in this endeavor.

Her mind raced as she wondered what would happen if they couldn't close it. Heart hammering now, she turned back to the archway. Her panting breaths steamed the glass in front of her.

Just then, something appeared in the center of Riven's magic. As his power sparked and swirled, Remi squinted, trying to see Moldize within its middle. She wanted to see her sister standing there with open arms, but there was only darkness. Her heart pounded, and her palms sweated as she looked harder—still nothing.

She looked back at his shaky limbs, strands of slick hair falling over his forehead. He wasn't going to make it. Twelve Hells, he wasn't even going to finish the portal, let alone be able to close it.

Then as though on queue to her doubts, the lightning settled and the archway hummed, the portal complete. A buzz loud enough to make Remi's teeth vibrate swept through the room and movement shifted within the entryway.

Bekka, Remi thought, unable to contain the giddy joy she felt at the prospect of seeing her sister again. She rushed to the door that led down to the portal entrance and swung it wide, hurrying down the steps to the portal.

Her breath quickened at the rush of excitement pumping through her; she couldn't wait to throw her arms around her twin once more. Then something stepped through and Remi skidded to a halt mere inches from the face of a creature unlike anything she had ever seen before.

She sucked in a stunned breath and stumbled backward, her steps faltering. The creature had bone-white skin stretched tight over an angular skull. Its eyes were black smoke and its yellowed teeth were carved into dangerous points.

Its focus shifted to her, and its expression morphed into the darkest and most terrifying snarl she'd ever seen. She turned and shouted, "It's not Bekka!" Blind desperation drove her as she ran to them, waving her hands over her head. "Close the portal! Close it!"

Her mind ran a frantic race as the beast roared, the sound guttural and so loud that the windows rattled. A war cry if she'd ever heard one. It had a large scythe that it held over its head, gleaming black with magic under the dim light.

It had been a trap all along; Bekka didn't send that message at all. Someone had set them up. Her mind raced through how this could have happened, but she came up blank. The code, the message, the handwriting; it had to be her sister. None of it made any sense.

Or at least, it didn't until she caught the feral, joyous gleam in Madwyn's eyes and the dark, grim expression in Riven's. Her stomach dropped, her adrenaline skyrocketing as

Madwyn smiled at her. It was the single worst expression she had ever seen a deity make.

The note wasn't a trick, she realized as she ripped open the door to the observation area. Madwyn and Riven's help had been.

Panic seizing her, Remi glanced over her shoulder as the door slammed into the opposite wall and saw thousands of creatures crawl like sinister spiders from the open gate. Their scaly bodies, either the darkest ebony or a sickly cream-color, scrabbled into the travel bay, sharp claws scraping along the metal floors, walls, and ceiling. They were the stuff of nightmares—all vicious and terrifying harbingers of death.

She held out her hand, intending to blast them all to kingdom come with her fire, when a feminine voice stopped her. "Don't even think about it. Keep that fire leashed, or I swear, I'll kill her."

Remi whirled to face the voice and saw, with gut-wrenching horror, that Madwyn had a hand locked around Ellarah's throat. A knife was pressed against the soft, bronze column of it. Remi froze.

Knives couldn't usually inflict damage on a deity, but this didn't look like any ordinary knife. Instead, it shimmered like black obsidian, with a blade that seemed to vibrate with every movement Madwyn made. The same kind of magic that had swirled around that terrifying creature's scythe.

She turned to Thayne and saw that Riven held him in a similar position. Only he needed no charmed knife to keep Thayne captive. Riven could tear Thayne's celestial essence from his body anytime he chose. Only, could he? Remi's mind raced as she tried to process everything that had just happened. Did his governor chip prevent him from doing that? If it didn't, would he be too tired to manage it after making that portal? She didn't know, and didn't dare test the theory.

She couldn't make sense of the betrayal, the terror, and the danger right in front of her. This had never been some distant Nefaral threat, but her new allies; Thayne's closest friends and Ellarah's Riven. They had been the real threat all along. But how could they do this to them? A sob crept up her throat as terror bucked inside her.

She heard the door slam shut behind her and decided to take a risk that might buy them some time. At least from the terrible creatures that still flocked through the open gate to whatever dimension Riven had accessed.

She pressed her hand on the knob, heating her skin and melting the mechanism shut, hoping this small use of power would go unnoticed. It wouldn't hold long against the creatures clamoring to get out below, she thought, but it was something. The plexiglass of the observation bay flexed under pressure as hoards of creatures swarmed from the open portal and filled the travel bay. The glass would explode soon enough, but every moment she bought them was precious.

Unfortunately, Madwyn saw the resulting melted metal and clicked her tongue in disapproval. "And here I thought I'd made myself clear." With that, she rose her hand up high and plunged the dagger into Ellarah's gut. To Remi's horror, it pierced the skin, sliding into Ellarah's flesh like butter. The sound of rending tissue as Madwyn ripped the knife back out made her gorge rise. She thought she heard a strangled cry but didn't know if the sound came from Ellarah, Riven, Thayne, or her.

Remi stayed frozen in stunned horror as Madwyn tossed Ellarah aside, her body crumbling as it hit the ground.

Blood gushed through Ellarah's slender fingers as she coughed and sputtered. Finally, snapping out of her stupor, Remi cried out and hurried forward, kneeling before her injured friend and putting pressure on the wound. "It's OK, Ellarah. It's going to be OK," Remi whispered, her voice breaking, tears streaming down her face. She could still hear thundering footfalls in the observation bay below, but it was drowned out by the sound of her pulse in her ears.

A second later, Riven was at her side, pressing his own hands onto Ellarah's seeping wound. "What the fuck, Madwyn?!" he roared as both he and Remi struggled to control the flow of blood. Riven moved one hand to brush down Ellarah's cheek, his voice sounding agonized when he said, "Ellarah? Ellarah! Say something! Please, baby, talk to me!" But Ellarah's golden eyes just stared from his to Remi's as she sputtered, blood beginning to seep from her lips.

Madwyn's voice crooned, calm but loud enough to be heard over the growing roar of creatures still trapped in the room below, and Remi could hear a cold cruelty that hadn't been there before. "Sorry, brother, I had to improvise. No empty threats, you know."

Riven growled, "That wasn't part of the plan, Madwyn." Remi spared a glance at the chaos deity, who stood beside Thayne now. She'd moved quickly, using their momentary shock against them, Remi realized, that sense of disbelief and rage still churning inside her. She held the same blade she'd used to stab Ellarah to his throat, the threat clear. Try anything and die.

Remi's heart ached as she watched Ellarah gasp for breath, skin growing more ashen by the second.

"Why are you doing this, Madwyn?" Thayne asked, his chin tilted up to avoid the sharp edge of the blade. "How could you do this to me, after everything we've been through together?" His voice seemed to break with betrayal, and a visceral kind of emotion.

Remi could still hear Riven whispering to Ellarah, begging her to stay with him, when Madwyn's laugh filled the room. "You mean after what you did to me, my love?"

Remi's mind fractured for a second, her fingers trembling as Madwyn's words clicked into place. She kept her eyes trained on them as realization dawned. Thayne's ex-lover was Madwyn?

The goddess sneered. "You left me for this Valerian whore, and yet you still expect my loyalty?" She *tsk'd* him as though he were a naughty child. "You know me better than that."

Madwyn looked at Remi then, disgust and distaste plain on her beautiful face. Remi had no doubt that her own expression must have shown her shock. "Oh, he didn't tell you about us, did he, Remi? You didn't know?" She laughed again, tossing back her blond hair as though this were the most hilarious thing she'd ever heard. "Typical Thayne. Full of half-truths and omissions."

More bangs and creaks issued from the glass behind them, a sign that they didn't have much longer before they got overrun by those creatures. Madwyn spared them little more than a glance, a satisfied smile on her face before she focused back on Thayne and unleashed a small bloom of purple smoke from a single finger. It seemed to drift in the air for a split second before absorbing into Thayne's skin. His eyes turned glassy, apparently under her thrall now. Madwyn pointed with the knife. "Move, lover boy; we're going to the control panel."

Ellarah's teeth began to chatter, her body quivering in pain as Madwyn's and Thayne's footfalls clicked on the hard steel floor. "Thayne, my love," Madwyn said, "I think it's time to get rid of these pesky governor chips, don't you?" Remi felt the blood drain out of her face in response to Madwyn's plan as Thayne obeyed and moved to the holo control without question.

"Thayne, don't!" Remi yelled, voice breaking as Ellarah's blood continued to pulse through her fingers, spreading across the floor beneath her. But Thayne didn't react, and his face remained void of any emotion, of any consciousness. She must have taken Thayne by surprise when her magic hit him, Remi thought. He'd be useless to them until it wore off, and she resisted the urge to scream in frustration and rage.

Riven's voice broke through the roar of Remi's emotions, "Hurry, Madwyn. I need that chip gone now!" Sweat sheened his forehead and his breaths came out ragged.

Startled by the sheer panic she saw in his eyes, Remi focused her attention back on Ellarah. "Shit," she breathed, horrified at the sight of her friend's celestial essence beginning to seep from her pores, her physical body preparing to ascend.

"Stay with me," Riven whispered, one hand on Ellarah's cheek. "Just a few more seconds, baby, and this will be over." Remi glared at the death god then with open disgust. How could he sit there and act like this whole fucked up situation wasn't his fault? Like he gave a damn about Ellarah?

Remi wanted to hit him, to pummel him with her fists and burn Madwyn to ashes for what they'd done today. But she couldn't. Madwyn still held Thayne captive, and she didn't dare move her hands from Ellarah's abdomen. Even with Riven's help, neither of them seemed able to stop the blood flow.

She turned her murderous gaze on the chaos deity, who muttered directions to Thayne as he obeyed without question, not seeming to know what he was doing. A loud groan issued from the window below and Remi winced in reaction just before Madwyn spoke, "Good, Thayne. Now get up." He did as she commanded and turned to face Madwyn at her behest. She rested the knife against his abdomen and then leaned forward and pressed a kiss to his mouth.

Remi squeezed her eyes shut in horrible realization of what would come next if she didn't act soon. She looked down then, sorrow and regret consuming her, because she knew what she had to do. She had to strike before Madwyn could eliminate her and Riven's governor chips, before they could unleash even more destruction. The only problem was that she would have to let Ellarah go. And if she did that, then Ellarah would die.

She swallowed a sob, hating the decision she'd been forced to make, and readied her body and her magic for what came next. Just as she started to make her move, Riven's hand gripped her wrist. Surprised, she tried to yank it free, but dark magic swirled around his fingers, and she looked into his eyes, stunned. Rage, grief, and a kind of determination seemed to churn in their blue depths. "Don't even think about it, princess," he warned, the threat clear.

At the sound of her brother's low, dangerous voice, Madwyn broke the kiss with Thayne and smiled. "Thank you, Riven, for rejoining the party. Here I thought you'd abandoned me altogether."

Then, before Remi could fight back against Riven's hold in earnest, Madwyn lifted her hands, and purple smoke bloomed from her palms. It ripped around the room so fast Remi didn't had time to process it before everything went hazy, her mind fogging over with confusion. Finally, she collapsed on her side, sticky hands slipping from Ellarah's belly as her eyes fixed on the portal entrance below.

She'd known it was bad, but it had grown so full of creatures that they were pressed bodily against the plexiglass, the ceilings and the walls of the room below. They snarled and banged their fists against the window in an attempt to free themselves, and yet still more came.

Unable to bear the sight of the heinous monsters below any longer, Remi's head lolled back to look at Madywn, who's eyes gleamed with triumphant excitement. "I've waited so long for this moment," she said, finger hovering over the holo display that would destroy the governor chips. "Soon, we'll all be free." Then, she executed the command that would change everything. Color flashed across the holo as Madwyn dropped to her knees, hissing, fingers pressing the column of her alabaster throat. Remi felt her own neck burn in sympathy as despair swallowed her. Madwyn's final words had been more terrifying than anything that had happened before. *They'd all be free*. Meaning, the Nefarals would no longer have inhibitors to stifle their power, to keep their darker nature in check.

She tried to fight the haze of delirium Madwyn had put her under as Riven groaned in pain beside her, but it was no use. She was powerless to stop them. They'd won, and she knew that what came next for her, for Thayne and for the rest of the Twelve Realms would be disastrous.

Exhaustion and a bone-deep sorrow took hold of her then as she watched the last vestiges of Ellarah's light seep out, her friend's body starting to turn insubstantial. But before she could ascend entirely, Riven's hands exploded with black magic, its mist swirling around Ellarah and trapping the pieces of her essence that seemed to drift away. His power shoved them back into her body as Madwyn rose to her feet, her cawing laugh ringing out around them.

Remi could hear cracks beginning to form in the observation bay glass behind her, as well as the hinges of the door groaning. The time to fix anything had passed. They'd lost, and she damn well knew it.

Madwyn's voice carried above everything else. "Oh, that feels so much better!" She ran her red-tipped fingers through her hair and over her body as though luxuriating in her newfound power. Then, she prowled across the floor, eating up the space between her and her brother and leaving still-controlled Thayne behind. "Thank you all for breaking us in here. You know, we could never have pulled this off without your help. This is the only place in all of Bicaidia with the access to overload those damn chips. So, let's just say we owe you one."

Madwyn's feet stopped right in front of Remi's face. She wanted to reach out, grab her ankle, yank her to the floor, and beat her to a bloody pulp. But her limbs felt limp, far-away and useless, her senses thick under Madwyn's fog. So, she could only watch as Riven rose to his feet beside his sister, Ellarah cradled in his arms like a child. She was alive but unconscious; she looked despicably pale and fragile as glass.

Then, without warning, Madwyn tossed back her head and unleashed the full force of her magic. It erupted from her, spewing in all directions. Electricity wove through it now, purple lightning amongst the smoke; it shattered the glass to the portal entrance, and the beasts roared through. The windows out to the palace grounds blew out too, and her power exploded out with it.

It decimated the unused portal and shattered the control panel, frying the palace archives and mainframe. Sparks flew everywhere as Madwyn destroyed their only way out of Bicaidia and locked the portal Riven had created open.

Remi could hear smaller explosions go off all around the palace, her hazy mind registering the severity of the situation. Communications were down, the Nefarals were freed, trans-universal travel was cut off, and they were all alone at the mercy of these monsters that spilled through the portal like water from a fountain. The uprising had begun.

"Give the order, brother," Madwyn commanded, standing at the death god's side. No longer did he look weakened or flagging. Rather, his skin seemed to glow with ethereal power.

Riven glared at his sister and spoke through gritted teeth, "Damn you, Madwyn. You know it wasn't supposed to go this way."

Madwyn rested a hand on his shoulder, drawing his gaze to hers. Her face softened a little as the beasts swarmed around them. "Give the order now, or this will all be for nothing, and we'll never be free." His jaw flexed as he slammed his eyes shut. Pain etched over every line of his face and a snarl ripped from his throat as the creatures emerging from the portal scrambled over each other to get into the immortal world.

He knelt to the ground and set Ellarah down gently before he stood, holding his hand up high. A large, black sword materialized in it, almost as long as Remi was tall. The blade itself seemed to devour all the light around it as his magic began to pour out from him. It wrapped around his body, draping him in blackness, cloaking him in his death power.

The beasts all stopped, seeming drawn to him like moths to a flame. They watched him; their black, depthless eyes fixed on the blade. He pointed the ebony sword toward the palace then. Toward the inauguration ball. Toward all the most powerful deities and all of the leaders of Bicaidia. "Attack!"

And that was when Remi realized just how serious the situation really was. That this wasn't just an uprising—it was a full-blown coup d'etat. Suddenly, she felt a hand grabbing her arm, and when she turned to her right, she saw Thayne's face. His expression looked horrified yet befuddled, and she could tell that he was trying fight Madwyn's hold over him.

But before either of them could say or do anything, the beasts rushed from the depot and out into the night. Seconds later, the screaming started. Close at first and scattered, but then further away and louder as more and more of them piled into the godly realm and scurried into the palace grounds, and toward the inauguration party.

There was an equal number of Nefarals to the regular deities in attendance tonight. If two deities as high up in the Bicaidian government as Madwyn and Riven were a part of this insurrection, Remi hated to imagine how many more would be on their side in the palace tonight.

She, Thayne, and Ellarah had screwed up. They had screwed up so badly. Tears pricked at the corners of her eyes as Riven and Madwyn focused their attention on her and Thayne. "Kristos Hellborn," Riven called, gesturing to a beast who seemed more sentient than the rest, less animal.

The creature stopped, a forked tongue slipping from its lips. "Yes, master." It prowled closer to them, its massive, scaly body looking like something from a horror movie in the mortal realm.

Riven pointed to Thayne and Remi. "Take them to the dungeon below the castle."

"Yes, Master," the beast hissed. The monsters were demons, Remi realized, the beast's name and obedience to its master, causing the connection to click into place. Her mind reeled as she realized that this was a portal to hell. They were responsible for opening a portal to and from hell in the godly dimension.

As the creature approached them, Riven turned his attention back to Ellarah, kneeling before her. He looked reverent yet agonized as he moved to lift her body once more. Madwyn stood behind him, her expression anything but worried. Instead, she looked gleeful, triumphant even.

Remi wanted to scream, unleash her fire, or claw Riven's face to ribbons. But before Riven could secure his grip around Ellarah's limp body, or the demon could haul Thayne to his feet, a shadow darted through the portal. It knocked Madwyn and Riven off balance, and then Thayne disappeared.

"What the f—" Madwyn growled, but something blasted back into the room and ricocheted off the walls. It took form inches from Madwyn's body, and a large male deity blasted a front kick straight into her chest. She stumbled backward and slammed into the wall, head smacking against it. Riven shot out his power, but the male disappeared as the mist blasted where he had been moments before.

A hint of recognition sparked in Remi's mind just before Riven yelled, "Pietyr, you bastard! Come out and fight me god-to-god." He swung that ebony sword in tight circles and showed his teeth.

Pietyr shimmered into form right behind his back. He whispered in Riven's ear, "Not today."

Riven whirled, sword swinging, but Pietyr was gone. The death god roared in frustration as a dark shadow swirled around Ellarah and Remi.

"No, don't let him take her!" Riven bellowed at his demon ward just as Pietyr materialized directly in front of it. His fist still a shadow, he reached into the demon's sternum. It sucked in a stunned breath as Pietyr's hand materialized inside the creature's body and ripped its still-beating heart straight from its chest. Before anyone could react, he threw the heart aside, hand soaked in gooey black blood before he gathered Remi and Ellarah into the protection of his shadows. Then, Remi watched in stupefaction as the depot fell away.

CHAPTER 9
BEKKA

Vacant

I twisted my hands together as I paced. "Nothing's happening." I turned to my companions and fixed a panicky gaze on them. "Why is nothing happening?"

"Just be patient," Arrick reassured. His soothing voice grated on my ragged nerves. Most of the time, his ability to remain calm in the face of inevitable disaster was enviable. But today, it irked me.

Deklan was no better. He stood with his arms crossed over his chest as he leaned against the far wall of the Moldizean Communications Depot. According to Arrick, the room hadn't been used for its intended purpose in quite some time. But it still had a trans-universal travel archway and the technology needed to power it.

Like so many of the other depots that Moldize maintained in their mortal realm, this room was lined with metal storage containers packed with supplies. Weapons of all shapes and sizes hung from the walls, and a sparring mat sat in the center of the room. Erykha told me that they'd used this room to train their deities in human combat prior to going to the mortal realm. The whole process fascinated me, so different from how things were back in Valeria.

Focusing back on the issue at hand, I narrowed my eyes at Deklan, who looked as though he might nod off any minute now. I swore to the Ascended that if he yawned, I would kick him in the shin.

Caden, the ever-present voice of reason, interjected. "Arrick's right. Remi's message didn't state a specific time, just a two-hour window. And we're only one hour into it."

I ground my teeth. Of course, they were right. Most likely, I was just getting worked up over nothing.

Maybe it was fear that the hope I had of seeing my sister again would be shattered into a million tiny pieces if this portal didn't appear. Or maybe it was because she was trapped in a world brimming with Nefarals who wanted nothing more than to overthrow the Bicaidian government. My best guess was that it was both.

I gnawed on my lip as a hand settled on my shoulder. "Just be patient," Arrick said. "Everything is going to be OK."

Erykha had powered up the control center's holo to keep an eye on the readings. "Anything?" I asked, resisting the urge to wring my hands together.

"Nothing yet. You have my word; I'll let you know as soon as we get our first readings," she answered, both apology and promise in her eyes. I sighed, trying to remind myself that everyone was just doing their best. Damion had been called away on some critical duty, and we'd said our goodbyes earlier. But I found that I wished he was here right now. I found his presence comforting.

Deciding not to bite either Erykha's or Arrick's head off, I turned to Deklan. "Don't you have any words of wisdom to impart? An opinion, perhaps?"

Deklan offered me an arrogant smirk. "How about *calm down?*"

"You're just saying that because you know it will piss me off."

He shrugged, grin spreading. Then he threw a knife at my head. His hand had moved so fast that I barely registered it. I caught the blade inches from my face and gaped at him. Then, without thinking, I snapped my mouth shut and chucked it back at him. He caught it in turn, and, using the distraction to my advantage, I launched myself at him.

An hour later and my breaths came in ragged gasps, my hair disheveled and black, tank top askew. After everything that had happened in Moldize, my new friends had taken it upon themselves to teach me how to fight.

Mostly Caden and Deklan had used it as a distraction for me while Arrick had been in the underworld, just as Deklan was now. But when Arrick returned just over a week ago, he had begun to participate as well.

As a result, I had become a sufficient fighter hand-to-hand and proficient enough with a sword too. Of course, there remained the slight possibility that they let me win from time to time. But I preferred not to believe that. It messed up my mental image of myself as a fierce, warrior goddess. Granted, it was more like a human warrior who fought with crude weapons, but it summoned a fearsome image to mind nonetheless.

Deklan wiped the sweat from his brow. "Good fight." Then he gestured to the holo that Erykha manned, which housed a countdown timer. "But now might be the time to worry. We're outside the window."

I looked up at the clock and grimaced; he was right.

I appealed to Eryykha, hoping that maybe we'd missed some spike in the readings. That perhaps a portal had started to open while we were sparring. But she shook her head in anticipation of my questions. "No readings have come through yet, and I see no presence of a portal." She swiped through pages of holographic readings before she looked up at us, "I think it's time to worry."

Anxiety coursed through my veins like a drug. "What do we do?"

"We wait, and we don't make any rash decisions," Caden answered. "Something may have delayed them. So we hold our position."

"But what if something's wrong? What if we wait and something bad happens to Remi?" I asked, trying to calm my rising panic.

Arrick turned to face me and rested his hands on my shoulders. His eyes held mine, and I could feel my breathing begin to steady. "Caden is right; we need to stay in this position until we're certain that Remi has failed. But, don't forget, we have a backup plan."

I groaned as frustration built inside me. "I hate that plan. That is the worst plan ever conceived in the history of the entire Twelve Realms." I stared at Arrick and settled my hands onto my hips in an attempt to try and control my emotions because the truth was that I was starting to panic. My sister was the most reliable person I knew, and if she wasn't on time, then something serious had to be keeping her.

Had the pillar leadership and royals changed their minds and revoked the portal's approval? Surely, if they had, we would have received word of it before now. Or had something more sinister happened? Had the Nefarals attacked when they heard that I would be returning to Valeria?

Hairs raised on my forearms as I ran through everything that might have gone wrong. Then, a couple of seconds later, Deklan said, "Bekka's right. The backup plan is an irredeemably shitty one."

Arrick shrugged a broad shoulder. "It's all we've got right now."

Erykha cleared her throat, drawing our attention to her once again. She gestured to the holo. "We can wait another hour, just to be certain no readings come through. But if they don't, I think we need to consider that something has gone seriously wrong in Bicaidia. If the leadership had decided to revoke the portal, there's no way Remi wouldn't have already sent word to us. So I think it has to be something else."

Her thoughts mirrored my own, and I turned to Arrick. He rested a hand on my shoulder, reading my fear. "Don't worry, Bekka; we'll get to her. We might have to change our plans to do it, but we'll get it done."

We hadn't talked about the backup plan since we'd received Remi's note. With her confirmation that the Bicaidian leadership had agreed to open a portal, we hadn't thought we'd need it. But if we did have to use it, that changed things.

I knew, as well as everyone else did, that if we went through Bicaidian hell, then Erykha wouldn't be able to come with me. Instead, Arrick would have to escort me into Bicaidia and, once there, I'd have to figure out a way to keep a governor chip out of his neck. I didn't know if it would be possible, but maybe my word would be enough, as long as we got to Valeria quickly.

Arrick touched a finger under my chin to turn my attention back to him. "But for now, we wait here until we're sure."

I clasped my fingers behind my head, trying to calm myself. "An hour tops, right?"

Erykha was the one who answered, "If nothing happens by then, Arrick, you'll need to go with her."

Caden and Deklan stepped forward then, Caden speaking for both of them, "We're going too. Whatever is happening in Bicaidia, we can help."

My eyes softened as I looked at them, grateful that they'd be willing to follow us into…well, literal hell. "You don't have to do that. Arrick and I can handle it alone."

Deklan scoffed, rolling his eyes. "You really think you can leave us behind when you have no idea what you'll be walking into? Nice try, sweet cheeks."

I snorted out a bubble of nervous laughter. The demigod had such a way with words. I smiled at them, appreciation for them blooming within me. I owed them so much, and I vowed then and there to repay them as soon as I got back to Valeria.

"Okay, then, we'll all go together if it comes to that," I said, turning back to the single Moldizean trans-universal archway. "Until then, though, we wait."

The words hung between us as we all stared at the space where the portal was supposed to appear. I could tell that we all hoped that it wouldn't come to plan B. That Remi would come through for us and that the portal would open any minute now.

I chewed on my thumbnail as I tried to keep my mind from venturing into dark territory. The kind where I imagined Remi getting killed by Nefarals. I swallowed thick spit down my dry throat as I willed the portal to open, begging with my inner voice.

Arrick, Caden, and Deklan stood close together, whispering about something as Erykha stayed focused on her data feeds. Then, after a quick huddle, the three males broke off and began to gather supplies from the locked storage containers that lined the room, shoveling them into their packs. They were preparing for hell, but my eyes stayed fixed on the doorway, not ready to give up hope just yet.

I saw Arrick set his pack down out of the corner of my eye and then move toward me. His confident gait and strong body radiated power and, no matter how absorbed I was in my fear, I was drawn to him like a moth to a flame. My body craved him.

But then there was the other part of me—the practical one who knew just how tenuous our relationship was. I sighed, pressing my back to the wall and sliding down it, still staring at the empty space where the portal should have appeared over forty minutes ago.

I felt Arrick settle in beside me as the brothers moved on from the packs and began to pull weapons from the walls and stash them in their Itorian battle leathers, which they still wore most days despite my best efforts to convince them otherwise. For whatever reason, they felt more comfortable in their battle attire. Perhaps old habits died hard.

Arrick didn't speak, and I could tell that he just wanted to offer his presence as comfort. What was there to say anyway? Before I could question the wisdom of it, I leaned into him and rested my head on his shoulder. He slung an arm around me and gathered me closer to him.

We sat in silence as the final minutes ticked away. Finally, with seconds left, a delicate ringing sounded, and Erykha lifted her head from her work. "Wait, hold on, something's coming through."

Excitement pulsed through me, and I could feel my breath quicken in anticipation.

"What is it?" Arrick asked, stepping closer to the holo Erykha manned to examine the readings. Light shimmered in the portal, but just a tiny, fragmented beam of it. Confused, I stepped closer as the light winked out. I squinted, eyes locking onto what had just been deposited on the floor beneath the archway.

A slim, folded piece of paper.

"The reading just stopped. It wasn't—" I heard Erykha say, but her voice was far away as I pushed up to my feet and hurried to the archway. Something cold had begun to form in the pit of my stomach. Something was wrong, and I knew it. A few quick steps and I picked up the paper, unfolded it with shaky hands. What did this mean? Why was there a letter and not a portal?

Arrick stepped away from the holo and closer to the archway as I scanned through the note. When I finished, the letter fell from my hands, and my knees buckled—the last tiny fragment of hope I'd held onto cracked, shattering into a million tiny shards. Arrick caught me before I could slump to the floor, as Erykha moved next to me, too. "What is it?" She picked it up and skimmed through it while Arrick held me steady.

"Just breathe, Bekka. Take a breath," he urged, his voice full of concern. Hot tears had swelled in my eyes, and I shook my head, my breaths coming in quick now. I was about to have a full-fledged panic attack, and there wasn't a damn thing anyone could do about it.

"Arrick," Erykha breathed. "You need to see this." I'd curled my body around his, trying to draw on his strength, to use him to keep me in one piece. I felt his hand leave my back as Erykha passed him the letter.

"Shit," he said, and I couldn't have said it better myself. The first half of the letter was in Remi's writing, detailing that this note had been some kind of a contingency plan. A way to let us know that they'd failed. She'd said something about going around the Bicaidian leadership, which by itself was bad enough. But it was the second half of the letter, written in some unknown deity's hand. That had been what sent me into this state of utter despair.

"What is it?" Deklan asked, and I could just make out the blur of his booted feet standing nearby. "What's happened?"

Erykha answered, "Remi's failed. The Nefarals have launched an attack on the Bicaidian palace and the capital city of Helverta."

"What?!" Caden half-shouted. The sound jerked me out of my stupor. I needed to get control of myself. Right now. We had to do something. We had to fix this somehow. I couldn't curl into a fetal position and leave my sister to deal with this on her own. We had a contingency plan, and we had to use it immediately. No more wasting time.

"I recognize this writing," Erykha said. "It's from Datania, our source inside of Bicaidia. Remi must have tracked her down and used her to send this communique. In the beginning, Remi says that she went around the Bicaidian leadership and that this letter is to let us know that they'd been caught. But that's scratched out and replaced by what Datania said about the Nefarals."

I extricated myself from Arrick's arms and swiped thumbs under my eyes to catch the tears. "She lied to us about the approval all along," I said, cursing under my breath. "I wish we knew more. How serious is the attack? We could be walking into a full-blown war zone or we could be walking right into a pissed off government's palace. There's just no way to know."

Arrick rose to his feet beside me. "You're right," he said, tapping his chin in thought. "You know, we have an open line with Datania. Maybe she can give us more information, just in case we're walking into a trap."

He strode over to the holo control panel and began swiping at the display. Erykha followed hot on his heels as Deklan, Caden, and I just stared at each other in shock. Then, snapping her fingers to get our attention, Erykha said, "Bekka, come here. You need to write a response, just in case Remi is there and able to answer. She'll trust it more if it comes from you."

I did as I was told, a numb feeling creeping over me. I felt like we were wasting time we didn't have, seeking more intel. Though logically, I knew that we needed to know what we were walking into. But in my heart, I wanted to burst into Bicaidian hell and leave a wave of destruction in my wake until we made it into Helverta.

Cooler heads prevailed and I let my logical brain take over, grasping the pen Erykha handed me and began writing as she dictated.

Datania, what happened? How serious is the threat? How many Nefarals are we talking about? Do they have other allies? Has the Bicaidian leadership quelled the attack yet? Please report.

When I finished, and Arrick and Erykha had updated the settings on the holo, Arrick jogged over to the arch and placed the note beneath it. Erykha fired up the machine a second later. Light crept around the arch as it harnessed raw energy magic tapped from Ascended knew how many deities, and the note lit up like a miniature sun. After a few seconds, I had to look away from the vivid brightness before the whir of the machinery died down.

I blinked to refocus, staring down at the paper, sitting unmoved beneath the archway. "Is that supposed to be there still?" I asked, already knowing the answer.

Erykha's response made nausea creep back into my belly. "No, it's not." She swiped her fingers urgently over the holo displays; concern clouded her face. Her eyes were vivid green, and her skin pale as she worked. After a few moments, she stopped, resting her hands on the control panel and shaking her head in helplessness. "I can't get through. The communication line has been shut down. Datania must have gotten this out just before that happened. We're not going to get any more intel than what's in that letter. And we can't send anything back."

Arrick crossed his arms over his chest as he surveyed the readouts on the holo. "She's right. We're going to have to go in blind. We don't have a choice."

Urgency spread through me like a wildfire, and I grabbed a pack from the floor. "Then what are we waiting for? Let's go."

Deklan strode over to the weapons wall and called over his shoulder, "I agree with her. We need to move fast. The sooner, the better. They might need reinforcements."

Arrick and Caden rushed behind him, grabbing even more weapons for themselves and distributing some to me as well. Caden slipped his swords onto his back and tossed me a pistol while Deklan handed me a short sword. I strapped the holster and scabbard around my torso and added a hunting knife to my thigh.

When they finished, Arrick carried his signature two swords, three guns, and a knife, while Deklan carried his crossbow and throwing knives. We were armed to the teeth, and I hoped that none of it would be necessary—because even in hell, Arrick and I should have access to our power.

We each picked up our packs and strapped them on our backs over our weapons. It was all very uncomfortable as we turned to Erykha, who'd shut down her holo and stared at us, concern etching every line of her face. I knew she was reticent to let her son come with us, but we had no choice now.

Over the past few days, I'd helped them double down their warding even more. After the news concerning their uninvited visitor, I'd insisted that we make it stronger and swore that I wouldn't leave if they didn't let me do that one last thing for them. I could only hope they'd hold until Arrick could return.

She reached out a hand to her son, and he took it. "Be careful," she said, and I could see a mother's concern in her eyes.

"Don't worry, I will be. I'll contact you the first chance I get," he said, wrapping his arms around her in a tight hug. My heart melted. They weren't just deities; this was his mother, and he was her son. For a moment, her eyes glistened before she squeezed them shut.

She whispered something inaudible in his ear before she pulled away and turned to the rest of us. We all gave her a bone-crushing hug, and I tried not to cry, knowing I might never see her again. She'd become a friend to me, someone I cared about, and I hated that politics would get in the way of that. Maybe I could change things once I became Peacekeeper of the Twelve Realms.

If we succeeded.

If we survived.

I could only hope I would hold that kind of sway.

She waved us off, watching with intensity as we strode through the depot door that led to the palace and toward hell.

We walked in silence as we contemplated our bleak destination and what we might face once we got through hell and to Helverta. Finally, as we wound around our third turn, Caden broke the silence. "Arrick, can you tell us what we are walking into here?" We had all avoided talking about plan B since we had hoped that it would never come to this. So, we hadn't prodded Arrick for details.

But now, no matter how much I wanted to rush headlong into hell and help my sister, details were exactly what we needed. No matter the urgency, I agreed with Caden. I wanted to know what to expect.

"It's hard to say since all hells are different, depending on who created it," Arrick replied. We turned down yet another hallway, white walls and wooden doors flying by as we hurried.

"Well, haven't you been to Bicaidian hell before?" I asked.

"Not to Bicaidian hell, no."

I stopped and stared at him. The last time we'd talked about this, he'd made it sound like he knew what to expect, like he'd been there a thousand times. But then he dropped this bombshell, and I didn't like it. Caden and Deklan followed suit, each of them looking just as dumbstruck as I did. "What do you mean *you've never been to Bicaidian hell'?*" I asked, narrowing my eyes at him.

Arrick stopped. "There was never a need for it. Valerian hell, I've been through dozens of times. But there has never been a reason to go to Bicaidia."

I pinched the bridge of my nose, reigning in my frustration with him. "So, you're telling me that you have no clue what we'll be walking into? You know it's the only realm with a living death deity aside from Moldize, right?"

He fixed a steely gaze on us. "Which is why I expect it to be worse than any I've been to before."

We all stared at him, expecting him to continue. Reading the room, he did just that. "Hell, when left unattended, usually means that there isn't much happening down there. Spirits have no way of getting from purgatory into hell. So, Valerian hell, like most others, is low occupancy."

He was right, of course. This was a key reason for my sister's marriage, to share resources. Bicaidia had a death god, a resource we'd needed. Valeria had been without one for millennia now, and the spiritual dimension was piling up with all those lost souls. Aimless and alone, with nowhere to go and no one to comfort them.

My stomach churned as I realized that this added another layer of complication to an already complicated situation. "You couldn't have mentioned this earlier?" I knew that it didn't matter in the grand scheme of things. No matter how bad this might be, we were going to do it, period. But I still wanted to know what I was getting myself into.

He ticked off his fingers. "First, we didn't think we'd need to go this route, so we never discussed the details. And second, you didn't seem too keen on the idea, so I decided it would be better not to add fuel to the fire."

"You're a real piece of work; you know that?" Deklan observed, shaking his head.

Arrick grinned darkly. "Keep telling me that, and it'll go to my head."

Deklan's lips pulled back in something that resembled a snarl before Caden stepped between them, putting an end to their bickering. "Enough. You didn't answer the question, Arrick. What can we expect when we get there?"

Arrick let out a long breath in frustration, and I could see a dark expression flicker over his face before he slipped his hands into his pockets. "There will be demons, a lot of them. There will be screaming, suffering and torture. Hell itself is a form of torture, but the demons facilitate it too. They'll leave us alone while we're there if we don't disturb the occupants."

"Occupants?" Caden asked, brows cinching together.

"The human souls. Since Bicaidia has a living death deity in its realm, there will be many of them. Only, they won't look like spirits there. They'll appear as flesh and blood, even though they don't have physical bodies as we know them here. Physics works differently in hell. As we journey through the circles, they'll beg for help and mercy, but we can give them no quarter. We let the demons go about their business, and we do not interrupt. Do you all understand that?" Arrick finished, looking at each of us with a stern, warning expression. He was in general mode, and I could tell that these were our orders. He expected us to obey them.

"What happens if we do…say…interrupt them?" I asked, venturing for a what-if scenario.

"How about you just do as I say, and we won't have to find out?" he answered.

I had an eerie sense of déjà vu. The last time I went somewhere with Arrick's half-assed warning not to do something, I hadn't asked enough questions. This time, I wouldn't make the same mistake. I wanted to know exactly what would happen, should we disobey his orders or accidentally screw up. The stakes were too damned high for blind trust. I shook my head. "That doesn't work for me. The last time you said that, we ended up stranded in the mortal realm and almost had to kill four people to get back home."

Arrick ground his teeth in annoyance. "In the interest of saving time, let's just say that they won't stop until they kick us out of hell. And that getting back in will be damn near impossible. Demons are spiteful creatures, and they know how to hold a grudge. On top of that, this doorway took me two weeks to create. I could only use the smallest drops of power each day so that I didn't tip off the Bicaidian death deity. If we get kicked out, the demons will tear it to shreds. Then I'll have to start over, and it would be weeks before we made it back through. Does that satisfy your curiosity?"

I held up a finger to stop him. "Wait a minute, what was that about your power and the death deity?"

He sighed and dragged a hand through his hair. "While we're there, I can't use more than the barest fraction of my magic. My power transforms the metaphysical realm itself. The death deity will be able to sense it if I go too far. Since there is a decent chance he's in on the Nefaral attack on Helverta, we need to avoid that at all costs."

Deklan and Caden both paled in reaction to this news, and I felt my mouth go dry. Deklan stepped closer. "You're telling me we can't just blast our way through hell and out to the other side?"

Arrick blanched. "Yes. We'll have to pass through the circles until we find the existing portal, just like a soul would."

Caden looked stricken, and Deklan made a low sound in his throat that sounded like a growl. "Of course we do."

"Well, what about me?" I asked, but I already knew the answer.

Arrick's intense green eyes fixed on me. "Same goes for you. Minimal interference allowed. But you won't be able to manipulate anything in the metaphysical realm anyway. Your power is biological and life-driven, and nothing in hell is technically alive."

I squinted my eyes, trying to grasp his meaning. "So, I'll be able to do what exactly?"

"You can create objects within hell, but you can't manipulate hell itself or the creatures within it. Your magic will be less of an irritant to the death god, but you're still too powerful. He'd be able to sense more than a tiny fraction of it. So, using it isn't worth the risk."

I let out a long and beleaguered sigh. This was going to come back to bite us in the ass. I could feel it. "For the record, I still hate this plan."

"Unfortunately, it's the only one we've got," Arrick replied. "And, there's one more thing."

We all waited with bated breath. To be honest, I was just relieved to get everything out on the table before we got there. If we were about to walk into a disaster, I'd like to know just how disastrous it would be.

"I don't know what level of hell we'll land in, so it might be a while before we find a way through this dimension and into the Bicaidian capital. Unlike Moldize, Bicaidia has ten separate planets that each have their own immortal and mortal realms. So, once we find the inner circles, we'll need to make sure we find the right portal for the capital."

"How are we going to manage that?" Caden asked, hand on the hilt of his gun.

Arrick sighed and closed his eyes. "Trial and error."

Deklan shook his head and laughed, though the sound held zero traces of humor. When he spoke, sarcasm dripped from every word, "Wow. This plan just keeps getting better."

I couldn't help but agree. This plan had bad idea written all over it, but what choice did we have?

Caden interrupted then. "I have another question; can't we just bribe the demons to tell us which portal is the right one? Wouldn't they have used them before?"

Arrick shook his head. "No, the portals are warded so that only beings with godly blood can pass through them. And, no, we can't bribe them. They'll be loyal to their death god, so we need to keep a low profile and try our best not to disturb them or draw attention to ourselves."

Deklan laughed in response to this, the sound anything but humorous. "Perfect. This doesn't sound like an impending disaster at all."

Arrick crossed his arms over his chest at Deklan's outburst, annoyance plain on his face. "If you have any useful suggestions or alternatives, now is the time."

Deklan gestured to me and then to Arrick. "Aren't you supposed to be two of the most powerful beings in the multiverse? Couldn't you just, I don't know, meld your power together and create a portal directly into Bicaidia?"

Arrick and I looked at each other and then gave Deklan a look like he was one knife short of a set. "Meld? Death and creation power?" My expression, along with the bark of laughter I expelled, let him know just how ridiculous I found this idea.

Deklan ground out every syllable, apparently to make sure we understood his level of irritation. He was getting quite good at that. "What is so funny?"

"You don't get how this all works, do you?" Arrick asked, gesturing between himself and me.

Deklan glared at us. "Obviously not. So, why don't you explain why my plan is any worse than the '*go through hell and get tortured then lost*' plan?"

I held up a finger. "All of the Twelve Realms have wards in place. Protections against unregulated portals getting created in the middle of their major cities from opposing realms. Or else we'd have done that a hell of a lot earlier."

Caden jumped in and said, "But, Deklan's right, you're two of the most powerful deities in existence. So why is teaming up such a bad idea?"

"Because you need to have the same power to meld or team up or whatever. And we don't." I cleared my throat and ran a hand down my braid. I could feel a flush creeping up my neck. "The only way gods can meld two different powers is if they're soulfused."

Caden scrunched up his nose in confusion. "Soulfused? What does that mean?"

I shuffled from foot to foot, growing impatient. This was taking up time we didn't have, but I tried to explain as best I could, "Soulfusion is like a blending of two souls. Magics are shared, connections are made, but the point is, it's extremely rare. The last soulfused pair I know of was my grandfather and grandmother. There haven't been any since."

Deklan frowned. "So, the bottom line is that hell is still our only option?"

I gave him a finger gun. "Yep. Unless you have another plan you'd like to share, I'm open to any viable alternatives. Please. Anything better will do." Deep down, I really hoped that they might have an idea that we hadn't thought of. They had fresh eyes and perspectives, which could be helpful.

When both brothers remained silent for a long beat, Arrick pointed to a door to his right. "Alright, then if we have no other ideas or plans, the portal is here. Are you ready?"

All three of us nodded, and I knew that we felt anything but ready. It didn't matter, though, because we were going to do it anyway. We had to. My sister was in danger; she needed our help. This was the only way we knew to get to her. So, it was our only choice.

With our consent, Arrick opened the door to a dark, cavernous vacuum. I held my breath, bracing for an onslaught of demons, and…wait a minute, I thought, peering into the darkness.

I took a step forward. Turned a circle. Looked around. Gaped.

I had expected a hell teeming with demons and mortal men screaming in torturous pain.

But instead, I saw nothing.

Hell was empty.

CHAPTER 10

REMI

Fallout

They were flying, blasting through the air.

She could still hear screams, roars, and fighting going on below. It was a slaughter; there was no other way to describe it. And it was all her fault. She squeezed her eyes shut, and when they stopped moving, solid ground beneath her once more, she slumped over.

She gasped for fresh air, eyes still closed, desperate to clear her head from whatever Madwyn had done to it. When her vision began to stabilize, she saw Ellarah on the ground next to her. Her friend's body was limp, sprawled with legs and arms askew, blood already pooling beneath her. Remi scrambled closer, rocky gravel scraping against her knees as she put pressure on the wound once more. She had no idea what Riven's magic had done to her. She couldn't imagine that he'd do anything to hurt her. But then again, everything else he'd done that night had been terrible.

Before she could breathe a word, a second pair of hands appeared next to hers. Remi looked up; it was the goddess from the party, the one who'd beckoned to Pietyr earlier. She laid a hand on Ellarah's forehead, and her power glowed yellow, a humming gold as she brushed her fingers down Ellarah's body. A healer, Remi registered through the lessening haze. She spoke as she worked, "You can take your hands away. You did well, princess, but now let me take care of her."

The words seemed to float from far away, and Remi didn't register them until the goddess gently pulled her fingers from the wound. The blood seemed to seep slower now, and Remi squeezed her eyes shut, praying to the Ascended that Ellarah wouldn't bleed out. The healer unleashed her molten gold healing magic, the soft glow of it running over Ellarah's skin. Remi breathed a sigh of relief and brushed a bloody hand over her forehead, not caring about the gory streaks it made across her skin.

Thayne's agitated voice pulled her attention from Ellarah and to the two gods behind her. "Why the hell did you bring us here, Pietyr? Take me to the courtyard, now!" Remi's brain struggled to fight past the still-lingering haze of Madwyn's power as she took in her surroundings. The moon was full and illuminated the area around her, and the familiar location registered in her mind—the secret cliffside where Thayne had taken her earlier that day. That interlude felt like two hundred years ago, considering everything that had happened since.

Pietyr dragged a hand over his pallid face. He shook his head. "I can't do that."

Thayne snarled, "I'm giving you an order, damnit! We won't make it in time if you don't shadow-walk us in there!"

Pietyr didn't move to obey. Instead, he shook his head again and repeated, "I can't do that." His voice broke, and Remi didn't miss the sorrow and regret in his eyes.

Thayne rushed forward and gripped Pietyr's shirt in his fists. Lighting snapped around him, and she could see that his face was a mask of rage and despair. "Take me, now!"

Pietyr didn't move. He allowed Thayne to shake him twice in desperation before he replied, "There's nothing left to save Thayne. We've lost the palace, the pillar leadership. All of it. It's all gone."

Remi felt like she'd been kicked in the gut and she let out a quiet sob, hand covering her mouth to stifle it. She'd just sworn to protect them. And with her first act as the high princess, she'd doomed them all.

Thayne let go and stumbled back, agonized horror washing over his face. "That can't be true. You're wrong."

Pietyr shook his head, staring up at the sky. "Whatever Madwyn did at the party, it turned any non-Nefs into gooey piles of stupidity. Then when Madwyn disabled the Nefs' chips, they attacked. It was coordinated and well planned. No one made it out except Charmelle and me."

The shock on Thayne's face was complete, his skin chalk white in the moonlight. "My parents?"

Pietyr looked stricken when he shook his head. He stepped forward and laid a hand on Thayne's shoulder. "I'm sorry, majesty, they're gone."

An urgent female voice sounded from behind them, the healer, Charmelle. "We only escaped through sheer luck. We were fighting along with some others who could get away from Madwyn's magic in time, and when we saw an opening and were on our way to look for the King and Queen, an explosion threw us close to the gates. We were the only survivors. By the time we got our bearings together, it was too late. We saw the Nefs making an example out of your parents. Then, we turned around and ran." Remi felt sick, bile crawling up her throat. Tears burned her eyes, and she shook her head, not wanting to hear any more, wishing she could take it all back. Then, without warning, Charmelle lifted her hands, extinguishing her power.

"We need to get Ellarah someplace safe. Now. Something's wrong. She's not responding to my magic."

Remi spoke through heaving breaths of panic. "What do you mean? Why not?"

Charmelle shook her head. "I think it's poison, but it's hard to say what kind. Her wound won't close. I need more healers to seal it and stop the bleeding, but she's lost so much blood already. We need to move, fast." She ripped a strip from the bottom of her dress and fastened a belt around Ellarah's waist to compress the wound. She pointed back to the doorway and the staircase. "Pietyr's right, there's nothing left to save down there, and there are too many of them for us to fight on our own. But we can save Ellarah, and we can live to fight another day. A retreat is our only option right now."

Thayne's jaw worked. Remi could almost see the wheels turning as he struggled to think through Madwyn's damnable haze. First, she rested a hand on Thayne's forearm. Then, hating herself for having to suggest that he leave his parents behind, she steeled herself against the pain of it. "We don't have a choice, Thayne. We have to save Ellarah. We can't let her die like this."

Thayne's voice cracked with grief, his muscles tightly coiled. "They're my parents, Rem."

From the corner of her eye, Remi could see Charmelle pull Ellarah up and cradle her in her arms. She walked closer to them, and so did Pietyr.

"I'm sorry, majesty," Pietyr whispered. "But I don't have time to ask for your permission." Then he reached out and enveloped them all in shadow.

A few moments later, Remi landed hard on her feet, stumbled, and fell to her knees. She sucked in labored breaths as she fought through nausea. She'd never shadow-walked before today, and she'd been under the influence of haze-inducing magic both times. Pietyr's gray shadows shifted around them, and she began to register her surroundings. But before she could get her bearings, the shadow god gripped her upper arm and yanked her to her feet.

"We need to move." His voice was as hard as steel, and she winced as she struggled to obey. Her head still felt foggy, entrapped by the awful purple haze of Madwyn's magic. Ascended, that bitch was powerful, she thought, needles prickling up and down her limbs. It felt as though they'd fallen asleep and were only just waking up.

Screams clanged in her mind, and a dull roar, like the constant hum of an ocean tide, broke through her foggy brain. A quick glance around connected the sounds to her current circumstances. To her horror, she realized that they were still in Helverta. No more than a few miles from the palace, close to the clandestine meeting spot that had set this entire disaster in motion.

Her head swiveled as she took in the scene around her. Lower-caste deities rushed from the apartments and condominiums that surrounded them, screaming to be heard over the deafening drone that came from the palace. This could only mean one thing—the uprising had breached the palace walls and had begun to pour into the city.

With an urgency that stunned her, Pietyr yanked her forward, forcing her to move. Her feet stepped, one in front of the other, without her brain registering the decision.

They joined the growing swarm of deities racing through the streets. Still more came. Running from their homes, what little possessions they deemed critical clutched under their arms. Those with strong enough power to transport using their magic did so, disappearing into swaths of shadows or blasts of light.

Some of the more powerful elementals dematerialized their physical bodies, transforming into whatever element they controlled. Those with lower power rankings used whatever magic they had to propel themselves forward, and if they didn't have that, they jumped into their domiciles, hoping to get away from the palace and the chaos spreading across the city faster than Remi could have imagined possible.

The chaos of battle grew closer with each passing second, that dull roar turning deafening. It was becoming clear that unless they dematerialized or translocated, they weren't going to be able to outrun it because the rebellion was coming for them. The demons, the Nefarals. The unholy union.

As her head pounded and gut-wrenching nausea threatened to overtake her, Remi dared a glance over her shoulder back toward the castle. She had to see what came next.

She had to know.

Behind her, Thayne and Charmelle ran at full speed, with Ellarah tossed carelessly over Thayne's shoulder. Her limp, unconscious body bounced and gyrated, her wound seeping blood down Thayne's white shirt. She looked further and saw a cloud of blackness blocking out the sky. Flashes of power rippled inside of it, and Madwyn appeared within it, hovering above the city like a vengeful goddess, Riven at her side.

They rained her chaos magic down on the city, decimating everything in their path. Madwyn's purple power sizzling with electricity pierced into the buildings beneath them, pillar embassies and other critical structures exploding into rubble. Beneath them on the cobblestoned streets, Demons roared through the city, sprinting into buildings, attacking anyone lucky enough to avoid Riven and Madwyn's power.

The gods fought back, their magic illuminating the night sky, as demons fell one after the other. But Remi watched more and more of the deities who stayed to fight fall victim to the horde of hell. There were simply too many of them. They were outnumbered and overrun.

Twelve Hells, she thought, her heartbeat skyrocketing at just how close that horde was to them and how badly everything had gone wrong. Why hadn't Pietyr transported them further? She wondered as the last vestiges of her brain-haze cleared. Why didn't he try to translocate them all again right now? But then, where would they go? What place would be safe from Madwyn and Riven's allies? Who could they trust?

"This way!" Pietyr yelled over his shoulder a second before he darted into a narrow alleyway between two massive, glass, and stone skyscrapers. Remi followed him without question, Thayne and Charmelle on her heels. Her mind assaulted her with even more questions. Why were they still in Helverta? Where the hell were they going, and why weren't they getting out of the city?

She drew in deep breaths, strengthening her resolve. They didn't have time for questions. They needed to evacuate, get the hell out of there while they still could.

Pietyr was leading the way, and he'd saved their lives before. Surely, he knew what he was doing, and Remi was smart enough to realize that anything less than full cooperation could get them captured, or worse—killed.

A thunderous explosion, louder than any she'd heard before, ripped through the city, and the ground began to shake beneath her feet. She wobbled off balance and slammed into the stone wall of the building beside her, her body chipping away at the solid exterior. She felt Thayne's strong grip on her shoulders, and she righted herself, not daring to break stride.

"What the hell was that?!" she yelled, her voice ripping through her throat as her muscles strained to keep moving.

"You don't want to know," Charmelle shouted, her voice muffled. Remi turned her head anyway and saw Charmelle looking back toward the palace. She followed her sightline and Remi's heart leaped into her throat. The Peacekeeper's embassy, the one that had belonged to her grandfather, and the largest building in Bicaidia aside from the palace, had been reduced to nothing but rubble. Her throat constricted with terror as she realized that there was no going back. Bicaidia had been overthrown.

Just then, a roaring battle cry sounded, and a horn blew, its ominous whine making Remi's skin crawl with fear. The ground shook beneath them from the impact of hundreds of thousands of footfalls, getting closer still.

In response to the descending army behind them, Thayne caught her arm and dragged her forward. "Don't stop!" They ran side-by-side now, and she could just make out his voice above the shouts of the demons bearing down on them. "If they get here and Pietyr doesn't have a way out for us, then you need to dematerialize and get as far from here as you can!"

"What?" she yelled, stunned at his suggestion that she just leave them behind. Thayne could call a storm and go anytime he wanted to, riding his lightning and wind to the ends of this planet. So, why did he just want her to disappear? She gritted her teeth. "I'm not going anywhere. If it comes to a fight, then we fight together." It was her mess even more than it was his, and she would damn well make sure she stood by his side to face it.

He growled in frustration but was prevented from arguing further when Pietyr's voice rang out above the melee. "Keep going! We're almost there!"

An arrow encased with black mist sailed past Remi's ear and embedded itself into the glass skyscraper at her side. Her breathing stuttered as she realized how close she'd just come to getting poisoned with it.

She dug deep, pushing her muscles harder than she ever had before. They turned a corner, rounding another alleyway, but were brought up short when thousands of demons filled the gap between buildings, cutting them off.

Remi skidded to a halt, following Pietyr's lead, as did Thayne and Charmelle. They stood in a loose circle now, back-to-back, as the demons filed in around them. They held their black, charmed weapons before them like omens of death to any who dared to challenge them.

The hideous creatures snarled and bared their teeth; their scaly skin, smokey-black eyes, razor-sharp teeth, and claws made Remi's stomach churn with terror. She knew that they'd have to stand and fight if they were to have any hope of survival. They had no choice now.

Thayne passed Ellarah to Charmelle, whose power would be useless in this battle. Healers were of little use in a fight to the death. Remi ushered her and Ellarah to the center of a circle encased by Pietyr on one side, Thayne on another, and Remi on the final one.

The demons licked their lips, closing in on them in a painfully slow crawl that made her muscles clench in terrible anticipation. Knowing what would come next, she closed her fists and fire licked up her arms. She'd never fought with her fire magic before. She'd only ever used it for the benefit of humanity and the gods, but now she would need to wield it like a well-honed weapon. Was she capable?

She drew inside herself and tapped into the well that she had struggled to control her whole life. Her entire body ignited, blue, yellow, and orange flames covering her, encasing her hair in a blazing hot inferno—no part of her burned. Neither skin nor clothes, a benefit to being an upper-caste fire goddess; nothing could burn you save the surface of a star.

Armed and ready now, she looked to her right and saw Thayne, electricity sizzling around him. She heard a crack of thunder and looked up as the billowing, black clouds laced with lightning began to fill the night sky. Then there was Pietyr, just to her right. With shadows surrounding him, gathering around him like pet eels, caressing his skin with their light touch.

They stood in a small clearing at the center of four skyscrapers, in the middle of what had once been a small quad of some kind. Was this where they would die? Remi wondered darkly, refusing to give in to any terror she may have felt at the prospect, while more demons piled into the crossroads between the buildings, surrounding them at least ten rows deep. There had to be 5,000 of them at minimum, maybe more, licking their lips in anticipation of tasting godly blood on their tongues.

Remi's heart hammered, and she bared her teeth. Heat radiated around her, and anticipation of the fight to come pulsed up her spine. She had spared a glance at Ellarah and noticed an eerie black trail of veins infecting that wound in her gut despite Charmelle's field medic ministrations. "What are they waiting for?"

Whatever poison those enchanted weapons contained, she did not want to end up on the wrong end of one. She had a feeling that if that happened to any of them, this fight would be over before it started.

Pietyr answered, "Reinforcements. Madwyn and Riven, or any powerful enough Nefaral that could help them. They know who and what we are. We're the first upper-caste deities they've fought on even ground tonight without the element of surprise."

Thayne and Remi shared a glance that spoke volumes before Thayne nodded his head in approval. Then, with his confirmation, she yelled, "Then I see no reason to wait."

With that, she lunged forward, thrust out her hands, and rained her ethereal fire into the horde of hell in front of her. Thayne followed her lead, and an explosion of light surrounded them as he sent a bolt of pure lightning down in the middle of the demon army. Their bodies flew into the sky, propelled by the force of the strike. The scent of the demons' burning flesh stung Remi's nostrils as she opened her palms and unleashed her fire down on their enemies once more.

A small path cleared before her, and she heard Pietyr shout above the mayhem. "Advance Remi! Thayne, we cover her flanks!" They moved quickly, straining to gain precious ground before more demons closed the gap she'd created. Despite their hurried movements, it took mere seconds for the demons to converge into the fragile opening.

Remi sucked in a breath and loosed her power again, the wind picking up as Thayne called his storm in earnest. Pietyr's power was on full display at that point, his body shadow-walking through the crowd of devils, reaching into their chests and ripping their hearts out at will. Every time they swung their black-coated weapons, he disappeared, reappeared behind them, and issued another deadly blow.

As her magic rang like a song in her blood, Remi had to admit that this felt good—in fact, she'd never felt anything like it. A surge of adrenaline soared through her muscles as she set fire to the evil that had killed all those deities back in the palace and even more on the streets of Helverta. Then, suddenly, a gust of Thayne's mighty wind sent her stumbling forward, forcing her to clothesline a rushing demon to catch her balance.

She risked a glance to her left and saw Thayne's body, coated in lightning. The magnificent electricity of it skittered over his torso, arms, and legs like a million live snakes. He touched the demons and electrocuted them with his hands as the black, billowing clouds above rained down bolts of lightning into the army at random.

They cut another hole before her, moved further down the path that Pietyr demanded they take. Unfortunately, it wasn't long before more demons encircled them yet again. It seemed that hell had an endless supply.

Charmelle shouted, "Pietyr! We need to shadow-walk again! They're not coming, and I'm losing her!" Charmelle's hands glowed a soothing gold once more. However, Ellarah's skin still didn't have the typical reaction of humming white in response to the healing power. Instead, it stayed pallid, and her blood pulsed in a constant stream onto the cobblestoned road beneath them.

Remi's belly knotted in concern and fear for her friend's life as Pietyr snarled and then said, "Don't you think if I could have done that, I would have already?! Damnit, Char, I'm doing the best I can here!"

"Well, it's not good enough!" Charmelle snapped.

In response, Remi kept pushing, drawing from that well of power deep inside her, but to her dismay, she could feel it begin to wane. The edge of it was approaching faster than she would have thought possible. She groaned, pulled hard, dragged more magic up.

But the further she delved into her reserves, the harder it became. She would burn out soon if she wasn't careful. She'd killed thousands of beasts with her magic alone tonight, but she couldn't sustain this much longer. Power was a muscle, after all, and she'd done more toward suppressing hers than using it since she'd come of age.

As the reality began to set in that she was not going to make it much longer, she looked to her right at Thayne and then to Pietyr on her left. She could tell that they had both begun to slow down as well. They must have been reaching the edge of their power too. They'd been using massive surges of their magic, more than they'd ever had to use in their entire lives, in just the past few minutes.

This wasn't good, she thought frantically. They were boxed in, the demons pressing them closer, growing more difficult to hold off with each passing second. They'd killed so many of them, and yet, they kept coming in relentless waves of gnashing teeth and guttural growls. Dimly, in her mind, she knew that Madwyn and Riven probably wouldn't be far behind, drawn to their power like magnets.

A large demon with sharp, yellow teeth and a scaly bald head lunged forward with a broadsword. Remi narrowly side-stepped it and sliced off its hand with a searing hot flame. The creature screamed, dropping to its knees before Thayne sent a bolt of lightning through its chest.

Remi picked up the creature's discarded sword and chucked it at Pietyr. After all, he was a spy, which meant he should be trained to use all manner of weapons, human and godly. Or at least, if he were a Valerian spy, he would be. Remi hoped that the Bicaidian customs were the same as the ones back home.

To her relief, it seemed they were. He swung the sword through the rush of incoming creatures, cutting five of their heads off neatly, then he plunged it into another's heart. Yet still, they lost more ground, the demons closing in tighter around them. Finally, Remi's fire sputtered, and she turned a panicked gaze on Thayne.

"Dig deeper, Remi!" he shouted, his own power showing signs of depletion. "We can't stop! We can't let them win!"

Remi's mind raced, wondering what hope they had to get out of this. They had no backup and nowhere to go. If Pietyr couldn't shadow-walk them out, then what did they plan to do? Refusing to give into blind panic, she concentrated and re-lit the fire on her skin just as it fizzled out.

She could feel exhaustion starting to drag at every fiber of her being and stepped back behind Thayne and Pietyr, moving next to Charmelle. Her heart hammered in her chest, her vision blurring with fatigue as her mind flew from one jumbled thought to the next, trying to formulate a plan that didn't involve her burning out.

But her panic wouldn't allow her to think clearly. After a few beats, she closed her eyes and calmed her breathing, practicing the same techniques that she'd used a million times to control her gift. The sounds around her slowed and then melted away as she focused on the inhale and then the exhale. In, and then out again, she thought, chanting the mantra in her mind.

She had always believed that she had a massive well of magic within her, one so damaging that it could never be unleashed. But if that were the case, then how could she have already reached its end? Power might be a muscle, but something in her gut told her that she had more. She just needed to access it, to find it.

Clinging to this hope, she dug deeper. She delved further inside herself in search of the power she knew was in there. Finally, after a few precious moments of hunting, she found it. More power, but not just a well. A veritable ocean of it.

She hesitated. If she unleashed that ocean now, what would happen? With that much power at her disposal, she feared that she'd incinerate everyone left alive in the city.

Was such a thing even possible?

In all the time she'd experimented with her magic, used it for her work with the mortals, she had never felt anything like this before. Of course, she'd always known that she had a lot of magic at her disposal, but that much power simply hadn't been there before.

So, what the hell was it doing there now?

Before she could even begin to answer that question, without warning, the demons stopped pressing forward and suddenly parted. Madwyn and Riven stood like deadly sentinels, filling the void their demon allies had just created. They advanced on them slowly, as though they wanted to savor every moment of this.

Dread trickled through every cell in her body as Remi realized that there was no chance they were getting out of there. Not with them there. Madwyn's voice sang out like a song through the wind, its beauty a horrible lie. "There you are." A victorious smile stretched wide across her blood-red lips, and she reached out a hand just as a blast of white light burst from the sky and landed right into the center of Remi's allies.

It disappeared as quickly as it had come, and Remi shielded her eyes, stumbling backward and blinking hard. Then, vision clearing, she shook her head to clear it as power pulsed through the air. The static electricity of it raised the hair on her arms, and she looked back to Madwyn and Riven, the chaos deity's arm extended out as though in warning. Riven's gaze had locked onto Ellarah with an urgency in his eyes. But both remained unmoving. That was when she realized they were frozen in time; in fact, everything surrounding them except for her allies remained immobile.

An unfamiliar voice behind them caused her to jump, and she whirled to face it, not daring to call her magic, uncertain she'd be able to control it. "You look like you could use a little help." A god stood before her, his youthful, smooth face surrounded by a flurry of curly hair.

Before she or Thayne could react, Pietyr hurried toward the newcomer and held out his hand. "Rackham!" They clasped each other's wrists and shook like old friends. "Thank the Ascended you found us. We tried to make it back to the rendezvous, but they cut us off before we could get there."

"We saw that you'd been pinned down on the security feeds. It took us longer than we wanted to put together a rescue effort, but Emorie got it done," Rackham said, just as the beam of vibrant light reappeared. "It's now, or never; I can't hold them like this much longer."

Remi stared at the disturbing stillness that surrounded her, so different from the roar of battle they'd been in mere seconds ago, and realized that he was a time deity and a powerful one at that. Time was a tricky gift in the immortal realm, and the fact that he'd been able to stop it at all there proved just how much magic he had at his disposal.

Without hesitation, Charmelle and Pietyr stepped into the light and disappeared, carrying Ellarah's unconscious form with them. But Remi hesitated, her feet feeling frozen to the spot as she gaped at her would-be rescuer. That had been Pietyr's plan all along, to find this time god, and who else? She wondered. Who else would be there once they went with him? Would it be safe? Or just another trick?

Exhaustion tore at her, and she looked at Thayne, desire to follow them to some safe haven, away from all this death and destruction, so visceral she could almost taste it. But, instead, Thayne stepped forward, his voice a low rumble in his throat, "How do we know we can trust you?"

Rackham shrugged his shoulders. "You can either stay here and die or take a chance with me; your call. But I can't hold them any longer." They looked at the demons and Madwyn, their bodies beginning to twitch as though skipping into fast-forward.

Remi thought about it for less than a fraction of a second before she and Thayne stepped into the light with Rackham at their sides. Then, when she turned again, she saw Madwyn shudder as time snapped back.

She could only hope that wherever she landed was better than the hoard of snarling, blood-thirsty demons. After all, what could be worse than this?

CHAPTER 11

BEKKA

Tormented

I stared into the void in front of me and felt my pulse ratchet up a few notches. "Why is hell empty?" There were no human souls, no demons, no...nothing. Our footsteps echoed from the tall, rocky ceilings, and the shuffle of gravel beneath our feet was so loud in the vast silence that I resisted the urge to shush us.

Arrick looked over his shoulder, scanning the massive cavern and endless tunnels that surrounded us. "I don't know, but I have a feeling it's not good." I followed his gaze, then turning my attention to him, I noted the stiff set of his shoulders and intensity in his eyes.

Chills pricked up my forearms at his apparent discomfort. Who could have guessed that the lack of tortured souls and hideous demons would be the thing that made me uncomfortable? "Should we be worried?"

Deklan looked confused but otherwise stoic, while Caden seemed reluctant to move away from the portal entrance back to Moldize as he eyed Arrick for answers.

Arrick halted his slow assessment and turned to face us. "You want the truth?"

I stared. "Always."

Arrick took in the silence and the void around us. "Yes. We should be worried. I've never been to an empty hell. Low occupancy, yes. But empty?" Arrick shook his head in disbelief as he surveyed the scenery. "Never."

We let his words settle for a moment, all three of us shuffling our feet as we considered what this could mean.

At last, I broke the silence. "Maybe this is a good thing." I forged onward, unable to allow my thoughts to take a dark turn. I already had enough concerns, knowing that my sister's life was in imminent danger. So, I nodded my head with a hopeful vigor. "Yeah, maybe it will be easier for us to make it through here so we can get to Remi faster. Fewer obstructions, right?"

Deklan and Caden stared at the cavernous twists of the sickly, yellow tunnels around us, dripping with eerie stalactites, and gave me matching, disbelieving looks. The tunnels jutted off in about a million different directions, with no discernible pattern. Add to that, it smelled like rotting garbage, and it was hot. Uncomfortably so. I yanked off my cargo jacket, leaving only the thin knit tank top beneath it.

Arrick shook his head. "I hate to disappoint you, but without demons or at least some humans here to guide us, it's going to take a long time to find our way out. Every hell I've seen has circles, levels of punishment that increase as you get closer to the center. The portals to the immortal realm are usually within that center circle."

He paused, his tongue wetting his lips, presumably to combat the dry conditions as I asked, "So, what does that mean exactly?" I didn't have any personal experience with hell, so he was going to have to spell this out for me. I imagined that Deklan and Caden probably felt the same way.

"With the way things are right now, I have no idea which circle we've entered. Usually, I can tell by the level of torture, to a degree of certainty at least. While the chambers themselves are part of the punishment, the demons play a critical role, too. Without them and without human souls here, it will make the chambers more difficult to interpret. So, we're...on our own."

"This just keeps getting better," Deklan muttered under his breath. "For the record, I hated this plan from the get-go."

Arrick sighed and rested his hands on his hips. "Thank you for that. That's very helpful."

Deklan lifted a broad shoulder. "It needed to be said."

Caden cleared his throat, interrupting Deklan's soapbox moment. "I take it that going back to Moldize isn't an option?"

Arrick stared over my shoulder to the doorway that still lingered in the middle of Bicaidian hell. It had shifted from an open portal, crackling with power to a simple wooden door. Strange, I thought as I squinted at it. I'd never seen a portal do that before. Arrick's voice pulled my attention back to him. "It's an option, but—"

I interrupted before he could finish his thought. "It won't get us any closer to Bicaidia, and we can't abandon my sister to the Nefarals. This is our only shot at getting to her." My belly clenched as I once again thought about the danger she was in. I hoped that we could hurry the hell up and make it to Bicaidia's capital in time to help quell the rebellion. Sinister imaginings niggled in the back of my mind, but I refused to acknowledge the possibility that it might already be too late.

Arrick nodded. "She's right; this is the only way now."

Caden's vibrant, blue eyes seemed to glow with electricity, his body shimmering with subdued godly light in the dimly-lit cave. "How long will this take us?" His brows drew together, and his lips pressed together with concern. "We only packed a week's supply of food and water. Maybe two, if we ration. Will that be enough?"

I could almost see the wheels turning behind Arrick's eyes as he considered. "I think so, but I can't say for sure. Just to be safe, we should go back and pack heavier before we move forward. We don't want to run out of provisions."

All the hope I'd previously carried that we'd make it to my sister within a day, two at most, deflated. I tried to swallow down my panic as he stepped in front of the Moldizean portal and opened it just like any other door.

But when he did, there was nothing behind it, only the empty cavern that surrounded us. He drew his brows together, closed it, and then reopened it as though a reset would do the trick. Sadly, it didn't. His eyes said, *what the fuck?* But the twist of his mouth said, *oh shit.*

My heart quickened as sweat pricked my hairline. "The portal's gone, isn't it?" I ventured, chewing on a thumbnail, my nerves getting the better of me. This was not a good sign. My mind whirled as I tried to piece together what this meant for us. One week's worth of food, a long journey ahead of us, no powers allowed, and Remi's life in danger? I unleashed a string of colorful curses under my breath that could have made a Puhari raider blush.

Either ignoring me or unable to hear my outburst, Arrick closed the door once more and rested his forearm against it, leaning into the useless portal. "Something has gone very, very wrong here," he grumbled to no one in particular.

"No shit," Deklan agreed, muscles in his arms flexing as he clenched his fists.

Arrick let out a long, suffering breath and tilted his head back as though in prayer. "Do me a favor and pray to the Ascended that this doesn't come back to bite us in the ass," he murmured as a tiny fraction of black mist swirled around his hand like a glove. Fingers encased in power now, he wrapped them around the handle and tried the portal one more time, apparently hoping to reactivate it with his magic.

Adrenaline pulsed through me, knowing exactly why he wanted us to pray. We weren't supposed to use more than the barest fraction of power in this place. So, how could he be certain that this wasn't too much? Simple answer? He couldn't. I watched, gritting my teeth in terrified anticipation, and resisting the urge to stop him.

After a few gut-wrenching seconds, his magic dissipated, and the door remained just a door.

We were trapped.

He let out a long breath and then kicked the door with enough force that it splintered, his booted foot piercing straight through it. Not terribly effective, but I appreciated the sentiment.

I pulled his attention to me with a quiet, "Hey." Despite my own dismay, I rested a hand against his cheek to comfort him, his chest heaving with frustration and anger. "It's going to be okay. We can do this; we just need to work fast."

He took a few more deep breaths before he nodded his head, his dark hair sliding forward just covering his eyes. "You're right," he muttered. He raised his hand to his cheek and covered my fingers with his. They were smooth and calloused, and I was reminded once again of the warrior beneath all that godly polish—the respected Itorian general lurking beneath the handsome exterior. His eyes locked onto mine just before a thought seemed to occur to him. "Shit, we have no way to get in touch with my parents from here."

Concern trickled through me like water. I knew Erykha and Damion could handle themselves, but whatever was trying to break through the Moldizean wards meant business. I didn't like the idea of abandoning them to deal with it on their own.

Arrick shook his head, his jaw flexing as he said the one thing that made me want to rail to the Ascended at the unfairness of it. "The only way out now is through."

"That's just fucking perfect," Deklan blurted, clasping the hilt of his favorite knife, the one I'd affectionately named Mr. Sharpington III.

Caden gripped Deklan's shoulder hard enough that he winced. "You're not helping, brother."

"We're trapped in hell, Caden. Should I be cheerful about that? Would that make you happy?"

"No, but being productive would. We need to scout a way out, which is something we know how to do better than anyone. So, why don't we make ourselves useful?"

Arrick surveyed each of the dozens of tunnels that split off from the circular cavern where we stood and grimaced. "Caden's right. We need to find the fastest route to the center circle."

Deklan stared into a tunnel on his right. Its mouth yawned wide, like a throat decorated with deadly-looking spikes, leading into utter darkness. Shivers ran over my skin despite the heat as I realized we would probably have to venture into a lot of these to find our way to the center.

"That seems like it's easier said than done," Deklan said, arms crossed over his broad chest. "Normally, we could check for fresh air, water, broken twigs, footprints, or something. But in hell? How are we supposed to know what to look for?"

Arrick chewed on his cheek as he considered. "Don't go too far down the tunnels. Look for signs of elemental changes or shifts in the scenery. Like water or fire, snakes or spiders, wind is good too, and then report back here."

"Spiders and snakes?" I asked, my voice filled with a sick kind of dread that I tried and failed to conceal.

"It is hell, you know," Arrick said, raising a dark brow in my direction. "Nothing we encounter will be pleasant. The tunnels themselves will lead to..." He cleared his throat. "...torture chambers. We'll have to endure that chamber and cross it to get to the next tunnel. It's the only way."

I could feel my expression tighten involuntarily, my lips pressing together as I took in this knowledge. I wanted to react, but I knew I couldn't allow myself to right now. If I gave myself a chance to consider this as my new reality, I might start to panic, and I had more pressing matters at hand. First, I needed to get to my sister, and then we needed to find a way back to Valeria. After all, I had to do the right thing here and take up my mantle as Gabryel's heir before it was too late.

Composing my frantic innards, I looked at Caden and Deklan to gauge their reaction as well. Their faces had turned to stone, the standard battle mask of Itorian warriors.

Deklan spoke first out of the three of us, "Then let's split up the tunnels and get to work. The sooner we start, the sooner we can get the hell out of…hell."

Agreeing, we split the circular cavern into eight tunnels per person. I found that after going a good, long distance down each of the tunnels, signs of change began to manifest themselves. Winds rustled, water began to drip from the ceilings, slithering snakes and furry spiders moved around my feet, or heat pulsated around me.

I labeled each cavern with a symbol outside its wall and surveyed them each with pursed lips. They all had themes to them. Torture by themes seemed horrific and meticulous, but I tried my best not to dwell on it and forced my imagination not to go too far down the rabbit hole. At least I didn't have to listen to the souls of the tortured scream for hours on end. So there was one perk to hell's eerie emptiness.

Once we all finished with our sections, we stood in the center of the room and took stock of our handiwork. Arrick read all of the labels I'd made and asked the brothers about their locations. They had made their own notations but in Itorian shorthand from their homeworld.

Arrick cupped his chin in thought. "So, we have four fires, four wind tunnels, four water chambers, four pitch black, four bright lights, four shrieks, four radiations zones, and four insect/arachnid/reptile rooms." I shivered at the last, relieved that I'd only happened upon one of the reptile rooms. I about pissed my pants when a snake began to slither up my leg.

My squeals of horror had been quickly chased by Deklan's belly laugh when I came sprinting back through the tunnel, flailing like I'd been set on fire—it hadn't been my most dignified moment.

"Any clue which way is the best one?" Caden asked. Something about the way his eyes drifted to the radiation chambers let me know that he hoped Arrick wouldn't choose one of those. I couldn't blame him for that. He and Deklan had just narrowly survived their most recent trip through a radiation zone, and it hadn't been pretty.

As for me, I dreaded both the critters and the water tunnels. All but the most intense radiation couldn't penetrate our godly skin anyway, so it was unlikely to cause any severe damage. But water...ugh. I hated the idea of slogging through the next however many days soaked to the bone. There was nothing more uncomfortable than wet boots. Or a wet bra, for that matter. And anything creepy crawly? No thank you.

"Let's try wind," Arrick answered. His voice filled with certainty, but there was a flash of hesitation in his eyes that didn't fill me with confidence. Instead, I got the immediate impression that he'd just picked the lesser of all evils. Which made sense if I thought about it, considering our location.

"You're sure?" I asked, staring down the tunnel he'd gestured to. I looked back at him. "'Cause, you don't seem all that sure."

Arrick shook his head. "You're right. I'm not. I didn't design this place, so I don't know what comes next, but we have to start somewhere. At least this way, we can establish a pattern. If we can follow one method of torture all the way through hell, it should get us to the center faster."

A thought occurred to me as I remembered something I'd learned a long time ago when I'd interned at the Nefaric

Pillar of Power. "Aren't the inner rings supposed to be the worst parts of hell?"

Arrick didn't mince words. "Yep."

"Then why wind?" Caden asked, a look of genuine confusion plastered on his face.

Arrick ran a hand over his hair in mild exasperation. "It doesn't matter at this point. Each form of punishment will lead to its own inner circle. It's all based on what each human feared most while they were alive. So, we just need to pick one and follow it to the middle."

I felt nausea and anxiety swell in my belly as I stared down the wind tunnel. I'd been the one who'd ventured down this particular one—the whistling and the way the breeze whipped through my hair did not bode well.

Despite my trepidation, we sallied forward, moving down the tunnel at a quick clip, the smell growing more rancid the further down it we went. I wondered if this would continue to worsen as we got closer to the center circle, but I refrained from asking. Honestly, I didn't want to know.

We hiked about a mile before we started to hear that subtle whistle once more and another hour before the howl started. By the third hour, it turned into a dull roar, and we entered another large, circular room filled with tunnels.

At the center of this room, swirling with ominous power, was a massive, green, glowing tornado. Within it whipped all kinds of consumer products from the mortal realm, like ground-bound domiciles, tiled roofs, and large panes of glass. Every so often, it shot one of these dangerous objects from its funnel cloud and shattered it against a rocky wall.

Lightning crackled within the cyclone and electrified everything swirling in its depths, and out of nowhere, it threw a sizzling toaster at me. It smacked me square in the chest, and the electrical cord swung around, the prongs slapping against my forehead. The force and shock of the blow sent me sprawling backward and crashing against a wall. After a moment to catch my breath from the sudden onslaught, I let out a tinny wheeze. "Ow."

Arrick stepped between me and the cyclone, presumably to give me a moment to compose myself before I got hit with something bigger. A riding lawn mower, perhaps? He gripped my upper arms to steady me and searched me with his eyes. Finally, he mouthed, "You OK?" and gave me the *OK* hand signal to further emphasize his point.

We were gods, so he knew that physically, I was fine. Only a killing event inspired by godly magic could do me genuine harm, but I assumed he meant the question in reference to whether I had composed myself enough to stand without his assistance. I nodded, then peered over his shoulder and eyed the tornado with suspicion. Clearly, it had a problem with me. Otherwise, why would it have hit me with a toaster? It hadn't picked on anyone else.

Arrick gave me a thumbs up since there was no point in yelling. Even a full-throated scream wouldn't enable us to hear a damned thing in this room. He pointed to a doorway on the opposite side of the cavern and gestured for us to follow him.

We shimmied along the edges of the rocky cave, the wind howling so loud that I felt like my brain might leak out of my ears at any moment. The force of it whipped my braid, causing it to swing around and slap me in the face, along with anyone else dumb enough to get in my general vicinity—namely, Deklan.

As we continued pushing toward the door and what I hoped would be our exit from this terrible place, I wished that we could just magic our way out of here. However, I had to remind myself of the possible repercussions, should we resort to that option. I did not want to unintentionally invite a Nefaral from Bicaidia to find us infiltrating their hell dimension.

As we passed around the massive, grey band of roaring winds, I counted the objects I could see within it. Finally, I stopped when a human skeleton, still intact despite the turmoil it endured, soared past us.

And that was when I realized what this particular form of punishment must look like from a human standpoint. People would swirl around in the tornado, getting pelted with objects and electrocuted for all eternity. Alone, with a demon presiding and probably adding their own elements of torment to the twister. Or maybe not all eternity, but at least until that presiding demon decided that they'd completed their sentence. Then they would just wink them out of existence, leaving nothing but a skeleton behind, as foreshadowing for those who remained.

The notion of it sent chills rippling over my skin, and I counted the seconds until we crossed the distance to the far doorway. Once safe within the precipice between caverns, I turned back to offer the cyclone a final, departing glance. I saw the skeleton once more and realized that there were no living or, well, undead inhabitants within it. This didn't surprise me but instead reaffirmed the eerie sensation that something didn't seem right here.

Turning my back to the tornado, we kept walking. The emptiness that existed in this place felt like both a salve and an irritant. The same question played on repeat in my skull. What happened here? Which was promptly followed by the secondary refrain of *'Why is hell empty?'*

And, on top of the sense of emptiness, I had this strange sensation of something watching me. Like eyes were fixed on the back of my neck at all times. But every time I turned to investigate it, I saw nothing. So, after a while, I'd written it off as some secondary layer of hell's torments. An uncomfortable feeling I'd just have to live with every moment we remained here.

As we traversed the rocky tunnels, I wondered if all hell dimensions were fashioned after giant ant hills or if it was just a Bicaidian thing. I wanted to ask Arrick but didn't want to interrupt our forward progress. As it stood, I felt like four massive bugs crawling through a foreign creature's nest. The worst part about that assessment was that maybe it wasn't all that off the mark.

Hours passed as we went through more tunnels, each one growing more minor in punishment from the last. A little sandstorm in the desert, but nothing insurmountable, was the last straw. After that, Arrick convinced us to turn back. We had gone in the wrong direction and had ventured into a more outer layer of hell.

I watched Arrick's back as we returned to where we had started. His muscles were tense beneath his sweat-soaked t-shirt, all coiled ribbons of frustration. We may not have known each other long, but I liked to think that we were battle-tested. That was my way of referring to a relationship that seemed disproportionately close for the amount of time spent together.

We had seen each other at our absolute worst and our absolute best, but there had been little of the in-between. I found that I longed for the mundane once more. Before I'd left Valeria, my life had been so simple. I'd been preparing for my role as the quasi-mortal defective granddaughter of The Peacekeeper of the Twelve Realms when Arrick had kidnapped me. Since then, everything had taken a sharp right turn into insanity, and I hadn't had a chance to take a breath since.

Then once we got to Bicaidia, we'd face something even more terrifying and dangerous than anything we'd witnessed before. We'd have to quell a rebellion. I hoped it hadn't gone too far. That the pillar leadership and the royals still maintained some level of control over their realm. That I'd have some allies to look to once we arrived. Because if not, then I had no idea what we were going to do.

After another careful circumvention, we cleared the tornado chamber, no accidents this time, and made it back to the unusable Moldizean portal. As we arrived, our breaths labored heavily from the effort we'd expanded.

"Which one next?" I asked, my throat dry as sandpaper. I reached into my pack, the exterior of which had been battered by our excursion through the tornado. However, I was pleased to find that all of the contents inside remained clean and intact, including my jacket. Dusting sand from our fingers and faces as best we could, we each sucked down greedy gulps of water from our canisters.

Arrick spoke between sips, "We keep pressing. We aim to get to the next circle before morning." I looked around the cave, wondering how we'd be able to tell when morning came. The cave was dank and dimly lit, like dusk just as the sun falls below the horizon. Time was impossible to tell in here, something I'd already begun to find disorienting.

I tilted my water container back to take another sip, but Arrick rested his hand on it to stop me. "You'll need to conserve that. We should ration, just to be safe."

Deklan stopped with his own canister halfway to his mouth and stared at Arrick. "You think we'll be here longer than a week? I thought you said we should be fine."

Arrick shrugged. "We should prepare for the worst-case scenario." We all put our canisters back into our packs and shifted them onto our backs.

Caden's electric eyes settled on his cousin. "Okay, we ration. One meal a day, no snacks. Eight ounces of water a day. If we do that, then we should make it the full two weeks."

My eyes widened. "We'll be starving by then." As gods, we could make it without food and water for a long time. But there was a caveat. Unless we maintained our bodies with regular, prolonged stasis sleep, we would weaken without that fuel. For obvious reasons, we didn't have time for long, lazy days of stasis sleep. We needed to spend every moment we could looking for the inner circle.

Then there was the issue of the twins. Being in the immortal realm seemed to have strengthened them, enhancing the demi-god part of their heritage. But could they make it on minimal food and full-body exertion every single day for two weeks?

Deklan answered my concern with a simple, "We've had worse. This is nothing we can't handle." I shook my head, stunned that they didn't consider this to be the monumental setback that I did. But then I thought back to my time in Itoriah and remembered how they had lived in that village. Minimal water, minimal food, and minimal resources. Half the people on Myhzrele, Moldize's only life-sustaining planet, had been starving slowly over decades. So, they were probably more equipped to handle this dietary restriction than I was.

"Good, we're in agreement," Arrick replied, shifting his pack onto his back. "We need to make sure we keep our packs as secure as possible. Most of our food and supplies are protected in water-tight packaging, but we're going to face some serious obstacles the closer we get to the center. So we need to make sure we hold onto these at all costs."

"Noted," Caden said, tightening the front strap of his pack and testing its strength. "Where do we go from here, Arrick?"

"We try all the wind torture chambers. The one we just went through was an outer circle. Eventually, we are bound to hit an inner one, and then we should find the portal from there."

We all nodded, and I tried not to remember the tornado. Arrick continued, "There will be other elements at play. Or at least, there usually are. Sand, water, and other objects that are part of the wind torment."

I remembered the toaster and grimaced. "This is going to hurt, isn't it?"

"Don't worry. Our bodies are physical, living. This realm is made for the metaphysical. Nothing in these chambers can kill your physical bodies, but they can hurt you. We just have to push through."

The determination on his face, the look of pure drive he wore made me appreciate him even more than I already did. He was doing this for me, for my sister, for the stability of the Twelve Realms. My chest swelled with gratitude as I watched his handsome face harden, the look of the warrior in place now. He was the general, and he was leading us into battle. So, without further preamble, we moved onto another wind tunnel.

This one turned out to be worse than the last.

We walked for two more hours before the cavern walls opened wide to reveal a sandy beach with crystal blue water. For a moment, it looked like we'd landed in a tropical paradise, but I knew that couldn't be the case considering our locale. Then I looked up as the wind started to whip around us, and the ceiling morphed into a blackening sky. Though I knew it had to be an optical illusion when I saw nothing but miles of gray-blue water and angry clouds as I looked out into the ocean.

One word rebounded through my mind as lightning struck the water and three massive waterspout twisters formed: Hurricane. Arrick yelled something, once again inaudible under the oppressive wind as the gigantic storm bore down on us. He took off at a dead sprint, and we followed without question, like obedient soldiers.

The waves grew taller, and we fought our way through the thick, ever-sinking sand. Though we all had some level of godly strength, the sand seemed to suck us down and sap our energy. Magic seemed to enhance every granule of it, I realized, my legs burning as I dug deep into my energy reserves.

I squinted and could see the exit that Arrick ran at full speed to reach. If we didn't make it, we would be sandwiched between the crashing waves and the walls of the cavern on the other side of the narrow strip of sandy beach.

We fought our way down the beach, and the sand and torrential winds seemed to be fighting back harder the closer we got to the door. In the dim recesses of my mind, I realized that this journey would be impossible for a human and that the exit would have existed to torment them. They likely wouldn't have known that it was the entrance into another ring of hell, probably worse than this one. They would have expected it to be their salvation, running toward it for decades and never reaching their imagined safe haven.

Waves lapped at our feet, then our calves, and all the way up to our thighs as we slogged through the slush of water and sand. The waves took over now, pressed onto us by the wind, and we swam for all we were worth. As the water rose and the waves crashed us into the cavern wall, I could see that the door had disappeared beneath the water. We swam forward anyway, a preternatural current dragging us backward as we fought against it.

By the time we, at last, reached the sea cliff where the arched doorway had once been, the wind whipped over the surface of the water and created a choppy disaster around us. Arrick made a follow-me gesture and pointed down; then, he sucked in a breath and dove. I followed without hesitation, as did the brothers.

My eyes stung from the salty water as I tried to see through the dark depths and locate Arrick. I caught sight of the light of his utility watch and followed it. Using my hand on the wall to guide me, I dragged myself down further and further into the dark depths. As a god, I could hold my breath indefinitely, so I wasn't concerned with drowning. I just wanted to get out of here before I got trapped underwater with no exit. I liked talking and breathing and couldn't do either underwater. Finally, I felt a break in the seawall and found the arch. I turned to the brothers, who were just above me, and gestured for them to follow.

As I crossed through a barrier of water and into fresh air, I fell on my knees and into a room that seemed too picturesque for hell, if you asked me.

I had about one second to get my bearings before the mountains of golden sand beneath me were blasted with gale-force winds. They hit my body full-on and sent me soaring across the room and smacking into the rock wall behind me. Again.

As I tried to detach myself from the rocky surface, my three companions flew right at me. Deklan slammed into the wall on my right, Caden on my left, and Arrick? Well, Arrick slammed into it right on top of me. Perfect. Absolutely perfect. He pressed his hands on either side of my body and struggled with gritted determination to detach himself from me. I groaned from the pressure of his rock-solid body against mine.

Just when he'd pried his upper body away from me, the wind abruptly stopped, and we all fell to the ground in a heap of limbs and weapons. I was straddling him then. Even better, I thought, exasperated.

"We need to move," Arrick rasped as I rolled to the side, rising to my feet. He pointed forward, and I saw the exit. This time, it was a large, carved stone doorway.

We started to run, but wind roared through the chamber once more. We flew into the wall and then fell into a heap for a second time. We repeated this process for a few joyous hours, making it about three steps before we got blasted each time. Correction, one time, we made it ten steps before the cursed winds started up again. The only positive thing I had to say about this experience was that by the time we made it to the last chamber, I was dry.

When we started toward the next installment of torture, I felt a little like a puppy who had been kicked too many times and was suspicious of all hell-related things. But when we entered the room, there was nothing. Instead, it was an exact replica of the first room we had gone through—a central tunnel.

Arrick smiled at me, dark hair grainy with sand. "This is a good sign. We made it through a circle."

I coughed up sand and spat on the ground beneath us, pulling my water canister out of my pack again. I gestured to fifteen new tunnels, all leading in different directions. "It seems like we're right back where we started."

Arrick shook his head. "No. If you look closer, there are fewer tunnels here than in the last cavern. That means we're making progress. We're getting closer to the center."

In response to this bit of good news, Deklan and Caden each leaned against a cavern wall and proceeded to puke up a disgusting combination of seawater and sand. I thanked the Ascended for my pristine godly constitution. Puking sans toothpaste was not an experience I hoped to relive any time soon.

I turned back to Arrick. "I defer to you since you're the expert. But we only made it through two tunnels today. What if we don't guess as well on the next go around?"

"Then we keep trying tunnels until we do."

Caden's face was ashen when he stumbled closer to us. "In the morning, though, right? We're going to make camp for now?"

Arrick's brows drew together as he looked at the utility watch on his wrist, frowning again. He looked back up to Caden, the expression on his face peculiar. He looked…surprised? He shook his head as though to clear it. "Yes, of course. It's 1300 Moldizean time right now, and it's been a long night. We'll rest for now." That meant we had been at this for twelve hours straight, without any sleep. No wonder Caden and Deklan had demanded that we rest.

With that, Caden nodded, pulled his pack off his back, and let it fall to the floor. We all followed suit, each taking conservative sips from our water cannisters. How were we going to make it through any length of time on eight ounces of water and one meal per day after we spent the entire day being tortured? I wondered, taking another measured sip.

As I looked around the cavern, I realized that it was so dark that I couldn't see two feet in front of me. I heard rustling right before a light switched on and provided some modicum of visibility. I blinked, trying to force my eyes to adjust, but still had to squint to see past my hand.

Arrick let out a frustrated breath next to me. "The cavern is charmed with magic, a common torture element of hell is to suppress visibility even in the hubs between chambers. That means that our lantern's light won't travel far here. This is as good as it's going to get."

I knew then, that it was going to be one helluva crappy night. Rather than voice that aloud, I thanked the Ascended that we still had our godly light. So, at least that way we could see each other. After sitting around the dim lantern, we each grabbed our food from our packs—dried meat and fruit, along with nuts, all non-perishable and easy enough to carry—and ate in silence, each of us a little shell shocked.

Or, well, most of us were. Arrick seemed fine, completely undisturbed, and I had the horrible realization that this was a typical day-in-the-life for him.

Sometimes I forgot what he did for a living, but my time here was making that harder to ignore. He ruled over a place for humans to be tortured for all eternity. Bad humans, sure. Evil pricks who deserved it because, according to him, he never sent any but the most deserving to the depths of Moldizean hell. But still, he ran the mirror of this place in his home realm.

What kind of a toll would that take on someone?

Of course, I knew the answer to that. I just had to look at the history of the death deities who'd come before him. Most of them had lost their minds, compassion, and ability to relate to the living before they even hit middle age. Most of the time, their lives had ended in blood or sizzling alive on the surface of a star. But when I looked at him, his golden skin, and vibrant, green eyes full of empathy and kindness, he seemed so different than his predecessors had been.

As I chewed, I turned my attention to Caden and Deklan. They each sat, one the mirror of the other, their legs stretched outward toward the fire.

Chewing absently, I observed Caden's deep, tanned face and his white-blond hair. Though we hadn't seen any specific magic from them yet, his skin glowed with his demi-god power. Every once in a while, I could swear that I saw an ethereal light pulse around both brothers. But then it would fade away again, and I'd be left wondering, had I really just seen that? Or had I imagined it?

"Staring is considered impolite, you know," Caden said as he bit into a piece of jerky.

I blushed and looked down at my food. "Right, my mistake." But a few minutes later, I looked back at him and found myself wondering once more. Would they develop powers? And if they did, what would that be like? Weaker than a normal god's? Or would their presence in the immortal realm make them stronger, more…godly? I looked back at them, assessing them with care as I pondered the possibilities.

He turned his attention to me and raised his brows. "You're doing it again." When I didn't reply, he sighed. "If there's something you want to say, just say it."

I shook my head and took another bite of jerky. "It's just that—" I paused, trying to think of exactly what I wanted to say or ask.

Deklan snorted. "For the love of God, or, well, your Ascended, just ask, Bekka. We all know you aren't shy."

He had a point, so I went with direct. "It's your light. It seems like it's getting brighter." Here, in hell, there was no need for the built-in dimmer switch we used when we entered the mortal realm. Death deities ruled over their demons, so they knew all about us and what we looked like.

In response to my observation, Caden and Deklan looked down at the skin on their hands, matching frowns of surprise in place. I tried not to snicker. They were so cute, I mused, moving my hand up to cover my mouth as I thought about the size of the brick Deklan would shit if he knew I thought of him as cute. Even if it was just one time.

"It does?" Deklan asked, twisting his hand to-and-fro, trying to get a better look at it.

"Yeah, it does," I answered. "What I wanted to know is…do you feel, I don't know…magicky?"

Arrick's eyes had fastened onto the brothers as he considered my observation. He leaned forward, forearms resting on his knees as he evaluated them.

"How do you mean?" Caden asked.

I looked at Arrick and tried to think about how it had felt when I'd come into my powers. It hadn't been all that long ago for me, so the memory was still semi-fresh. Though, a lot had happened since then, and add to that, my magic felt different now.

At first, it had felt like a massive, uncontrollable tsunami, overtaking every part of me without my permission. It had been terrifying, suffocating, but also invigorating. Now though, the magic felt fused to my body in seamless harmony, another limb that I operated with ease.

I opened my mouth to explain, but Arrick beat me to it. "When I came into my powers, it felt like a buzzing under the skin at first. Almost like I had millions of ants marching just beneath the surface of it. The energy started subtly, and it lasted for a few weeks before the magic materialized."

I raised my brows, a little surprised. "Weeks?" I asked, pursing my lips together. "Mine happened all in one day." I made an explosion gesture with my hands and blew out a raspberry to demonstrate. "But, I know for a fact that it's a little different for everyone."

Deklan frowned at both of us. "Then no, I don't feel *magicky*. I feel exactly the same as I always have." A pulse of light seemed to shimmer off of him, and I squinted my eyes, not sure if I'd really seen it or not.

Shaking my head in uncertainty, I looked at Caden. "What about you? Any tingles?"

Caden chuckled, shaking his head. "No, same as Deklan. Everything feels normal."

"Huh," I said, shrugging a shoulder. Maybe I was off base here, but I could swear that I sensed a change in them. I could be wrong. Twelve Hells, that'd be nothing new, but there definitely seemed to be something else at play here.

Before we could interrogate them further, I heard the unmistakable sound of gravel shifting and pebbles falling. I whipped my head around, hand on my knife, and rose into a crouching position. My companions reacted just as quickly, Arrick drawing his gun and Caden his sword while Deklan held Mr. Sharpington III. The sleek metal of the blade gleamed in the lantern light, and I strained to see into the darkened tunnel on the opposite side of the room where the sound had come from.

That was when I felt it again, the sensation of being watched. I could feel eyes boring into me as if I'd stumbled into some kind of a mortal-world horror film.

Were we truly alone here? Or were we just fooling ourselves? I wondered, hairs rising to attention on the back of my neck as Arrick jerked his weapon to indicate the tunnel we'd all fixated on. His lithe body had turned to steel now, and I knew he'd switched to general mode, a transition I approved of at this current juncture.

When he spoke, his tone brooked no argument. "I'll take point. Bekka, file in behind me, Caden and Deklan, you guard our backs." I could hear my pulse thrumming as I trailed behind Arrick, following his lead with my ears trained down the tunnel. The cavern had fallen into silence around us now, the only sound our combined breathing as we approached the tunnel.

I stared into it, my eyes narrowing into slits with the effort to see in the utter darkness it held. We moved in perfect harmony, all of us used to working together after everything that had happened in Itoriah. I understood how they moved, how they operated, and I knew how to complement that. I was no longer the broken cog in their well-oiled machine. I was a functioning member of it.

As our footfalls crunched, the sound barely audible, we entered the mouth of the tunnel. We took a few steps into it, darkness blanketing us like a cloak as we strained to locate what had made that sound. I tried to think through the thrumming pulse in my ears before I realized that maybe the sound had just been a natural part of this hell's caverns.

Maybe, we'd heard a rock come loose from the cavernous ceiling and nothing more. The further we ventured into the tunnel with no sign of anything living or, well, undead, the more I began to believe that we'd just overreacted, that I hadn't felt a sensation of being watched. That maybe, that had just been in my head.

After another minute of venturing through the pitch-black passageway, Arrick stopped walking. He held up his hand, the darkness swallowing everything but the glow of his skin. "There's nothing here."

Deklan whispered, "Something doesn't feel right."

I looked around the narrow tunnel; I couldn't see anything, and I didn't feel anything either. The sensation of being watched had disappeared just as fast as it had come. Caden's voice drew my attention back to him. "Deklan is right. That sound…it wasn't just a rock falling. You know that."

Arrick holstered his weapon and ran a hand through his hair. "I can't disagree with you. But whatever might have been here is gone now. So, we sleep in shifts and keep watch."

I grimaced as I realized that this meant less stasis sleep. With little food and constant torture, that would take a significant toll on all of us. Yet, I didn't disagree with him; I knew it would be for the best, just in case something was stalking us. But, we needed to find our way out here before those two weeks of supplies ran out, or we would be in bad shape when we got to Bicaidia. Two weeks of near starvation would make us little help to anyone if the conflict with the Nefarals had escalated.

Arrick's voice pulled me out of my dark musings. "Deklan, you lead the way back; I'll hold up the rear." We followed his orders, still alert as we made our way back to the central cavern. I saw zero sign of activity from anything, just a lifeless, empty tunnel. Finally, we turned a bend, and I could see the dim lantern-light from the opening of the central cavern where we'd left our packs.

I sighed in relief, ready to be out of the dark, enclosed area. We picked up our pace as the cavern focused into view, but when we reached the entrance, my limbs went cold with horror.

"Shit," Deklan breathed, and my stomach dropped. My hands flew to my mouth as a string of curses filled my mind. Panic swelled in my chest, and I tried not to fall to my knees and give in to it.

Arrick let out a growl of rage that echoed off the walls around us, boomeranging and rattling in my mind. He hauled back his fist and slammed it into the cavern wall. The impact resulted in a huge hole that sheathed his arm all the way to his shoulder as the ceiling shuddered. Rocks and gravel tumbled to the ground around us, and I sprung out of the way to avoid getting pummeled by one about the size of my fist.

Arrick's green eyes were feral, and his breath heaved when he extricated his arm from the wall. Then, shaking his smooth, unmarred hand, he snarled, "Whoever did this is going to pay."

I looked at him, understanding his fury, the rage that surrounded him like a shroud. Because I felt it too. I wanted to scream, pound my fists into the walls, and beat whoever had screwed with us to a bloody pulp. Judging by the fury on Caden and Deklan's faces, they wanted to do the same.

Because our packs, along with all of our supplies, were gone.

CHAPTER 12

REMI

The Rising

R emi landed hard on an unforgiving floor, her legs buckling as she went down on one knee...again. Adrenaline still pumped through her veins, and she rose to her feet without hesitation. Her heart hammered in her chest, and her breaths came in quick puffs, like an athlete's after a sprint.

The idea that they might actually be rescued, be safe, hadn't registered in her mind. So she whirled around and clenched her fists, too afraid of the vast ocean of power to dare dredging it up. Instead, she held her hands at the ready, prepared to fight with them if it came to that.

As she took stock of the current threat level, she saw nothing but a silent room. Thayne, Pietyr, and the god who'd shown up and given them an exit strategy all stood around her. What was it Pietyr had called the time deity? Rackham?

She unclenched her fists and forced her breathing to calm. Uncertain of her new surroundings, she used a calculating gaze to survey them. Sleek metal, white walls, and leather furniture in an array of bold colors filled the room she inhabited.

It looked like an ultra-fashionable office building. Or maybe the lounge area of one of the fancy apartment buildings that the upper-caste deities called home. But the eeriest part of it all was the silence—no roar of demon hoards, no thunder, and no screams of the dead or dying.

She squeezed her eyes shut, tears springing at their corners, as she tried to let the adrenaline that had been pumping through her body settle into some sense of normalcy.

But a thought interrupted her.

"Ellarah!" she shouted, turning to the god who'd gotten them out of that cursed battle. "Where's Ellarah? Please, I need to know if she's OK." Remi lunged forward and twisted her hands into the fabric of his shirt, her blood still high from the fight. She shook him as she snarled, "Tell me right now, or I swear to the Ascended—" She broke off, swallowing hard as she tried to control the full range of her emotions. Terror for her friend, edginess from the battle, sorrow for Thayne's family, and for all the innocent gods and goddesses who probably hadn't made it out of the city alive.

Then, of course, the guilt. It came last but most forceful of all. She closed her eyes for a brief moment and pushed it all down, pushed it back. This wasn't the time to come unglued. That could wait. Right now, she needed to focus on one thing at a time.

The god held up his hands, his face the picture of calm. "You'll want to take your hands off me, sweetheart."

Blood heating with renewed vigor at the disrespectful nickname, Remi twined them further into his shirt. Her nails bit against his skin, but she didn't care. "Not until you tell me—"

Before she could finish her sentence, the god disappeared. He reappeared two feet away from her, and her hands were suddenly at her side. She blinked. What the—?

She opened her mouth to yell at him, but he held up a hand to silence her. "Ellarah is fine. We thought it best to jump her straight to our surgical domicile. Charmelle and a few others are tending to her now. We'll join her in a few moments."

She let out a long sigh of relief as she ran her hands through her loose, fallen hair. Undoubtedly, if Ellarah had died, then they wouldn't be tending to her at all. She could feel her hands shaking as she took in long, deep breaths.

Rackham's eyes narrowed, and his jaw flexed as he turned his attention to Pietyr. "Now, onto the more important matters at hand. What the hell happened down there?"

Without warning, a loud crack issued from beside her. Remi turned to see Pietyr, shoulders heaving with anger, a large hole in the stone wall, and one leg covered in dust. "They betrayed us! That's what fucking happened!" He snarled and raked his nails through his hair, eyes wild with rage. Throughout the battle, he'd seemed so controlled, but in that moment, Remi could see the naked fury he must have been controlling all along.

"Madwyn and Riven?" Rackham asked, eyes widening. After a moment, he shook his head decidedly. "They wouldn't. There's no way...they've been dedicated to the cause from the start. They're founding members—"

Pietyr shook his head. "They did. Just like I said they would. I told you the intelligence was good. We should have had constant eyes on them from the second it came through."

"But that's the whole reason you were there tonight, Pietyr. That's why we called you home early from that bullshit mission for the royals—to keep an eye on them."

Pietyr stepped closer to Rackham, his shadows spilling all around him like liquid smoke now. Rage seemed to boil off of him in hot coils. "We needed more than exterior surveillance. We needed eyes in their home and an operative we could trust in their inner circle. Twelve Hells, Rackham, Madwyn unleashed her power with every pillar leader and the royals present; she didn't even bother to consider the consequences. She probably didn't care. And after that, everyone lost their damned minds. But before I could make sense of what happened, she'd disappeared. Along with these two, Ellarah, and Madwyn's slimy prick of a brother." He turned from everyone and paced, his hands locking behind his neck in evident frustration. "They opened a portal to hell, Rackham, and cut off travel and communication to all the other realms and the rest of Bicaidia. Then they killed every pillar leader that didn't side with them, along with the king and queen. It's all gone."

Rackham's mouth dropped open, a stunned kind of horror plain on his face. "Ascended."

Pietyr's granite expression said it all. Ascended, indeed.

Remi's mind whirled as she tried to process everything that they'd just said. Finally, she turned to look at Thayne, who seemed equally as perplexed as she was. What in the Twelve Hells was going on?

Thayne took one decisive step between the arguing gods, and static electricity filled the room. Remi felt the hair on her arms rise in response and took a step back, out of the line of fire. She could sense the fury vibrating from her husband, and she did not want to get in the middle of this one. Thayne's fists clenched as he growled, "What cause? Founders of what? What are you talking about?"

Pietyr and Rackham looked at Thayne, and they cringed in unison. The first cleared his throat and appealed to Rackham for support, but the time god just shrugged in response. "Cat's out of the bag now. Might as well read him in and hope he doesn't electrocute us until we drop into stasis sleep for the next two years."

Pietyr's jaw flexed and he looked over his shoulder and down the hallway. He seemed nervous, which was an odd look on him. Admittedly, Remi had just met him, but he didn't seem like the sheepish type. If she had to guess, she would say that there was something he cared about back there. Something he didn't want her or Thayne to see.

Thayne ground out each word with care. "Read me in on what?"

After a long hesitation, Pietyr finally said, "The Nefaral Uprising, or as we like to call it, The Rising. Welcome to ground zero."

Remi's mouth dropped open as she sucked in a horrified gasp. Shock overwhelmed her system for the thousandth time in the last hour. The Rising? Hadn't they just escaped the uprising and the Nefarals who'd planned it? So they were in the midst of it's what? Headquarters? Because upon second examination, that had to be what this place was, a command center of some kind. Why else would they call it base?

But before Remi could react further, Thayne rushed forward, gripped Pietyr's collar in his fist, and punched him square in the jaw. Remi heard a horrifying crunch and realized that Pietyr hadn't bothered to defend himself. Thayne hauled back his fist and slammed it into Pietyr's face once more.

"You?!" Thayne roared, his rage echoing off the walls. Remi could almost taste the anger pulsing off of him in white-hot waves, and who could blame him? His parents had just died, his city had been sacked, and his closest friend and the goddess he'd once loved had betrayed him. "You planned this?!" Without letting Pietyr answer, he went for another punch, but this time Pietyr shadow-walked, disappearing into darkness before reappearing behind Thayne.

Thayne stumbled forward, the sudden shift in weight disorienting him. He spun, his eyes wild with fury, and lunged forward, but Pietyr danced backward. He held up his hand in warning, eyes narrowed, and snarled, "I gave you two free shots, but no more, Thayne. If you bothered to listen to anything we just said two damn minutes ago, then you'd know that we didn't plan this. We were betrayed, same as you!"

Thayne's breaths came heavily as he clenched and unclenched his fists. "I do listen, you bastard. You said you came back just to keep an eye on them. You knew something was wrong. So why didn't you bother to say something?"

Pietyr's temper seemed to snap then and he roared in response to Thayne's accusation, "I'm not the one who gave them the keys to the damned kingdom. If I'd known what reckless bullshit you five had planned, I wouldn't have let it happen. I'd have stopped it. But the fact was I didn't know, and by the time I found out, it was too late." He paused and inhaled as the shadows that swelled around him seemed to shudder with frustration. Thayne's face was cold as winter ice as Pietyr stepped closer to him and continued. "All we knew was that Madwyn and Riven had been working to pull support from the more radical in our movement. Not all of us wanted a damn coup. We especially didn't want an all-out war. Before this happened, we were looking for the proof we needed to turn them both into the council."

Rackham stepped closer then, crossing his arms over his chest. "He's right, prince. They were going to ruin everything. Twelve Hells, they did ruin everything." He shook his head and looked out a window. Remi's eyes followed his gaze as silence descended once more, and noticed for the first time that the scenery hadn't changed. Her skin crawled as she realized that they were tucked into the Hylayah mountain range along the outskirts of Helverta.

The city skyline shone close at hand, and black smoke billowed in random sections throughout it. Her belly squeezed with the knowledge that they weren't out of harm's way just yet. Or at least, this sanctuary they'd found wouldn't last for long. The demons were coming, and she had a feeling it would only be a matter of time before they found this place. And if

Madwyn and Riven were a part of this movement, she assumed they already knew of its existence. They'd seek it out soon enough and come for anyone who hadn't sided with them in this movement.

Rackham cleared his throat, and she snapped her attention back to him. "What were you thinking anyway? Opening a portal without permission? Why did you do it?"

Remi drew her spine straight as guilt began to claw its way back to the surface. It was her fault. All her fault. Had she just listened to her instincts and gone to the pillar leadership and Thayne's parents for help, or not trusted Madwyn and Riven or... Twelve Hells, what good were what-ifs? The reality was that she hadn't done any of those things, and this is where that had landed them.

Remi's voice was raw with emotion when she spoke, "My sister is in Moldize. We were trying to bring her home to stop the Nefarals." She swallowed. The irony in that statement wasn't lost on her. When she spoke, she stared into Pietyr's eyes, "My sister, she's—"

"She's Gabryel's missing heir," Pietyr finished for her. His silvery eyes had grown wide. He rushed toward her, hands gripping her shoulders in his apparent excitement. "You found her then? Why is she in Moldize? How did she get there?"

Remi shook her head. "I don't know why or how. But Ellarah helped me get word to her." Pietyr let go, spun, and rubbed his chin with his hand in thought. "But it was—"

"A trick," Rackham interrupted. "It had to be. Madwyn and Riven were supposed to help you, but they faked it, banking on an opportunity like this one, right?" She thought about Riven's protests that day in the VR café, when they'd asked for his help. It had all been for show, but still, Rackham's explanation didn't ring true to her.

"I don't think so," Remi replied, shaking her head. "They couldn't have known to say some of the things that were in the letter. So it had to be from my sister." She paused, trying to logic her way through what had happened. At last, she said, "Actually, I think they used the situation to their advantage, which means that Bekka is still out there, trying to get back home." Remi clung to that hope unlike anything before. Because if it had all been some cruel trick, then that meant her sister might be dead, just like their grandfather. And she refused to accept that.

Pietyr and Rackham shared a speculative look before Rackham focused on her once more. "You're positive it was Rebekkah? You'd stake your life on it?"

Remi nodded, not daring to show the slightest hesitation. She couldn't afford to second-guess herself now.

Thayne scoffed in frustration. "Do you think we would have taken such a risk if we hadn't been sure?"

Pietyr shrugged. "I guess not, but still. You should have come to me."

Thayne scoffed at this suggestion and shook his head. "Why would I have done that? Because we're such great friends?"

Pietyr's eyes narrowed as he stepped closer. "No, because you know I'm loyal to the crown and Bicaidia. I'd never betray my realm."

Thayne laughed sardonically and threw his arms wide. "Aren't we in the headquarters of the Nefaral uprising? Or as you called it: The Rising? And yet you say you're loyal? You can't have it both ways, Pietyr!"

Before Rackham or Pietyr could retort, the sound of footsteps echoed down a long hallway at the far edge of the room. All of their heads spun in that direction as Remi tried to tamp down the immediate fear response to a new intruder. She had never been the jumpy type, but after everything that had just happened, who could blame her?

Before she could get herself too worked up, a goddess appeared around the corner, her tightly coiled hair springing with each harried step she took. She appeared at the edge of the hall and eyed them with a discerning glare. "Good, you're back. What in the Twelve Hells happened down there, Pietyr?"

Pietyr seemed to straighten, his posture tightening and leashing his shadows as he gave her the short version.

She held up a hand to stop him. "Got it. We can hash out the details later. But for now, you're all needed in control."

She spun on the heels of her ankle-booted feet and hurried back around the corner, barely sparing a glance for Remi or Thayne. Pietyr and Rackham rushed after her, Remi and Thayne hesitating for a quick moment before they hurried to join them.

As Remi turned the corner and walked down the hall, she saw that at least two dozen picture frames lined either wall— surveillance footage from all over Bicaidia. The moving pictures within them shocked her. Typically, these images from feeds in the immortal and mortal realms remained inside the royal palace or the sanctuary of the top pillar leaders' offices.

The fact that the Nefaral uprising had access to this much tech and intel horrified her. No wonder they'd known so much about their position only moments before, she thought as she squinted down into the very same alleyway where Rackham had rescued them. Pietyr must have led them down a path he knew would be intercepted by his militia, if that's what they were. The fact was, Remi had yet to see more than two gods here. How much of an army could it be?

She turned the corner, and the answer sucked the air straight from her lungs. She'd thought the picture frames were bad, but this new room was far, far worse. Holograms filled the massive area, along with at least a hundred deities. A buzz and flurry of sound and motion surrounded her as they all shouted, talked, and gestured wildly at all of the information flowing in from the holos.

She squinted, leaning closer to one particularly informative hologram, and found that they had the logs for every Nefaral across the entire Twelve Realms. The intel included names, contacts, close acquaintances, status, power level, and age. Next to this was another listing of names, but what they were for, she had no idea. Sympathizers maybe? But that was just a guess.

She noticed that the once-bustling room had gone silent, and when she looked up from the holo, everyone was staring at her in mute horror. Correction, everyone was staring at both her and Thayne in mute horror.

She squared her shoulders, her legs planting in defiance as a god she'd never seen before pointed in their direction. "What are they doing here?

Pietyr shot an accusing look at Rackham and the curly-haired goddess. "You didn't tell everyone we were coming?"

Rackham shifted from foot to foot, clearly uncomfortable to have the spotlight on him. Remi, however, was just happy to have it off her for a few blessed moments. "We didn't have much time. I decided it would be better not to mention the collateral luggage we'd picked up along the way. Rescuing your sorry ass took precedence."

Luggage? Remi seethed. Did he just call them luggage? She looked at Thayne, who seemed no more pleased by this term than she did.

The god who'd questioned their presence sneered. "You should have left them there. Especially this Valerian brat," he said.

Thayne narrowed his eyes, squared his shoulders, and stepped between her and this unbelievable jackass. "What did you just call my wife?"

Remi felt her spine stiffen at his protective reaction. She stepped to her husband's side and offered the jackass a scathing glare. She'd been through enough already, Twelve Hells, they all had. The last thing any of them needed was to deal with anti-Valerian prejudice on top of it.

Ignoring Thayne's inquiry, the god growled, his voice low. "I wouldn't have drained most of my power to build a portal for Rackham if I'd known he planned to bring *them* back with him."

The curly-haired goddess walked up behind the jackass and smacked the back of his head with her palm. "Ahlexei, shut up. We have bigger problems right now." Then she turned to address the room at large, the majority of whose eyes remained fixed on the showdown, apparently waiting for a fight.

Sensing this, she clapped her hands with authority and pulled their attention to her. "The rest of you, get back to it. We've got work to do." As though the queen had spoken, everyone obeyed, returning to whatever they'd been doing moments before. Only Ahlexei, the jackass, seemed miffed, and he spared a moment to glare at them as the apparent leader gestured for them to follow her.

She took off at break-neck speed and called over her shoulder, "Keep up. We don't have all day. Time is of the essence." Remi turned her gaze away from her antagonist and followed the goddess.

There was something about the curly-haired female, a sense of power and authority that emanated from her. She wasn't the type of goddess one ignored or defied, and clearly, she knew it.

She led them out of the main bustle around a corner into a glass room situated at the far end of the building. More gods and goddesses loitered around this area, maybe a dozen or so. They seemed less engaged in the pressing matters of Bicaidia, but Remi couldn't make out exactly what they were doing. Mainly because they'd moved through the room so quickly, she couldn't get a good look at any of their holos.

The goddess held open the door as they all filed in behind her—first Pietyr, then Rackham, then Remi, and at last Thayne. A large conference table sat in the middle of the room with a massive holo in its center.

Without preamble, she called up the picture, and a flood of images flashed between them all. Scaly, monstrous demons;

killing weapons; an aerial shot of the palace; and the distance covered by the hoard.

Flashes of light bolted through the city, similar to the one that had rescued them, and she cleared her throat. "In the interest of saving time, I'll give you the quick version." Then, she focused her attention on Thayne and Remi. "My name is Emorie, and I'm the founder of The Rising. Yes, I know, you've never heard of me. No, I'm not from Bicaidia. Yes, I'm an unregistered, upper-caste deity, and everything else about me can wait. I'm not important."

She then turned to address the room at large and swiped a hand over the holo, adjusting the image. "Right now, the evacuation of Helverta is our top priority. We're running rescue missions every two minutes into different sectors of the city. We have a group of well-trained energy deities here, who, thanks to that governor chip removal, are working with some serious mojo now. As much as I hate what Madwyn and Riven did, they leveled the playing field for us all, not just themselves. Though I imagine that was more due to incompetence than any intentional assistance."

Remi had a few seconds to absorb her words before she swiped a hand across the holo. The image blurred, moving back to a crowd of people looking bewildered and confused. "We've saved 400 deities so far, and they're under lockdown a mile north of here, but there are still more out there." She pointed, "Pietyr, I need you to lead a team of our top shadow wielders to head up the rescue effort. You're the most powerful, and we need to merge magics and save as many deities as we can before it's too late. The demons will have the whole city overrun within the hour. Now go." Without hesitation, Pietyr disappeared into a shadowy swirl of mist, and Remi noted his unquestioning submissiveness toward the deity in charge.

Emorie continued, "As for the rest of you, we all need a safe place to shelter tonight. The cover for this base has been compromised. Madwyn and Riven know where we are, and it won't take them long to realize that we have these two interlopers. Though I'll admit, it will shock the shit out of them. We've been working against them after all. But we need to get the hell out of here and torch this place behind us either way."

Rackham nodded as though this all made sense to him. But, to Remi, this course of action sounded insane. They'd just gotten there. It was an immense building, and they were going to just torch it? Like it was nothing? Then there was the whole part about the governor chips. What was she talking about? Remi shook her head, confusion taking hold. Energy gods weren't Nefarals. Why would they have governor chips? Emorie had to be confused or maybe just misinformed.

But before she could question anything the goddess had said, Rackham said, "On it. We'll get everything ready to relocate. Do you have a new base ready?"

Emorie nodded. "I've already ordered all field operatives to torch the other bases Madwyn and Riven know about. There is only one left, but no one is going to like the location."

Rackham's jaw flexed. "Better than waiting for them to show up and kill or capture anyone who doesn't side with them. It's a blood-bath out there, Em, and we're too close to the front line of it."

Her eyes registered pain for a moment before she clenched her jaw. "Don't I know it." Removing her thick-rimmed glasses, she pinched the bridge of her nose and sighed. "Just get everything ready to go. Check-in with me when it's done." Then she jerked her head to indicate Remi and Thayne. "Take them with you and make sure they carry their weight. We'll have no freeloaders here."

Rackham rose from his feet and started toward a door on the opposite wall from where they'd entered, expecting Remi and Thayne to follow. Instead, Thayne stood and took three long strides to the door and propped his arm across it, blocking everyone from exiting. "I'm not going anywhere or helping with anything until I get some answers."

"Are you going to be a problem, Thayne?" Emorie asked, her glasses settled low on her slim nose.

Lightning sizzled over his hand in a silent threat. "Only if you don't start talking."

She rolled her eyes, looking unimpressed. "Look, princeling, I don't have time for your temper tantrums. So move, or I'll move you myself."

Thayne's jaw flexed. "Temper tantrum? Do you understand what we've been through today, thanks to this uprising? I won't help you until I know what the hell you're fighting for. How do I know you're any better than Madwyn or Riven? Pietyr said he didn't want a war or a coup, but I still don't know; what is it you people do want?"

Emorie crossed her arms over her chest and glowered at Thayne. "It's a simple thing. We can hash over the specifics later, but the main gist is this: We want freedom. We want out of the gods-forsaken cage that Gabryel and his council put us in without due process or just cause. So, you can either get on board, or I will deposit you and that Valerian brat right back where I picked you up. Got it?"

Without any further hesitation, Emorie ducked under Thayne's arm. She called over her shoulder as she left them for the flurry of deities in the main room. "You better make your choice quick. The clock is ticking." Rackham, on the other hand, stood there, waiting for them to make a choice.

"Where are you taking us?" Remi asked, wondering if this was another trap or a trick. She might seem paranoid, but she'd been tricked enough for one day. Ascended, for one lifetime, she thought, pulse quickening.

"You'll see," Rackham replied, the shadows highlighting his facial features, giving his youthful face an air of severity.

Remi stepped forward, Thayne following her lead. "That's not good enough. Believe it or not, I'm all out of trust right now. So, if you don't tell me where we're going," she snapped her fingers, the tips of each on her right hand ignited in a blue and yellow flame. "Then maybe I'll start your little incineration party early." She was still afraid to let loose anymore of her magic than this small show, but he didn't need to know that.

Rackham's face glowed as he moved closer to the light of her fire. He crossed his arms over his chest and rested one shoulder against the wall, the picture of casual. "Cute," he said, eyeing her flames as though they were an amusing parlor trick. "But I saw you down there…fighting. I know you're running on fumes, honey. You'd need at least a few hours of stasis sleep before you could even attempt setting this place ablaze. So why don't you just—"

Remi took a step forward, coming nose-to-nose with him as she took a chance and tapped into that well. Her flames spread across her body and she resisted the urge the suck in a breath at the effort it took to contain them. They licked over her arms and down her torso and engulfed her hair. "Care to wager on that?" Her body hummed and the roaring in her ears proved deafening, but she needed to up the ante. She needed him to see that she wasn't weak, that she still had power to bargain with.

Startled by the sudden influx of light and heat, Rackham stumbled back a step, off-balance. Her lips quirked up in a half-smile as a throat cleared behind her. Thayne's voice rumbled out, low and just as threatening as hers. "I'd do what the lady says. Trust me; you don't want to see her when she's angry."

Rackham let out a sigh, rolling his eyes. "It's our supply room, and there's an undetectable speed tunnel down there too. We're getting the domiciles ready to roll, grabbing our go-bags, and backing up the hardware. Standard operating procedure when any of our bases are blown."

"That's all. You sure about that?" Remi asked, not bothering to extinguish her flames just yet.

Rackham looked annoyed when he said, "Yes. Look, I know you don't trust us, but guess what, honey, we don't trust you either. So, just do what Emorie said. Carry your weight. As long as you do that, no one will bother you. You have my word. Got it?"

Remi thought it over. Deciding it seemed like a reasonable enough agreement to her, she extinguished her fire. "Fine. But betray us, and I'll make sure you live to regret it."

"We won't," Rackham said, turning. "Now let's go," he called over his shoulder, finally moving.

Remi started to follow, but a hand on her shoulder had her pausing. Thayne leaned down and whispered in her ear, "Just give him a few seconds." His voice was raspy and full of its usual authority. She closed her eyes, pressing her lids shut in frustration. She wanted space from him just then. Time to process everything that had happened and maybe let some of the sting of his lie of omission regarding Madwyn dissipate. No wonder he'd wanted them to each be allowed their secrets, she thought, remembering the mad glee in Madwyn's eyes as she'd taunted Remi.

Thayne's grip tightened as though he could sense her pulling away. She made a conscious effort to relax in his grip. She wasn't stupid. She knew that this wasn't the time to let emotions take control. They needed to be able to trust and rely on each other at the moment. So, she pushed the anger aside and did as he asked.

When Rackham disappeared around a bend in the hallway just ahead of them, Thayne removed his hand. "We can't trust them. You know that, right?"

"Of course I know that, but we don't have much of a choice," Remi muttered, scrubbing a hand over her face. They shared a look, neither of them thrilled with their current circumstance. "Look, I think we'd better follow. If they're really going to torch this place, then we don't want to be here when Madwyn and Riven show up."

With one last, pained glance at the glass room with its damned holo, Thayne nodded. Once they'd caught Rackham up, he turned another corner and led them down a narrow hall to a large staircase that seemed to disappear into the darkness. "You made the right choice," he called over his shoulder. "Emorie would have done it, you know. Put you right back where I picked you up. She doesn't make idle threats."

Remi's jaw flexed, disliking how off-balance and out of control she felt in this place. "I inferred that, but thanks for confirming it." The blackness seemed to swell around them as they wound around a twist in a stairwell, and rocky walls appeared around them.

They took a few steps, Thayne's body close behind hers as he began to speak in a low voice, "I just realized that this is the main operation we've been hunting for the past month. We've had Pietyr's cohorts, the other shadow wielders, and some of the peacekeeper's council looking for the epicenter of the uprising. We kept getting tips about different locations, different hubs. But every time our people would find one, ready to infiltrate it, all that was left behind were charred husks of former buildings."

Remi processed his words, wondering why he hadn't wanted Rackham to overhear them. What difference did that make now? She wondered as they continued further down, deep into the underground chamber Rackham had described. Then a thought occurred to her. "It's no wonder you never found the places intact. Pietyr must have been their inside-man."

"Exactly," he breathed. "I get why he joined The Rising; he's a Nef. But the time god...I just don't understand why any non-Nefaral would want to be a part of this." She had been wondering the same thing herself. What the hell would an Altruist have to gain from siding with the Nefarals? What would be the point?

They finished their descent in silence as a faint light began to illuminate the stairwell from beneath them. By the time they hit the landing, she could hear the shuffle of Rackham's boots and the buzz of unbridled energy. She blinked, eyes adjusting as the scent of soil and damp filled her nostrils. A large, hollow tunnel surrounded them, with minimal comforts and frills.

Remi looked around and could sense that a combination of magic and natural engineering held the tunnel in one piece. After all, it hadn't been sealed with the traditional layer of the impenetrable, light trypton that an approved construction would have been. Instead, this was an illegal tunnel leading straight through the center of Bicaidia's primary planet.

Remi couldn't help but be impressed by it. The amount of work and level of secrecy it must have taken to create this place was just that—impressive.

She marveled that they had managed to keep it a secret. There had been no significant disruptions above ground in the city to draw attention to the construction going on right beneath it.

She gaped a little as she surveyed her surroundings. How long had this uprising been active? It couldn't have just been a couple of months, she realized. This had to have been operational long before her grandfather's death. When she looked at Thayne, his mouth had clamped shut, a tick pulsing in his jaw. His eyes had gone hard, and she could almost feel the anger emanating from him. She knew what he must be thinking. This had happened right under his nose on his watch.

She laid a hand on his arm, bringing his attention to her. His dark eyes seemed to blaze with fury as they fixed on hers. "I know," she whispered, her shock still fresh. "But—" she shook her head, indicating that they didn't have time to question how this had been possible. Besides, it didn't matter right now. Like it or not, she knew that they needed to carry their weight. Just as Rackham and Emorie had demanded, otherwise, they could find themselves on the wrong end of a demon's blade.

Rackham's voice echoed from behind a row of metal crates, "You two going to help, or what?"

Thayne released the breath he seemed to be holding and nodded at Remi. A confirmation that he would follow her advice; afterall, if Emorie gave the order to send them back to Helverta, there wasn't much they could do to stop a portal from forming right under their feet.

So, they walked along the soft, dirt ground past the crates and around a row of racking until Rackham came into sight again. He didn't look up from the holo he was manning. Instead, he flung a hand at a stack of crates. "Load those onto the rear domicile. There are three more large transport vehicles down the cavern that way." He pounded down the tunnel and toward another wall of racking, packs, and crates.

Remi and Thayne spent the next thirty minutes loading the domiciles while Rackham manned the holograph, backing up the data upstairs and sending it to the uprising's new location. Every so often, Remi could hear the thunder of footsteps above them, dirt sprinkling down on their heads as the sounds grew more hectic.

When they'd loaded everything and Rackham had finished his backup, the time god tapped and swiped at the holo. "Alright," he said. "Pietyr's sending the evacuees to our allies in Kilbralta. They're en route now." As he finished the last word of that sentence, gods and goddesses began appearing in bursts of bright-lighted energy or stepping through the eels of their shadow magic. Others came thundering down the stairs, and Remi smelled smoke. She turned her head and saw tendrils of it filtering down the stairwell.

Emorie appeared at her side, the resulting breeze of her arrival rustling Remi's gown. What was she the goddess of again? Remi wondered, narrowing her eyes. Clearly something powerful enough that she could translocate. Emorie's voice carried over the melee, "Alright, this bitch is about to burn. Time to go. File in!"

Everyone rushed to their spots in the domicile, the sheer organization of the entire operation surprising. Emorie eyed Remi and Thayne with something akin to distaste but seemed to force herself to swallow it down. Remi would need to remember to sleep with one eye open while in her company. She pointed to the domicile at the end of the line. "Ellarah's in there with Charmelle. You can ride with them."

Remi turned hopeful eyes on the final vehicle in the transport convoy. It was a small olive branch, but one she was grateful to receive. She nodded, a question popping into her mind. "What about Pietyr? Isn't he coming?"

Of all the deities, she had yet to see him file down the stairs with his fellow rebels. Then again, from what she remembered of Bicaidian geography, Kilbralta was far. Some 300 miles away. Maybe they would just meet him at their next destination.

Emorie shook her head, her curls swaying with the motion. "He'll be along soon enough. He doesn't need transport. Nor do the other shadow wielders still out there with him. They'll get the coordinates once they're done with the refugees."

Thayne squared his shoulders, "Where exactly are we going?"

"Somewhere far from here. It's need-to-know, and you don't. So, either get on board or stay behind and wait for the cavern to cave in. Your call." With that, she turned on her heel and headed to the lead domicile, a few other deities hurrying after her. Remi and Thayne locked eyes, wondering what they were about to get themselves into. Did their presence here make them rebels? She shrugged this notion off as unimportant. At this point in time, they needed to escape the city. They needed to put distance between them and Madwyn and Riven. She'd remembered the sick gleam in Madwyn's eye as she and Riven had ordered her and Thayne's imprisonment. She couldn't imagine what horrors would await them in that dungeon.

So, without another word, they hurried to Ellarah's domicile. Remi could feel the tightening of anxiety in her chest with each step that drew them closer to the vehicle.

When they opened the door, a sterile whiteness hit them. Clinical, clean, stark. Everything one would want in a hospital transport domicile. To Remi's surprise, at least a dozen deities were convalescing around them. She tried not to stare at the array of injuries as she made her way through the white, pristine beds to the back of the room.

A long, white curtain had been pulled between this main part of the room and the one beyond. Without warning, it pulled back, and Charmelle, disheveled with the soot and blood from the battle, locked eyes with them. She blew out a sigh of relief. "There you are." She offered them a follow-me gesture and led them inside. Remi and Thayne obeyed, hurrying behind her.

Thayne's voice betrayed the strain he must be feeling as he asked, "Is she—is she going to be OK?" Remi could see the grief and fear in his eyes, though they remained dry. She reached out and grasped his hand, needing to comfort as much as to be comforted. Ellarah had paid the price for their reckless plan, and Remi couldn't stop the guilt that assaulted her as a result.

Charmelle winced, and Remi's heart caught in her throat. The healer gestured to a bed in the far corner of the room. Machines, powered with a constant flow of healing magic, whirred and chimed, the image of Ellarah's internal organs and cellular structure projecting onto a holograph above her sleeping form.

Charmelle led them further into the room and pointed to where Ellarah'd been stabbed on the holo. "She's stable, but this poison—" Charmelle broke off and shook her head. "I don't know what it is or how to stop it. So far, we've been able to slow the spread and stop the bleeding. But I'm just a—" She cleared her throat and shook her head. "I'm sorry, but I'm just a middle-caste healer. We need someone with more power, someone who can identify the origins of the poison and create an antidote. The only thing I know for certain is that it's magical in nature. Otherwise, her body would be fighting it off on its own in stasis sleep."

Remi's eyes blurred with tears.

The self-loathing chant played on repeat in her mind, *all her fault*, and she shook her head to clear it. This was not the time to fall apart, she reminded herself. On the contrary, she had to hold it together if she had any hope of helping her friend. Or of striking back against what Madwyn and Riven had done. Despite how desperate and hopeless things seemed now, she knew that she had no intention of giving up. Not now, not ever.

Thayne's fists clenched at his side, and Remi could all but feel the anger pulsing off of him. "Do you have anyone here who can do that? A higher-caste healer with the rebellion who can help her?" he asked.

Charmelle shook her head. "No, we don't. I'm sorry. The best I can do right now is slow the spread and keep her in stasis sleep to manage the pain."

Remi moved to her friend and wrapped her fingers around Ellarah's limp hand. "How long do we have before the poison wins?"

In response, Charmelle stared at the holo and shook her head. "It's hard to say. My best guess is a few weeks. Maybe a month. I'm not really sure because I haven't worked with this specific type of poison before. But based on the limited analysis I've done so far, it's similar to what the Nefs used during the last war. The problem is that we haven't had to treat it since they outlawed it 900 years ago and, like I said before,

I'm just a middle-caste healer. I don't have the knowledge or the power to do more than slow it down, and since Madwyn and Riven killed Wren at the inauguration—" She turned to Remi to elaborate. "He was the leader of the healing sect. The only healer left in Bicaidia with enough power and the knowledge to save her, at least that I know of. So, if we're going to get help, we need to do it fast." She brushed a loose lock of hair off her filthy face, "And it's going to need to be off-world, somewhere where they still have an upper-caste healer."

Thayne's eyes darkened and Remi felt helpless as she realized that this left them only one option. Thayne seemed to come to the same conclusion, his eyes locking onto hers. She felt, for a moment, that she could read his mind.

He nodded at what he saw in her expression, the understanding clear between them. They knew what they had to do. They had to get back into that palace. They had to make a doorway out of Bicaidia and back to Remi's homeworld of Valeria. And they had to do it without getting caught. The only question was, how the hell were they going to manage that?

CHAPTER 13

BEKKA

Fatigue

We had spent the last week traveling down empty tunnels to various levels of torture and despair. With every passing day without our supplies, we grew hungrier and thirstier. Though it hadn't been long in the grand scheme of things, I could already feel my pants sagging low on my narrowing hips.

We'd just passed through our fourth chamber of the day, burning hot, gale-force wind that had left me feeling raw and even more sapped of energy than the tunnels before it.

On top of the physical strain we'd been forced to endure, my concern for Remi was an ever-present specter. Unfortunately, we were not blessed with a favorable time differential between hell and the immortal realm. They moved along the same timeline, marching forward in an endless, unstoppable stream. I worried we might not make it to Bicaidia in time to do anything to help. I could only hope that the royals could hold it all together until we reached them, or even better, that they already had it under control.

Still, a ringing sense of urgency plagued me as each hour ticked by. In an effort to make up as much of that time as possible, we worked until we dropped, collapsing at the next central tunnel each night. It became a sick kind of routine. Torture, starve, sleep, repeat, like an evil shampoo. Sometimes, on the bad days, we had to turn around and go back to where we'd started. Those were the worst.

Today, to my profound gratitude, hadn't been one of those days. Instead, we'd gotten through to the next circle of hell and made camp in an inner circle with twelve caverns left.

Arrick believed that based on the level of torture we had endured today and the number of tunnels remaining, we could make it out of here within the next three days. Give or take a few.

I hoped that his hunch was correct because if we stayed here much longer, I was going to lose my mind. Worry and exhaustion dogged me every waking moment, and it didn't help that I felt claustrophobic, paranoid, and irritable. Not the best combination when in tight quarters with three other people.

I let out a huff of breath and gnawed on my lip as I stared at the crackling flames of our fire. Caden had started it using two rocks and some of hell's shrubbery. Though minimal underbrush existed in the caverns, there were barbed and thorny bushes aplenty. We used those for burning each night.

The dim firelight danced along the cavern walls, casting long shadows off our bodies. Arrick sat nearby, Caden on the other side of me, and Deklan across from me. I could just make out the white gleam of his hair and the severe angles of his features above the flames. He seemed just as content with silence as me, which worked. What was there to say, after all? This day had sucked, the day before sucked, and so had every single day since we'd arrived here. Shocker. It was hell, after all.

As I surveyed my friends, I had to admit that we looked like a rag-tag group of ruffians. It was going to take some doing to convince the royals that I was who I said I was once we got to Bicaidia. Well, if we ever got there. Think positive, Bekka, I chastised myself. We're going to make it in time. A jaw-cracking yawn from Caden cut off my thoughts.

He stretched beside me, and I could hear the vertebrae in his neck pop. I surveyed him, noticing, not for the first time, that the golden sheen of godly light that had once surrounded him seemed dull now. He looked frail, almost human, and I wondered how much longer his and Deklan's bodies could endure this torment before they buckled under the weight of it. Hell might not be able to kill them on its own, but starvation and dehydration still could.

After a long silence, Caden spoke at last, "Do you guys feel that?" His eyes scanned the cavern around us, devoid of light outside of our meager fire.

Sweat trickled down my back and between my breasts as I followed his gaze, unsure what he meant. Arrick did the same, his sharp, green eyes vivid despite the soft lighting. Heat radiated around us, both from the fire and from hell itself. It seemed to be growing hotter with every progression we made toward the inner circle.

Deklan sighed, throwing another piece of scrub into the fire. "If you mean do I feel the eyes on the back of my neck, then yes."

Oh right, that, I thought. That, of course, was the main reason we bothered with a fire at all. Though we'd seen no tangible sign of it since our packs had disappeared, we knew that something must be watching us. I had the sickening sensation that whoever or whatever it was, was biding its time—waiting for us to grow too weak to defend ourselves.

Then, it would strike. Ascended only knew what it wanted from us. I didn't imagine it would be anything good.

Arrick ran a hand over his dark hair, salty and stiff from sweat and seawater. "We've searched every inch of this cavern. We agreed that there's no sign of anyone or anything for that matter."

Caden shook his head, his near-white hair shining golden in the firelight. "Doesn't change the fact that I can feel them…or it. Whatever it is, it's close, Arrick, and you know that as well as we do. No one survived for long in The Burning without developing a sixth sense for situations just like this."

Despite the heat, chills prickled up my arms. "What do you think it is?" I asked, my voice barely above a whisper.

Caden shrugged a lean shoulder as he and his brother, the mirror image of him, looked at Arrick. I followed suit, eyes settling on the only death deity in residence at the moment. He sighed. "You're right; I feel it too. And, you're not going like this, but I used my power earlier." My eyes popped wide as my heart issued a loud thump in my chest. We'd agreed. No magic. Not after that first time. The risk of the Bicaidian death god finding us here and in this state? It was too much.

"How could you do that without telling us first? We agreed," I hissed, a sense of betrayal washing over me. I could see my own outrage mirrored in the expressions of Caden and Deklan, though they remained silent.

He closed his eyes, winced a little at the accusation in my voice, my expression. "I know, but something felt wrong here. It has since the moment we arrived. I had to do something before—" He broke off, his eyes churning with frustration. "—before I couldn't anymore. We're getting weaker every day, and soon…" He shook his head, his meaning clear. Soon, he might not be able to do anything at all.

Deklan, the most pragmatic of us, seemed to recover first. "So, what did you find?"

Arrick rubbed his hands together, an agitated gesture as he stared into the flames. "Nothing. Whatever's down here with us, it knows how to hide. Even from me."

I licked my lips, an eerie sense of dread washing over me. "That doesn't sound good."

"It isn't," he said, fixing his attention on all of us. "And I can't risk using my power again. Not so soon after this last time. We just need to watch our backs, stay vigilant, and stick together."

My hand went to the grip of my gun, still strapped to my outer thigh. We'd managed to keep hold of most of our weapons, despite the chambers we endured each day. So far, we'd only lost Mr. Sharpington III, along with one of Caden's swords and one of Arrick's guns. But we still carried most of what we'd come with.

Deklan's expression hardened into the warrior I knew him to be. "Don't worry; we've had it worse before."

I resisted the urge to smack some sense into him. "When could you possibly have had it worse than this?" I snapped, my nerves stretching too thin to control the frustrating edginess of my mood. "We're in hell with no supplies, no food, no water, and something is stalking us. Not to mention the fact that the entire Bicaidian realm, and possibly the peace of the entire Twelve Realms, hinges on us getting out of here."

Deklan smirked at me, utterly unperturbed by my outburst. "Feel better?"

"You're an asshole," I spat, taking a fist full of dirt and chucking it at him.

He dusted it off his Itorian battle leathers, glaring at me, while Caden and Arrick watched us with intensity. I could feel my breath heaving in my chest as I glared at Deklan, but before I could continue my tirade, he said, "You don't know where I came from or what I've been through before this. Moldize? Hell? It all looks pretty much the same to me." His eyes narrowed with his assertion as he glared back at me.

He couldn't be serious. I'd been to Itoriah, had lived there with them. Granted, it had been for only a short time, but it hadn't been an active torment like this was. Then again, what did he mean about where he'd come from? I knew his family had migrated from the northern part of Myzhrele, but I didn't know much about his or Caden's origins. They'd never talked about it, and I hadn't asked.

"What are you talking about?" I asked, eyes flicking between the brothers as my anger dissipated. I almost dreaded the answer because I had a feeling it would make me look like a jerk. That was why I hated getting angry. I always ended up feeling like an idiot afterward.

Deklan fed another branch to the fire. "We were young when the worst of The Burning started. It had been in motion for years, but like many people, our parents didn't believe that the situation would get as bad as it did. So, they were slow to migrate south. We'd barely made it 200 miles when the government collapsed in Djorn, our home country in the northern part of Myzhrele. And once it was gone, the riots ensued. People started burning, looting, stealing, and the worst ones, like Lorus, started killing. We were a young family of regular people, caught right in the middle of it."

I felt my heart contract, guilt permeating me like a shroud. I knew it, I thought, I was such a grade-A jerk.

Deklan's eyes never left the fire as he continued, "We were kids then, maybe 5, but I'll never forget the smell or sounds as we fled the city. Blood, smoke, ash, and death. So much death."

On an impulse, I reached over and grasped his hand. He jolted in surprise and looked down at my slim fingers. He cleared his throat, and I slid them away, an apology in my eyes now. He acknowledged it with a nod as he continued. "That was when the world really went to hell, at least where we're from. It happened earlier in other places and later in more. But my parents got us out of the city, hid us in abandoned homes as we made our way south on foot."

He sighed and chafed an arm with his hand. "Because we traveled on foot, we were in the north for a long time. And the more time we spent on the road, the more we noticed that people started dying from radiation sickness all around us. But, we never got sick. I didn't know it at the time, but it must have been Afryel's lineage that saved us. Only, it didn't save our parents for long. They died when we were thirteen, trying to rescue two kids from a tribe of cannibals. So, I'm sorry Bekka, but you've never experienced true hell until you smell the flesh of your parents roasting over an open pit."

I resisted the urge to gag with the disgust that his words elicited as I swallowed the lump in my throat. A combination of sadness and horror fought for dominance in my mind as I tried to tamp down the guilt I felt for losing my temper. Deklan was right; they had had it worse before. "I'm sorry," I said. "I never should have snapped at you or made you relive that."

I looked from Caden to Deklan, each carrying a haunted look in their eyes. As though they could witness the scene happening all over again. It was my fault. I'd dredged up that past when it should have been left alone. They'd had such hard lives, and I realized then that this was just another chapter of that difficulty.

"It's fine," Deklan said, rubbing his hands on the leather of his pants. "It was a long time ago. I think I'm going to call it a night. Wake me when it's my turn for watch duty."

Without another glance in my direction, he eased away from the fire and toward the cooler, outer edges of this new cavern. Despite his assertion that it was fine, I knew he wasn't. I could tell. A darkness had come over his eyes, a shadow of pain passing through them. I wished I could take it back, turn back time and eat my own words before I'd said them. But I couldn't.

Caden rose to his feet then as well. "I'm calling it too. Let me know when I'm needed."

I watched as he disappeared into the darkened outer edges of the cavern and rubbed my eyes. I felt terrible, guilt and anxiety pulsing dual beats in my chest, and I knew that I wouldn't be able to dull the edge of either enough to sleep. Though the insomnia wasn't anything new, the guilt was an unwelcome addition.

Logically, I knew that my sour mood wasn't all my fault. Lack of sleep and sustenance had worn my temper thinner than a gossamer nighty, but still. It didn't excuse how I'd treated Deklan tonight. I'd need to find a way to make it up to him. I looked to the outer edge of the cavern, saw his back turned on us as he tried to sleep, and decided that I would take both his and Caden's shifts tonight.

It was the least I could do after how I'd acted. Besides, it wasn't like I was going to be able to sleep anyway; I hadn't been able to since our packs had been taken that first night in hell. I couldn't shake the unmistakable sensation that someone was watching us.

Though I knew that I needed to get at least some stasis sleep each night, every time I closed my eyes, the same vision came to mind—Remi murdered by Nefarals, her dead eyes staring up at me in lifeless horror. Then I would see Bicaidia burning to the ground; every ally I sought to make dead before I could even get there. Next, I'd watch in my mind's eye as the rebellion spilled into Valeria and the other ten realms, causing a war unlike any we'd experienced in over 900 years. Then, at last, I would picture myself as the Peacekeeper, the leader that the deities of the Twelve Realms would expect to end this war. To know what to do to stop it, unaware of the awful truth—I had no idea what I was doing.

I thought for the millionth time that Arrick should have saved Gabryel that day in Moldize instead of me. Everyone would be better off if he had.

I shifted on my sit bones and rubbed my eyes again, begging my mind to turn off. To let me rest. Then I could at least use the small window of Arrick's watch to get some stasis sleep.

I heard a rustle of dirt on the ground as Arrick inched closer to me. "You should get some sleep. I'll take the first shift tonight."

I resisted the urge to say *No way, you think?* and nodded instead. "I know; I just can't seem to shut it off." I tapped my temple to indicate the troublesome thing that was my brain.

He rubbed a hand over the shadow of a beard lingering on his jawline. "Is it Remi?"

I watched his face, the rugged contours of it softened by the dancing light. The compassion I saw in the depths of his eyes melted me just a little. "Yes, well, that and the brothers. I shouldn't have pressed Deklan tonight. I don't know what came over me. I'm just so tired and hungry." As though in answer, my stomach growled, and I pressed a hand to cover it as I continued, "Then, with Remi, I don't know what I'll do if we're too late." I'd lost too much already, I thought, still thinking of my grandpa as I toed the gravelly dirt beneath my feet.

After a brief hesitation, he looped his arm around my shoulders. I leaned into him, inhaling the musty scent of dust, sweat, and saltwater. It suited him somehow, and I winced as I imagined how I must smell. Something told me sweat and seawater wouldn't be a winning combination on my skin like it was on his.

Arrick's thumbs traced tiny circles on my upper arm. I shivered as each contact with my bare flesh caused tiny flames of pleasure to rocket up my spine. Then, he soothed, "Don't worry about Caden and Deklan. They'll forgive you in the morning. They know, better than most, what hunger and thirst can do to a person. As far as Remi is concerned, I'm sure she's

OK. She's a powerful, upper-caste goddess, and she had the royals to protect her."

I let that settle, hoping that he was right about the brothers, thinking that he probably was. He knew them well, better than almost anyone. But Remi?

"How can you know that she's OK?" I countered. The truth was that we were walking into this blind. We had no idea how far it had gone or how bad it was. We could show up right in the middle of a war, or the rebellion might already be over, quelled by the Bicaidian leadership. I hoped for the latter, but I didn't want to lay all my bets on that.

"She's royalty—"

I interrupted before he could finish. "But that's part of the problem! She's royalty. If the Nefarals overthrew the leadership, then there's no way they'd leave her alive. You know that as well as I do. Then, if she really did go around the royals, like she said, how do we know that they aren't exacting their own punishment on her? All around, this is bad, Arrick." I stopped, my breath heaving, my body vibrating with anxiety.

Sensing the storm brewing inside of me, he wrapped me in his arms and pulled me into his lap. I went willingly, my body craving the comfort of his touch more than I craved a cup of steaming coffee each morning. He stroked my back as I gulped air and tried to get my emotions under control.

"As far as the Bicaidian leadership is concerned, they'd never risk a war with Valeria. They wouldn't punish her without first consulting your parents," he reasoned, fingertips tracing my spine to soothe me. "And as for the Nefarals, I'm sure the royals have it under control."

"But my grandpa is gone now—"

"And the leadership of each of the Twelve Realms is a formidable force without him. They should be able to quell an uprising without his help. A Peacekeeper will just deter anyone else from trying the same thing, which is why they need you. It won't be on you to stop it all. Your presence should keep it from happening."

With each stroke of his hand and the smooth tenor of his words, I felt the fist that clenched around my gut ease. I heard the logic in what he said and knew that he was probably right. But there was something there, in the back of my mind, that made me uneasy. I couldn't explain it, but I knew something was off.

For now, though, his arms and his presence quieted that uncertainty. I felt safe there. Protected. Like I could let it go, even if only for a little while.

I let out a long breath as I pulled my cheek away from his chest. "How do you always stay so level-headed? You never seem to panic or lose your shit."

A soft laugh rumbled out of him. "Oh, I lose my shit plenty. I wouldn't have left after our fight a few weeks back if I hadn't lost it then."

My mouth turned down as I remembered his absence. While I hadn't admitted it to anyone, his abandonment had cut me. My emotions had been so raw, and maybe the distance had been good for me, but it still stung that he could just pick up and leave. Meanwhile, forcing myself away from him proved far more difficult on my end.

I ran a hand through my hair and scooted off his lap. "You know what I mean. How do you keep everything together? It seems like you always have it under control. Like you always know what to do next."

He looked into the fire and rubbed a hand over the back of his neck in thought. "I'd say it comes from growing up in a place like Moldize." I stayed silent, waiting for him to elaborate. He shrugged a broad shoulder and leaned back to rest on his hands. "We're from two different worlds. You understand that, right?"

"Thank you for stating the obvious," I said, rolling my eyes. "But what does that have to do with anything?"

He shook his head at me, fighting the exhaustion I could see in his eyes. "I'm getting to it, but it's not a question with a simple answer." Settling in, he stretched his legs out. I moved to sit next to him, mirroring his posture, wondering why the hell I'd gotten off his lap. It had been so cozy there, so comforting. Interrupting my internal chastising, he sighed. "My whole life, I've known that the rest of the multiverse hates us. They view us as scum beneath their boots." He paused again, and I could see him thinking over his words, chewing over the right way to explain. "It's a hard way to grow up, and it can shake out a couple of ways. Either you live up to the reputation everyone else gives you, or you fight with everything you have to prove them wrong. I shook out the second way."

I thought about it, not understanding his point. "So, you're able to stay calm because you want to prove everyone wrong?"

He pressed a finger to my lips and said, "Shh." I narrowed my eyes at him, fighting amusement now. He always knew how to distract me when I needed it the most, I thought as he continued, "Not exactly; I'm still working my way around to it. Moldize is a hard place, whether you're in the human or the godly realms. Nefarals, like me, live amongst us, ungoverned, and we have nearly all lower-caste or servant-caste deities making up the rest of our godly ranks. As a result, we fight for every scrap of improvement we make in either of our realms. And most of that improvement, we've had to make up close and personal, not through the use of magic or power. But through influence, by reading the situation and understanding our adversaries better than ourselves. So, I don't panic because I understand how people think, human or deity. I can read a situation well, and I usually know what people will do before they do it. That's how I know that the Bicaidian government won't risk punishing your sister without due cause. They will also do everything in their power to stop this uprising. Not doing either could cost them the peace that everyone cares so damned much about in the Twelve Realms."

I traced lines into the dirt with my fingers as I considered. It made sense. He'd become confident, self-reliant, and self-assured. But one point of his explanation stuck out to me. "You don't care about the peace?"

He ran a hand through his hair, his triceps flexing as one arm held his weight. He had such nice arms, I thought, waiting for his answer. They were toned with a lean bulk to them. Strong, but not obtrusive, and I knew from experience just how good it felt to be held by them.

He explained, "I don't know. I care because you do and because I don't want to see anyone die. But the laws that bind the Nefarals—They're not right."

My eyes widened in surprise. Of course, he was a Nefaral, so it shouldn't have shocked me that he would have an opinion on the matter. Nevertheless, it did. "But look what happened before the laws. The death and destruction and all that suffering. It ended once the regulations were put into place. Once the governing chips were enacted."

His jaw flexed. "Maybe, but don't you think it's wrong to put someone in a cage before you even give them a chance to prove whether or not they need one? I don't have a governor chip, Bekka. Do you think I need one?"

I flushed. "No, of course not, but—" I broke off, unable to find the flaw in that logic.

"I just think people should be judged for their actions, not for how they're born. I can't help being a death deity any more than I can help that my eyes are green. But what I can do is fight to bring good into this world instead of evil."

I swallowed and rubbed my temples as I thought it through. He wasn't wrong. "Do you think all Nefarals feel this way?"

He shrugged his shoulders. "I'd be surprised if most didn't. I've never lived with a chip or under the scrutiny of The

Peacekeeper's council. Still, I'd imagine that that resentment has been festering for centuries. I'll grant that it made sense at first. Gabryel put the Nefarals who'd fought against him under a governor chip. But then he kept doing it, even with deities born centuries after the conflict ended. So, if I had to guess, I'd say that's where the seeds for this uprising come from."

I stared at him in surprise. "So, you think they're right to revolt? To risk the lives of thousands of gods and mortals if this conflict were to break out into the open?"

He looked into my eyes, and, shaking his head, he turned back to the fire. "I'm not saying whether I agree or disagree. I just want you to see it from a different perspective. We're not all bad, you know. Not all Nefarals give into the darker temptations that come with our powers. So, don't we deserve to live our lives free of obstruction? Don't we deserve a chance to prove ourselves, one way or another?"

I cut my eyes from him to the fire. "You think I should consider changing the laws once I'm Peacekeeper, don't you?"

He moved, turning to face me and trailing his fingertips over my cheek. He looked into my eyes, those green irises glowing in the soft firelight. He brushed a thumb over my lips. "That's up to you, Bekka. But think about it this way, would you put a chip in my neck?"

He already knew the answer to that. I hadn't wanted him to come with me to Bicaidia for that exact reason. But I hesitated. My heart thumped in my chest with his casual touch as his gaze held me captive, as hypnotic as ever, butterflies taking up residence in my belly. The idea of taking his power away, modifying it, and then tracking him like he was some criminal made me feel sick.

"Never. You know I would never do that, right?" I covered his hand with mine, so he understood that I meant it. I had meant it the first time I'd said back in Moldize.

"They'd force you to if I stayed in Valeria with you."

I knew that, of course, but my heart pounded, and I could feel each beat acutely as I imagined it. This was the main reason I'd asked for distance and time, why I had planned to take Erykha with me instead. Our worlds were so different. I had no idea how they could ever coalesce into something even remotely resembling cohesion. I knew, someday, I'd need to make a choice. I had ties to both Moldize and Valeria now; I couldn't deny that.

Moldize held the promise of freedom of both choice and the substance of my life there; and Arrick of course. I could be whomever I wanted in his realm. I would not be required to lead the council that held all Twelve Realms in check. I could just be *me*. But then there was Valeria. It was my birthright, my responsibility. I couldn't show up there, put things to right and then disappear like a shadow wielder in the middle of the night, never to be seen again.

The gods and goddesses who lived there would expect me to stay. My parents would expect me to get married. Probably to some other god from another realm, some alliance that would help us keep the peace or provide resources that we needed. But then again, even if by some miracle, they allowed me to choose my husband...My mouth went dry as I thought about Arrick—with a chip in his neck, his power diminished so that he was less than me. An unfair advantage and a sickening realization. I didn't want that for him. I knew I couldn't let that happen to him.

Our eyes still held, and despite all of it, all the impossibility and the strife that us together would cause, the heat of longing flooded through me. I might not be able to have him forever, but at least I had him here and now. Maybe, just maybe, that could be enough for me.

The firelight danced around us, and a hot wind rushed from one of the tunnels, causing the loose tendrils of my hair to rustle around my shoulders. I looked at his lips, full and sumptuous. I wondered what his newly formed beard might feel like scraping over the smooth flesh of my body.

I swallowed, licked my lips, and made up my mind. To hell with space and time. I didn't need to have it all figured out; we could do that later. Deep down, I knew that I was setting us both up for hurt further down the road, but we'd cross that bridge when we came to it.

He trailed an index finger over my lips, and I reached up and twined my fingers into his hair. Twelve Hells, I wanted him. More than I wanted air in my lungs, I wanted his mouth on mine. If I were honest with myself, I wanted a lot more than that.

I tilted my head up to his, inviting him to taste my lips, so he leaned down, and my nerves skittered. It felt too damn good, too damn right to be wrong. Our breaths mingled, and he stroked a thumb over my cheekbone. When his lips met mine, my entire body lit up from the inside out. The kiss started sweet, tentative, and then it exploded. We poured all the longing and need from weeks of physical separation into this single act.

His mouth took mine, and I matched his tongue stroke for stroke. His hands roamed, slipping under my shirt, and I met him there too. We were wild, untamed, each wanting to fill the other. He pulled me onto his lap once more, and I wrapped my legs around his waist, taking the kiss deeper. I never wanted this to stop. My heart thrummed, my head swam, and my emotions somersaulted, but he was my anchor. It wasn't the result of heightened emotions or circumstances—it was real. My heart called to his, and our bodies were meant to be one. I never wanted this to stop; I never wanted to lose him. Valerian politics and rules be damned.

A cleared throat from across the room jolted me, and I broke the kiss. The voice behind me effectively doused any flames we'd been generating in metaphorical ice water. "Some of us are trying to sleep over here."

It was Deklan, and my face flushed bright with embarrassment. I'd completely forgotten about him and Caden in my haste to bang Arrick. Glad it hadn't gotten that far. That would have been really awkward. He muttered something about *"horny"* and *"perverts"* before the cave went silent.

I slapped a hand over my forehead and hauled myself off Arrick's lap. I groaned. "So…that was humiliating."

When I peeked out from between my fingers, I saw that Arrick looked amused and not embarrassed in the least. Typical. He shook his head and grinned. "I've had worse." Intrigued, I was about to ask him for more details when he said, "You should get some rest." Then he leaned in close, whispered in my ear. "We'll revisit this soon, Bekka. When we have a little more privacy."

My lady-parts burned, clenched, and seemed to sigh with excitement. Yet, despite their reaction, I managed to sound confident and coy when I answered, "Maybe. You know, if you're lucky."

CHAPTER 14

REMI

Blindsided

Awhole week had passed since they'd escaped Helverta in the underground domiciles. They'd since arrived at the rebel safe house in the Devanos Mountains. From that point forward, Emorie, Pietyr, and Rackham had fallen off her radar. Yet, despite their lack of visible leadership, the entire operation seemed to unify under one goal: Disaster relief.

So, rather than sit around and twiddle their thumbs while they waited for Emorie to grace them with her presence, Remi and Thayne had taken action. They'd spent long, tireless days helping the refugees displaced from Helverta.

They'd used the complex network of secret tunnels that the rebels possessed to funnel evacuees from all over the city to one of the few secret safe houses The Rising had left. Or at least, they were safe for now. They had no way of knowing what or where Madwyn and Riven would strike next. Neither she nor Thayne were naive enough to believe that they were finished with their coup. There had to be some kind of a bigger plan at play here.

This theory was evidenced by the fact that they seemed to hear reports and rumors of demons occupying different parts of Bicaidia's home planet every day. But, of course, they had no way of knowing if this had bled into the other habitable planets in their realm since communication lines had yet to be restored. All they knew for certain was that demon and Nefaral patrols had swept across the capital planet, enforcing new curfews and laws.

Remi had yet to be stopped by one herself, but from what the refugees she'd rescued told her, the punishments ranged from random beatings to imprisonment. Unfortunately, though, no one could be certain what happened to the gods or goddesses they hauled away to the royal dungeons.

Despite the disastrous state of their world, there was still one small mercy that produced a modicum of hope in Remi's mind. From what she'd seen on inauguration day, she'd expected the streets of Helverta to be lined with the dead and injured. But the casualties had been nowhere near as traumatic as she'd anticipated.

She wondered if that meant that Madwyn and Riven had held back, waited for those buildings they'd decimated to be evacuated before they'd gone to work on them. Or, if it had just been blind luck that news of the insurrection had spread as fast as it had, and the survivors had quickly evacuated to the outskirts of the city.

Either way, it had been fortuitous that Madwyn and Riven had been focused on tearing down the institutions of leadership first. The urban sprawl of Helverta's design kept the official government buildings removed from most of the residents. So, the destruction to those areas had proven minimal.

Though the injuries and deaths hadn't been as horrific as Remi had feared, there were far too many casualties. Gods and goddesses injured during the mayhem or due to one of those beatings were provided medical care by Emorie's people. Unfortunately, the enchanted weapons still mystified even the best rebel healers in their midsts. It sent every god who had been struck by it into what seemed to be a perpetual state of stasis sleep. But that was only if they were offered medical care within the first hour of infection. If the poison ran through their veins unchecked any longer than that, then they died. Without exception.

When she wasn't aiding in the rescue effort, Remi spent most of her evening hours with Ellarah, at her bedside in the stone-walled room of the mountain lodge that doubled as the rebel hideout. Though lodge might be understating it. It was more like a compound fortress owned by a wealthy upper-caste deity. Remi had yet to learn who that person was, but she imagined she'd find out soon enough.

A fire raged in the fireplace of Ellarah's room, and she was covered with the softest fur blankets that currency could buy. Remi ran a cool cloth dipped in peppermint-infused water over her friend's forehead in hopes that a simple, less complicated remedy might jar her awake. Unfortunately, she had no such luck.

Giving up the effort for the moment, she sat on a cozy, suede chair and reached for Ellarah's hand, depositing the cloth back into the porcelain bowl on the nightstand. She leaned down and rested her head on Ellarah's knuckles. "I'm so sorry." Her tired eyes felt drained of moisture. She tried to blink away their sand-paper stickiness to no avail. "This is all my fault."

She sighed and rubbed her thumb over Ellarah's hand before she looked up and stared out the large window; burgundy, plaid curtains pulled open to let in the natural light of the waning sun. Snow flurried outside, and she let out an involuntary shiver, despite the cozy temperature indoors.

She wore a thick pair of black leggings reinforced with leather knees and a thick, forrest green sweater to combat the chilly temperatures of the fortress without using her fire. She had pulled her wool socks over the leggings, and she'd left her damp snow boots by the door. It seemed wrong to soil the room that Ellarah slept in without good reason.

Momentarily hypnotized by the barren beauty of this part of Bicaidia, she rose to her feet and strode to the window, arms crossed as she stared into the winter tundra outside. "I should have listened to my intuition. We should have taken Bekka's letter to the pillar leadership, or at the very least, I should have told you about Pietyr's warning—" She chafed her arms and sighed in frustration. "But, I let my personal feelings about my sister sway me. I was just so damn desperate to get my family back. Not to lose someone else."

Her eyes burned, too tired and dry from lack of sleep to cry now. But her emotions didn't matter anyway. What good were her useless tears to Ellarah? They couldn't heal her, or bring her back to them. She sighed. "I know it's useless to apologize. But I promise, Ellarah, I'll find a way to cure you. I won't let you stay like this forever. You have my word."

Remi strode over to her and kissed her forehead. The remnants of peppermint stung her lips as she turned and strode to the door, slipping on her boots before she opened it. She clicked the door shut behind her, jumping when she heard a voice. "That's a hefty promise." Pietyr stepped from the shadows, the lines of his tall frame materializing from them.

She tilted her chin up in defiance, attempting to hide her surprise at his sudden appearance. When she replied to his observation, her voice didn't quaver. "I meant every word of it." The sun had begun to set, and she could see the purply, cloud-laden sky from the window at the end of the hall. She began walking in that direction. Pietyr hurried to catch up, and she surveyed him from the corner of her eyes. "Just how much did you overhear in there?"

He offered her a semi-guilty expression. "All of it."

"You know, spying on personal moments is frowned upon in polite society."

He lifted a shoulder. "It's what I do, as you may recall." Of course, she thought. He'd been born a spy by nature and then trained for his entire life to do just that. What made her think he would have any respect for personal boundaries?

"Any reason why you're listening in on my personal conversations? Or am I just lucky?" she asked, letting her displeasure at the intrusion show without dismissing him out of hand. She hadn't seen him in days, and right now, she wanted to know why he'd sought her out at all.

Rather than look remorseful, he half-grinned at her in amusement. "Don't be so self-important; I'm here on orders. You've worked every shift of the rescue mission since you arrived at the safe house and Emorie sent me to tell you that it's time for a break."

Remi eyed him from beneath her lashes, her expression hostile. "How would either of you know that I've worked every shift? It's not like you've been around since you dropped us into this rebel's nest."

Pietyr offered her a shrug of his shoulder. "First, I have my sources. And second, would you rather I left you in that comm station? Or how about in that alleyway with the city crumbling around you and the demons, Madwyn, and Riven closing in on you? Or even better, would you prefer to be in the palace dungeons right now? Because without our help, that's exactly where you'd be."

Goosebumps raised along Remi's arm. She pressed her lips together, and, swallowing her pride, she shook her head.

Pietyr gave one succinct nod before his mouth tilted in a wry expression. "They say war makes for interesting bedfellows. I guess they were right."

Remi turned the corner, him tight to her side as she lengthened her stride. "Is that what this is now? War?" Her voice felt tight, strained. In her lifetime, she'd never had any experience with war. She'd always had her grandpa, protecting the realms and keeping the peace at all costs. He'd never failed once in his task. But now, he had been gone less than two months, and it had already begun to fall apart. It let her know just how fragile their peace had been all along.

Seeming to sense the turmoil roiling inside her, Pietyr laid a hand on her shoulder and pulled her to a stop. He spoke, but not with his lips, mouth, or tongue. Instead, he shadow-spoke, his voice brushing over her ear. Not wholly unwelcome, but still disconcerting. "What else do you call everything that's happened since your inauguration?" he asked. The words seemed to linger between them as his eyes stared right into hers. Green and gold flecks that she hadn't noticed before penetrated the silver. They were even prettier than she'd given him credit for, but more unsettling this close up.

She blinked, breaking the spell that seemed to bind them, and shook her head. "You're right. I just—" she sighed. At first, she'd clung to hope that this had been a localized rebellion. Something that they could quash with the correct application of force. But with all the news coming in from all over the planet, she'd had to let go of that hope. "I just can't believe how quickly 900 years of peace fell apart."

This time he spoke aloud, "But it wasn't quick, Remi, not even close. You know that, right?"

She looked up at him, back into his disquieting eyes. "What do you mean?" It had seemed pretty quick to her. One minute everything was fine; the next, an insurrection was underway, and the stability of their world had crumbled around them. The thought made her feel sick.

Pietyr gave her a pitying look that would have infuriated her if it hadn't also been laced with genuine sympathy. "The seeds of this rebellion have been sown for centuries now. Gabryel kept the Nefarals in a chokehold for decades, even after most who'd fought against him in the war had died. I mean, governor chips, regulations, rules against the use of their magic? Those practices are akin to imprisonment for committing no crime whatsoever. What did you all think the outcome of that kind of oppression would be?"

Her mind seemed to tumble as she processed the picture he painted. Then, finally, she turned her back to him and moved to the window at the far end of the hall, needing some space and a moment to think. The sun had slipped behind the white mountains outside, and the hanging iron and glass sconces had turned on to light the stone-laden halls.

She'd never really thought about The Peacekeeper's laws in that way before. She considered his perspective, eyes on the white of the snow, still visible despite the darkness outside. As she ran through his logic, she had to admit that she saw sense in it. Though she knew the Nefarals had been an immediate threat a thousand years ago, hadn't they stopped being one centuries ago? Well, at least until The Rising.

But then, was this really a threat of their own making? If her grandpa had loosened the rules, allowing the Nefarals more freedom, could he have stopped this before it started? She rubbed the bridge of her nose between her thumb and her forefinger, a headache beginning to form.

She sighed, knowing that her family would never have considered that an option. She knew all too well that there was no cost too high for Gabryel if it meant that the peace held. She had no illusions of this fact because her parents and Gabryel himself had told her as much. An old, unwelcome memory flashed in her mind, and she did her best not to wince, not to show the emotion that it dredged up inside of her.

Instead, she focused on the present. She could feel Pietyr's presence looming close behind her, his reflection displayed in the glass just above her shoulder. After a few careful breaths, she got her mind and her emotions under control and turned back to face him.

She replied, the words eerily similar to her parent's and the council's. She tried not to hate herself for it. "He put those laws in place to protect mortals and immortals alike. Everyone knows that the Nefaric gifts have a way of turning sour when they're allowed to run rampant."

Distaste flashed across his face, his lip curling. "So then the means justify the ends? That's what you want to go with?"

She squared her shoulders and spoke, finding that her words tasted bitter on her tongue, "It's better than what we had before. You've heard the stories. We all have."

He stared at her, those intense eyes boring into hers for a long while. "Do you really believe that? That this is the best we can hope for? That systematically condoned oppression is what must be done to maintain peace?"

"What would you suggest? A free-for-all? Let the Nefarals run wild and do as they wish? That didn't go so well for anyone before. If we let that happen, then we'd end up right back where we started over 900 years ago."

Something like surprise flashed in Pietyr's eyes. "You honestly don't know what they did, do you?" He looked astonished, his brows rising high on his forehead. Then, he stepped closer, so close she could smell the woodsy scent of his skin.

Her heart pounded as the warmth from his body enveloped her. "Know what?" she asked, uncertain what in the Twelve Hells he was getting at.

He shook his head and a bitter, arrogant laugh issued from his lips. "I can't believe they didn't tell you. We thought you knew. That's why Ahlexei and Emorie were furious that we'd saved you."

Ahlexei. The god who'd slandered her the moment she'd arrived. She held Pietyr's eyes still, then stepped forward and gripped his forearm, her nails biting into his flesh. "Know what?" she asked again, the sharpness in her voice unmistakable. She didn't like the way he looked at her, as though she were a clueless child to be pitied.

He looked down at her hand, but she didn't remove it. Instead of yanking out of her grasp, he stepped closer so that mere inches separated them. Shadows swirled around them and their presence made her feel uneasy. In her ear, his magic whispered, "Nefarals weren't the only ones with governor chips, Remi. They chipped a lot more deities than you think. Thousands of non-Nefs have them, or at least they did before Madwyn and Riven disabled them all."

Her breath caught in her throat, burned there for a brief moment as her mind reeled, trying to process what he'd just revealed. What did he mean by that? Who else, if not just Nefarals, had them and why? Did she want to know? She stood frozen to the spot, her mind filled with disbelief and suspicion. Then, before she could make a conscious decision, the words were out of her mouth. "No, you're lying. That can't be true. The law is clear, and only Nefarals are subject to chips."

He stepped back, the shadows shifting and absorbing into his skin as he leashed his gift. He shrugged his shoulders, an affectation of casualty, but she could see the tension in every muscle of his body. "I'm not lying and I wouldn't level an accusation like this without proof. So, you can deny it all you want, but you'll find out the truth for yourself soon enough."

Her mouth felt dry as she tried to swallow. She shook her head, unable to believe him, yet he said he had proof. Before she could formulate a coherent retort, he changed the subject, "But that's not why I'm here. We have more pressing issues to deal with right now. Emorie wants—"

She held up a curt hand to stop him, and he paused mid-sentence. She didn't care what Emorie wanted at that moment. He'd just dropped a bomb right into the middle of her life, something that went against everything she knew. Her mind whirred as she tried to process it, what it would mean for the

Twelve Realms if the allegations were true. Her family couldn't have—no, they wouldn't have. Would they?

She felt denial take hold. "I don't believe you. My family, they would never—"

Pietyr's cold, harsh laugh interrupted her. "You don't have to believe me. Emorie will show you the proof, but you might not like what you see. She has good reason to hate Valeria."

Remi swallowed, her throat bobbing. Her face felt hot, and her limbs cool as she tried to control her racing thoughts.

Despite her best efforts at denial, she thought back to that old unwelcome memory once more. She remembered the PAB, that archive, and the words *"whatever it takes"* beat like a drum in her brain. Those were the words her parents had used when they'd found her there, in their secret place that no one else was meant to see. The exact words her grandpa had used when he'd made her promise never to tell Bekka what she'd found. With the memory of what they were capable of fresh in her mind, her resolve that her family would never do what Pietyr alleged weakened.

The shadow deity watched her, his eyes fixed on her as she grappled with the possibility that he wasn't lying, and that everything he said was true. When she didn't say anything else for a long while, he spoke, "Look, Emorie expects both you and Thayne to report to command first thing in the morning. You can ask her about the chips then, if you like. I'm sure she'd be happy to enlighten you both to what your families have been up to."

Pietyr stepped back then, and she could see shadows trailing beneath his feet again, sheeting down his back. She knew instinctively that he was about to disappear, but she lunged forward and gripped his forearm again to stop him. "So, you throw that on my lap, and now you're just going to leave?"

Pietyr stared at the hand that gripped his forearm, and then he looked up. Back into her eyes. "I'm guessing I've given you enough to think about for one day. Oh, and don't forget to take the night off. Emorie won't be happy if she sees you on the front lines again. She needs both you and Thayne rested for tomorrow."

Remi's jaw flexed as her teeth clenched in anger. She didn't like these accusations against her family, but deep down she knew that they carried weight, no matter how much she wanted to deny them. If someone like her, someone who should be loyal to the Valerian royals couldn't dismiss them out of hand, then what would the rest of the Twelve Realms think if these allegations were ever made public? She hoped that Pietyr was bluffing, that Emorie had no proof, but a pit had taken up residence in her stomach. She hated to admit it, but her gut told her that they must have something to back up their claims.

Whatever it takes. Whatever it takes.

Pushing aside the dread that enveloped her, she chose to focus on the less horrifying reason for his visit. "Are you giving me an order?" She asked, chafing a little at both his and Emorie's presumptuousness

"No, Princess. I'm just relaying one from Emorie," Pietyr replied. He offered her a lopsided grin, full of swaggering confidence. "And you'd do well to follow it. She isn't the most pleasant person to receive an order from. Trust me; you don't want her coming to your chamber. I'm a much more charming messenger."

Irritation spiked within her without warning, indignation flaring. She resisted the urge to roll her eyes. At least she was on familiar footing now, and he wasn't hitting her with mind-boggling accusations against her grandfather and her family. "You keep telling yourself that."

Before she could utter another word, his shadows enveloped him, and he was gone. She could hear a throaty laugh in the air as she ground her teeth. As much as she wanted to tell him to take Emorie's order and shove it up places unmentionable, curiosity outweighed that urge. She wanted to know what Emorie had to say. Maybe there'd been a new development in their current situation, something that could help Ellarah and the dozens of others poisoned by the demons' blades. Or maybe they'd found a way to turn the tables on Madwyn and Riven, she thought, not allowing herself to get her hopes up too much on that front.

But then she thought about Pietyr's assertion just moments before. Did Emorie truly have proof? Or had he been exaggerating? She stood alone in the hall for a few moments and felt a sick kind of dread wash over her as she consider the possibility. What would it mean if Emorie actually had concrete evidence of what Pietyr alleged? What would that do to the Twelve Realms? The trust in The Peacekeeper's council? The entire thing would implode, she thought, dragging her hands through her hair. Maybe she'd take that break Emorie had ordered. But not because she'd demanded it. Because right now, Remi knew that she needed it.

As she approached her chamber doors a few minutes later, weariness seemed to weigh down her every step. That conversation with Pietyr had been a lot to process and had dredged up old memories. Ones she'd thought long buried.

Whatever it takes.

She tucked a tumble of red waves behind her ear as she opened the double doors to her chambers. The instant she stepped inside, she spotted Thayne.

Since their arrival at the rebel safe house, the room selection had been limited. They'd recruited at least another 30 gods and goddesses from the melee in Helverta and ten more from the cities outside the capital. The additional recruits were the reason they shared a room.

It had been forced and uncomfortable at first, but they'd managed it well enough. He'd slept on the bear-skin rug on the floor while she took the bed. Despite her insistence that they switch off and share the bed, he had never allowed it.

Guilt over Thayne's inevitable discomfort nagged her each night, but she still couldn't bring herself to invite him to share her bed. Granted, she was no prude, but they had yet to discuss anything that had happened with Madwyn during the night of the inauguration. At first, she'd told herself that they were too busy with the rescue effort to even think about anything else. Then she blamed the need for her temper to cool off before she bridged that topic. Now though, she knew the truth. They were both cowards, avoiding a subject they knew would probably end in a fight. Honestly, she just didn't have the energy for that anymore.

She sighed, and as she peered into the room, she saw him standing at the far edge of it, where a rough-wooden desk sat, a holo station at its center. He had turned it on and was flicking through the news feeds. While just a few days before, there would have been sect representatives talking through their pillar leader's agendas, at that point, every feed showed nothing but an empty, black screen.

Madwyn and Riven had done their jobs well—no news, no intranet, no contact with the outside realms or the other Bicaidian planets. Total Isolation. She could only guess how the other planets were faring. There were still so many questions left unanswered. How coordinated had the attack been? What was the extent of the damage? How many of the other Bicaidian planets had been targeted?

But, rather than worry about questions she had no answers to, Remi turned her attention to her husband. "Hey," she said, her voice soft as she lingered in the doorway. Thayne turned toward her in surprise. He'd clearly been so absorbed in his task that he hadn't heard her enter. She slipped off her boots and moved toward him, socked feet padding on the cool stone floor. A fire roared on the far wall, warming the otherwise cold, gray stone room. "No luck?" she asked, peering at the blank holo.

He shook his head. "No feeds, no feedback. Nothing. They've shut the entire system down, and there's no telling when they'll pull it back up."

She leaned over the rough-wood table and switched off the device. The low hum of machinery quieted, and she straightened, crossing her arms in thought. "You think they will?"

Thayne sighed, running hands through his hair. "I'm working on the theory that they'll have to. Emorie said they had followers, right? So, they'll eventually have to communicate with their allies. It can't stay down forever."

Remi nodded and pursed her lips. "That's true. Let's hope they do. Some of the science deities say there's a shot we can use their communication system against them once it's online."

Thayne's intense gaze landed on her. She couldn't help but notice the change in it. It had once been full of good humor and authority, but since the inauguration, she could see the torment and anguish in his eyes. Another of the list of reasons she hadn't wanted to broach the topic of Madwyn. He'd been grieving his parents, for Ascended sake. What kind of a selfish brat would she be if she picked a fight over his ex-girlfriend when they had so many bigger issues?

"I agree with them. That's why I keep checking," he said, rising and moving over to the closet, where a small selection of clothing had been provided to them. He opened it and pulled out a casual, lightweight jacket. He slipped on the black material and zipped it up. "Were you visiting with Ellarah again?"

"Yes, in a moment of desperation, I decided to try some peppermint oil. I thought maybe there was the off chance that something simple like that would work." She pinched the bridge of her nose and shook her head. "It didn't."

After a long pause, where he seemed to stare straight through her, he covered the distance between them. Then, to her surprise, he wrapped his arms around her and pulled her close to him. His hands twined themselves into the fabric of her sweater, and she felt a tug in her belly in response. The firm muscles of his chest felt good against her cheek as she returned the gesture, squeezing him tighter. Her heartbeat seemed to intensify, taking solace in the comfort he offered her. After a long moment passed, he released her and set her at arm's length, strong hands still gripping her upper arms.

She peered up at him, confused and a little thrown off guard. "What was that for?"

His loose, dark hair framed his angular face as he looked out the window for a moment. The sharp line of his jaw and cheekbones were more pronounced in the firelight. She couldn't help but think that he looked like a tragic hero from one of the mortal novels she often devoured.

When he looked back at her, his eyes seemed heavy with emotion. "It's an apology." He let out a long sigh, and she could see the pain cut into sharp relief on his face.

"For what?" she asked, unsure what he meant exactly. There was so much to apologize for, and she knew that not all of it was on his end either. She understood her part in the current disaster as well.

She still believed that their plan to get Bekka home and in her seat as Peacekeeper had been well reasoned. They'd had to help her, and that it had been the right thing to do. But in execution, it had all gone horribly awry. And she knew, deep down in the pit of her celestial essence, that they had done too much damage. She could think of no remedy to repair it. So, they could help as many refugees as they wanted, but she knew it would never fully clear her conscience.

After a pause long enough that she'd begun to question whether he would answer, he whispered, "It was my plan, and I miscalculated."

The absolute despair in his voice made her chest convulse with involuntary pain. She moved forward, resting a hand on his forearm. She saw it then, the agony that washed over his features. He had taken this all on himself. All the responsibility and all the blame. "Thayne, don't do that."

He shook his head. "Madwyn and Riven were my call. And you tried to tell Ellarah and me to go to the pillar leadership and my parents instead, but I wouldn't listen. I had to do it my way."

Remi clicked her tongue in disapproval. "How could you have known what they'd do? That Riven would betray Ellarah and Madwyn would betray you?" As angry as she was with him for not telling her about their past, she knew logically that all that knowledge would have done was made her second guess herself. Madwyn had never shown signs of hatred or loathing before her betrayal. So she couldn't say for certain that knowing their secret would have made a difference.

Thayne shook his head. His eyes traveled past her out the window to the last vestiges of sunlight waning behind the frosted mountains. "I've asked myself a similar question every minute of every day since it happened. But it goes more like this: How could I have missed it? How did I miss how unstable she'd become? How angry?"

"Hey," she said, shaking his arm gently to bring him back to her. "They were good liars, Thayne. They had me fooled too. There was nothing about them that I didn't trust. Twelve Hells, I liked them even. I envied Riven's relationship with Ellarah—" her voice broke on her friend's name, and she swallowed to wet her throat. Thayne watched her, his eyes intense before she shook her head. "All I'm saying is that they had me fooled too. I'm just as much to blame as anyone.

Though…" She looked away before her eyes met his again. "I wish you'd told me Madwyn was the one from your past."

Thayne's gaze burned into hers and after a brief silence, he reached for her hand. Taking it, he wrapped both hands around her fingers, and his eyes softened. "I'm sorry. There's no excuse. I just wasn't ready to share that part of me yet. She used to mean a lot to me, and I'd be lying if I said her betrayal didn't cut deeper than I could have possibly imagined. But I never expected her wrath to go this far, Remi, I swear it. I had no idea—"

Remi pressed her finger to his lips, stopping him from going further. He didn't need to defend himself or his innocence in Madwyn's scheme. She knew he hadn't known, and she understood not wanting to share everything with her. They'd said no lies, not no secrets, after all.

"It's not your fault, Thayne." He scoffed, raking his hand through his hair. She grabbed his hand once more and refocused him on her. "You had no idea what she'd do, what they'd do. They were your closest friends, and besides, all I'm saying is that there is plenty of blame to go around. We both played our parts in what happened."

"But I'm the one who made the call, who arranged the entire operation. I'm—" His voice broke, "I'm the one who got my parents killed."

Remi took a step forward then, closing the gap between them. She wrapped her arms around him, standing on her tip-toes. She'd known that he'd been in pain since the moment Pietyr had given him the news of his parents. Now, as she held him, she wondered how he'd managed to hold it together for the past week. He'd hidden his grief from the world, working on the rescue effort to keep it at bay. Guilt assaulted her as she realized that she should have given him the chance to talk about them before that moment. But instead, she'd let her own sorrow swallow her like a cocoon.

She could almost understand the anguish he must be feeling. Before, when her grandfather had died, and her sister had been missing, she'd nearly torn the palace apart with her fire. She could see that same despair in her husband's eyes then.

Rubbing his back, she spoke into the warmth of his body, "Thayne, you can't do this to yourself. You couldn't have known. You trusted them. Anyone could have made the same mistake." Though she wanted to comfort him, to find the right words that would make him see that this hadn't been all his fault, she knew that anything she said would fall on deaf ears. His parents were dead, ascended to the next plane of reality. He would never see them again, and no kind words or platitudes would change that fact.

A long time passed as they clung to each other, each taking whatever comfort the other could offer before Thayne stepped away. His face had turned ashen despite the warm, orange light from the fire.

Thayne's eyes hardened as he focused his attention back on her, and she could still see him struggling to control his emotions. This close to him, she could see the circles under his eyes and the paleness that hadn't been there before. He'd lost weight, and his hair had lost some of its signature sheen.

"Did Emorie get in touch with you?" he asked, changing the subject.

Her heart squeezed, knowing that this conversation was done and that there was nothing she could say or do to fix his pain. The least she could do was let him change the subject and answer his question. "No, but Pietyr did. Did you hear about the mandatory break?"

He nodded, his demeanor distant now. "Did he tell you that we're needed for some kind of meeting in the morning?"

"Yep, but he didn't say why. I'm just hoping that she wants to talk about what comes next and how we can fight back. I have to be a part of fixing this, you know?"

The first night of their arrival, Emorie had spent hours dissecting every tiny second of their time spent with Madwyn and Riven. She wanted to uncover any possible detail that might give her a clue as to their plans. Something that they could use to get one step ahead of them. Unfortunately for all concerned, Madwyn and Riven had never let anything slip.

"You don't think they want to discuss the binding again, do you?" she asked, this thought occurring to her for the first time.

Thayne shook his head in response. "I don't think so."

The binding between Ellarah, Madwyn, Riven, Thayne, and Remi had been a source of great interest for Emorie. At first, she'd been curious about the contents of the deal. But after they'd provided those details, she'd brushed it aside. Remi tried to remember Emorie's exact wording, but to be fair, exhaustion had begun to take hold. She'd been awake for over a full day at that point, and all the adrenaline she'd mustered from the battle had flowed out of her veins like tea from a kettle. The gist of Emorie's conclusion, though, had been that the language of the binding allowed for far too much wiggle room in the deal.

Basically, as long as no one divulged the specifics of their plan to anyone else, then they could undermine the entire bargain and still manage to betray the others to whom they were bound. All that the pact had required was secrecy. It made sense. It also made Remi want to go back in time and berate her past self. Why hadn't they asked for the same pact that she'd made with Thayne? Then maybe all of this could have been prevented.

She couldn't help but wonder, had Madwyn worked her magic on them without them even realizing it? Making them all fuzzy-brained enough not to think through all possible angles? But not so stupid as to give them a hint to their own impairment? She ran a hand down her face and stopped to press her fingertips over her closed eyelids.

Without warning, she thought of the pact Thayne had made with her on inauguration night: no lies and half-truths, just honesty between them. "Thayne, there's something else I need to tell you. Pietyr told me something tonight. I need to know if you've heard anything like it before."

He raised his brows in surprise but remained silent, waiting for her to speak. She obliged, launching into the accusations Pietyr had leveled at her family and the other royals. After all, the other royals would have had to be complicit for something like what he described to work.

When she finished, she asked, "So? Did you know?"

Thayne shook his head. "No, but there's no way something that coordinated across all Twelve Realms could have happened unless people at the top were involved. Right? I mean, why risk it, though? That kind of a scandal—" he whistled through his teeth for emphasis.

Remi thought about it and shrugged helplessly. "Pietyr didn't cite any reason for it. Instead, he told me to ask Emorie if I wanted proof." She sighed, raking her nails over her scalp. "I'm not sure if I do, though." *Whatever it takes. Whatever it takes.* She flinched as the words rushed unbidden in her mind.

Thayne rubbed a hand through his hair, his jaw flexing as he considered her assertion. "Remi, you know we have to ask, right? We can't just let an accusation like that stand."

She groaned as though in pain. "I know, but can you blame me for not wanting to know? Besides, she might be able to give us facts, but she won't have the reason. We won't know that unless we can talk to my parents and get the answers straight from them. They're good deities, Thayne. So there must be a reason why they'd do something like this." Her voice had taken on a desperation that she didn't care for at all. Was she kidding herself? Giving herself false hope?

Whatever it takes. Whatever it takes.

Thayne rested a hand on her shoulder. "Don't worry, Remi. We'll figure it out."

"You're right," she agreed, thinking about their meeting with Emorie tomorrow. She would be ready for whatever she threw their way.

CHAPTER 15

BEKKA

Alachary

Three days had come and gone over four days ago. I wasn't even sure how many days had passed after I stopped caring. Arrick's low-ball estimate had been just that, a lowball. My confidence that we would find our way to a portal had begun to wane, along with most of my strength. Nevertheless, Arrick remained certain that we were close to the center. Close to a portal that would get us the hell out of this hellhole.

But Caden, Deklan, and I had become convinced that his constant certainty was just a front to convince us not to panic. The funny thing was, it wouldn't have mattered if he didn't have a clue where we were. We were all too tired for sheer, unadulterated panic anyway. Such an emotion required too much energy, and we didn't have it.

On the edge of the circular cavern, as far away from the fire as I could get, I laid down on the hard, dirt surface and propped my arm under my head as a makeshift pillow. Before this experience, I would never have thought that I could get tired enough to sleep on rocks. Of course, I would have been wrong. Insomnia had given way to sheer exhaustion, though the limited amount of stasis sleep we got each night between watch shifts did little to restore our strength.

Arrick settled in beside me, and I took comfort in his closeness. It had been an entire week since our interlude by the fire, and we hadn't given in to the temptation since, mostly because there hadn't been any. After enduring endless days of agony, torture, dehydration, and starvation, my libido had fizzled out like a candle drenched by a tsunami. Strange, because I had been swept away by that exact torrent of nature just a few hours earlier in the last circle we'd completed. I tried not to dwell on the irony of that.

Despite this momentary lack of interest in anything sexual between us, we each stuck close to the other. As though each of us contained a gravitational pull that the other couldn't seem to resist. He made me feel safe, even though he led us all into new, horrifying levels of agony each day. It wasn't his fault, after all. I knew that. This was a means to an end that I wanted to realize so badly that I could taste it.

I closed my eyes, exhaustion pulling me down into that toasty place of near sleep. But before I could fall under entirely, I felt his fingers wrap around mine. I opened to him and held fast. Comfort was all we had down here, and I would take any that he had to offer.

As I started to drift once more, the unmistakable crunch of a footstep brought me rocketing into an upright position. My breath gasped in my ears as my heart rate soared into overtime. What in the Twelve Hells was that? I thought, startled. Deklan and Caden were supposed to be asleep, and I could hear the soft rumbles of their breaths nearby. Arrick had bolted up as well, and I struggled to make sense of the look on his face in the low-dancing firelight.

"Did you hear that?" I hissed, adrenaline pumping through my system. None of us had been able to shake the sense that something was following us, watching us as it lurked behind corners that we couldn't see. Could whatever it was finally be making its move?

In response to my question, Arrick pressed a finger to my lips and rose into a crouching position. I'd take that as a yes. I followed suit, hand traveling to my thigh holster and clasping around the knife strapped inside. I flicked open the top of the holster and slipped the blade out of the leather. With no magic allowed and my energy sapped anyway, I'd have to rely on the human weapons to defend myself.

Arrick moved away from me, his steps as silent as a panther as he moved closer to the sound. Then, I heard it again, a scuffle and a flurry of shifting pebbles. The slow, steady breathing of the brothers stopped then.

I heard them shift to their feet and then nothing but utter silence. My heart pounded in my ears as I tried to listen. But the sheer anxiety and creep factor of this whole situation made that difficult. I had a bad feeling in the pit of my stomach, and I could feel eyes boring into the back of my back. Nothing about this felt right.

Before I could tumble down my self-made rabbit hole of fear, I heard the loud thump of bodies colliding. First, flesh hitting flesh, and then someone hitting the ground, the resulting gravelly skid unmistakable in the near silence. Groans and grunts of pain came next, and I heard Arrick snarl, "Stop fighting me."

I took off at a dead sprint in the direction of the sound, which fell just outside the perimeter of the light provided by the fire. Typical, I thought, hurrying to catch up to the melee. Caden caught me up within seconds, but I didn't see Deklan. I wondered dimly if maybe there had been some kind of misunderstanding, and he hadn't been asleep nearby after all.

I'd hate to think that Arrick might have attacked him just because he'd had to tinkle.

Without warning, light bloomed brighter around us just as I reached Arrick. I skidded to a halt and stared in mute shock as I took in the scene before me. Arrick held a small woman, blonde, roughly thirty years old, in mortal terms. He had her arms pinned behind her back as she kicked and bucked, trying to break the hold.

Without thinking, I stepped closer and regretted it instantly. Her booted feet connected with my chest and sent me stumbling backward. I coughed, wheezed, and rubbed the point of impact. For a human—she lacked the obvious glow of divinity that we deities had—she packed a serious wallop, I thought, rising to my feet. Either that or I was even weaker than I'd thought.

Ire rose within me, and without thinking, I jumped back into the melee. I dodged one kick and then another, dropping into a sitting position on her legs, thus rendering them ineffective. I ripped a strip from the bottom of my filthy cotton shirt and began to bind her ankles. She struggled against me, but weak as I might be, she'd pissed me off. And unfortunately for her, that had renewed some of my vigor.

Rising to my feet to survey my handiwork, I wiped my hands over my pants. "She packs one hell of a punch." I drew closer and squinted as Deklan came up behind us. "Especially for a human." The fire burned brighter and taller from the corner of my eye, and I realized that Deklan must have stopped to feed it. Probably the reason I didn't see him earlier. Good thinking.

The blond hellcat still fought, the chords of her neck straining as she struggled to break free from the bonds I'd tied. To her immense and evident frustration, she had no luck budging them. I might be weak and tired, but I damned well knew how to tie a knot.

Arrick chuckled, the sound terrifying and low as he crept closer to face her. As he scanned her from head to toe, he tossed a response to my observation over his shoulder, "That's because she's not a human."

I jerked my head to him in surprise as realization took hold. I stepped closer to stand beside him, and she hissed at me like a cornered feline. "Demon?" I whispered, stunned.

He dipped his chin to say yes. I looked closer and immediately saw what he meant. Her eyes were huge, overlarge, and had an ebony color that seemed to eat away at the light. Her features shifted between human and monster as the firelight danced across her face.

Arrick crossed his arms and rubbed his chin with a thumb as he observed her. Rather than answer my question, which worked for me since it was rhetorical anyway, he settled his focus on the demon. I didn't miss the tiny flash of victory in his eyes. Then, with a sense of urgency I sympathized with, he turned away from her and gestured toward the three of us to follow him.

Once out of earshot from the beast and close to the fire, I hissed, "She's the one who stole our packs, isn't she? I'd like to ram my boot straight up her ass."

Deklan snarled. "I second that motion. But, it should be my boot. It's bigger, and it'll hurt more."

Despite his subdued manner, a mask Arrick wore well, I could sense a pulse of energy ripple through him. He spared one quick look at the demon and then turned back to us. "We can use her. She'll know where the portal to Helverta sits. If I can convince her to help us, she can lead us to it."

I squinted one eye and peered over Arrick's shoulder, watching the creature writhe, still fighting her restraints, futile as her efforts might be. I eyed him dubiously. "She doesn't look like the helpful type, and besides, I thought you said we couldn't enlist the help of demons here. That that would be too risky."

Arrick grimaced, remembering his own warning before we'd come here. "Given our current state, I don't think we have much of a choice. This is the best chance we have at getting out of here. Besides, I have a plan."

I looked at the spitting mad demon, who looked like she'd knife us as quick as help us, and then raised my brows at Arrick. "You really think she's going to cooperate?"

This time Deklan replied instead of Arrick, "We can be very persuasive when we need to be." His lips spread into a grin then, the feral disposition of his teeth not lost on me. The alarm bells that should have been ringing in my head at this observation seemed to have taken a vacation. Instead, I heard a chorus of tiny chirps of protest, barely audible over my sheer desperation to get out of this place and find my sister. I had priorities, and a demon's feelings didn't rank very high on them right now.

I offered him a acquiescent nod. "You make a good point. I'll allow it."

Arrick chuckled, and Caden rolled his eyes as a ripple of excitement pulsed through us. This was our first break since we'd gotten to this Ascended-forsaken place. We'd found a demon, Arrick had a plan, and suddenly, things seemed a little less hopeless than they'd been just moments before.

Caden crossed his arms and stared at her, his face displaying an open curiosity and surprise. "She's really a demon? She could just as easily pass for a human."

Arrick looked over his shoulder back to her as well now, nodding his head. "Don't be fooled. She's one of the alachary." When we all stared at him with blank expressions, he elaborated, "They are part of the lower class of hell. Like I've told you all before, only the worst of the worst humans are sent to hell. After they've served their sentence here, they are given a choice. They can either exterminate their souls and cease to exist, which is the fate that most choose. Or they can become demons themselves and continue to punish the evil-doers from the mortal realm long after their souls should have expired."

My eyes widened. I'd not heard of such a practice before, but then we didn't have a living death deity in Valeria. I wondered for the ten-thousandth time why my tutors had never mentioned more than the barest outline of the afterlife to us. Probably because without a death deity, we had no way to manage or maintain it, which meant that no one bothered to visit. But it still didn't explain the lack of records in Valeria. When, or at this point if, I ever got home, I swore to the Ascended I would get to the bottom of why.

Caden's lip pulled back in distaste. "What sort of human chooses to stay in hell and exact the same torture that they endured?"

Arrick rubbed a hand over the back of his neck. "The worst kind. Most of the evil men and women sent here break at some point. The alachary don't, instead they transform into the thing they hate the most. But, what they don't realize is that their choice makes them into a servant class of demons, and this just furthers their torment."

I swallowed, gulping down the horror that this thought elicited. Caden was right. What kind of person did you have to be to choose to become a demon and torture human souls for all eternity? Demons, those made by a death deity, were a necessary evil. They kept the balance of good and evil in proportion; otherwise, humanity's worst instincts and baser needs would run rampant and unchecked. But to choose to become one? The thought sickened me.

"So, tell us again, how is she the break we've been waiting for?" Deklan asked. "From what you just described, how could we trust a word that comes out of her mouth?"

Arrick's face split into a smile. "That's where the plan comes into play. You're just going to have to trust me." Then, without further permission or discussion, he broke from our small circle and stalked back to the snarling alachary. Hesitant, we followed behind him, unsure of what this plan might entail. Hopefully, nothing terrible. Or torturous. I didn't think I had the stomach for that, despite my recent experience down here and knowing what she was.

As we approached Arrick's back, he held up a hand for us to stay behind. "Caden, remove the gag. I want to speak with the alachary."

Caden stepped forward and tugged down my makeshift gag, narrowly avoiding the snap of her sharpened teeth. He stepped back, looking unruffled and composed, as though her gnashing teeth didn't startle him in the least. His calm had to be a holdover from his experience with the Puhari in Moldize. They hadn't exactly been tame either.

Gag removed, the alachary's black eyes bored into Arrick, and her nose twitched. Her gaze skipped to Caden, Deklan, and me, and her mouth twitched upward, her shoulders relaxing. "Gods and…whatever these two are," she said, gesturing to the twins and eyeing them up and down like an apex predator. "This is an unusual treat." Her voice was a feral yet seductive purr, and she shook her head so that her hair rustled from side to side. She ran a tongue over her lips as though savoring the taste of us despite the distance we kept from her.

Arrick remained silent, keeping his arms crossed over his chest as he surveyed her. Nothing about his posture or gaze seemed friendly, and I grew more impressed by the alachary's resolve. She never flinched or showed a single sign of backing down.

After a long pause, she let out an annoyed sigh. "Who are you? Not Master Riven, clearly." She sniffed again. "Someone new. You smell…foreign."

Apparently, demons had an epic sense of smell. How could she have known something like that? Arrick lifted a broad shoulder and offered her an arrogant smirk. "All that matters is that I'm someone who can help you."

She tilted her head back and laughed, the over-sharp canines in her mouth made more apparent by this gesture. "Oh, can you?" Her amusement dissolved in an instant as a snarl crept into her voice. "What makes you think I need your help?"

Arrick rubbed a hand over his chin in thought. "Tell me, alachary, what's your name?"

Her eyes flashed, and she shook her head back and forth. "I'll show you mine if, well, you know the rest. Or at least, you get the picture."

"I'm Arrick of house Brannon and death deity of the Moldizean realm."

I cut my eyes to him, surprised that he'd shared that with her. What if the death deity, her Master Riven, came back, and she told him we were here? I worried, trying to stay focused on the issue at hand instead of the nerves that prickled at my neck.

She jerked her chin to the rest of us. "What about them?"

Arrick clicked his tongue in disapproval and matched her seductive tone. "Now, now, alachary. I showed you mine, and well, you know the rest." A slight throb of jealousy pulsed through me, irrational as it was. But, what was he doing? Flirting with a demon? A creature so abhorrent that she chose to torment souls for all eternity rather than accept a true death? I tried not to let the disgust I felt show on my face.

She rolled her eyes and sighed. "Fine. A deal's a deal, I guess. But, to be fair, we didn't shake on it."

Arrick stepped forward, inches from her body, and gripped her chin in his hand. Black smoked eased from the fingertips that touched her face, and she cringed in horror. He smiled, the expression terrible. "Don't push me. I'd planned to be generous. But, I don't have to be."

"Mina!" she cried out, eyes attempting to track the black swirls that marred her skin. "My name is Mina. Now let go! Please!"

Arrick released her face and leashed his gift, lifting his hands in a gesture of peace. I tried not to react at the sight of his power, but I couldn't help but wonder what the hell he was thinking. Hadn't he just said he couldn't risk using anymore power? He must know something we didn't, and we'd just have to go along with it. Nevertheless, I felt my nerves skitter as I wondered how many times he could wield his death magic before it would be one too many.

"There. See Mina, that wasn't so difficult. Now we've established some civility."

Her skin was flushed, and I could still see the traces of fear on her face. Whatever he had done to her had shaken her up good and proper. She was scared, and that arrogant edge had been dulled. "What do you want from me?"

"Your help." Her eyes widened ever so slightly, betraying her surprise yet again.

"But you're a death deity. What could you possibly need from me?"

"I'll tell you soon enough, but first, call your friends, Mina. I'm willing to offer you all the deal of a lifetime."

My mind raced. Friends? What friends?

With a look of utter stupefaction, she glared at him. I'd never seen someone look simultaneously furious and dumbfounded before, yet somehow she managed just that. "No."

Arrick ran a finger down the side of her cheek, his threat implicit. "Do it now, Mina, or you won't like what happens next."

She hissed again, her expression murderous as she gritted her teeth. Then, after a brief pause, she shouted over her shoulder as best she could, considering that she was bound, "You can all come out now. He knows we're here." I spun around, searching for who she was talking to. That could not be good. What did she mean they could all come out? Then after a few electrifying beats, I heard the shuffle of gravel and the whisper of voices. Demons appeared all around us—two filling each of the tunnels. There were over a dozen of them, all feral and vicious-looking as they crouched in an animalistic battle stance and snarled at us.

They had the same human appearance, with an edge of vicious monstrosity within them. I wondered how they had transitioned into something different than mere spirits. Was the power or transition bestowed upon them by the death deity? Or was it part of some natural progression that changed them from the inside out once they'd made their final choice to turn into demons? I'd have to ask Arrick about it later.

Arrick stepped away from Mina and held up his hands in a gesture of welcome as though he were greeting some long-lost friends. Then, he shifted his body toward us. "Caden, cut her free." Then he addressed the room at large. "Consider it a gesture of goodwill."

I stared at him, mouth agape. Stepping closer, I gripped his arm. "You can't be serious."

He tore his eyes away from the alachary, his reluctance to do so obvious. He fixed his attention on me, and the smoldering intensity of his gaze produced beating butterfly wings in my belly. Even at a time like this, I could feel the allure, the pull, our undeniable connection. His eyes conveyed the words he couldn't utter. *Trust me. I have a plan,* he seemed to say before he turned to Caden. "Cut her loose."

Caden and Deklan stepped forward then too. Caden's eyes assessed the room, and he shook his head in disapproval. He lowered his voice to a mere breath. "Are you sure this is the right move? She's our only source of leverage. How do you know we won't be attacked once she's free?"

He gestured to the other alachary, all of whom blocked any hope of exit. If we had to fight our way out, we would make a downright ruckus. Especially considering how strong they seemed to be and how weak we were at that point. We'd probably need to use our powers to defeat them, and I didn't love the idea of the resident death deity coming to this realm to investigate and finding three Moldizeans and the Valerian creator hiding out in his realm. And to make matters worse, something told me he wouldn't come alone. He'd probably have friends; Nefaric ones.

That possibility became even more pressing when I factored in the very real likelihood that he was a part of the coup in Helverta. And if I was right in my supposition, I didn't think he'd be too happy to see me if he caught up with us.

Arrick nodded at Caden, unaware of my inner turmoil, and crossed his arms over his chest as he spoke, "Like I said, I have a plan. A little trust would go a long way right now."

He arched a brow at all of us, his expression full of confidence. "Caden, release her now." Though he seemed calm on the exterior, I could see the intensity roiling within him. He needed us to do as he asked. He needed to be in charge right now, and seeming to sense this, Caden obliged him. He moved forward and pulled out his double swords. With an ease I'd grown accustomed to, he sliced through her restraints.

Free now, Mina slumped to the ground on her knees. She filled her lungs with exaggerated gasps for air. Dramatic, if you asked me. I hadn't even made the bonds that tight. Well, OK, maybe a little tighter than was strictly necessary. But still, she was overreacting. Once she caught her breath, which took nigh an eternity, she rose to her feet and eyed Arrick with a combination of fear and anger.

"What do you want from us, hell-god?" Distaste was plain in every line of her face.

"A way to the immortal realm. Helverta, specifically."

Her eyes widened, and I could hear the shifting of her pals as they inched closer. Whether it was to listen or to attempt to capture and detain us, I could only speculate. I hoped it was the former. I could feel the room close in around us as they converged closer again when she said, "You can't be serious." She eyed Arrick like he was a toad with a defective croak. "You're a death deity. Why don't you just translocate?"

Arrick flashed her his thousand-kilowatt smile. "I would if I could, but sadly, I can't."

She narrowed her eyes in suspicion as her alachary pals drew closer yet again. They stood a few feet behind us in a semi-circle, and the hairs raised on the back of my neck in reaction. I didn't like it. Not one bit. I gripped my dagger tighter and slipped my hand over the butt of my pistol. If it came to a fight, I wanted to be ready. Arrick held up a hand to stay me, not bothering to turn to face me.

"Can't?" she asked, the invitation to explain clear to anyone in the room.

Arrick held up his hands in a mock helpless gesture and shrugged. "Since I'm not from around here, I don't have permission to go around opening unsanctioned portals into Bicaidia's capital city. If I tried, the other guy might come to investigate. We were hoping for a stealthier option."

Mina smiled, the unnatural look of it unnerving. How the hell had I ever mistaken her for human? She folded her hands behind her back in a casual stance that didn't fool me one bit. "So...you're stuck here then?"

The brothers shifted uncomfortably on either side of me. They could feel the alachary pressing closer, too. Deklan's finger hovered right above the trigger of his crossbow, and I could practically see Caden resisting the urge to unsheathe his sword lest we start a battle right here and now.

Arrick titled his head from side to side. "Not exactly. More, temporarily lost than stuck."

She threw back her head and laughed, apparently recovered from whatever Arrick had done to her moments before. The sound echoed off the halls, and she shook her head. She was mocking us. I could tell because the laugh held no real humor in it. Plus, it didn't reach her eyes. I didn't like Mina. Not one bit. After a long moment of that shrill laugh and the other alachary joining in on the faux levity, she held up her palm. They quieted instantly.

Apparently, she was their leader, and when she spoke, her voice was full of venom. "And why shouldn't I summon Master Riven right now? It sounds like you're not willing to risk using more than the smallest piddling of your powers. He must really hate you. I bet he'd reward us grandly for your capture."

Arrick stroked his chin as though in thought. "I don't know about that." He let out a long sigh. "You can summon him if you want. It's your right as his subjects, but before you do that—" He stepped closer to her, right into her space bubble. I could see a small flash of panic in her eyes, and I couldn't tell if he was trying to seduce her or intimidate her. Maybe both. He leaned close to her ear and whispered in a low voice, "Don't you want to hear my offer, Mina? Don't you want to know what I'm willing to do in return for your help?"

He pulled back and eyed her up and down. A pang of jealousy shot through my belly again—the green monster rearing its ugly head. I wondered if this was how he was with all other women who weren't part of his family circle. Did he always use his natural allure to get his way? I found that I didn't like that picture in my mind.

Her eyes jerked up to his, her mouth open in amazement. Or maybe it was shock? She looked absolutely stunned, as though she had just learned the answer to the meaning of life. "You mean…?" She swallowed, the sound audible, and her breath caught, causing her chest to rise with the sudden effort of breathing.

"Oh yes," Arrick replied, and I didn't miss the smug triumph on his face. Then he spun to address the small group behind us. "If you help us find our way to Helverta, I'll give you what you desire most."

As I surveyed the dozen demons around us, I could see the hope and disbelief gleaming in their eyes. The sheer shock and astonishment evident in every single one of them just by the rise and fall of their chests. I had the distinct feeling that this was good for the demons but not for anyone else. I looked to Caden and Deklan, who each seemed as bewildered as I did. But before we could say or do anything, Arrick said, "I'll get you out of hell. I'll give you a second chance at redemption."

All eyes locked onto him as he began pacing the crowd, appealing to each of them with a fist to his chest. "I'll make you human again."

My mouth dropped open as he spoke the words. Humans so evil that they had gone to hell in the first place, who then chose to torture their fellow kind rather than let their souls perish? And he was offering them absolution? Was he insane? What kind of havoc would these monsters wreak once they were back in the mortal realm? My heart thundered as I imagined the sheer damage this could cause.

"Impossible," Mina breathed. "The Master would never allow it." Her voice was breathy and filled with a mixture of hope and disbelief. She wanted to accept his terms. I could tell from her hesitant denial, but she still needed convincing.

Arrick smiled once again and lifted a shoulder. He'd already won, and he knew it. "You'll have to come with me into the immortal realm. You'll be under my protection. From there, I will take you all to my home realm, Moldize, where you will be reborn. Free from the memories of your old life and all you did here. A fresh start. A second chance. A chance to never come back here again."

Mina's eyes darted to a male alachary, his red hair vibrant in the fire-lit room. Murmurs rippled through the crowd, their whispers inaudible despite their nearness. An ability they must have learned from their subservience in hell.

Arrick held out his arms, a gesture of complete generosity. A king to his subjects. "It's your choice. Come with me and live free as humans again or you can stay here and keep serving in hell." He smiled once more. "An easy choice, if you ask me."

Another rush of harried whispers before the redheaded male stepped forward. "Mina, this is our chance. To start over. To never come back here again. We must take it."

I looked around and saw the naked desire laid bare in all of their eyes. Arrick was right. He did have a plan. He'd offered them the one thing they could never refuse. Their lives back. A second chance.

Mina's head jerked in a nod before she turned back to Arrick and smiled. "You have a deal, Master Arrick." She held out a hand to seal the bargain.

"Do you speak for all present?" Arrick asked before he extended his own hand. "I'd hate to have one of your friends here sound the alarm after I'd already made a pact with you."

A rush of assurance rippled through the room, and Mina's lips twitched into a near snarl at his question. Apparently, she didn't like her authority questioned. I'd have to remember that. "I speak for all of them," she hissed. "Now shake before we change our minds."

Arrick strolled over to her, lazily, as though in no hurry whatsoever. Then, when he was within spitting distance, he grasped her hand hard in his and yanked her closer. As soon as he did, a sliver of his power snaked up her arm. She hissed and dropped to one knee in pain.

I heard panic rush through the other alachary, and they surged forward two more steps. But Arrick held up a hand to hold them back. "It's all part of the bargain. It's a binding."

This stopped them dead in their tracks, but my mouth dropped open. Had he just executed a binding with a damned demon?

"Arrick!" I snarled in fruitless protest as the ink of the bond traced up her arm, then his before it disappeared. "What the hell?"

When it was done, he withdrew his hand. "A necessary evil," he assured everyone, including me. "It makes the pact binding. If either of us breaks our end of the deal, the pain will be unbearable. It might even kill Mina here. I can't say for sure, though. No demon I've made one with has ever been stupid enough to break it."

The red-haired, male demon rushed to Mina's side, who clutched her arm to her chest and sucked in ragged breaths. "You didn't have to do that!" the creature yelled, his cheeks flushing with anger. "You could've killed her!"

Arrick shrugged. "I had to have some assurances that you wouldn't stab me in the back. I never make a deal with a demon without a binding. Personal rule."

He turned to Caden, Deklan, and me and smiled his best grin at us. "Now, are you guys ready to get the hell out of here?"

CHAPTER 16

REMI

Revelation

Remi could hear the wind whistling outside the window of the lodge, winter in this part of Bicaidia hitting with a vengeance as they hurried down the gray, stone hallway. They'd been summoned just moments before by a loud banging on their door. They'd dressed in a rush and opened their chamber door to find Rackham standing there, his youthful visage looking impatient.

"About time," he'd said before turning on his heel and striding away from them. "Keep up, Emorie's expecting us," he tossed over his shoulder. Remi and Thayne had shared an irritated look; neither used to be given such curt orders. But, they decided to obey anyway. At this point, aligning themselves with Emorie still seemed like their best option, if they wanted to stop Madwyn and Riven. Mutual interests and all that, Remi thought, trying not to let Rackham's abrupt manner chafe her.

They followed him past the large wooden doors of the residential bedrooms and into a bustling great room filled with deities. Familiar to them both, it had been used as the epicenter of their disaster relief efforts.

Thayne and Remi navigated the make-shift work stations with ease, following Rackham past the flurry of motion as small teams of gods and goddesses, each responsible for its own sector of Bicaidia's capital planet, planned and executed rescue missions.

Gods and goddesses surrounded holos with live feeds and freshly created portals. Deities disappeared and reappeared in varying states of disarray before they were shuffled out the hall and into one of the three temporary shelters erected since they'd arrived here. All three had once been grand, massive ballrooms in this sprawling estate. Now, they were packed with cots, medicinal supplies, healers, and provisions.

A collection of discarded comms and travel tech sat on one table at the far end of the room. Instaportal spheres and traditional comm devices were all stacked high there, useless lumps of scrap now. Whatever Madwyn and Riven had done to fry all off-planet communications had rendered those two pieces of tech useless too.

Rackham led them to a tall wooden door next to the table of worthless tech and opened it for them. Uncertain what to expect, Remi walked inside, her posture straight and her eyes steady. They immediately locked onto Emorie, who stood on the opposite side of a long, wooden table. Her wild curls were gathered into a massive ponytail, and she wore leather pants and a thick, creamy sweater that dipped low over one shoulder. She looked more like a model from the mortal realm than the leader of the Nefaral uprising.

Yet there they were.

"You're late," she said, her eyes never shifting away from the hologram that she manned.

Thayne moved next to Remi's side then and offered Emorie an expression filled with distaste. "Nice to see you,

Emorie. We were wondering if you'd ever grace us with your presence again."

Emorie's lips twitched, but she didn't bother to look at Thayne. "I thought it was clear that you held no authority here, so why should I adapt to your wants and wishes, your highness? I don't need to give you an explanation, especially when it should be obvious that I was cleaning up your mess."

Thayne's jaw flexed as anger flashed in his eyes. From their conversation the night before, Remi knew where that anger really came from—guilt. He already felt responsible for everything that had happened since inauguration night. He didn't need some holier than thou goddess rubbing salt in his wounds.

Before he could snipe back, Remi stepped between them and held up a hand. "Look, Emorie, you called us here for a reason. I'm assuming that means you found something, or you have some new information to share about Madwyn and Riven. Something that can help us get a leg up on them. Let's focus on that instead of throwing blame at each other. After all, there's plenty of that to go around."

Remi's eyes were hard and cold, trained on Emorie, who at last looked up from the holo. Her expression seemed annoyed but otherwise unruffled. In some ways, she reminded Remi of Madwyn, minus the cruelty factor. Emorie seemed practical, almost to a fault.

"Fair enough," she replied, gesturing to the oversized, overstuffed leather seats that surrounded the table. "Have a seat. We have many things to discuss."

Remi looked up at Thayne, checking to see if he was ready to move forward, to let Emorie's slight go for now. His dark eyes found hers, and he gave her an almost imperceptible nod. At his affirmation, they moved toward the chairs Emorie indicated.

Once settled into the plush cushions, Remi took the short lull that followed as an opportunity to scan the room. Floor-to-ceiling windows on two of the walls provided a stunning view of the blizzard outside. Though it had been repurposed into a conference room, this had obviously once been a study. She could tell because books lined the other two walls and a cozy desk sat at the far end of the room. The table and chairs seemed to have been added later to accommodate more people.

As far as the deities present went, she knew Rackham and Pietyr from their rescue. And of course, Emorie, but there was one more. Male, dark-haired with wire-rimmed glasses, he glared at her and Thayne with a palpable dislike. He was the god who'd said that they should have let them both die when they'd first arrived.

Remi leveled a disinterested, bitchy glare on him as Emorie continued to call up images on the holo, lining them up so that they spanned the entire length of the table. Then, she flipped them so that everyone present could see the full contents of them.

Remi turned her attention to the images and immediately felt nausea crawl up her throat. They were all images of destruction, chaos, and suffering. But, despite her immediate reaction, Remi knew she needed to see them. They needed to understand the full scope of what they were dealing with. So, she squinted, leaned closer, and tried to identify where each of those terrible images had been taken.

As she did, she saw that buildings had been torn to rubble and bodies of servant-caste gods, whose lack of magic made it impossible for their physical bodies to ascend, had been left to rot in the streets. In some cases, demons feasted on their flesh, consuming them as though they were food. Her eyes stung, but she kept looking. She knew she couldn't look away. She had to see the devastation for herself. After all, she'd been an unwilling participant in making it happen.

Patrols of demons and Nefarals seemed to march everywhere, gods hiding in their homes for fear of losing their lives. She saw how those brave enough to disobey received beatings so brutal that she winced in sympathy. Others were chained together with a golden metal that seemed to glow with power. The gods who wore them looked drained and pallid, as though the chains had sapped their celestial essence.

Dread crawled up her spine as she realized that these scenes were from each of the ten capitals across the Bicaidian planets. Not just from the planet they inhabited at that moment. It seemed, though, that the images held the answer to one of their questions. How far had the rebellion reached? They'd wondered. The answer? To every planet in the Bicaidian Realm.

Rather than explain or elaborate on the images, Emorie chose to remain silent, and Remi presumed that she wanted to let the reality of their situation settle.

The death.

The agony.

The destruction.

Remi's tutors had taught her about demons, but they'd said that these creatures represented a necessary evil. They kept the mortal evil-doers in line. But never in her wildest dreams had she imagined they would turn against the gods and use their abhorrent methods against their creators.

Emorie rose to a standing position and rested her palms on the table while all eyes were fixed on the screens in mute stupefaction. However, at her movement, the spell-like effect of the images dissipated. She locked eyes with everyone there, making sure that she had all of their collective attention. "Three days ago, Madwyn and Riven of house Senagal staged a well-coordinated and well-funded attack on Bicaidia. Backed by most of the Nefaric pillar of power and some Altruists, they used the inauguration as a distraction to gain access to a gateway from hell into Bicaidia across all ten capitals on all ten planets."

She pointed to each image and the distinctive landmarks within them. Everyone remained silent as she continued, "Since then, we've worked tirelessly to restore communication across the other factions of our movement from the other ten planets. These images represent most of the intelligence we've gathered at this point. Still, it's fractured and inconclusive regarding how broad the reach of this rebellion has gone into each of the planets. The only other intel we received is this message."

She swiped her fingers, and to Remi's relief, the pictures disappeared. She wasn't sure how much longer she could stomach looking at them. In their place, a video appeared, a god's face filling the screen. In the background, the rumble of explosions and roars of battle hummed. The building surrounding him shuddered, dust falling from the stone ceiling.

His dark eyes darted to a door behind him before he refocused on the recording and his raspy voice filled the room, *"Emorie, I don't have much time. I'm sending this through the secret channel in hopes that it gets to you. All other communication lines are down, and my time is almost out. I'm done for, and I know it. But maybe what I have to say can help you fight back. Help you win."* His image blurred, the camera shaking as though rocked by an earthquake. Remi watched in horror when a metal-reinforced door behind him flexed as though someone strained against it from the other side. He held out a palm, and fire shot out, melting the hinges shut and fusing it closed, buying him some time.

"It's bad, boss. Demons came into the city through an open portal. None of our pillar leaders were here. They were all at the inauguration, and you know we aren't the realm's prime capital. We don't have the concentration of power that you have there. The city fell in minutes, and half our ranks turned on us, all of the Nefarals and some of the more radical inside our organization too. They attacked us at the base, killing almost everyone. Except me. But they'll manage that soon enough." The door flexed again; one

hinge groaned and snapped under the pressure of whoever pressed against it.

Remi shifted to the edge of her seat, her heart hammering in her chest. Even though she knew that it had already happened, she couldn't help but feel a sense of urgency. She wanted to cry out, beg him to run, to fight back. To do something other than sit and wait to die.

"First, you need to know that if we've been betrayed here, then you might have traitors in your midst. Zealots who want to take our cause too far. They don't want equality under the peacekeeper law; instead, they wish to overthrow it. Second, you need to find the new creator, the one who's meant to replace Gabryel. Only the creator can restore order, the balance. I have intel on who she is, and her current location—" The door flexed again, and another hinge gave way.

He spun back, talking faster now. *"She's in Moldize, Gabryel's granddaughter, the blonde one, the one who destroyed the high prince's wedding. My source says that she was meant to travel to Bicaidia tonight. I think that's why this is all happening. They wanted to strike before she arrived here, to prevent her from making it back to the Twelve Realms. But there's more—"* The building shook once again, throwing the god to the side, causing him to lose his footing.

He gripped the table and hauled himself up. *"My source said she had a backup plan. She's with the Moldizean prince, the death god, Arrick of house Brannon. His house is protecting her in some way. My guess is that they're using that backup plan. Emorie, they're still coming, and you need to intercept them before Madwyn and Riven, or any of the other traitors, do."* More shudders as the door flexed once again. The final hinge groaned, but the door held.

"They're coming through Bicaidian hell and into Helverta."

Every muscle in Remi's body clenched as this new, horrifying information set in. *"They won't know, Em. They won't know what they're walking into. You have to be there to help them when they make it through. She's our only hope to put things right—*

" He looked back at the groaning door. *"If it's not already too late."*

The door flexed wide enough that the scaly head of a demon pressed through. It gnashed its teeth, snarling as it tried to squeeze through the crack. The fire god shot his magic out once more, and the demon screeched. Its flesh turned black and charred in seconds flat, and the god looked back at the recording. *"There's one more thing. The weapons, Emorie. The poison, the black poison in them. It's not new. We've seen it before, and we can fight it, harness it to our advantage even. You have to look back to the last war—"* The door gave way then, flinging off its hinges and flying off the frame. The god spun around, the feed still running as another being stepped through. His face was beautiful, youthful, and vibrant. Remi's mouth dropped open then, as recognition slammed into place. He was the consciousness deity, the one who'd given her Bekka's letter. Her mind spun as she tried to focus on the events playing out on the holo.

"Davendrie, don't—" the fire deity pleaded. *"You don't want to do this."*

Davendrie smiled, his teeth sickly white in the dim lighting. *"Oh, but I do."* He stared at his prey, and Remi could tell that he enjoyed tormenting him. Then, with a quick twist of his finger, he said ever so softly, *"Ceryn, why don't you turn that fire on yourself now?"* She remembered his immense power from before the governor chips had been removed. But with his gone? She couldn't imagine what kind of magic he would wield. As though in a demonstration, the fire god's hand lifted. She could see it shaking with the effort to stop on the screen.

Fire bloomed in Ceryn's palm, and they all watched in horror as the flames absorbed him. As a fire deity, one had a natural immunity to their own magic. But this god must have been lower-caste. It took a long time, minutes, but soon the fire began to burn his hair, then his clothing. After another minute, his skin began to boil.

The consciousness deity watched, a disgusting kind of glee on his face as Ceryn screamed. Then with a quick nod at one of the many demons who flanked him, he stepped out of the room. The hideous creatures advanced on Ceryn, one stabbing him through his eye socket. The fire winked out instantly, and they converged on him. Remi could hear grunts and bones crunching before Emorie turned it off.

She waited for a beat, staring at each of them before she shook her head. "Ceryn's dead. As far as we can tell, the rest of our factions are gone." She gestured around the room and to the door, indicating those left in this compound. "This is all we have left." She let that sink in. "The only chance we've got hinges on the intelligence about Remi's sister. He must have gotten it just before he died, or else he'd have briefed me sooner."

Pietyr's fists clenched on the table, and he stood, slowly and with exacting purpose. He glared at Emorie. "How long have you had this information?"

"Since yesterday afternoon. I've assigned a team to scour the records we have on the War of the Nefarals for any evidence they can find on the weapons and—"

Pietyr's eyes flashed with anger. "And you just chose to brief us on it now? We're your command staff, Emorie; you can't just sit on intel like this."

Thayne stood. "Pietyr's right. You've wasted precious time we could have been using to find a way back into Helverta, to intercept Rebekkah." Remi, still too stunned to speak, tried to control her spinning thoughts amongst the rising voices.

Emorie pressed a finger onto the table for emphasis. "Apparently, you didn't watch the same video I did. Ceryn said that there might be traitors in our midst. So, I didn't waste time, I did my research. I made sure everyone I wanted to read in on this could be trusted."

The room split straight down the middle then. Pietyr, Thayne, and Emorie began talking all at once, the dull roar of it throbbing in time with the beats of Remi's heart. Remi, Ahlexei, and Rackham sat still as statues; their faces pale in the white light of the blizzard outdoors. She could tell that they must have been just as stunned as she was. Twelve Hells, probably more so.

They'd lost a member of their ranks, a friend, and someone who'd obviously been old enough to remember the war. They didn't seem quite ready to move on from that point. As for her, she felt sick about what had happened to Ceryn, but her mind had stuck on her sister. She planned to go through hell to get to Bicaidia? Why didn't she mention the existence of a backup plan?

Then, there was the contingency plan of her own. The letter she'd written. Had it made it to Bekka? She hadn't exactly been in the state of mind to tell time while Madwyn and Riven were betraying them. Even if the letter had made it, it was just a generic warning that things hadn't gone according to plan. She didn't dare to hope that the water deity had had enough time to alter her letter and get more information to Bekka. So, most likely, Bekka would be walking into a trap without even knowing it.

Then there was the Moldizean prince Ceryn had mentioned, a death deity? A Nefaral and a sworn enemy to the Twelve Realms? Was he really helping Bekka? If so, why? None of it made any sense. The realms had truly lost their minds, she thought as she rubbed her hands hard down her face and through her hair. She'd let the messy waves stay untamed today, and they tumbled down around her shoulders. She felt the room go quiet around her even though deities still shouted over one another, her mind traveling a million miles away as she thought about everything she'd just seen and heard.

Then the cruel actions of the consciousness deity bloomed brightly in her mind. She knew, deep down, that he had been a part of this from the beginning. The question was, how did it all fit together? And, what would come next?

At last, anger seemed to surge within her at everything that she'd just witnessed. Without thinking, she slammed a hand down on the table. Fire exploded out of her so fast she didn't realize what she'd done until it had already happened. The blast knocked everyone out of their chairs and off their feet, slamming them into the glass and book-lined walls.

In the same breath that it had exploded, the flames evaporated—apparently, her magic's version of a slap on the hand. But what disturbed her more than she dared to admit was how fast it had happened, how out of her control it had been. She hadn't even thought about using it. Instead, she knew without understanding how, that it had come from that well, hidden inside her. The one she had only recently discovered.

Her heart beat fast in astonishment as everyone stayed motionless where they'd landed; only Pietyr was still on his feet. He must have shadow walked to avoid it, she realized, shaking her head to clear it.

At last, everyone began to sit up, and she addressed the room. "Everyone shut up and stop talking over each other." No one dared breathe a word; even Emorie remained silent. She squared her shoulders as they rose to their feet and dusted off their singed clothing.

The fire hadn't stayed long enough to do any real damage. Just enough time to get the attention of everyone present. She continued as they eyed her, a new wary appreciation in their eyes. Thayne seemed to shine with a combination of astonishment and pride, but she did her best to ignore him for the moment. She needed to get this out before chaos descended once more. "Your best shot at getting my sister to trust you and follow you out of Helverta is with me at your side."

Her eyes tracked the room, daring anyone to speak out of turn. No one did. She continued, "Thayne and I have stayed here and helped in the disaster relief, and we haven't asked any questions since that first day. To tell you the truth, we haven't wanted to. There have been other more pressing issues at hand, like saving as many lives as possible. But I'll be damned into the seventh pit of hell if you get any more help from me than you've already gotten before you give us answers. So tell me, Emorie, what is it that you people want? Who are you all? Because you're clearly not all Nefarals. And what do you expect in return for any help you deign to give us?"

Though Remi felt semi-confident that Emorie hadn't been in on whatever conspiracy had driven the consciousness deity to give her the letter from her sister in the first place, that didn't mean she trusted her. She needed to unravel this tangled mess of a web before she would ally herself any further with this organization. She needed to hear the truth and believe it deep into her bones.

She stared at Emorie, waiting for a response. The leader's once perfect curls looked frizzy and disheveled from the blast of heat. However, she still managed to affect an otherwise composed appearance. Remi expected her to evade and argue, give half-truths, but she did none of the above. Instead, she said, "Glad you finally decided to flex your muscles, Remi. I was wondering if that governor chip in your neck had been useless all these years."

Remi's brain did a mental stutter-step. What had Emorie just said? She blinked, trying to process that last remark, her confidence wavering.

Emorie jumped on the opportunity. "You see that expression on your face? That feeling in the pit of your stomach? The violation, the betrayal? That's why we exist. That's what we fight against here every day. Everyone calls this the Nefaral Uprising, or The Rising, but we aren't just Nefarals. Shit, we aren't even mostly Nefarals. We're a coalition of anyone who's been forced to live in a cage their entire lives. So you see, this movement began with that very feeling that you have in your gut right now."

Remi tried and failed to process what Emorie had just said and reconcile it with her conversation with Pietyr the night before. Instead, her eyes darted to the shadow god, and she saw that he stared, watching her with exaggerated caution, as though she might break under this revelation.

Or maybe just explode.

She pushed the emotions aside as best she could and tried to think. As she did, a realization hit her. That well of power. The one that had just unleashed a shockwave without her even thinking about it.

When she'd found it on the battlefield in Helverta, she'd thought the reason that she hadn't felt it before was that she'd never needed it. But now, with this new information, she realized it was because it had never been there before.

It had been blocked by a governor chip.

And probably by her own family, no less.

Before she had time to process that revelation, another connection snapped into place. The sting on her neck the night that Madwyn and Riven had destroyed the governor chips. It hadn't been a pang of sympathy at all, but her own chip imploding inside the fleshy part of her neck. Questions swirled in her mind. If she hadn't been hazy from Madwyn's magic, would she have noticed it more acutely? And how in the Twelve Hells would someone have put a governor chip in her without her permission? Surely, she would have noticed.

Thayne stood then, resting a hand on her shoulder to coax her back to them. "Remi—" his voice sounded far away. "You should sit." After a moment of speechlessness, she did as he requested, unable to do anything else.

Slumping back into a chair, her mouth opened and then shut again. She took a deep breath, feeling out-of-sorts and detached from her own body. She shook her head. Despite how much sense it made with the well of power and that stinging in her neck, she was still stuck on one part. She didn't remember getting one.

"Why would I have had a governor chip? And why don't I remember getting one?" Remi asked, her mind wanting to hang onto denial. The idea that her family would do that to her without her knowledge or permission was too painful.

Emorie held up a finger and called up a document on the holo with her free hand. A list of names, dates, power rankings, and patient notes. It was the same list she'd seen that first day, the one she'd mistaken for potential sympathizers. Remi leaned closer and examined the writing as Emorie explained, "This is a list of everyone still alive who has received a governor chip. They chipped thousands of non-Nefaric deities over the past 500 years and then wiped their memories. You can see the notes here."

Remi leaned closer and found her name. Her heart hammered in her head as she tried to take in all this new information. "Wiped their memories?" Remi squinted her eyes, confusion taking hold. "How?"

"Consciousness deities," Emorie replied, her voice breezy and calm. "For you, a god named Vangyle did the honors. He ascended a few months ago, and Valeria didn't have another upper-caste one. That's one of the main reasons Gabryel arranged your marriage." She gestured to Thayne and then Remi, encompassing their union. "He needed to make sure one stayed in the family. Haven't you ever found it a little odd that all Twelve Realms are required to have access to an upper-caste consciousness deity by Peacekeeper law? After all, what possible use could that serve?"

Remi stood, shoving away from the table, her breaths turning shallow. She spun as fire licked up her arms, igniting again without her permission. She squeezed her eyes shut and forced herself to extinguish the flames. Pain rippled in her mind as the effort of controlling her magic took its toll.

So, if this was true, then her family had put a chip in her neck and then had her Uncle Vangyle wipe her memory. A heady sense of violation and betrayal coursed through her veins, making her entire body feel fragile, prickly with rage. Vangyle had been her grandfather's brother. The only one of her grandfather's original family to leave their home realm of Ipopulca to join Gabryel when he created Valeria. He'd fought beside the Altruists in the war, despite his status as a Nefaral, and had been a critical player in their victory.

He had been a part of her family, and her favorite person to talk to about mortal books and entertainment. He'd always shared her interest in the art their mortal wards created. No one else seemed to care, even Bekka. But him, he'd understood her passion for it. Her interest. She thought back on all her memories of him and found them tainted by this single act of betrayal. The sheer invasiveness of it made her want to close her eyes and shut it all out. He'd tinkered with her mind. Been inside her head and wiped her memories.

What else would he have seen in there? What other memories would he have rifled through before wiping the one he sought? Because, as far as she knew, consciousness deities had an open line with limited control once they made a cerebral connection. Especially if the person they accessed trusted them and wasn't guarding their thoughts.

She squeezed her eyes shut as they burned with unspent tears. It was too much. It was all too much to process. But she could not, would not cry. Not right now. Not where Emorie could see her. When she opened them again, they were dry, emotions controlled, yet still raging beneath the surface—her specialty.

"Why?" she croaked, her voice hoarse from the effort of self-restraint.

Emorie offered her a pitying, smug look that made Remi clench her hands into fists to keep from throttling her. "Every non-Nef who received a chip, every single one had a power ranking over the 85th percentile according to their coming-of-age test. Once the governor chip got put in place, they read lower, usually in line with the family's average across a few generations. We don't know exactly when or why they started chipping Altruists, but we know that it started well after the war."

Rackham jumped in, seeming to have recovered from his shock after Ceryn's video. "Power. They must have wanted to keep the royal families in power throughout the Twelve Realms."

Remi shook her head, denial still fighting for a foothold in her brain. Even though she could see her name right there on the roster, the notes about her original power test visible, somewhere at the 98% level, and then her power after the chip had been inserted, 90%. Still, she couldn't fully accept it. "Nefarals are one thing, but Altruists too? My grandpa, my family, they wouldn't have—"

Pietyr cut her off, though his voice was gentle as he did it. "But he did. These are the cold, hard facts, Remi. Like it or not, it was happening. Hell, it has been happening for hundreds of years."

Thayne dragged his hands through his loose, long hair and fixed his attention on Remi once more. He moved toward her, his eyes intense as he seemed to struggle through his own reaction. "This doesn't make any sense. Why would they do this? Why keep it from us? And why do it to you? You're a part of the Valerian royal family, for Ascended sake." He turned to Rackham. "Think about it, why do this to Remi if all they wanted was to keep the royals in power?"

Pietyr replied then, and his answer stunned her, "If you ask me, this isn't about power. It's about stability." He paused for a moment settling his attention on Remi. "Some powers are more difficult to control than others. Isn't that right, Remi?"

Weary and drained from all of the revelations and betrayals of the past few moments, she shifted her gaze to him.

Pietyr stepped closer, moving toward her, eyes locked onto her like he was in a trance. "I'm guessing you've always had trouble controlling your gift. Most fire deities do, but your power?" He whistled through his teeth. "Now, imagine if they'd let you keep it all. Let you just hold onto everything you have right now." He gestured around the room. "That little outburst you had a few minutes ago is nothing. You would have had a hundred more like them, only a hundred times worse by now. Then spread that possibility across every deity they chipped. So, like I said, Rackham, I don't think it's as much about power as it is about keeping order, balance, and stability across the realms."

Remi cleared her throat and shook her head, trying to fight through the noise of her internal screams of rage and frustration. She had to be logical about this, or else she'd break down into a puddle of pathetic tears, wailing to the moon and cursing her family to the depths of the Twelve Hells. She trained her eyes on Pietyr's and tried not to let the intensity of his examination intimidate her.

"Some powers are harder to control," she allowed, but the admission cost her, as she felt her face crumble just a little bit before she could compose it again. Standing up taller, she continued, "And if my family did this, then they would have had a damned good reason for it." She thought about Pietyr's assessment and thought it held a ring of truth to it. It was a hell of a lot more likely than Rackham's. But the question remained, was something this extreme really the right thing to do? Could she forgive them for it?

Whatever it takes. Whatever it takes. That old memory still hovered at the forefront of her mind.

"Reason?" Ahlexei scoffed, speaking up for the first time since they'd entered the room. "There's no reason good enough for doing what they did." He shook his head as though disgusted by Remi's defense of her family. Then he turned an accusing stare at Pietyr. His voice held a nasally quality that made the strain of emotion he attempted to control even more apparent, "And dangerous powers can't be the only reason they did this to us, and you damn well know that. You know what this bullshit did to me! To my family! And what about Emorie and Rackham? None of us have dangerous or unstable powers."

Emorie shifted closer to him and rested a hand on his shoulder in sympathy, her face softening. "Ahlexei, you don't have to—"

But he shoved away from her and took two quick steps closer to Remi, leveling a finger right under her nose. "There's a reason for the 85% cut off, you know. That's the threshold for upper-caste status, and the only deities allowed to keep more than that are those with the right heritage. Royals and long-running upper-caste family lines. So, you can drone on all you want about this not being about power, but you're only fooling yourselves. They wanted to keep us down."

Remi let the accusation sink in, anger blossoming where the betrayal had been. "You don't know that! You don't know them!" She argued, her voice growing higher and louder than she'd intended.

In reaction, Ahlexei turned on her. His skin crackled with raw energy as his nostrils flared. "You have no idea what you're talking about, princess!" He yelled, the room buzzing with his magic. "My sister, mother and I were all turned into lower-caste energy gods because of this barbaric practice. So, I had to work in the energy mines for centuries, letting the upper-caste pricks suck me dry day after day. It eventually killed my mother and my sister, and I wouldn't have been far behind them if Emorie hadn't found me."

He looked at his leader then, his eyes glistening with outrage, and then he turned back to Remi. "None of us had to be there; we could have been upper-caste gods. Part of the leadership of the pillar. But Gabryel and the Valerians, and all these arrogant, entitled royal families made us suffer instead." He sneered, not bothering to hide the hatred he so clearly felt. "They chose our fate for us without giving a second thought to the consequences. So you can take your *they must have had a good reason*' speech and shove it up your ass." With that, he turned on his heel and stormed out the door, slamming it shut behind him.

Remi stared, stunned by everything he'd just said. The implications of it, the accusations so monumental and mind-boggling that she had no idea what to say or do.

Even though she didn't know Ahlexei at all, her heart broke for him. He'd lost his family from this practice. But then, was it really her grandfather's fault that Bicaidia continued to allow energy mines? They'd outlawed anything like that in Valeria, and she made a mental note to do the same in Bicadia. Of course, that was if anything ever got back to normal. If she were honest with herself, she had begun to doubt the possibility of that.

Still, the heat of his hatred, his vehemence penetrated her shell even as she tried not to let it. After all, it wasn't her he was angry with. She'd been violated, same as him. Though, obviously, her outcome hadn't been as drastically changed as his or his family's.

Whatever it takes. Whatever it takes. Her parent's mantra continued ringing through her mind, adding to her confusion and wavering certainty of her family's good intentions.

She looked back to the listing with her name on it, followed and preceded by so many others. If The Rising had had that much dirt on the Peacekeeper's council, why hadn't they aired it? Why not drop that bomb, then sit back and watch the fallout? It would certainly have ended the council and the practice. But then it probably would have started a war too, which Pietyr had said that they didn't want.

Emorie's voice broke through the chorus of thoughts raging through Remi's mind. "So, Remi, you asked what we wanted. You wanted to know what our goal is for this movement? It's a simple thing, really, same as I told your husband that first day. We want freedom. Freedom to rise within the ranks of deities. Freedom to choose our destiny and an opportunity at a chance for a better life than the one we have right now. We've committed no crimes, neither have over 99% of the people who received these chips." She pointed to the screen and let her words settle. Her amber eyes blistered with heat and passion, then her mouth turned up with a satisfied smirk. "So, what do we expect in return for help, you ask? We expect a seat at the table, and we expect these practices to end. And we expect you to convince your sister to get that done for us."

CHAPTER 17

BEKKA

Elucidation

After the deal of a lifetime for the alarchary and a glimmer of hope for us, we learned why hell was empty at last. Once Mina had relayed the entirety of Riven's plan and his collaboration with the coup, all hope had evaporated like a shadow in the night. My insides curdled like they'd been dipped in acid, and bile crept up my throat.

Arrick's face, previously filled with confidence, looked stricken. We'd underestimated just how bad the situation was in Helverta. Demons unleashed in the immortal realm? An alliance forged between them and the most powerful Nefarals in Bicaidia? Black-as-death killing weapons they'd spent months developing?

When Mina described how Riven had eradicated the souls of every human left in hell the minute my grandpa had died, I realized just how naive we had been. Of course, they wouldn't wait; they'd strike while the chips were down.

While there was no Peacekeeper to stop them.

Sweat trickled down my back as I pressed my fingertips to my eyelids. A headache bloomed there from the intense panic and resulting adrenaline rush that this revelation had caused.

"You mean, the death deity unleashed hell into the immortal realm?" Arrick asked, his voice filled with horror. He dragged a hand down his face and settled his gaze on me. Was that panic in his eyes? Was he panicking? Arrick never panicked. This was so very, very bad. I dragged breath into my lungs and tried to calm myself.

Mina nodded, as did the other alachary. They all had the same semi-human appearance that had grown far less so once they'd moved closer to the fire. Once adequately lit, you could see the monster that lurked beneath the surface. It was as though a skeletal shadow shone through if the light hit them just right—all jagged jawbones, sharpened teeth, and bulging eye sockets.

I felt my chest get tight, and my nails bit into my palms from my clenched fists. "Remi. She could have been—" I swallowed, unable to finish the sentence. The idea that my twin could have been killed in the violent assault Mina described had not escaped me, but I couldn't accept it. It felt as though if I said it aloud, that would make it real. And I didn't want to lend that possibility any more credence than absolutely necessary.

Arrick stepped close to me and rested his hands on my shoulders. "Don't do that. Don't assume anything until we know for certain."

Caden spoke, and I pulled out of Arrick's grasp, turning to face him. "Arrick's right, Bekka. We don't know what's happened to her. Riven could have lost, and we could have just missed Remi when she tried to open a portal to Moldize for us."

Arrick shook his head somberly, his expression filled with regret. "If he'd lost, then he would have retreated back here."

"How can you know that?" Caden argued, his words full of passion.

Arrick's jaw clenched, daring someone to defy him. "It's what I would've done. He could have transported back here before anyone was the wiser. In hell, he's untouchable. After all, he could lock this dimension shut behind him. He's the only one with a key. Except for me, that is."

Mina cleared her throat, her face a mask of passive indifference. "He's right. That was the Master's plan in defeat. But he said something else, something more, something about freeing his power. He said that they would all be unstoppable once their powers were freed. This is how he convinced the demons to join his war, by promising them riches, glory and protection in return for their service."

My jaw dropped open, unable to believe the deal the death deity had given them. The implications behind everything she'd just said, the consequences, they were all deadly. Everything she described was world-ending. At the very least, such an action would send all Twelve Realms into upheaval, maybe even all-out war.

Arrick seemed to recover first, his shrewd mind zeroing in on a point that hadn't even occurred to me. "Then why are you still here? Why didn't you take the deal?"

Mina shifted from foot to foot, the ripple of muscle in her legs shifting beneath her bare skin exposed by her ragged shorts. She looked around her to the other alachary, but they all seemed unwilling to speak.

After a long pause, she answered, "What he offered—" She rubbed a thumb over her chapped lips, her eyes unsettling in the warm light. "I know when something sounds too good to be true. Others, high ranking demons, refused at first, too. But then he executed them for everyone to see. No one refused him after that. At least, not to his face."

Arrick crossed his arms over his chest, a defensive and suspicious gesture. "But you did?"

Mina's throat bobbed. "We did, but——"

"Ah," Arrick said, his expression showing that he'd made some kind of connection. "That's why you didn't have to think about my offer. You want out of here as much as we do because when he finds out you're missing, he'll kill you himself."

A hushed whisper rushed through the alachary, their heads bobbing their ascent, sharp teeth bared in a collective smile. They seemed undisturbed by Arrick's pronouncement.

When Mina spoke again, I began to understand why. Her chin tilted up with smug arrogance. "You know, we'd been watching you for days before we showed ourselves. We knew what you were, where you wanted to go, and why weeks ago. We destroyed your packs the moment you arrived. We needed you as weak as you are now. That way you'd need us."

Anger spiked within me, and I caught movement from the corner of my eye. Caden and Deklan had both shifted into a fighting stance, their hands hovering above their weapons. They looked furious beneath their exhaustion. Of course, we knew that they had to be the ones who'd stolen our packs and that it had been an intentional move. But hearing them admit to wanting to weaken us, make us desperate, sparked a rage within me that I fought to control.

Mina continued, "Don't you see? We could have let you find us any time."

Arrick's eye's sharpened, and he leaned closer. "But you waited until we were desperate enough to make you an offer."

She tapped a finger to her nose in confirmation, an oddly human gesture that I found unsettling. Then she smiled, all of the alachary joining her again in the motion. They peered at each other, proud of their deception. My skin crawled, and I felt sick. Arrick had promised these creatures, these monsters, a fresh start. A new life. And they'd played us for fools.

They'd let us languish here, waiting for weeks for us to grow weak, all while a battle raged in Bicaidia, knowing that we planned to stop it. They'd left untold numbers of deities to die while we toiled in this shit hole just to save their own hides.

I charged forward, taking three quick strides toward Mina. When I was within spitting distance, I whipped my hand across her face, palm slamming into her cheek. Her head swung to the side, and I wrapped my fingers around her throat before she could recover, squeezing. I kept moving, charging forward, lifting her and slamming her into the rock wall of the cavern. Her head hit with a sickening crack, and I resisted the urge to smile.

I waited for her eyes to refocus on me, adding pressure to her neck. "Look at me, you worthless bitch," I snarled. I could feel my power pulse through my veins, and I tried not to groan at how weakened it had become. Anger swelled inside me, and I wanted to unleash what little power I had left and turn her to dust. But, like it or not, I didn't have dominion over the metaphysical, and I needed this despicable excuse for a creature alive. We all did.

Mina's black eyes seemed to glaze for a few beats before she managed to focus on me once more. I bared my teeth, and her eyes widened with fear. "If my sister is dead because you decided to play games with us, I will snap you out of existence. I don't care what kind of a deal you have with *him*—" I threw my free hand out to indicate Arrick. Then I leaned closer and spoke in a vicious hiss, "You'll answer to me, do you understand? You will answer to me."

Mina's feet scrabbled at the ground as she tried to regain her footing, but I held her just out of reach. I could hear Caden and Deklan, along with Arrick, keeping the other alachary at bay. They snarled and spit, but no one had dared approach me. Smart move. Who knew what I would do if one of them tried to attack me? I wasn't feeling charitable at the moment, and we didn't need all of them—just one.

The alachary leader gargled with an effort to breathe as she nodded her understanding. "Good," I growled, just before

I dropped her on her ass. I turned back to the other alachary and realized that all three of my companions had their weapons drawn. Apparently, an all-out brawl had been closer at hand than I'd realized. I addressed all of them now, sliding my knife from my holster and gesturing with it for emphasis. "If you don't get us out of here within a few hours, you can all kiss your deal with Arrick goodbye. Do I make myself clear? Don't forget; I'm not bound to any of you."

Their eyes flicked to Mina, who still coughed and sputtered, her back pressed against the wall. They jerked their heads from side to side, each looking at each other before they nodded their agreement with me.

Within minutes, they began leading us on what they promised was a shortcut through hell and to the inner circle. I let the others pull ahead, unwilling to leave my back exposed to the alachary. I didn't trust them.

Finally, after an hour, Arrick moved beside me. He hadn't said a word about my outburst, never once contradicting me. But since we'd fallen far enough behind everyone to be out of earshot, he whispered, "You know if you break my deal with them, I'll still suffer the consequences, right? The binding goes both ways."

I swallowed, nodding my head. "I know. But they don't need to know that, do they?"

He offered me a proud grin. "Well played."

I shrugged a sharp-boned shoulder. "I thought they needed proper motivation. I couldn't let them think they'd gotten the upper hand on us." We walked in silence for a few moments, watching the alachary slink along this secret passageway as quick as mice, their thin legs spindly. Their clothes were little more than rags. Ripped, soiled shirts and tattered shorts with no shoes. That left their feet bare to traverse the rocky ground, and I wondered how long it must have taken them to become accustomed to the pain.

After my outburst and my threat, Mina had cut her hand with a knife she'd kept hidden in her boot. She pressed the blood against a wall of the central cavern, and it wavered, then evaporated into nothing, revealing a long tunnel.

Since then, the rock walls and tunnels had seemed endless, and I breathed a sigh of relief at the lack of torture. Each tunnel we turned down remained empty, like we were walking through an employee entrance or something. Which made sense. How else would demons get around down here?

Sweat, an ever-present obstacle, dripped down my back, and it grew hotter with each passing second. My exhaustion had ebbed just a little bit with the end in sight, but I could still feel it beneath the surface. It tugged and dragged at my legs and forced me to push harder than I'd ever imagined possible. After a few ragged breaths, I breathed in deep through my nostrils and caught the scent of sulfur. Arrick assured me that these were both good signs. A couple of hours later and the rocks began to change from tan to red. Another hour and the rocks changed to the deepest black. Another positive indication, according to the death deity next to me.

Wiping a hand over his brow, Arrick looked at me, clearing his throat. "There's something we haven't discussed yet, but we should do it soon. We're getting close to the center. I can feel it."

I blew out a breath, a kind of nervous expectation coursing through me. "What do you want to talk about?"

"If what Mina says is true, then Helverta will be overrun with demons and Nefarals. There might not be much left for us there." He let that sink in for a minute before he stated the obvious. "And we might have to fight our way out, depending upon what's waiting for us on the other side of the portal."

I'd been thinking about this very conundrum during our entire journey, and apparently, so had he. I had some ideas, but without all the information I needed, I couldn't be sure any of those ideas would work. I decided to voice my secondary concerns. Why not heap more onto an already massive problem, right? What could it hurt?

"Even if we did manage to fight our way out, where would we go? I don't know anyone in Bicaidia. Remi is the only person I trust there, but we don't even know if she's—" I broke off, still unable to say the worst possible outcome. I settled on, "in trouble. And if she is safe, how would we even begin to find her?"

We were no longer whispering, and Deklan and Caden were close enough to hear our conversation, so they slowed their pace to walk alongside us. Deklan's dour expression spoke volumes. He didn't seem enamored with our prospects either. He looked to Arrick. "What about the contact who sent that message from Remi through? Datania? How high profile is she? Would she have been a target for the Nefarals, or could we use her?"

Arrick sucked his teeth as he thought over the suggestion. It sounded like it could work to me. Besides, no matter how much I racked my brain, I couldn't think of many other options. After a few moments of consideration, Arrick responded, "She's on the lower end of the upper-caste. She's not the type to draw attention to herself."

That sounded encouraging. "So, do you think she could have avoided the worst of it?"

Arrick pursed his lips, thinking about it. "That depends on how far the assault spans. She lives in the city but not close to the palace. She's a water goddess whose sister escaped the energy minefields in Bicaidia around eleven years ago. She came to Moldize through Valeria as a refugee."

I winced in reaction. The energy mines were a sensitive topic for most of the Twelve Realms. They consisted of extraction cables that a licensed operator attached to the wrists and temples of an energy deity. The cables then siphoned the magic from the subject by force and stored it in a massive battery created by science deities.

My grandpa had banned this practice in Valeria, preferring to use more compassionate and voluntary means of extracting the energy that powered both the immortal and mortal worlds. Some other realms had followed his lead. But sadly, Bicaidia wasn't one of them. They still required any lower-caste energy deities to participate in the extraction process. From what I understood, the experience was grueling, painful and exhausting. And the side effects? Even worse. Vision and hearing loss, tremors, seizures....

And even premature ascension.

I cringed as I tried to imagine what this goddess's sister must have gone through to get out of the mines and into Moldize. It couldn't have been easy. But, on the other hand, it bolstered me to know that we would be meeting with someone used to subterfuge. We would need that on our side.

"Good, we find her then. Can we translocate rather than fight our way out?" Caden asked, and I saw a tinge of hope in his eyes that I sympathized with, but I shook my head in answer.

"We can't. My power is too weak, so I'm betting Arrick's is too. I don't think either of us could manage a portal in our current state. I think we'll have to go it on foot."

"She's right," Arrick said, agreeing with my assessment. "My power is depleted as well. So, we keep to the shadows and try to move through the city unseen. We used a map her sister gave us to set up the initial correspondence point. I remember it well, so I should be able to manage a route on my own."

"What about them? Do you think we can trust them to stay in line?" Deklan asked, staring at the alachary ahead of us. Their heads rotated on a swivel, as though suspicious of every tiny shift in their surroundings. I realized then that they lived in a constant state of paranoia, probably learned from the years that they were subjected to torture. I tried to feel sorry for them, I really did, but I just couldn't muster it. Not after what they'd done to us since our arrival.

Arrick shook his head decisively. "Don't worry about them. The minute we cross into the immortal realm, they'll turn into souls. I'll absorb them until we get back to Moldize."

I blinked in surprise. "But Riven—" I broke off confused. "He offered them freedom here to fight. How could he do that if they turned into souls?" I thought about the eel-like creatures that slithered into Arrick whenever a human died. How could they participate in any kind of combat?

Arrick elaborated. "I could forge them a more corporeal body if I needed or wanted to. But I think we'll all be better off with them out of the way."

I resisted the urge to stare at him in wonder. Sure, my powers were incredible. But his? They had so many facets and nuances that I didn't think I'd ever learn them all.

"We agree then?" Arrick asked when none of us said anything for a few beats. "The instant we're in Bicaidia, we'll travel on foot to the coordinates leading outside the city? Then we'll find Datania."

I nodded my head. It was as good a plan as any. At least we had something to work with, some kind of ally. Caden and Deklan nodded their ascent as well just before a voice called up ahead of us.

Mina's sharp tone cut through the hot wind. "Master Arrick, it's just up here."

CHAPTER 18

REMI

Solace

Thayne gripped Remi's hand, pulling her aside as Emorie, Pietyr, and Rackham breezed out of the room. Pietyr shadow-walked into nothingness, off to handle the next steps of the rescue they'd just formulated for Bekka. Meanwhile, Emorie and Rackham hurried to the command center to gather as much intel as possible from Helverta, specifically around the palace. They'd assumed that since the only portal to hell that existed on this planet at the moment was in the palace, all other regulated ones having been destroyed on the night of the inauguration, that this was where Bekka would have to come through.

Thayne watched their departing, tenuous allies from the corner of his eye until he was sure they were out of earshot. "This is insane," he hissed, his deep voice coming out raspier than usual. "We're just supposed to trust that the same movement that enabled Madwyn and Riven to stage this coup is going to help us? Be on the same side of this as we are?" He shook his head. "I don't buy it, Rem."

Remi paused for a moment to consider. Then she glanced out of the corner of her eye to the hustle and bustle of the control room. She understood his reservations. She had some of her own. "I know," she whispered and caught the wave of a relief shadow over his face. "But—" she said, and that relief seemed to harden into disbelief. "They're our best shot at getting Bekka back, and she is our best shot at saving Bicaidia."

He gave her a look that let her know just how naive he believed her to be. "You can't be serious. You want to just trust them?"

She looked over her shoulder to be sure no one was listening before she replied. "Look, this isn't the right time or place for this conversation. But I'll say one thing. They have no reason to lie to us. No reason to read us into this and let us be a part of something this risky if they didn't need our help."

Thayne scoffed. "Unless you count access to the new Peacekeeper."

Remi glared at him. "They told us what they want from her. It's no secret."

She watched as skepticism cut through every inch of his expression. "And you believe that all they want to do is talk to her? Convince Bekka of their cause? How do you know they won't just hand us all over to Madwyn and Riven once she gets here?"

Remi had never found that trust came easily to her, but Thayne had never struck her as the untrusting type until that moment. She supposed that their experience with Madwyn and Riven had tainted him.

She knew logically that he was right to question Emorie, to be suspicious of her motives. She hadn't said they wanted to restore the remaining Bicaidian royals to power once they defeated Madwyn and Riven.

And she definitely didn't say what she wanted to happen to the Bicaidians pillar leadership or the Twelve Realms when this was all said and done. But for some reason she couldn't quite pinpoint, Remi found herself on the opposite side from Thayne on this one. Something in her gut told her that she could trust these deities.

Maybe it was their sense of purpose or the way they helped everyone from the fall out of Madwyn and Riven's coup. She sensed that they felt some level of responsibility to fix everything as well. After all, it had been their intel and their movement that had allowed Madwyn and Riven to recruit so many to their cause.

As she dug deeper, she realized that maybe it was because she was one of them. One of the chipped and the violated. Probably, it was a combination of all of it. Despite her desire to cling to the idea that there had been some kind of grand reason for her family's betrayal, some sort of "greater good" that they had been striving for, the betrayal still cut through her like a knife.

Suddenly, a deep yearning seized her. She yearned for a time when she was naïve, happy, and free, running around the Valerian palace with her sister, letting Bekka drag her into her schemes. She yearned for her mother's warmth and her father's soothing words. She yearned for her grandpa's hugs and stories of battles and victories.

But that time was over.

Her grandpa was dead, her parents were unreachable, and her sister was missing, traipsing around in Moldizean hell. No more laughing, no more warmth, no more soothing words, no more hugs, no more stories.

And no more trust or naivete, because three of the four of them had betrayed her.

Pain seared her heart, and she had to recognize that maybe the most significant reason of all to trust Emorie's group was because she agreed with them. She wanted this practice to end. No one deserved their fate chosen for them or their power taken from them. She closed her eyes and tried to think of a way to explain her empathy, her understanding to Thayne.

Finding no words, she sighed. "I can't explain it but, I believe them. And really? After everything that Madwyn and Riven have done to them, to their cause? You think they'd side with them?" She shook her head firmly. "I think they'll honor their side of our bargain, and I damned well plan to honor ours."

Thayne shook his head. "Fine, but I'll be watching our backs and waiting for that knife." With that, he turned and strode away, the tension in his shoulders a clear indicator of his anger.

She watched him leave, and tried to feel guilty that she'd caused him more anger, but couldn't manage it. She was standing up for what she believed was right. It was all that she could do in this situation. So, he could be as mad as he wanted, but she wouldn't change her mind.

She ran a hand through her hair, and deciding that she needed to clear her head, she began to walk toward Ellarah's chamber. She wanted to visit with her friend if only to be alone in the quiet for a few minutes.

As she moved in that direction, she thought about her sister and what she'd say to her if she were here right now. How would she react knowing that Remi was working with The Rising? The very movement Bekka sought to quash? Surely, she'd have somewhat of an open mind. After all, she was working with a death deity, if Ceryn's intel proved correct.

Her sister had always been the more trusting and more innocent of the two of them. Bekka liked to believe the best of people, no matter how many times they showed her their true colors. As a result, Remi had always felt responsible for her twin, to protect her and help her keep some of that innocence.

For Remi, she'd lost that optimism, that bright-eyed look of wonder long ago. She thought back to the night she learned that things in Valeria were not all peaches and rainbows. That there was a dark side to what they did to keep the peace.

She remembered that secret archive buried deep in the belly of PAB, known only to her parents and her grandfather. She licked her lips as the image of the golden strings of prophecies long-past and a massive holo flashed in her mind. What she'd discovered that night was the real reason why she'd believed Emorie about the chips. After all, her family had done a lot worse than just chip people and suppress their power, as despicable as that was.

Her mother had sworn that the end justified the means, but this secret had burned a hole in Remi's celestial soul since the day she'd learned of it. She'd told no one, not even her sister. How could she tell Bekka that their family had used the PAB and their legion of shadow deities to carry out assassinations when their efforts to subvert a prophecy turned sour?

And judging by the vast archive of golden strings, there had been thousands of failed attempts to prevent an apocalypse of one kind or another. Though, apocalypse might be too strong of a word. A destabilization or a disruption of the peace would be a more apt description for most of the situations she'd witnessed.

Before her mother had caught her, Remi had plucked through about a dozen viscous strings. The sticky, golden cords were the result of a prophecy from a true seer, and she'd allowed the liquid fever dreams to play out on the holo one after the other. Apparently, she'd set off some kind of an alarm because before too long, her mother had appeared, her father close behind.

Oh, how she'd raged at them. They'd killed so many people. Gods, goddesses, humans. Anyone who'd threatened the peace or the stability of their godly world. How could they stomach it? How could they live with themselves?

"Whatever it takes to keep the peace. More would die if we didn't do it. You can see it for yourself in the prophecies. We had to do it to save more lives." That's what they'd told her. The only reason she hadn't melted down and told the rest of the godly world everything was because they'd been right.

The prophecies had been terrible. But the part that still stuck with her was that the people, god or human, who caused the disruptions, weren't always evil or even bad for that matter. They were often the victims of circumstance, or their mere existence threatened the peace. Yet, they'd put them down like rabid animals, given no choice.

In the end, she'd sworn a binding not to breathe a word of this to anyone. That was when she'd started spending a lot more time in the Valerian mortal realm. That was also when she'd begun taking sexual partners, mortal men who were pretty to look at but offered little in the way of substance. She'd needed to escape from her family for a while, to rebel against them.

Now she found that same razor's edge of anger spiking within her. Where was the line? Did they even have one? Was there anything they wouldn't do or anyone they wouldn't trample to maintain order? Peace?

As she exited the control room and strode into the residential portion of the compound, she felt the tears begin to well. The moment she opened Ellarah's door, the first tear slipped down her cheek. She shut it behind her, closing out the world, and looked at her friend. Ellarah's pale face looked peaceful despite the reality of her slowly dying body, and Remi pressed her back to the door and slid down it. She broke then, and when the tears started, she feared they'd never stop.

Later that night, eyes dry, at last, she made her way back to her chambers. She thought about Thayne and his anger, and she sighed, knowing that she would have another fight on her hands. The truth was, she was exhausted, too spent to fight, and she just didn't want to be at odds with him anymore. She wanted them to be on the same side and the same page.

She scrubbed at her sandpapery eyes as she walked down the empty halls; most gods were either resting, helping in the shelter, or assisting in the relief efforts in the control room.

She ran through their plan, or at least, the pseudo plan they'd come up with after Ahlexei had stormed out. It was little more than a shot in the dark and a prayer to the Ascended that it would work. Most of what they needed to do was gather information. So far, they hadn't been able to glean a good entry path into the palace. Patrols of demons guarded it at all times.

All they knew for sure was that they needed to find a way behind those patrols when Bekka showed up. But the tricky part was when? When would Bekka show? And when she did, how would they know?

That was all part of what Pietyr was trying to figure out. Rackham, meanwhile, had started to head up the research on the weapons along with Ahlexei. Emorie would use her contacts to find a safehouse near Helverta where they could hide in the meantime.

She swung around a corner, and her chamber door came into focus. She squared her shoulders and pulled open the door, exhaustion dragging at her. To her surprise, Thayne lay on the floor, asleep, his steady breathing a calming rhythm in the empty night. A fire crackled at the edge of the room, and she wondered if she could bathe in it, let the energy of it wash through her. Fire was her omen, after all, the very source of her power.

She moved closer to her husband, a sudden pulse of lust rushing through her as she appreciated just how attractive he was. Arranged marriage or not, she couldn't deny the allure he offered. His smooth skin glowed in the orange light, and his shiny, long hair draped over the white material of his pillow.

His full lips and strong jaw contrasted with the slightly slanted eyes. Handsome, she thought, tragically so.

She slipped off her snow boots and, before she could question her actions, dropped down beside him. He lay on his back, one arm tossed over his head and the other across his broad, muscular chest. She traced a finger down the middle of his chest, between the sharply formed muscles there. He shifted slightly but didn't wake. Slipping off her leggings and her sweater, she curled up next to him, wearing nothing but a tank top and her panties.

Heart hammering, she snuggled closer and pressed a kiss to his shoulder. His breathing stopped for a second and then resumed as he lifted an arm, offering her a spot on his side. She took it, shifting closer and resting her head on his shoulder. He wrapped the arm around her, enveloping her in his warmth. He ran his thumb over her arm in soothing circles. "I'm sorry, Remi. About… everything." His pause let her know that he meant for the revelations and their disagreement about their new companions. But her mind had gone elsewhere, away from all of the bullshit that had happened earlier.

Instead, desire pooled in her belly as she appreciated the hard line of his body against hers. Then she reached out to touch his face and pulled it toward her. "I understand why you don't trust them. It's probably smart for one of us to keep our guard up. But I don't want to talk about that now. I don't want to think about any of it." She looked up at him from beneath her lashes, making her meaning clear.

His lips tilted upwards, and he rolled onto his side. "What did you have in mind?"

In response, Remi wrapped her hand around his neck and molded her body to his before she covered his lips with hers. His mouth was liquid fire, and his tongue did torturous things to hers as they delved into the kiss. The heat of her desire burned inside her as she trailed her fingernails down his back and then tangled them into his hair. She twined his legs with hers and groaned when Thayne wrapped his hands in her hair and pulled her head back, exposing her neck to his lips.

He sank his teeth into the column of it, the nipping pain causing her to groan in ecstasy. When his lips found hers again, she pressed a hand to his shoulder and rolled on top of him. Their mouths were ravenous as they kissed, and she felt that empty hole, that ragged despair soften just a little. Wanting more, wanting to escape, she rose above him, breaking off the kiss. She gripped the end of her tank top and made to pull it over her head, but Thayne's hand on hers stopped her.

Surprised, she looked down at him. His eyes had grown dark and full of concern. "Wait," his voice was gruff with desire, but she could see him hesitate. "Are you here right now, Remi? Are you with me?"

Remi's body burned, the ache between her legs almost painful. She reached for him, wrapped her fingers around his wrist, and guided his hand between her legs in demonstration. She ground her hips against it and moaned in a breathy whisper, "Can you feel it? I want this, Thayne."

In a move that stunned her to her core, he grabbed her by her waist and lifted her off of him. She moved with him, disappointment and despair crashing into her so hard that she struggled to breathe. Silence lingered between them for a few moments, and all she could hear was his ragged breathing and her own pulse in her ears.

She sat beside him now. "You don't want me?" she asked, humiliation washing over her, but she didn't dare break his gaze. Instead, she stared into his eyes, awaiting his response.

His fingers brushed over her cheek, their touch heartbreakingly tender. "Damnit, Remi, of course I want you."

"Then what's the problem?"

She tried to crawl closer, to press herself against him once more, but his hand on her cheek stopped her. So she gave up and waited for his answer. "The problem is that you aren't with me. Your body might want this, but your mind is somewhere else. The first time we do this, I want you to want *me*. Not just someone to fill a void, because that's what this feels like right now. I don't know why, but I'd be surprised if you were even thinking about me or us at all."

She sank her teeth into her bottom lip, looking away from him for the first time as she felt her heart plummet to her toes. She wanted to tell him that he was wrong. That she wanted him for his own sake, and that's what this was all about. But she couldn't bring herself to say it.

The truth was that sex had been her outlet for a long time. She'd sought it out whenever the world had hit her with more than she could bear. And to her dismay, she'd resorted to using her husband for it. Treating him like a warm body to offer comfort, not thinking about any of the possible repercussions of her actions. Thayne wanted more, and she knew it; he'd told her as much. So, what in the Twelve Hells was she doing?

She swallowed and shifted away from him. "You're right; I'm sorry. I just—" she shook her head, looking back into his eyes.

He reached for her hand, twining his fingers in hers. "Today hasn't been easy, and we have a lot of pressure on us right now." He ran a hand over his five-o-clock shadow. "I'm here if you want comfort, but not like that. When we do that, and trust me, we will, I want it to be about more than convenience and solace."

They stared into each other's eyes, an understanding passing between them. Before she could reply, he reached out and pulled her close. She went willingly as he gathered her into his arms. Then he lifted her from the ground and stood, moving them to the bed. He pulled back the covers and set her on it.

It felt so damn good to be in his arms and even better when he scooted onto the bed behind her. He wrapped his arms around her from behind and pulled her close to his chest.

As his heartbeat drummed against her back and his breathing turned rhythmic, she wondered if this was what it felt like.

Love, or at least something building toward that.

She couldn't be entirely sure. But she knew they were building toward something. She hoped with all of her heart that it was toward all those possibilities Thayne saw when he looked at her. She realized then, with a sweet feeling in her chest that made her feel warm rather than fiery hot, that she saw them too.

CHAPTER 19

BEKKA

Explosive

ina's words sent a shot of relief through my entire body. Ascended be praised! We'd finally made it. I resisted the urge to break out into a victory dance. Mostly, because I feared I might look stupid in front of my friends. But also because I lacked the energy and vigor required to shake it.

The four of us looked at each other, each glowing with excitement now. Then, after a quick pause of disbelief, we picked up our speed and rushed forward. All we had to do was get through hostile territory and locate the coordinates on a map, all from Arrick's memory. How hard could it be?

We passed under a large archway and into a dark cave. My heartbeat quickened in anticipation as the sulfur smell dissipated, and a warm breeze of fresh non-hellish air greeted me. I filled my lungs and closed my eyes, elated at the prospect of getting out of this cesspool, back to a place with soft beds and warm showers, no matter how unstable the situation topside might be. I was fairly certain that I smelled like a hairy yak at this point, and a shower would do a lot to revive me. Hell, I'd even settle for a non-salt water submersion of any kind.

We turned a sharp right, and I could see it. The center circle of hell, the place we'd been looking for for the last three weeks. I wanted to fall to my knees and kiss the dirt beneath my feet, but I restrained myself in favor of sensibility. Dirt in my mouth didn't sound like fun right now. I already had enough hygiene issues.

Relief swallowed me as I stared into the massive circular cavern and surveyed the ten portals that hovered in midair. Black mist swirled around them, and I could see scenes of the worlds they led into beyond them. I couldn't help but notice that these portals weren't secured, and they weren't up to Peacekeeper regulation standards either. They stood wide open, and I knew it was the result of Riven's insurrection. He must have opened them with his newfound power, allowing a revolving door to exist between hell and the immortal realm. But I couldn't let worry over what came next drown me now. I needed to focus on the positive. We were here, at the center circle of hell. We'd made it.

I started to rush forward, but a tug on my hand stopped me. Arrick cleared his throat, and Deklan and Caden halted as well, faces turned toward him quizzically. Arrick stayed frozen, rooted to the spot, and didn't bother to speak. The hairs rose on the back of my neck as I realized that something was wrong. Deklan and Caden seemed to sense the same thing I did, and they each drew their weapons.

Caden whispered, "Arrick, what is it? What's going on?"

Arrick remained still as a statue. Every muscle in his body had tensed, and I could see him resisting the urge to use his power. Mist swirled at his fingertips, and his jaw flexed with the effort to leash it. "Someone's here." He looked at me then, the green of his eyes sharp and vivid. "Not a demon, a god."

That was when the screaming started.

I heard Mina's voice first, her high, shrill shriek cutting through the silence. It was stopped short by a wet-sounding *thwack*. I turned back to face the alachary and watched three of them disintegrate into red mist. It looked like blood but smelled like a sickening combination of iron and sulfur, and my stomach churned.

I tried to rush forward, to help them, but Arrick's hand on my shoulder stopped me. We stayed in the darkness at the edge of the cavern and watched as the alachary attempted to flee, each of them trying to escape with their lives. But it was no use. Their bloody fluid spewed all over the walls as they exploded and popped one-by-one. It was the single most violent thing I'd ever witnessed. And I'd seen a lot in the past couple of months of my life.

No matter how much I despised Mina and how little I thought of the alachary, this torment, the screaming, and their sheer terror tugged at my inherent compassion. I looked at Arrick, my eyes pleading. "We can't just leave them to die. What about your binding?" I hissed, my voice quiet and almost inaudible beneath all the cries of terror and despair.

"Don't worry about the binding. We didn't break it, and there's nothing we can do to help them now. We've been discovered. He's here."

And I suddenly knew who had come calling. There was only one explanation, and it was not a good one—the Bicaidian death deity.

Arrick had warned us, after all. Any power he used here could be sensed. According to him, a death god could feel another god's power if they used it in one of the metaphysical realms where they held dominion. Sweat pricked at the back of my neck, and I prayed to the Ascended that we could still somehow avoid detection. Maybe if he couldn't find us, he would think it was all a big mistake. We were exhausted, depleted of our power, and in no position to have a knock-down, drag-out fight against anyone. But I knew, deep down, we'd never be lucky enough to avoid it. Trouble had turned into my middle name, not just my nickname, and I so did not appreciate it.

I heard one final scream and a final wet pop before the room fell silent. A few more seconds and I heard shoes crunching on gravel and a low chuckle. The cavern was bathed in red, the substance dripping from the walls in a sickening malaise. Then a voice, smooth, deep, and cultured, called out, "You can come out now. I know you're there."

With that, he stepped into view, and his ice-blue eyes locked onto mine for a split second before they flicked away. Black mist swirled around him, his slick, dark hair gleaming in the low light. His black suit and black shirt looked impeccable. If I didn't know from first-hand experience, I'd never have guessed that he'd just committed mass murder. He wore a long wool coat and a smile so vicious that it made the hair on my forearms stand on end.

"Arrick, Rebekkah, I know you're in there. And I'm sure these alachary told you all about our…extracurricular activities."

Then, without warning, demons filed in, six on either side of him. They were varying sizes. Gigantic, medium huge, and absolutely mammoth. Their scaly, black and white heads and gnashing, sharpened teeth made my belly clench. They carried a mass of weapons, all surrounded in black mist. My immediate thought was, *oh shit, we are so screwed,* but it was immediately followed by another.

I turned to Caden and Deklan and gripped Deklan's forearm with my hand. I leaned close, and he followed suit, Caden and Arrick leaning in too.

Before I could speak, the death god crooned again, "We can be civilized about this. Come out, and we'll go easy on you. But if you make us come in there after you, it won't go so well." I knew why he wanted us out. We were in a prime location. This tunnel created a bottleneck where only one or two of his gigantic beasts could get through at a time. If they had to come down the tunnel and face us, it would put them at a disadvantage.

All three of my friends looked at me, waiting for what I had to say. I dropped my voice low and whispered, "Caden, Deklan, he doesn't know about you. He thinks it's just me and Arrick." I nodded, feeling encouraged that we might have some kind of a play here. An advantage we could work with, other than location.

The slime bag spoke again. He kept interrupting. It was irksome. "I'll give you until the count of 5. If you're not out by then, I'll be forced to come in after you. And you know what that means. It starts with a T and rhymes with scorcher." Damn, he meant torture. I didn't like the sound of that.

"One."

Ignoring the horrific implication of the Bicaidian's threat, Arrick picked up on my idea, and ever the general, he began to strategize. Without hesitation, he pressed his hand to the wall and let loose his magic. I could barely see it in the darkness, but I could just make out the thin slivers of mist as it slid along the rocky crevice and around toward the Bicaidian death god's blind side. A quick shimmer, like a mirage, and a tunnel appeared, the entrance forming next to us. When Arrick finished, his breath heaved and I could see that the exertion had cost him.

"Two."

I peered into the center circle's cavern and saw a small tunnel appear behind Riven. Arrick gestured to each of them and whispered, "We'll split up. You two, go now. On my signal, you advance and hit the demons from behind. We'll lead Riven and as many of the demons as we can into this bottleneck. Then we can sandwich them in and pick them off one at a time."

"Three."

Deklan hissed, his words hurried, "How do we kill them?"

"Four."

Arrick answered, "Aim for the head."

"Five."

With that, Arrick gestured to me to hold my position as Deklan and Caden took off down the tunnel. Then, without hesitation, Arrick stepped out of the shadows and into the light of the center circle of hell.

"Ah, there you are," the death god sneered, that horrifying smile back in place. "And here I'd worried that you would try to hide from me." His power seemed to pulse out of him as the clawed demons raked their nails across the dirt in anticipation of a fight.

Arrick threw out his arms. "Here I am. You caught me." Arrick let his power off the leash now, too, his own cloak of mist enveloping the area around him.

I couldn't imagine how much effort it cost him. I could feel my magic, weak inside me, and hoped he didn't try to use too much too soon. I inched closer, unsure what he wanted me to do. Stay hidden? Join him? We hadn't had a lot of time to discuss it, given the five-second countdown. I slipped my knife out of its scabbard and my gun out of its holster. I remembered what it felt like to burn out, the memory of the day I'd saved Moldize solidifying in my mind, and I had no intention of repeating that experience. So, I'd keep my magic leashed unless absolutely necessary.

The god laughed again, and a goddess stepped through one of the portals and into view. She was beautiful, her blond hair silken, and her full lips painted blood red. She wore a red silk shirt, black, fitted ankle-high trousers, and a pair of black ankle boots that would have made me green with envy had this situation not been so dire.

No magic emanated from her that I could see, but she had a presence about her; she seemed to radiate power out of every pore in her body. I knew then that she had to be part of the upper-caste in Bicaidia. This did not bode well—two upper-caste deities and eight demons versus the four of us. We were exhausted, half-starved, and on the borderline of dehydration.

Granted, I had some serious mojo, but I'd need a week in stasis sleep just to get back to full power. So, long story short, I'd have to be an idiot not to be afraid. My powers could be blocked or deflected by an upper-caste deity, if that god or goddess knew what they were doing. Add to that, my powers weren't as all-encompassing here. I could only create new objects, not manipulate anything in hell. Like Arrick had said, I held dominion over the tangible, living world, but not the metaphysical realms of the dead.

I realized with a sickening dread that these two probably knew all of that. And they felt confident in their ability to win. Why else would they want us out in the open? For what other reason would they expect us to surrender?

The goddess spoke now, her voice every bit as lovely as she was. "And where's that creation deity friend of yours? Rebekkah? Are you there?" I swallowed, not daring to answer, but then she said the one thing that would make me leave my post without Arrick's say-so. "I have news you might be interested in, you know. It concerns your sister."

I rushed forward, thinking only of my sister's safety, and stepped into the clearing. Light enveloped me as I tried to ignore the terror that bucked inside me at the mention of Remi. The sulfuric scented blood of the Alachary suffused the room, and a feeling of dread grabbed at my insides while I felt my throat go dry. One thought pulsed in my mind; these people might have killed Remi.

I snarled, "What about my sister? I swear to the Ascended, if you hurt one hair on her precious skull, I'll tear you to pieces with my bare hands." I tried to lunge forward and make good on my threats, but Arrick stopped me with an arm around my torso.

The goddess's lips twitched. "My goodness. Such colorful imagery." It seemed she found my threats amusing. I'd have to disabuse her of that notion. She let out a laugh that sounded like a purr. Over her shoulder, I saw movement and tried not to focus on it. Deklan and Caden had taken up their positions. Good.

The goddess continued, "My name is Madwyn, and this is Riven. We're friends of your sister. Or well, we were. Until we betrayed her and killed the royal family and anyone in the pillar leadership who wasn't already in our pocket. Oh right, I almost forgot…We also sacked Helverta along with the ten other capitals of Bicaidia. So, I hate to break it to you, but you're too late. The Nefaral uprising has already happened."

Her face glowed with pleasure as she bragged about their conquests. I felt sickened and heard my voice whisper, so weak I could barely get it past the lump in my throat. "You killed them all? Remi?"

Madwyn shook her head, her hair swinging. She stepped in front of Riven, making it very obvious who was in charge, and it wasn't the death god. Rather, he seemed to be subservient to her. A lover, maybe? Or a family member? They had a closeness, a comfort with each other that I couldn't quite pinpoint.

"Oh no, your sister's still very much alive, though not through any fault of ours. You see, we need you to help us get her back, and you'll make a rather lovely hostage. Don't you think she'd make a lovely hostage, Riven?" Madwyn stepped closer again and looked me up and down. "Such a pretty goddess. All those long, graceful limbs and wide, doe eyes." She clicked her tongue in approval, and my skin crawled. Relief swam through me at the knowledge that my sister was alive. That relief was chased by a single observation: This bitch sure liked to hear herself talk.

Instinctively, I reached for Arrick's hand and stepped close to his side. I needed the solidarity and protection he provided.

He growled, "Sorry to disappoint you both, but the only thing you're getting from me today is my boot up your ass."

"Oh, come on now, don't be a spoilsport," Madwyn purred. "If you choose to side with us against the Altruists, we're happy to offer you a spot in our ranks. We could use another Nef with powers like yours. With your gifts, you'd be a top general. And when it's all over, how about a post as ruler of Valeria? What do you think? And all you have to do is turn over pretty little Rebekkah to get it."

Arrick's jaw flexed, and he narrowed his eyes. If you didn't know him better, one might think he was considering her offer, but I could read the disgust in his expression as easily as a page in a book.

Madwyn continued, speaking to Arrick as though I wasn't even there. "You know you're far more powerful than she is here. This is your realm, after all."

Arrick laughed in response to her proposal, but the sound held no humor in it. "Lady, you're a real piece of work. And let me tell you something, if you want her, you're going to have to come through both of us." He let a slow smile spread his lips, the menace in it unmistakable. His beautiful face sharpened, and his teeth gleamed, making me realize in that precise moment that he was every bit as scary as Riven and Madwyn.

Thank the Ascended for small mercies, I thought, knowing where this would go next.

Madwyn looked at her nails and sighed in disappointment. "Very well then. I'd hoped we could come to some kind of an agreement, but since you're being difficult…" She looked at Riven, and his eyes seemed to sparkle with anticipation.

He turned his gaze away from hers, and black mist exploded around him, filling the room as he yelled, "ATTACK!"

CHAPTER 20

REMI

Liberation

"**G**et up."

Still in the depths of her dream, Remi wasn't sure if the words were real or just part of her imaginings. She chose to believe the latter and sunk further into the abyss. Sleep felt so blissful, so comforting compared to the harsh reality of life.

"Damnit, Remi! Thayne! Get up! I'm not screwing around here!" She jolted as someone yanked the covers off her body. Her eyes flew open and cold suffused her. She blinked, trying to clear the sleep from her eyes. The room was dark; the embers of the fire had gone a deep, glowing red. It must have gone out sometime during the night, she realized dimly.

"What the hell?" Thayne growled as they both sat upright on the mattress. He'd still been sleeping beside her, the warmth and comfort of his body a welcome reprieve after the previous day's revelations. Or at least, she thought it had to be the previous day considering how drowsy she felt.

At last, her vision cleared, and she saw Pietyr standing at the foot of their bed. She could just make out the lines of his face, and he looked panicked, his chest heaving with the effort of his breathing. Darkness swirled around him, and she realized that he'd just shadow-walked into their private chambers.

She looked down, saw the panties and camisole she wore, and jerked the blankets up to cover her body. "What the hell Pietyr? Haven't you ever heard of knocking?"

He shook his head. "There's no time for that. We need to go right now—"

Picking up on Pietyr's anxiety, Thayne narrowed his eyes in concern. "Go where, Pietyr? What's wrong?"

Pietyr raked his hands through his hair and spun in a circle; his expression strained with fear. "It's your sister. It's happening right now. We have to go, or it'll be too late."

Without a second thought, Remi lept from the bed. All concerns about her state of undress evaporated as she rushed to the armoire, Thayne at her side. They pulled clothes out and slipped them on, not bothering to think about what they grabbed. Pietyr's anxiety and fear had rubbed off on them, and her hands shook with adrenaline, the urge to hurry overwhelming.

"What happened?" Remi demanded, tugging a pair of soft, leather pants into place and yanking the button to close it. Next, she grabbed a thin, long-sleeved shirt and thrust it over her head. The black material fell into place without effort, and she yanked on her snow boots.

As they dressed, Pietyr gave her the condensed version. "After yesterday, I followed Emorie's orders. I've been monitoring Helverta and the front lines of the demon army, trying to find a path through it and a way to stay concealed once inside. But the army is massive, hundreds of thousands deep, all surrounding the city and swarming inside it. I found a way through, but—"

He paused, his shadows rippling around him as though they spoke to him, and Remi took the opportunity to jump in. "Pietyr, can you get to the point here? What happened? Is Bekka okay?" Thayne slipped on a pair of heavy boots, and Remi pulled her hair up into a high ponytail, both of them ready to go.

"She was when I left her," Pietyr replied just before he stepped closer to them and wrapped them in his shadows. Remi's head spun, and her stomach lurched as they hurtled through a tunnel of shadows. When they came through it, they were standing on the edge of a cliff outside the compound. A blizzard roared around them, and the cold air cleared all remnants of the disorientation that always came along with shadow-walking. Remi clenched her fists without thinking, and flames erupted all over her body, warming her instantly.

"Get to it, Pietyr," Thayne growled. He stepped closer to Remi, as though drawn to the warmth her body offered.

"I found Bekka, but so did Madwyn and Riven. They know she's in hell."

A raging fire of terror burned in Remi's belly. "No, no, no, no." All hope that they might intercept her and keep her safe from them fled like a thief in the night.

Pietyr interrupted before she could descend into full-blown panic. "Like I said, I found a way past the patrols. The army had split, and half of it began retreating into Helverta. The other half maintained the line around the palace. But I followed the ones who left back into the heart of the city, and once behind the line, I shadow-walked my way into the palace." The sky had begun to lighten now, the only indication of daybreak beneath the cloud cover. Remi's attention was so laser-focused on Pietyr that she didn't notice the sound of boots crunching behind them until she felt breath on the back of her neck. She whirled around and saw Emorie there, Rackham flanking her.

Before she could question them, Pietyr continued his explanation, the words tumbling out in rapid succession, "I went deeper into the palace, staying in the shadows and trying to get close to the portal you guys created on inauguration night. I thought maybe if I could get through without anyone seeing me, I could help your sister. Keep her safe and lead her back to us. But, instead, I found Madwyn and Riven—" He broke off, running a hand through his damp, wind-tousled hair. "They were talking about Bekka and the Moldizean death god." She squeezed her eyes shut, fighting through panic to stay focused, to listen. Pietyr's eyes were filled with determination now, and he locked them onto hers. "They know Bekka is there. They said that Riven had sensed her and the Moldizean death deity in hell. They were surrounded by demons, dozens of them inside the palace walls and an army of them close at hand. They were in the control room, where they created that portal to hell. They walked right through it and I managed to follow them, sticking to the shadows and staying out of sight. They want to kill the death god and use Bekka as bait for the Valerians. They said that they don't plan to stop with Bicaidia." The distress he felt was plain on his face. "I'm sorry—I couldn't stop them. There were too many demons, too many Nefs to risk showing myself. So, instead, I came back here as soon as I could. But we have to go now, if we have any hope at saving them."

Remi felt every muscle in her body stiffen in response to the threat. Her sister. Her best friend. Her blood. She had to help her. "How long since you last saw them? You're sure you can get us all through that portal undetected?"

Pietyr nodded. "Yes, I can get us through the patrols to the portal. It's been ten minutes, give or take a few." Remi's mind whirled, leaping from thought to thought. None of them were good.

She pictured her sister, captive in the palace. Then she imagined her dead in Bicaidian hell. Both thoughts made her sick with dread. Finally, Pietyr's words broke through the haze of terror in her mind. "I followed Madwyn and Riven and watched for as long as I could, to see what they would do. They wanted to make a bargain with the Moldizean; Rebekkah in exchange for his life. But if he refused...I think we can all imagine what they'd do. So, we need to decide our next move right now."

Rackham stepped forward, close enough that Remi could see the fog from his breath and smell it in the wind. "It's not getting in I'm worried about, it's getting back out. Once they know we've broken through their lines, they could lock the palace down, converge the army around it and surround us, trapping us inside."

"We can't worry about that now," Pietyr appealed, his eyes wide. "We don't have the luxury of time to discuss every possible nuance, Rackham. My guess is that Riven and Madwyn didn't get the deal they wanted. Which means that Rebekkah and the Moldizean are outnumbered. And to make matters worse, they looked weak and like they'd been in hell without supplies for a long time. But even if, by some miracle, they manage to make it out of hell and past the Nefarals and demons in one piece, they'd have nowhere to go once they do. No matter how we slice it, they need our help."

Remi listened, trying to process everything he said. Time was ticking away and Bekka was in danger. As far as Remi was concerned, the risk that they might not be able to get out of Helverta and back to safety meant nothing. They needed to go now. They had to save her, and then they could figure out their exit strategy later. After all, Bekka was their best hope at salvaging what remained of their world. But more than that, she was Remi's twin, her flesh and blood.

Before she could rush forward, take the fabric of Pietyr's thick, wool jacket in her fists, and beg him to take them to Bekka, Emorie's voice pierced through the roaring wind. "We go now. Saving the creator is our top priority. If we ever hope to restore the balance, we'll need her to do it. We'll figure out our exit plans later. If we all go together, then we'll have the ability to slow time and translocate on our side. We'll make it work. We have to because we can't afford to lose her. Once they have a chance to imprison her and dangle her like bait to the Valerian royals, any hope we have to get to her without dying goes from slim to none."

Rackham looked pale, stricken at the prospect of going in there half-cocked. But as far as Remi was concerned, they didn't have much of a choice. They either went right then or lost Bekka for good.

Emorie stepped closer to Remi to form the beginning of a circle, and Pietyr and Thayne fell in line with her. Only Rackham hesitated, his jaw working as the snowstorm dumped flurries of ice on them.

Steam rose around Remi's fire-laden body, and she stared at Rackham, desperation welling inside her. Emorie was right. They could use a time god on their side no matter what they walked into. The ability to slow the action around them would give this dangerous mission a critical advantage. "Rackham, please," Remi appealed. "We need to get to her, and we need your help." She made sure her eyes held the pleading desperation she felt in her heart. She needed him to say yes.

He hesitated for a moment. Then he sighed, looked up at the sky, and groaned, his frustrated resignation obvious. Then, with one last growl, he stepped into their circle. Remi let out the breath she didn't realize she'd been holding and said a silent prayer of thanks to the Ascended. They needed all the help they could get.

Rackham locked eyes with her. "If this turns to shit, don't say I didn't warn you."

Without another word, Pietyr's shadows began to swirl, ensconcing each of them in a flow of scentless smoke. It swirled around them and Remi's heart hammered. She looked at her husband, his face fierce and filled with determination;

she reached for his hand and wound her fingers through his. He looked down at her, and his words traveled along the wind as they shot through time and space, hurtling toward Helverta. "We'll get her back, Remi. I swear it."

CHAPTER 21

BEKKA

Combat

Riven's roaring command followed us as we turned and rushed back down the tunnel. My heart hammered in my ears, and I could feel the impact of every footfall as I sprinted over rocks, gravel, and dirt. Finally, Arrick's hand on mine yanked me to a stop and I spun around.

"Gun. Now," Arrick ordered, the sing of his sword as it exited its scabbard causing the hair on my arms to stand on end.

I did as I was told and lifted the barrel to eye level, sighting down the open end of the narrow corridor. I could hear the blood rushing in my ears, and my limbs vibrated with adrenaline. Snarls, growls, and scraping footsteps sounded from the main cavern, growing louder with each passing second. They'd be on us soon.

I took one deep breath, then another, and steadied my nerves. I'd trained for this; I could handle anything these bastards tossed my way. I was a goddess. A warrior. I didn't need my magic to rid us of the demons chasing us down. I would save that for later. For our true enemies: Madwyn and Riven.

Breathe in. Breathe out. Focus. I thought, preparing myself for the fight ahead.

The first demon cleared the corner, the bend in the tunnel creating that chokepoint I'd hoped for. Arrick lunged forward and, with one quick swing, relieved the thing of its scaly, black head. Its glowing, ebony sword hit the ground with a clang. Two more turned the corner, their massive bodies filling the entire opening into the main cavern. Arrick swung his sword in a long arch, but the first demon lifted its own weapon and blocked, its mouth twisted into a horrifying snarl.

These were no alachary, no slave demons in rags masquerading as semi-human. They were the real deal, 100% demon. They wore thick leathers, the black every bit as light-swallowing as their scaly skin. Their yellowed teeth and bald heads gleamed in the limited light. I watched in mute horror as the second, bigger creature leveled a kick straight into Arrick's ribs. The sickening crack split through the sounds of scuffled fighting and battle cries. The blow knocked Arrick off balance; his body weakened from so much time without food and water. The creature drew back its hand and slammed a fist into Arrick's face so hard, his head snapped back and hit the rock wall behind him.

The second demon raised its sword above its shoulder and rushed forward with its glowing, black blade aimed straight at Arrick's belly. Time seemed to slow as realization of what I had to do hit me, all hesitation and fear exiting my mind at once. I sighted my gun and fired. The bullet flew through the air, inching forward at what felt like a snail's pace. Then, when the demon was within inches of Arrick, the bullet hit home, blasting a hole straight through the demon's temple. The sword fell to the floor, the demon collapsing atop it.

The remaining demon whipped its head to me, its eyes filled with vitriolic hatred as it lunged in my direction. Before it could take two steps, though, Arrick swung his sword and severed its head. It slumped to the ground next to its two comrades, and I let out my breath in a whoosh. Arrick looked up at me, his face smeared with the brown, gooey blood of the demon. He smiled his thanks before another creature turned the corner.

It rushed at us faster than I would have thought possible for a non-god. Its body blurred with the speed of its forward motion, making it difficult to sight my gun. With his free hand, Arrick raised his palm and black mist speared out. It poured out of him like a geyser, the magic encapsulating the demon within seconds. It screamed, the sound hideous as the blackness spread all over its body, absorbing the face last. Arrick clenched his teeth and squinted his eyes, and I could tell that this effort pained him.

Once he'd coated the demon in his magic, he closed his hand into a fist. The mist and the demon evaporated, disappearing entirely. Of course, it made sense. The demon was from hell; he could control and manipulate the metaphysical realm. That was his power. When he finished, his breaths came out in ragged gasps, and he swayed on his feet.

I rushed forward and caught him just as he began to teeter. I dropped my shoulder under his arm to steady him when another demon came through the opening. I raised my gun and fired, the bullet hitting home and dropping the demon flat on its face. It slid across the gravel, still carried by its momentum, and stopped mere inches from our boots.

I heard grunts and snarls coming down the tunnel, the footfalls getting closer. I turned my head up to Arrick. "Are you okay?"

He shook his head as though to clear it and nodded. "I'm alright." His face had grown pale, and I could see that the use of his magic had been too much. If he used much more of it, he'd risk burning out altogether. But he pushed away from me and lifted his sword, steadying himself through brute effort.

"Are you sure?" I asked, fear licking down my spine. We couldn't afford to lose Arrick, not right now. He was the best fighter and the most powerful of all of us in this place. The mere idea of him not making it through this ordeal felt like a dagger through my heart. We had to get through this. I refused to accept any other outcome.

More than that, I couldn't lose him.

He sighed and closed his eyes. "I just used too much too quickly. Power is a muscle, and we haven't been feeding it." I knew he meant that both literally and figuratively. We'd been in this place, starving and on the border of dehydration for the better part of a month. Add to that, we hadn't used more than the barest fraction of our power, which meant that that muscle hadn't been flexed in far too long.

Another demon swung around the corner and bolted for us, and I realized that we weren't even close to done fighting our way through these sickening creatures. At this rate, Madwyn and Riven wouldn't have to bother to face us; they would just keep sending in demons until we were too exhausted to go on. I knew we didn't look great. They only needed to have eyes in their skull and the brains of a moderately intelligent human to see that. We were ripe for the kill or the kidnapping, depending on their master plan for us.

I raised my gun and fired again. The bullet veered wide as the demon dodged. Shit. The creature ping-ponged off the wall like a super-sonic parkourer and slid on its knees to duck my second shot. Close enough to feel the heat of its body, the creature swung its sword down, aiming to cleave Arrick's head in two. We both jumped out of the way. I hit the ground and kicked my body backward, sliding a few feet on my back across the gravelly dirt. I extended my arms outward, fingers gripping my gun and exhaled as I focused.

I fired one shot, then another, hitting the hideous thing center mass. Once, twice, a third time. It did no good. Like Arrick said, I had to aim for the head. The thing launched a bevy of attacks straight at Arrick, but he managed to block and dodge all of them. Even as he evaded, I could see him weakening, his body tiring from the effort of his magic and the fight. A single thought permeated my mind, and I tried not to let it swallow me whole.

We weren't going to make it out of there alive.

In desperation, I screamed out, "Caden! Deklan, A LITTLE HELP HERE!" My voice bellowed down the tunnel, possibly giving away the entirety of our advantage. But it didn't matter. We needed them at that precise point, or else we were going to lose. I could feel my body wearing down, even without using my power, and I didn't want to risk tapping into it. Especially not after seeing what that had done to Arrick. I needed stasis sleep; we both did.

But there wasn't time to worry about that now. We had to fight our way out or risk losing more than our lives, because these deities had no intention of stopping with Bicaidia. That little comment about a post as ruler of Valeria for Arrick replayed in my mind. Fire burned in my belly, and hatred flared there, just as another demon came through the tunnel, leaping over the pile of its fallen comrades and crunching the back of one as it landed.

Just then, a knife flew from behind me and pierced it straight through the eye. I turned in surprise and saw Deklan standing there. He must have come back through the tunnel rather than attack from the flank. Caden advanced then, his swords spinning in his hand. He looked even weaker and more drained than Arrick and I did, but he forged ahead anyway. We had no choice. We would either fight, or we'd succumb to our enemies right there in hell, never making it back to Valeria.

Two more demons squeezed their way through, and Arrick and I retreated backward, allowing Caden and Deklan to advance. We'd taken six of them out and I knew that the brothers could handle these two. And they did, each slicing into one and working back-to-back. Slashing their way up their torsos and then cutting off their heads with stunning ease. When they finished, their chests heaved, and they turned to us. Deklan's voice held a dire warning as he said, "More demons are streaming through the portals. There was no way we could get to you in time if we hit the flank, like we planned. We need to retreat further into hell and hide in the middle circles. It's our only shot at getting out of here alive."

He and Caden squeezed by us, each sparing Arrick a quick glance filled with concern. Caden started to wince at the sight of him but then controlled his reaction. This wasn't the time for weakness and soft feelings. We had to survive. The peace was at stake. The realms were at stake. I couldn't let them fall to those psychopathic murderers. I couldn't leave my family, my people, and the mortals we protected without a Peacekeeper.

We turned and bolted back down the tunnel. Deklan in the lead, followed by Caden, then me, and Arrick held up the rear. I could hear his footsteps behind me, his feet dragging and stumbling even as he tried to run. But before we could make it too far, something strange happened. Shadows began swirling all around us, their tendrils licking over the walls. If I didn't know any better, I would swear it was Arrick's magic. But it had a different quality—shadows rather than mist.

My stomach dropped.

Another Nefaral. A shadow god.

I grabbed Caden's shirt and skidded to a halt, yanking him with me. Arrick slammed into my back and we all stumbled forward, our collective balance teetering. I cried out, my heart racing and hairs standing on end. "Deklan! Wait! Another Nef—"

Then the mass of shadows solidified into a large, male body right in front of Deklan, who managed to stop just in time. He scrambled backward, raising his crossbow and sighting. The shadow god's body rippled with muscles, and his eyes were hard with determination. I'd never seen him before, but I raised my gun and leveled it at his head. It would do little to intimidate him or injure him. He was a god after all, but it felt good to have him in my sights. Besides, there was the slight possibility that it could slow him down, even if it was only for a second.

Before I could pull the trigger, more gods appeared in the shadows, filing in beside and behind him in the narrow tunnel. One on his left and another on his right, with two more behind him. More Nefs; it had to be. Dread pooled in my belly. That would be just our luck, I thought, grimacing at the stupidity of our entire backup plan. It had all gone to shit.

Despair filled my mind, and I looked to all three of my friends; love and grief spilled into my chest. In all likelihood, they would die here and then I would be kidnapped to use as bait. I choked back a sob and felt my finger tighten on the trigger when a voice called out from behind the shadow-wielder. A voice that caused my entire body to convulse with a combination of relief and shock.

"Bekka!"

It couldn't be, I thought, heart rate skyrocketing.

The shadow-wielder shifted to the side, and Remi shoved her way through. Her red hair was high in her signature ponytail, and her face was flushed. She ran to me and a relieved sob forced its way out of my throat. I stumbled forward, shoving my way past Caden and Deklan in an effort to get to her. My sister. Remi. She was here.

How the hell is she here?

It didn't matter when we collided, wrapping our arms around each other. Tears streamed down my face, and I clung to the solid warmth of her body, always a little hotter from that pesky fire gift she managed so well. She cried too, her body shaking in my arms.

After what felt like an eternity but could only have been a few seconds, she rested her hands on my shoulders and pushed me to arm's length.

Her eyes, the mirror of my own, searched me. I watched as a range of emotions passed over her face. Worry, pity, and then fear before she composed herself. She flicked her gaze back to her companions. Mine followed. I counted five of them in total. The only one I recognized was Thayne, and I said a small prayer to the Ascended that they would have a plan to get us out of here.

Remi's voice cut through the myriad of thoughts that tumbled through my brain. "We need to hurry. Rackham can't hold it much longer. Come on!" She waved a hand in a gesture to follow her and slipped by Deklan and me, then Caden and Arrick, and rushed down the hall back toward the demons and Madwyn and Riven.

"Hold what?" I shouted, wondering what she was talking about as her back disappeared around a bend.

"Time!" she shouted, her voice carrying well in the otherwise silent, echoing chamber. I looked back at the gods she'd brought with her, so many questions in my mind that it was unreal. But I didn't have the luxury to ask them at once. Instead, I noticed how one of the gods' hands glowed in a green light so vivid that it looked like freshly cut grass. A time god. A handy ally at a time like this and, also, not a Nefaral. At the moment, this seemed like as good of a reference as any.

I nodded my approval and turned to follow my sister. Caden and Deklan seemed to hesitate, looking between Arrick and me. They didn't seem to want to go back into that death den any more than I did. But Remi was my sister. She wouldn't lead me in there without a plan. So, I followed, rushing down the tunnel and back toward the psychotic Nefs who wanted to destroy everything I loved.

As we got further down the tunnels, I could see a massive line of demons. All of them a single pile down the narrow passageway and frozen in time like statues. We squeezed our way around them, going as fast as we could manage without getting nicked by their weapons per Remi's direction.

At last, we surpassed them, rushing into the cavern that contained the portals. The time god behind us grunted with effort, and time seemed to skip forward for a brief second before he got it back under control.

"We need to hurry," he hissed, the strain in his voice unmistakable. "It's slipping." Another groan, followed by another, longer time-stop stutter. And we all took off in a mad dash for the portal. Remi still held the lead, Arrick behind her and me at his back, watching his every step. He still seemed weak, but he moved at a decent clip. If I had to guess, he was running on pure adrenaline now. Nothing else made sense.

A few seconds later and we reached the portal that the goddess had come through. Remi turned, crimson hair whipping to the side. "Come on! Hurry!" she yelled, waving an urgent hand.

As we rushed to the entrance to the godly realm, my heart raced, and I dared a glance behind me. Caden and Deklan kept pace with minimal effort, and I breathed a sigh of relief. Despite our combined weakness and frailty, we were going to make it out of there and into Bicaidia. Once out, maybe we could translocate. I could only hope that our new companions had enough mojo to help in that endeavor because we were going to need to find a place to hide and quick.

I had one foot inside the portal, about to pass through and out of hell, but a sound behind me had me spinning back. It was the time god. He cried out and fell to his knees, not five steps from the portal. The glowing power in his hands flickered, and time slipped once more. Then it fizzled a second and third time, the figures of death around us rocketing forward each time it guttered.

At last, it gave way entirely, the green glow disappearing from his fingers. He looked up at us in absolute horror, his curly brown hair falling over his face in a sweaty mop. "I'm sorry, I can't keep—"

Time snapped back, the full speed of it a shocking contrast from the utter stillness just seconds before. I looked beyond him to Madwyn and Riven, who whirled around, sensing a shift in the time-space continuum. They locked their eyes right onto us, all hope of escape evaportating in an instant. I had spoken too soon. Celebrated too early.

Madwyn wasted no time.

Before any of us could react, purple power swelled around her. Smoke and lightning crackled through it. Then, with that sickening, saccharine smile, she flung her hands forward, and the world exploded.

CHAPTER 22

REMI

Reunion

The purple blast smacked into Remi's side, blowing her off her feet and flinging her across the room and away from the portal like a rag doll. Unfortunately, it had a similar effect on the rest of her team. They all went sprawling, skidding across the ground and slamming into the rocky wall behind the portals.

Remi coughed, struggling to her hands and knees. She turned her head from side to side, eyes scanning the room to find her sister and Thayne. Both of them seemed dazed but mobile. They struggled to their feet, and she followed suit, adrenaline rushing through her.

But before they could get up, another blast of purple smoke crashed into them. This time it knocked loose the boulders and rocks above, embedded in the ceiling. One by one, they began to fall, smashing onto the ground around them with devastating impact. Emorie scrambled out of the way as a massive boulder dropped, landing inches from her booted feet. Bekka rushed backward and fell on her butt as a rock narrowly missed smashing into her skull.

Bekka's eyes darted to her right, locking onto the Moldizean death god. Or at least, Remi assumed he was the death god. Bekka's other two companions looked like identical twins, and they definitely weren't gods. At least not quite, but she didn't have time to worry about their origins. They carried weapons, which meant that they could fight. Maybe they couldn't take the gods, but they could help them handle the demons streaming through the open portal, which was good enough for her.

She opened her mouth to rally her sister and her own allies together, but before she could get a sound out, another blast of magic slammed into them.

Madwyn kept it coming, wave-after-wave of unrelenting power shooting through the cavern so fast and furious that no one had time to get their bearings before the next surge hit. The tunnels surrounding the main cavern began to crumble, and then, in a sickening domino effect, they all caved in on themselves. Remi could hear demons shouting their war cries as Madwyn's magic seemed to breeze right over them. Her head rang from the sheer chaos that surrounded her as she tried to pull her senses together.

Bekka crawled toward the death god with each brief let-up in the onslaught of Madwyn's attack. When they found each other, he reached out to grasp her hand. Their fingers gripped each other, and Remi watched in curious shock as he pulled them both up against the wall. They huddled together under a cut-out in the rock wall to wait out the insanity.

A brief pause in the onslaught of chaos magic, used so differently than at the inauguration after party, made Remi's body stiffen. Was it the removal of the governor chip that allowed Madwyn to use it in that way? To sow destruction rather than mere disorientation? But before Remi could gather

her wits enough to strike back, a voice she recognized too well filled the room.

"You ready to surrender yet, Emorie?"

Emorie coughed, growling under her breath in frustration. "Not even close."

Madwyn laughed. "I was hoping you'd say that." She unleashed another round of pure destructive chaos, and Remi braced herself for impact. A hand reached out and gripped her shoulder, yanking her backward as a rock plummeted from above. It slammed to the ground where she'd just been sitting, and she looked up to see who'd helped her. Thayne. He wrapped his arms around her and scooted her backward, despite the rumbling floor and away from Riven and Madwyn.

From the corner of her eye, Remi saw a shadow flicker. Through the haze of power and the chaos that surrounded her, she realized that Pietyr had just shadow walked. What the—? How was he even upright right now? She thought as his body disappeared and then reappeared beside a demon. His hand closed on the creature's blade so fast, Remi barely registered the motion. Then he disappeared again and solidified behind Madwyn, holding the knife right at her throat.

All onslaughts of power ceased as Pietyr yanked her back against him and dragged her away from the demons and Riven. Pietyr pressed the blade into the chaos goddess's neck, not quite hard enough to draw blood, but enough that the threat was implicit. "That's enough, Madwyn," he hissed, his voice low and dangerous. "Make one move, and I'll cut your throat."

Her eyes had grown wide with surprise, and Remi tried to dampen the elation she felt at this turn of events. In reaction to the threat on his sister, Riven stilled, his power swelling around him.

Pietyr twisted, planting Madwyn between him and Riven, using her as a shield. He leveled his deadly-calm glare on the Bicaidian death god. "Don't even think about it, you prick. Just one little slice, and she'll be gone."

Riven's lips curled, the mist hanging above his hands, the threat implicit. Remi could see the lines of concern etched into his face. She wondered briefly if he'd even spared a thought for Ellarah since inauguration night. At the sight of the lethal dagger at his sister's throat, he seemed to seethe with anger. Yet, despite this, quiet descended on the cavern, Madwyn's power leashed for now.

Remi let out the breath she hadn't realized she'd been holding as Emorie's voice rang through the chamber, the command in her tone unmistakable. "Listen to him, Riven, back down now, or she dies."

Remi swallowed and tried not to choke on the dust that seemed to clog her throat. Thayne still had his arm wrapped around her shoulders, and she detangled herself from him, rising to her feet and dusting off her pants. Everyone else on her side followed suit, each person looking as dazed as she felt. She shook her head to clear it and executed a quick survey of the cavern. No one seemed to be injured from Emorie's team. And Bekka and her friends had managed to dodge the worst of it too, but they all looked like they'd been raked over the coals for weeks on end.

They needed stasis sleep and medical attention. Probably a feast large enough to feed a small village too, she thought, wincing at her sister's protruding collar bones and over-large cheekbones.

Emorie barked another order, this time directed at everyone on her team. "Lock and load people." She clenched her fists and red magic, a signature of the Science and Technology pillar of power, swirled around her. Remi stared in mute astonishment. Emorie had never mentioned her gift before, but of all the things that she could have been? Then again, it answered many of the questions Remi had had since the first minute she'd entered their compound in Helverta.

She remembered all of that technology and the state-of-the-art control room at both of the bases. Then how The

Rising had been able to build state-of-the-art domicile tunnels through the Bicaidian realm in utter secrecy. This explained how they'd been able to accomplish all that.

Remi wondered what good it would be in a fight and how she'd been able to translocate with it, but didn't ask. It appeared that Emorie knew something she didn't. So, without any further questions or hesitation, Remi shook out her hands and lit her fire. Thayne's lightning sparked up his arms, and he stepped closer to the line of demons, away from the rest of their group. He, along with the two non-gods, had taken up posts between the demons and Riven and Pietyr and Madwyn.

Rackham didn't obey, and neither did Bekka nor Arrick. As for Rackham, Remi already knew why. He'd been holding time for over an hour as they wound their way through the palace stuffed with demons and into hell itself. Pietyr had only been able to shadow-walk them so far before he'd had to stop. To complete the journey, they'd had to rely on Rackham, and time was a notoriously tricky thing to control in the immortal realm. It amazed her that he'd been able to hold it as long as he had. If he tried to use his magic now, he might not make it back out.

As for Bekka and Arrick, she may not know exactly what the issue was, but she could guess. They looked like shit— Arrick in particular. And with Madwyn to use as leverage, they probably didn't need the extra help from Bekka and her companions anyway.

Just then, a laugh sounded around them, the sound melodic, and Remi knew without question who the owner of it was. Madwyn's laugh had once sounded pretty to Remi's ears. It was one of her better qualities. But now, it grated and made Remi's skin crawl.

Remi turned her head and fixed her eyes on the chaos goddess. Hatred, visceral and white-hot pulsed through her. That bitch had killed so many people, her in-laws included, and destroyed her new home. Not to mention the 900-year peace her grandfather had fought so hard to maintain. Hatred didn't even begin to cover it. She wanted to eviscerate the evil witch. Without thinking, she strode toward her, Emorie on her heels.

Rackham followed suit, his eyes filled with rage and betrayal. Remi stormed right up to Madwyn and spoke through clenched teeth, "I'm sorry, but what's funny?" Fire began to ignite over Remi's body, and she could feel the power of it, ready and at her disposal. But she kept it under control, for now, knowing she couldn't afford to release it in such an enclosed area lest she risk the lives of everyone present. She'd need a lot more practice controlling this new mass of magic before she felt comfortable letting it off the leash.

In reaction to Remi's question, Madwyn only laughed louder. Bekka stepped forward, joining them, as the death god moved to stand with the twins and Thayne. The four of them stood like a shield, eyeing a simmering Riven and the edgy demons. The death god and his hell-spawn seemed like they had no interest in exercising restraint. Instead, they looked like they wanted nothing more than to tear Remi and her friends' throats out.

Emorie stepped in then, hauled back her hand, and slapped Madwyn so hard her head whipped to the side. Emorie leaned close as the laughter cut off abruptly. "That's for Ceryn, you crazy bitch."

Emorie's eyes danced with red power and rage, her entire body alight with both. She looked like she wanted to take Madwyn apart piece by piece for the sheer pleasure of it.

Riven snapped in response to the assault on his sister. "Madwyn!"

But Madwyn addressed her brother directly. "Stand down, Riven. I have this under control." A thin trickle of blood pooled at the corner of her mouth. She glared at Emorie. Emorie must have hit her with some magic; otherwise, she wouldn't have been bleeding. "Call off your dog."

Pietyr's arm wound tighter around her body, and he pressed the knife harder against her throat. Emorie laughed, a demonstration of just how ridiculous she found this notion. "Not a chance, Madwyn."

"I'm not so sure about that," the chaos goddess replied, her voice casual. "If you don't, the consequences could be dire."

Pietyr hissed. "No one's buying your bullshit anymore, Madwyn. It's over."

Madwyn's eyes grew cold, and her expression bordered on smug. "Oh, it's far from over, hun. Now let me go, or you will lose that ridiculous winter compound you've been hiding in. Oh, and what's left of your pathetically small army too."

Surprise flickered over Emorie's face before she could control it, and Rackham snarled, "Bullshit." His young face was filled with a venomous kind of hate. At least they were all on the same page. "You're a liar. Always have been."

She smiled, blood outlining her teeth now. "Am I? Are you sure about that?"

Riven stepped forward again, his power swelling around him. Madwyn's gaze flicked to her brother, and she shook her head in warning. He stopped, his power still blooming but not advancing as she turned back to Emorie. "Why do you think we haven't bothered to attack you in that compound yet?" Madwyn asked. "We killed everyone else in your pathetic movement who didn't side with us. Haven't you ever asked yourself, why not you?"

Emorie's eyes narrowed, but other than that, no reaction. Remi had to admit, she had nerves of steel. Because Remi's insides had turned to slippery eels, and she felt certain her face reflected that. Pietyr's shadows coiled and slithered around them, amplifying in his anger. But he also held his neutral expression.

Thayne snapped his attention away from the demons and surveyed Madwyn. For a split second, he turned to Remi and their eyes locked, an unspoken thought passing between them. If she had infiltrated the compound, then...Ellarah.

Ellarah was in danger. Because whether Riven cared for her or not, his sister clearly didn't.

Madwyn continued, "How sure are you that everyone is still on Team Emorie there?" She paused as Emorie continued to glare at her. She looked both impassive and murderous, a terrifying combination. Meanwhile, Madwyn oozed confidence from every syllable she spoke. "I wouldn't be too sure if I were you. Think about how effective we've been at taking apart your little organization. It would be awfully coincidental if we couldn't get a mole inside your cell, don't you think?"

Emorie bared her teeth. "Bullshit." The word came out in a clipped snarl, but Remi could sense the hesitation in it. The quiver of uncertainty. Remi felt it too. If the rest of the cells had fallen, just like Ceryn's, then what was the likelihood that Madwyn had zero allies inside the Helverta cell? The only one left standing?

Madwyn's voice cut through once more. "Don't you get it?" She paused, waiting for her words to sink in, letting everyone feel the full effect of them. "We let you all in here. Twelve Hells, we practically rolled out the welcome wagon, and you idiots fell for it." She let that settle for a minute before she continued, "We knew about Rebekkah the instant she walked into Bicaidian hell, and we've watched Pietyr sneaking around our borders for days now. It was all part of the plan. We hold all the cards, Emorie. We always have. We just wanted you all in one place and away from that pesky compound of yours."

A sick kind of dread pooled in Remi's belly, and she looked at her sister, then her husband. Her mind whirled, her world turning on its ear in a second. They'd played them like a fiddle. They'd let Bekka wander aimlessly around hell for Ascended knew how long, getting weaker every second she stayed there.

They'd bided their time and waited patiently. They had always known where the compound was and what The Rising was doing; they had been plotting. They'd set the perfect trap. They'd gotten the creator and the leader of The Rising, the segment of it that opposed their movement, along with her commanders, in one place. Remi's thoughts tumbled one over the other, making connections as Madwyn continued, her voice smooth as silk.

"Didn't you ask yourself, Emorie, why you couldn't find Ahlexei tonight? Aren't you curious what he's been up to?" The hairs rose on Remi's arm, and shock registered on Emorie's face as Rackham grew pale. But Madwyn didn't let up. "We attacked the minute you left. The compound is ours now."

Thayne left his post and moved to stand next to Remi as she looked at her sister, whose face was filled with horror and disgust. And then Thayne growled. "What did you do with them, Madwyn?"

"Oh, don't you worry, my love, they're alive, for now. As long as I stay alive. Oh, and as long as you all surrender right here, right now." Pietyr didn't loosen his grip, and Remi remembered the veiled animosity of their first meeting at the inauguration. But now, that naked disgust was plain for all to see. He hated Madwyn just as much as any of them. That was clear enough.

Emorie had tried to maintain her composure, but Remi could see traces of panic now. "I don't believe you," the science goddess whispered, stepping closer. "How do I know you're not lying?"

Madwyn jerked her head at Riven, and he took a step closer. The two non-gods who traveled with Bekka gripped their weapons tighter, bared their teeth. For that alone, Remi liked them already. But the Moldizean death god held up his hand, and they stood down.

They let Riven approach, and he pulled something from the pocket of his wool coat. A portable holo. He stopped a reasonable distance away from them, flipped it on, and then rolled it toward them. The second it stopped, a holo appeared. Terror filled every pore of Remi's body. The compound. Only not as they'd left it just a couple of hours ago.

Fires sprouted from every piece of machinery in the command center, and debris littered the floor. In the middle of the control room sat about fifty gods. All of them cuffed with those same golden, glowing manacles they'd seen used throughout Bicaidia. No one fought back, all of their heads drooping low. If she didn't know any better, she'd say they looked drugged.

Before anyone could react, Ahlexei stepped into the feed, a brilliant smile on his face. "We have the rest of the rebels rounded up in the domicile tunnel. We're standing by for orders." With that, the holo flicked off.

They stayed silent, all hope of escaping back to the safety of their compound evaporating. Remi's mind beat a refrain, one she couldn't quiet no matter how hard she tried to think of a way out of this situation. But she could think of nothing. They were screwed.

Bekka had moved back toward Arrick and the non-gods, her hands shaking with shock. She stared at Madwyn in a way that told Remi that she would rip her limb from limb if given half a chance.

But Remi couldn't think past one reality. All of their good intentions and efforts to stop a Nefaral uprising had had the exact opposite effect. They had been the ones to bring it about.

Add to that, Emorie had lost control of her movement. The goddess who seemed to have it all together. The one whose sense of command no one ever seemed to question. It had all been a ruse. Madwyn was right; she and Riven had held all the cards. She realized then that they had all along.

Riven had been the one to give Ellarah the contact with Bekka's letter. Likely, he'd orchestrated the entire meeting with the consciousness deity. She imagined that they had been the puppeteers of the entire disaster the whole time. No wonder they hadn't bothered to attack or seek out Emorie's movement right away. No wonder Emorie had been able to keep them hidden in that supposedly secret compound for so long. The truth was, they hadn't been.

"Now release me, or Riven will send the order to kill them all," Madwyn purred. Remi looked at Riven, whose eyes widened just before he controlled his expression.

Pietyr hesitated before looking to Emorie for confirmation. He seemed to hope, as Remi did, that maybe she had a plan. A way to take back the advantage. But she didn't, not any more than the rest of them did. It seemed that none of them had predicted this. They had all underestimated just how far Madwyn's reach went. And when Emorie nodded her command to release Madwyn, Remi realized just how fucked they really were.

Pietyr obeyed, looking disgusted as Madwyn strolled away, snapping her fingers in a single order. Another dozen demons filed through the portal, each carrying the same golden chains as Ahlexei had used at the compound. The chaos deity turned and smiled once again, gloating in her victory. Remi couldn't believe she'd ever liked that hideous creature, that she'd ever imagined that they could be friends. "I'm afraid this won't be too comfortable for you all. I'd say I'm sorry, but—"

"You're not sorry," Thayne growled. "Not yet, but you will be."

Riven sneered. "I wouldn't make threats you can't follow through on, Thayne."

Thayne's fists clenched, his dark hair gleaming in the low light. "It's not a threat. It's a promise."

Riven seemed to radiate with smug satisfaction. "One you'll never be able to keep."

Thayne's face turned to marble, his expression murderous. She thought about the despair in his eyes when Madwyn had stabbed Ellarah, but that seemed to be gone. She'd thought, maybe, he would rein in his sister. Maybe he was the reason behind the lower death toll than what she'd expected. But seeing him then…he felt different. More angry. More dangerous.

She thought about unleashing her power as the demons advanced. One last effort to destroy their enemies, but she knew that she couldn't. If she did, she could wind up killing them all along with Madwyn and Riven. Or, they'd stop her and order everyone else at the compound killed.

So instead, she watched helplessly as the demons stepped forward with those shackles. The ones that seemed to absorb the power in the room, their mere presence making her dizzy. It was over. They'd played their hand, and they'd lost. Remi felt tears swell in her eyes as she watched the peace her grandfather had fought for, and that her grandmother had died for, disintegrate into nothing.

CHAPTER 23

BEKKA

Bound

I stared in disbelief as the demons advanced, snapping shackles on Remi, then Thayne. They moved on to the one they'd called Emorie and then the time and shadow gods too. Each of them fell to their knees and winced in pain. Their light dissolved the second the shackles clamped shut. The essence that gave them their power dissipating like fog in burning sunlight. They slumped to the ground as the demons advanced on Arrick and me.

A helpless kind of despair infused me, and I gripped Arrick's hand harder in my own. I turned my head up to his, and my eyes swam with tears. I'd found my sister at last, only to have our freedom ripped away from us in damn near the same breath.

My mind scrambled as I imagined what they would do to Deklan and Caden. To Arrick. Would his flat-out refusal to join their side cost him his life? And then, what would they do with the demigods? What would these shackles do to them?

The way they pulsed and seemed to absorb all the energy in the room hinted at their true purpose.

Even a complete moron could tell that they suppressed celestial powers. But we were full deities, and Deklan and Caden didn't have anywhere near the power we did.

I watched in motionless horror as the demons advanced on them. Arrick moved forward, but Deklan snapped his gaze to us and shook his head in warning. Then he turned his attention back to the approaching demon as he and his brother snarled, baring their teeth in a primal show of rebellion. But we all knew it was just that—a show.

We had no way to fight back, each of us too weakened by our time in hell and by the leverage Madwyn and Riven held to do more than let ourselves be captured. Deklan's warning and the resigned look in those electric blue eyes said it all. We'd lost. I realized then and there that I made a piss poor substitute for my grandfather. Why had I ever thought that someone like me could fill his shoes?

Bile rose in my throat as the demons snapped shackles onto Deklan's wrists, then Caden's. Their eyes went blank as they each crumpled to the floor, their bodies limp and slack. I cried out, the desperate scream wrenching from my lips. Arick and I moved in unison, a growl low in his own throat as we lunged forward, both of us knowing we could never cover the distance in time to help them.

But it didn't matter. Deklan's warning be damned. How could we just sit back and let this happen to them? I thought, my head pounding. They'd been through so much already and survived so much. And we'd just led them here, like lambs to the slaughter.

Before we could make it two full steps, a massive demon cut us off from them. Their bodies were obscured behind the creature's immense frame as it strode toward us. Arrick gripped my arm and tugged me behind him, walking us backward in a rapid quickstep. We gained precious ground before our backs hit the cavern wall, but we still had a few seconds before the vicious, snarling thing reached us. I turned my head and saw one more approaching from the other side. We were trapped. There was no way out.

Sweat trickled down my back as the demons closed in around us, any hope of escape diminishing with each step. I yanked Arrick's hand to spin him around, and his eyes locked onto mine. Even dirty and starved, his irises held the same electric quality they'd had from the first moment I met him. And as I stared into them, the world around me disappeared. I felt it all. That undeniable draw, the sensation that we had become inextricably intertwined. Our fates tied together no matter what. I knew then that I would never have wanted that to change. Only, I'd realized it all too late.

He touched a hand to my face and smoothed it into my hair. I could see a sadness in his eyes that matched my own. The truth was that we had lost, and our paths would diverge in the worst way possible. I didn't know what I would do without him in my life. And if they killed him? I could feel my heart wrench in two at the mere thought of that possibility.

I leaned forward and pressed my forehead into Arrick's, tears slipping down my lashes. It was goodbye, and we both knew it. I thought about everything we'd done together since that first day in Moldize. How my decision to stay and help them had brought about so much unintended destruction— our good intentions all for naught. Maybe my grandfather and my family were right to keep it secret. To try to keep me from living out my destiny.

Yes, we'd saved the mortal realm in Moldize and with it millions of lives. But how many more would die because of this insurrection? Or be tormented by rogue Nefarals until the end of their days because of our good intentions? Would Valeria fall? With both my sister and me to use as bargaining chips against my parents, the possibility seemed sickeningly high.

The tears flowed freely now, and I hiccuped as I tried to catch my breath. Arrick's whisper was gruff and filled with his own raw emotions, "Bekka—" he grasped my face in both hands. "Just in case we don't get another chance. I want you to know—" He wiped a tear from my lashes with the pad of his thumb. "That I love you. With every, single part of me. I love you."

As I absorbed the full meaning of his words, something broke deep inside of me. A dam that I'd been holding back for months cracked, and a flood of emotion that I couldn't seem to control rushed out. Warmth, despair, loss, and most of all— love. I loved Arrick. And I had for Ascended knew how long.

No matter how much I'd tried to push him away, we always seemed to find our way back to each other. The truth was that I would never have let him go. And I sure as shit wasn't ready to do it now. Not after I knew how he felt about me. It was too bad that I didn't have much choice in the matter.

I gripped his hands on either side of my face. We didn't have much time, and I wanted to make sure I told him before it was too late. "I love you too."

As the words slipped from my lips, something happened.

A heat bloomed inside of me, so hot and so alive with power that I gasped in reaction.

My lungs burned at the sheer magnitude of it, the realization of what had just happened sudden and acute.

My body seized with the shock of it as our souls fused faster than light or sound could travel. I could feel a tiny piece of his spirit, along with his magic, twine to mine, as mine did to his, and I knew that we would be joined, soulfused for eternity. However short that eternity might be. And just as the bond solidified, clicking into place for each of us, the demons snapped those damned shackles on our wrists.

Our eyes stayed locked as all the power and the *knowing* that had coursed through each of us seconds before evaporated. My body, already depleted and drained of any nutrients aside from my power, collapsed with its absence. Because these damned bracelets did just that, they didn't just suppress power. They took it away entirely.

My knees buckled, and I fell to the ground, slumping atop Arrick's prone and motionless form. I could feel the rise and fall of his chest beneath me, the only indication that he still breathed. I blinked, a film of exhaustion forming over my eyes even as I clung to the knowledge that he wasn't dead. At least, not yet.

I could hear my own ragged breaths in my mind as two high-heeled feet appeared in my line of sight. They belonged to Madwyn. I heard a laugh, the sound melodic as rough hands yanked me to a standing position. The demon's, I realized as its nails scraped against my skin, cutting ragged holes through my shirt. It held me upright, but my head lolled, my neck muscles lacking the strength to bear its weight. Ever so helpfully, Madwyn grasped a handful of my hair and jerked my head backward. Pain raced over my scalp, and I resisted the urge to grimace. I wouldn't give her the satisfaction.

Her smile widened, and the sight of her filled me with a hatred unlike anything I'd ever experienced. Of course, I'd never been the type of person to hate someone before. But as I'd learned so well over the last few months, there was a first time for everything. And not all firsts were good. She called from over her shoulder; I could only assume she spoke to her brother. "Tell Ahlexei to kill all but the most powerful. Bring the living back to the palace for re-education."

I heard a strangled cry from across the room. "No, please, Madwyn, you can't!" The plea was weak and breathy, the strength in Emorie's voice gone now. "We surrendered. You promised you'd spare them."

Madwyn's head jerked to the side, giving me a clear view of her flawless profile. I wondered again how someone so beautiful could be so damaged. So evil. "You heard me, Riven. Give. The. Order."

Shoes crunched on gravel as he moved to the hologram on the ground a few feet away from me. Madwyn's face turned back to mine, and she showed me her teeth again. With one hand still fastened to my scalp, she gripped my chin with the other, forcing me to focus on her. "You, my sweet, little creator. You're the key to it all. The keys to the kingdom, as it were. When we go to work on you and your sister and start sending pieces of you both back home, there's nothing your parents won't do to get you back. They'll be far too busy worrying about their daughters to notice anything else we're doing. And by the time they do, it will be too late to stop us. So really, thank you for coming here and walking right into our trap." She sighed, shaking her head as though nostalgic. "It truly was just *too easy.*" She leaned forward and kissed me on the mouth, and I resisted the urge to gag. She let go, and my head lolled to the right, watching as a demon hauled Remi to her feet.

Terror bucked inside me as I pictured the reality she'd just painted for my sister and me. Pieces? They planned to cut pieces of us off and send them back home? Bile crept up my throat at this prospect. I felt helpless. The most powerful being in the multiverse, and yet there was nothing I could do to stop them.

I turned my head to the left, and I watched as a demon hauled Arrick to his feet. A strangled cry escaped my lips as it began to lead him away from me. Surely, he wouldn't live much longer. My heart felt like someone had shoved their hand through my chest cavity and ripped it out. My soul seemed to rebel inside me, and I used what little strength I had left to kick out and fight the demon's grip. It did little good. The demon's hands held me in an iron-clad grasp.

In response, Arrick fought too. Shoving against the demon who held him in an effort to get to me. I felt like the rest of the room had gone black, and all that mattered was him. I couldn't be separated from him. I had to stay with him at all costs. It felt like something had taken over every sense in my body and laser-focused it on him. On my soulmate.

Though I understood logically that this was an effect of our soulfusion, it didn't matter. I felt frenzied, terrified at the prospect of separation. Or worse, of losing him forever.

"Take them to the cages," Madwyn said, waving a careless hand at the demons surrounding us. "We'll deal with them later. After we clean up that little mess at the compound."

One by one, they hauled the rest of us to our feet, shoving us toward the portal. I fought them every step of the way, jerking against my bonds to little effect. Arrick twisted and shoved, trying to see me over the shoulder of the demon who pushed him forward. But no matter how hard we all fought it, we couldn't stop the march toward imprisonment.

At last, Arrick's voice rang through the cavern. "Wait! Just stop for a second!" He panted, his weakness and his despair at the prospect of what was about to happen to us painted on his face. His chest heaved with the effort of his struggle, and sweat lined his forehead, wetting his hair.

Madwyn arched a brow as she stared at him. "Something wrong, Arrick?"

His eyes flicked to mine. I could see the apology in them, as though he was begging me to understand what he was about to do. My stomach dropped all the way to my toes when he focused back on Madwyn and said, "You said you could use another Nef with powers like mine on your side, right?"

"Arrick, no! Don't!" I gasped, my words coming out in a rush of breath.

Ignoring me, Riven scoffed, his slicked-back hair gleaming in the shimmering light of the portal. "That offer expired the minute you decided to kill my demons."

Madwyn tapped her chin with a painted nail. "You know, my brother's right. I seem to remember you countering my generous offer with a boot up the ass."

In reply, Arrick yanked his arm free of the demon's grasp and stepped forward. He wanted to follow, but Madwyn waved it off, unconcerned. "What if I sweeten the deal?" he asked, his eyes careful to avoid my pleading gaze. What the hell was he doing? What was he thinking? He couldn't be serious.

"Now, what could you possibly offer me that would change my mind?" Madwyn asked, genuine curiosity in her eyes.

Arrick stayed focused on her face with no hint of hesitation. "Moldize. I'll give you Moldize's support in the war. Because that's what you're angling for, right? War? You just want to win it this time."

A flash of greedy delight flitted across her face, and she turned to Riven, brows raised. A slimy smile spread across his lips as he stared at my mate, the love of my life. The most noble deity I'd ever met. And here he was, gambling away everything he believed in, his very soul. I knew why too. Deep down in the pit of my belly. He was doing it for me.

Madwyn stepped closer to him now, her slender frame damn near pressing against him. She seemed to radiate sensuality as she drew a fingertip across his jaw. "I assume you want something in return?"

He looked at me now, his eyes full of resignation. I shook my head at him, begging him not to do this. "Arrick, don't," I mouthed, despair choking me. "Please." Tears burned my eyes and closed my throat as he looked away from me, his message clear.

He pointed to me. "I want her kept in one piece and treated well. Along with all the others. No dungeons or cages and no torture. You can't cut her and her sister into pieces and send them to Valeria. You'll have to find another way to bargain. I'll help you do it. And lastly, you spare the ones in the compound. I can't watch you murder war prisoners after they've surrendered and still serve your cause."

Madwyn pressed her lips together in thought. "You drive a hard bargain. We need a moment to consider." She turned to her brother and jerked her head in his direction. They stepped aside for a few moments and spoke in hushed whispers.

I stared lasers at Arrick, trying to get him to meet my eye. But he refused to look at me, as though he knew that seeing my despair would break something inside of him and cripple his resolve. After less than a minute, Madwyn and Riven turned to face Arrick, smug expressions on their faces. "And you'll serve faithfully? Follow our orders when given? Even if you disagree with them? And you'll pledge Moldize's support when the time comes?"

Arrick closed his eyes as though this agreement pained him, and nodded. "I will as long as she and the rest of those present today stay safe and cared for. And those who are trapped in the compound remain unslain by your orders or your hand. They have to stay in one piece too."

Madwyn smiled then as she pulled a key from her pocket. It was gold, old-fashioned, and looked like it would fit perfectly into the lock of the manacles that had been clamped around Arrick's wrists.

She slipped the key into the lock, and as the shackles fell to the ground, something broke inside of me. "Arrick, no, please don't do this. This isn't you! This will destroy you! We'll find another way. Don't do it!" Even as I panicked over the prospect of losing him to death, this seemed somehow worse.

He looked at me, his eyes lined with despair. Then he looked to Caden and Deklan, who remained slumped unconscious and tossed over two demons' shoulders, and the rest of the people who'd come to rescue us. Finally, when his attention fixed back to me, he whispered, "There is no other way. I hope you can forgive me, Bekka."

Then he turned his back on me; his mind made up. I fell to my knees, sobs racking my shoulders, and I felt a hand grip mine. Remi was there, holding me as I cried. My despair knew no bounds. Even if we found our way out of this by some miracle, Arrick would be on the opposite side from me.

We could never be together again.

As tears blurred my vision and agony clawed through my guts, Arrick held out his hand to Madwyn and said the words that would seal the deal forever, "A binding?"

ACKNOWLEDGEMENTS

Diary of a Deity - The Rising has been a long time coming. It feels like I had to set aside my writing more than I would have liked to over the past year. I got pregnant, had a baby, and our lives transformed along the way. This book traveled with me through all of it. Now that it's finished, I feel so grateful to have had the love and support of my family and friends throughout the process.

There are a lot of people who helped make this book possible. So, without further preamble, I want to give a big thank you to my editor, Melissa Bourbon, who gave me lots of insightful feedback and a wonderful line edit. Her canny eye helped me polish this into a final draft.

Another big thank you to Leoneh Charmell, my mind-twin and editor. Without her plotting prowess, there are so many elements of this story that never would have happened. Trust me, they would have been sorely missed. And, lastly, a special thank you for this GORGEOUS cover art. I'm in love!

So again, to everyone who supported me and continues to support me today: Thank you!

ABOUT THE AUTHOR

Loryn Moore lives in Northern California with her husband and two young sons. She and her husband are avid DIYers, backyard gardeners, proud chicken owners, and recreational soccer players. Her eldest son is in non-stop motion and keeping up with him proves ever more challenging as his ability to sprint like the wind grows with each passing day. Her youngest is an infant and his epic smiles are the absolute highlight of her day, every single day. These three men are the loves of her life, and her inspiration in all that she does.

Loryn knew that she loved writing by the time she hit sixth grade. She took a poetry class that year and enjoyed every second of it. This led into a passion for reading, which further spurred her passion for writing. The place she cultivated a large part of her acumen was with friends in high school, passing long, funny notes between classes. They would always try to one-up each other with ridiculous stories that they would fabricate over any mundane detail they could find. It always left them with aching bellies and stitches in their sides from laughing so hard.

By the time college hit, she switched her major four times. Business, Journalism, Creative Writing and then back to Business, which stuck. But she continued to take creative writing workshops all through her coursework. This was where she wrote her first book. And to be blunt. It sucked.

But she kept at it, writing a new story that allowed her to stick to her strengths. A mere eighty drafts later and she had come up with her debut novel. She learned that writing is a labor of love and that characters do the damnedest things, constantly destroying the author's carefully crafted plotlines. But to her, that's what makes characters so real. They all have minds of their own.

VISIT Loryn's Website at www.LorynMoore.com

Follow Loryn on TikTok @LorynMooreAuthor
https://www.tiktok.com/@lorynmooreauthor?lang=en

Follow Loryn on Facebook @LorynMooreAuthor
https://www.facebook.com/LorynMooreAuthor

Follow Loryn on Instagram @LorynMooreAuthor
https://www.instagram.com/lorynmooreauthor/

OTHER BOOKS BY LORYN MOORE

Diary of a Deity Series

Published
- The Burning (Book 1)
- The Rising (Book 2)

Upcoming
- The Fall (Working Title Book 3) - Coming Soon
- No Title (Book 4) - Planned

Jenna Torrence Series

Upcoming
- Jenna Torrence Book 1 - Coming Soon

Made in the USA
Middletown, DE
19 September 2024

60684100R00239